JOSEP

IN DAR
IT DWELLS

Gold Imprint
Medallion Press, Inc.
Printed in USA

DEDICATION:

To Susan Finley, for reading and believing.

Published 2006 by Medallion Press, Inc.

The MEDALLION PRESS LOGO
is a registered tradmark of Medallion Press, Inc.

Cover Illustration by Adam Mock
Character Illustration by Joseph Laudati

Printed in the United States of America

10 9 8 7 6 5 4 3 2 1
First Edition

Like one that on a lonesome road
Doth walk in fear and dread,
And having once turned round walks on,
And turns no more his head;
Because he knows a frightful fiend
Doth close behind him tread.

—*The Rime of the Ancient Mariner*

Fau'Charoth alammash'ta rashag muku tu

Wavering beams of flashlight pierced the darkness, accompanied by a chorus of whispers. Six figures splashed ankle-deep through the muck. Their dark sacerdotal robes were soaked from the downpour. Loose sleeves dangled heavily from their wrists. With faces hidden beneath ceremonial cowls, they resembled monks escaping the siege of a monastery. As they trudged onward, the ground began to elevate. The receding waters revealed a parallel set of iron bars with decrepit crossbeams: railroad tracks. The figures sighed through labored breaths, grateful to step on dry earth, as they marched wearily along the rusty ties.

One by one they removed their hoods, revealing the drenched, frightened faces of four men and two women. They looked about the tunnel as though they had entered a primordial cave last visited by Neanderthals. The stale, musty air smelled of dead stone. The leader stepped forward, brandishing his flashlight boldly. His flash beam fell upon black plastic bundles, piled high along the wall. He reached for the first bag, placed his foot on it, and with his free hand tore through the plastic sheet. Inside was a used soda bottle filled with water and some packaged food. He unscrewed the lid of the bottle, took a swig, and then tossed it to the others, who grabbed out thirstily for a drink. The man reached for the second bag and pulled out fagots of bundled wood, a can of kerosene, and a box of dry matches.

As he fumbled with shivering fingers, the flashlight in his left hand danced its beam across the ceiling above, revealing a desolate arch of tortured stone. The tunnel was his cathedral. It would serve him as surely as Notre Dame. Here, he would commune with his gods. He would pray, and the gates of heaven would open for him.

Jacob Tornau discovered the tunnel quite by accident, wandering in from his estate at Crohaven. It lay hidden in a nest of hills and evergreen, a relic from the past, like Crohaven itself. No one had ventured into it for decades. No one but the bats. He had designs on it almost instantly. The tunnel would prove a useful rendezvous point should their plans go awry. He had stashed it with firewood and provisions, converting it into a safe house. It was as though, on some intuitive level, he perceived a threat and was preparing for the worst-case scenario.

But Tornau was not precognizant in any way. No magical prescience guided him, or he would have anticipated betrayal and identified the traitor in their ranks. He was blinded by confidence and paid now for his shortsightedness.

The others found the box of cheese crackers he had stashed in the bag and were greedily munching on them. They were like famished children, exhausted and frightened. Were it not for his strength and leadership, they would fall to the ground weeping in despair. They had suffered a terrible defeat, and it crushed them to the core.

What a waste.

What an utter and terrible waste it had been: eight months of magical preparation, four of his group killed in ambush, and of course the *sacrifices*. Six human lives, dead for no purpose. They were being hunted even now. Their enemies were closing in. All seemed lost.

But there was still a chance to put things right.

Tornau gestured with his flashlight, making a circular motion above the ground. "Here." There was a bite of frustration in his voice. "Make a circle with the stones. Now!"

Without question, they dropped to the ground, clawing at the stones imbedded in the loose earth. Dry patches erupted with clouds of dust, and they choked with raspy coughs. Kicking chunks of fallen slate from the base of the walls, they formed a pile with a deep pit in the middle at the center of the tracks. Dust streaming from the crater, it resembled a volcano about to erupt.

The bundles of firewood and fagots of kindling were hastily emptied into the stone basin. They splashed kerosene over the wood, and a match was struck, igniting a blaze with a soft *flump*!

Tornau reached into his leather satchel and took out a chunk of bright yellow chalk. He hastily scraped it over a region of wall that was smoothed over with concrete. The crayon made a rasping sound against the stone. In long, smooth gestures, he scrawled a series of lines and circles. Chalk dust assaulted his nostrils, but like a graffiti artist, he persisted until a pattern of ceremonial emblems adorned the crusty surface.

The fire was already growing in the pit. They gathered around it, seeking its warmth.

Healthy yellow flames sent eerie shadows across the walls. Reflecting the light, the chalk symbols seemed to glow with their own radiance.

Tornau pulled a clay jar from his bag, ripped the seal off with a snap, and poured a dark viscous liquid in a circle around the fire. The smell of rancid blood filled the air, and one man stepped back in revulsion as the liquid splashed over his shoes.

In a commanding voice Tornau issued an evocation.

"Aga mass ssaratu. Ia mass ssaratu. Ashshu kashshaptu u namaritum!"

He raised his arms; his long delicate fingers stretching out in graceful strokes. The flesh of his wrist showed scars from years of ritual bloodletting. He was a lean, sinewy man in his middle fifties, with sparse gray hair surrounding a bald dome. A silvery goatee wreathed his mouth and chin. His piercing blue eyes were like shards of ice that could skewer a man's soul. As he stared into the flame, he spoke a language that wreaked havoc on his vocal cords.

"Shadu yu liktumkunushi! Zi Dingir Anna Kanpa!
Zi Dingir enlil la lugal! Ninkurkurrage Kanpa!"

Clinging above, the sickly bat twitched as though offended by the ancient verse.

The fire sputtered, fanned by a supernatural wind. It reached high; its warm yellow glow shifting to a lavender-purple, until peaks of flame licked the ceiling. A throbbing hum filled the tunnel.

Tornau felt his blood race. He pulled a third object from his bag a wooden idol with the crudely chipped visage of a snarling dog-creature. The beast was cloaked with bat wings.

Quickly, now. He held the idol aloft and recited.

"Fau'Charoth a Lammashta ra shagmuku tu.
Fau'Charoth ud kalama shagmuku tu.
Aga mass ssaratu. Alakti limda.
Fau'Charoth kur amda lu amesh musha tu!"

Something stirred in the flames. They could not see it so much as *feel it.* A consciousness seeped forth from the blaze, filling the ætheric space of the chamber like a mist. It was a frightening presence that lurked at the very fringes of perception, devoid of shape, starving for sustenance.

Tornau felt hairs bristle on the nape of his neck. He knew the demon was about him, clinging close, drawing essence from him like an orchid nourished by sunlight. He could feel his head go light, a sudden blood rush, as the demon sucked energy from his soul. It was feasting off the luminous emanations of his aura. He closed his eyes to concentrate his thoughts on the wooden figure in his hand, visualizing its every contour. The demon lapped up the mental impression like nectar, and it grew stronger. It was for this purpose that he had summoned it: to join it to his soul and create a powerful slave for his command.

He shuttered—a moment of fear perhaps—and withdrew from the demon's suckling. The sensation was more visceral than he'd imagined. Fighting a swell of nausea, he motioned to his companions.

Cut off from the magician's mind-waves, the demon drifted. It sensed a tiny life force clinging to the ceiling. Still hungry, it swelled around the sickly bat and fed!

The bat carcass made a loud flop as it fell to the ground.

Tornau faced the pillar of fire, which thickened like a tree trunk, spilling its canopy across the arched ceiling of stone. His hands reached up like a maestro conducting an orchestra. The flame responded by billowing outward. It seemed eager for something.

Tornau looked to his followers. Harsh, weather-beaten faces, mostly old. Of the women, the first was a shrill-looking crone with a mat of overlong gray hair, but the younger was barely thirty and pretty. She had delicate, highbred features and tawny blond hair that was cropped short in a pageboy. Tornau stared directly at her.

Sarah Halloway blinked under his gaze and looked away.

Tornau thrust his hands openly before the fire. No, not openly. Mockingly. He pretended to cradle an object, a *child*, in his empty hands.

"The fire is hungry," he said to Sarah. "But we have nothing to feed it!"

Sarah trembled with dread.

"We have nothing to feed it, *Sarah*!" With his single gesture, two men grabbed her arms and restrained her.

"No!" she gasped and fought them off fiercely.

The older woman snatched at her robe, tearing it off until she struggled in a soaked flannel shirt and jeans. The chill of the tunnel cut deep into her form. They quickly tied her ankles and wrists with the twine from the firewood bundles and then lifted her aloft.

"Let me go! Please!" she implored. "*Jacob!*"

"You dare cry to me for mercy? What arrogance!" Tornau stood cold like a monolith, glaring at his former consort. His lips trembled. An arsenal of cruel taunts echoed in his mind, and brutal disclosures that would burn her as effectively as the fire. But he held his tongue. She was irrelevant. She had violated his trust, bringing his designs close to ruin, and was no more to him now than a cog in the great machine he was building. An ingredient in his devilish brew. Like the others before her, she would serve the faction in one manner alone, as fuel for the flames.

Tears of outrage filled Sarah's eyes. And then panic. She turned her attention to the fire and stared with unmitigated terror at the roaring blaze. She screamed to the others in a desperate plea. "Plea-eeese! Jonathan! Abigail!" The names fell on dead ears. Each muttered "traitor" in response.

Her head swam in delirium. She murmured into a swoon, but then her whimpering became a hysterical giggle of triumph. "I defied you. I defied you, Jacob!"

The words were like a balm for her soul. Jacob Tornau was high priest of her congregation, her master, and her lover. To know him was to live in obeisance. And yet she betrayed him. She broke free of his dominance to save a child from horrible death. Now she would pay for her impudence. But she felt liberated. Exhilarated, as though her soul had broken free from its shackles and soared now to salvation.

"I defied you!" she laughed, almost with song. "It's over for you! Over!"

"Traitor!" the old crone shouted, but Tornau gritted his teeth in silence.

Sarah's captors lifted her high, ever closer to the blaze. She gasped aloud, expecting a terrible heat.

But the burning sensation was not heat at all but *cold*—blistering, diabolical cold like the vacuum of space. She closed her eyes tightly. It would be over in a moment. If only she could faint. How merciful that would be? To pass out and be spared the agony? She prayed that her end would be swift, that her spirit would not be lost in the terrible abyss that awaited her. She heard Tornau give a final word, felt herself shoved toward the flame, and then she—

Fffffhht!

Magnesium-bright flashes caused all to blink.

Tornau watched as Sarah's body vanished. For one millisecond, it was wreathed in fire, and then she was gone!

What? Tornau barely contained his surprise. He stared in bewilderment. *Where did she go?* The six before her had not vanished. Their bodies dumped heavily onto the coals and were consumed violently in the blaze. But Sarah had passed completely through the wall of fire. It had entered a fissure of bright white and disappeared.

Tornau blinked in realization. The portal.

More flashes from the pit. Belches of white fire.

"It's open!" he shouted. "The portal is open!"

A bright igneous star materialized within the core. Tornau gazed, astonished. It was the vortex they had labored to create, the gateway to another world! It pulsated like the heart of a god, the throbbing hum almost unbearable on his eardrums.

With a hiss, the invisible demon withdrew deeper into the tunnel. It hovered warily beyond the reach of the vortex, looking to escape its insatiable pull back to the abyss. Lingering between realms of reality, Fau'Charoth watched and waited.

A shrill sound pierced the hum.

The cultists recoiled from the deafening peal as the pillar of flame began to gesticulate wildly. A thunderbolt of plasmic energy shot out of the vortex, striking one of the cult members in the chest. The man screamed, engulfed by a tenacious fire. He fell to the ground in a fetid heap of smoke and flame.

Tornau fell back in alarm. No! This shouldn't be! The forces were raging out of control. Another bolt of energy stabbed into the stone behind him.

"Fau'Charoth!" he shouted. Where was the demon? The demon should have guarded against this.

"Fau'Charoth!" he screamed again. "Fau'Charoth!"

Something was terribly wrong!

PART 1

CHAPTER I

September 1, 1980

PERCHED ON AN OUTCROP OF STONE, THE DRAGON Gothmaug surveyed the landscape of its rocky domain. A crocodile grin was frozen on its jaws as the blaze of three suns glistened off its snake-pebbled hide.

Click went the shutter of the Nikon Super-8.

Five feet away, Tom DeFrank stood behind his beloved home-movie camera. It was a handsome pistol-shaped device built of slick black metal and plastic. Its zoom lens gaped like an enormous eye, shielded from glare by a funnel of black rubber. The camera was supported on the sturdy legs of a tripod and resembled, appropriately, a Martian war machine. Tom bent to peer through the viewfinder, squinting against the rubber eyepiece, and through its aperture studied the dragon model standing on the tabletop. The synthetic creature was frozen in time, captured in marble stillness as it awaited the next fragment of life from its creator.

Satisfied with the exposure, Tom returned to the set and

stared into Gothmaug's eyes. The orbs were half-spheres of yellow glass ordered from a taxidermy supply catalog. Feline slits of black gave them a catlike gleam.

With a surgeon's precision, Tom pressed his fingers onto the dragon's back, holding it secure as he gripped the articulated foreleg. The dragon's skin was latex foam, warm from the glow of three overhead movie lights. Rubber flesh pulled tight over steel bones as the limb carefully advanced a tiny increment. Taking the head gingerly between thumb and forefinger, he carefully tugged the chin forward a fraction and lowered the jaw a single hairbreadth. With further increments the claws grasped, the tail whipped into an arc, each move barely perceptible to the eye. The boy grinned, noting how well the joints functioned, even after two years of animated battles. Gothmaug always emerged victorious—his champion.

The new pose completed, Tom stepped out of frame. He reached for a black rubber bulb the size of a lemon. It had a tail of plastic cord that snaked its way like licorice to the trigger of the camera. He squeezed the bulb, activating the camera shutter with a metallic *click.* A frame of Super-8 film was exposed, granting the dragon another twenty-fourth-of-a-second of life. Not in this world, but in the "netherworld" of stop-motion animation.

Stop-motion, also known as *three-dimensional* or *puppet* animation, was a cinematic process first pioneered by Willis O'Brien in the dawn days of Hollywood. O'Brien, a hard-drinking former prizefighter, discovered it by manipulating clay pugilists and photographing them with a newsreel camera. As the father of modern special effects, he would go on to create such classics as *The Lost World* in 1925 and his masterpiece *King Kong* in 1933.

The technique was simple yet painstaking. A jointed mannequin was placed on a set, and a single frame of film was shot of its position. The mannequin was then moved slightly, each limb adjusted, and another frame exposed, so on and so forth for *hours* until the end of the sequence. When those still photographs got projected rapid-fire on a movie screen, the mind, through a miraculous process called "persistence of vision," perceived them as continuous movement.

Persistence of vision. It was a philosophy Tom lived by.

He went back to the dragon and repeated the process. Each journey to and fro brought him through alternate universes. One-half of the room was a movie studio, replete with its rampaging monster and alien landscape. The other was a typical teenager's abode.

The set was built over his dresser bureaus, and it held a landscape of Styrofoam mountains. Plastic fern trees sprouted from a forest of lichen and dried orchid. The sky was a sheet of painted butcher paper tacked to the wall. Beyond this façade was an unmade bed strewn with clothing. The wall space was plastered with movie posters of *King Kong*, *The Valley of Gwangi*, and Raquel Welch's cave girl pinup from *One Million Years B.C.*

There was also an autographed portrait of the grand

master himself, Ray Harryhausen. A protégé of O'Brien, Harryhausen refined the craft of stop-motion into alchemy and was renowned as its king. Among his triumphs were the epics *The Seventh Voyage of Sinbad* and *First Men in the Moon*. He destroyed Washington D.C. in *Earth vs. the Flying Saucers*, and his battle of sword-fighting skeletons in *Jason and the Argonauts* was considered a milestone in the annals of cinema. The brute spectacle of his animated creatures bewitched Tom at an early age. Something about that jerky stop-motion strobe made them alluringly supernatural. While his peers were idolizing ballplayers, his passions were Talus, Mighty Joe Young, the Rhedosaurus, and the Ymir. He awoke at ungodly hours to catch late showings of Harryhausen flicks and read countless articles about them. Lured by the siren of fantasy, his interests sailed into realms of myth and magic. A book cabinet was stuffed with issues of *Famous Monsters of Filmland*, *Starlog*, and other 'zines, while sci-fi and fantasy novels cluttered into overflowing heaps. Each literary jaunt, from Edgar Rice Burroughs to Tolkien, brought him macabre visions of lumbering beasts. For most kids the journey ended there, but for Tom it just began. It fueled in his belly an insatiable desire to create.

At sixteen, some prodigies were musicians. Others danced in ballets, composed sonatas, or flaunted their intellectual prowess in Ivy League schools. Tom made monsters, and his expertise rivaled the masters in Hollywood.

A shelf above his desktop held a menagerie of puppets. Dinosaurs and dragons. Nightmare beasts of movie legend.

Here, a giant ape, with mini–Fay Wray in its paw; there, a single-horned Cyclops with fleecy cloven hooves. Fangs and claws abounded. Nothing survived on this shelf without teeth or talons. They were his handmade progeny, the spawn of years of intense labor.

Already an avid sculptor, Tom literally stumbled onto stop-motion through mechanical mishap. His dad had left him an old spring-driven eight-millimeter movie camera, and while fiddling with it, he mistakenly pressed the exposure lever *up* instead of *down.* The conventional *clackety-clack* of the shutter was replaced by a single ominous *click*! Tom discovered quite by accident that the camera could expose *single frames*!

In a flash, a world of possibilities opened before him. Time-lapse photography! Clouds speeding across the sky, the sun a fiery meteor. Flowers bursting open like slow-motion popcorn. But those were mere trifles in the bag of tricks offered by that simple grind of gear and shutter. Tom could make his clay monsters move! That single *click* was the clarion call of his true vocation. He would become a dragon maker, so that the St. Georges of the world would never lack for an adversary.

Even now, Gothmaug awaited his touch of life. He resumed his task.

An hour passed. Eight seconds for a dragon.

Tom paused to stretch his knotting muscles and ran fingers through wavy brown hair.

He wore a loose flannel shirt that dangled from his

jeans. The boy was short for his age but lithe and well built. Push-ups and strenuous outdoor labor gave him a sinewy physique and a tan like roasted peanuts. He had large brown eyes with long lashes that softened his appearance, but his gaze was generally intense and far off, like a feral creature hunting or being hunted. It was an image he fancied.

Another squeeze of the bellows. *Click!* He returned to Gothmaug.

With a twist, the dragon's head tilted. The tail swept. The jaws opened wider. Another click. Another exposure. Endlessly over, stop-frame by stop-frame. Somewhere in the world, winds were blowing, and the Earth was turning. Seasons were changing, winter–spring–fall, but not in this room.

Not so long as dragons needed life.

"*Tom!*" A voice dragged him to Earth.

Startled, Tom glanced to the door. "What?"

Maggie, his mom, was standing there, one arm pressed to the doorframe. The aroma of roast pork wafted in from the kitchen. She sighed and repeated, "I asked if you can move your stuff out of the living room."

"Mom, I'm in the middle of a shot."

"You have books on the coffee table, and that *thing* of yours is on the couch. Paul's coming over for dinner in an hour. I need you to clear space in the garage so that he can park inside."

"He's staying over?" Tom asked, without looking up.

Maggie fidgeted. "He might. We talked about this."

Tom stifled a scowl. "All right, all right, I'll move my

thing. Just give me a minute." He completed a move on the dragon and recorded the film frame.

Maggie lingered in the doorway, wrestling with another request. Tom could feel her eyes at his back. Their communication skills had diminished over the past seven years, since the breakup of his parents. It consisted mostly of hesitant exchanges and abrupt, sometimes curt remarks. The lines between mother and son were corroded like ancient telegraph cabling, and the message often arrived broken and misconstrued. She glanced over his movie setup with typical disapproval and didn't see a mysterious dragon-world or recognize the sovereignty of its king, Gothmaug. She saw an ugly rubber puppet in a fake landscape.

"Are you going out with your friends tonight?" she asked.

"I was planning to. It's the last night before school," he answered as though defining a sacred tradition. "Danny and Kev are picking me up for a drive. Why?"

"I was hoping you could spend some time with Paul before you go, so that he doesn't feel like such a stranger around you."

"Well, he *is* a stranger."

"That's the point."

"What do you want me to do?"

"I thought maybe . . . we could show him one of your Godzilla movies."

"I don't make 'Godzilla movies,' Mom. Godzilla's a man in a suit."

"He's really interested in seeing one."

Tom rolled his eyes. “Right. That’s what you said about Mitch. Remember? The cop?”

Maggie frowned. “Forget Mitch. He was a jerk. Maybe if you gave Paul a chance—”

“Maybe if *you* did.” As soon as he said it, he regretted it. It was a low blow.

Maggie fumed. “Why do you have to give me a hard time?”

“’Cause you keep putting me on the spot with these boyfriends of yours.”

“Just one film,” she persisted. “Then you can go out.”

“No!”

“Why not?”

“’Cause it’s my *stuff*!”

She sighed, exasperated. “Then I’ll do it. Where’s the projector?”

Maggie searched the clutter and noticed the film projector lying in a corner below the shelf of creatures. The puppets glared down at her with objection. She stepped around the tripod—

“Careful!” Tom shouted.

—and bumped one of the legs ever so slightly.

“Thanks, Mom!” He leaped to steady the camera. “You just ruined a two-hour work!”

Maggie flushed. “I just ‘nudged’ it. Can’t you put it back?”

“*No.*” He peered through the lens with a pained expression. The camera was looking squarely at the dragon’s tail. “The shot’s ruined. You caused a ‘glitch’.”

"A what?"

"A glitch! A glitch!"

A glitch was a shift in the visual continuity. It could be caused by a temperature change in the lights, an accidental nudge of the camera or model, or even the crimping of film in the gate. On screen, it created a distracting jump in the image. In life, a glitch was just about anything unexpected that affected the normal flow of events.

Tom spent much of his time avoiding glitches.

His mom shrugged. "Sorry."

"Just go. I'll set the projector up later."

"All right. Dinner's at six. And I didn't mean to cause a silly 'glitch'." She left.

Tom set about dismantling his camera from the tripod. It was pointless to continue. He dropped his eyes and stared pensively at the floor. Switching the lights off, he detached the dragon model from its perch and set it on his shelf beside the T. rex.

Gothmaug would not live this day.

CHAPTER 2

A DUCK-BILLED PARASAUROLOPHUS PLODDED THROUGH a verdant prehistoric valley. The herbivorous dinosaur had a shovel for a mouth and a bony crest extending back from its skull. It stepped cautiously through the moss, sniffing the air in realistic mock-movement, then set about grazing on tree ferns.

The image flickered on the portable viewing screen in the DeFrank living room, accompanied by tinny music on a cassette tape. Fragments of film score accented the footage. The film was *Primeval Kings*, Tom's newly completed masterpiece and the product of a year's work. With eyes cast to the screen, he hid behind the glowing projector to avoid having to watch his mom and her date.

Maggie sat with Paul Franklyn on the sofa, still holding a half-empty glass of wine she'd begun drinking at dinner. As they watched the film, she cuddled him affectionately. The projector's loud humming masked her intimate whisperings, sure to prove embarrassing to Tom. Occasionally they got "cute," and she gave off little giggles like a schoolgirl. Tom withdrew into the darkness as best he could.

The flutter of animated birds disturbed the duckbill. Then the menace appeared—Tyrannosaurus rex. It snarled in close-up at the plant eater. With a mighty stride, the predator bounded after its prey. Its sinuous neck darted forward, jaws agape. Tom gazed in wonder. Though he had seen the footage countless times, his eyes remained fixed, enthralled by his own creation.

The T. rex made short work of the herbivore, snapping its jaws onto the neck and wrenching it to the ground. The Parasaurolophus writhed in death throes and then lay still. With a savage yank, the T. rex pulled a chunk of dripping flesh from the carcass. His mom gasped on cue.

"Ugh! That's the disgusting part!"

Tom glanced over for a reaction from Paul. Whether the man was fascinated or bored he couldn't tell. Dinner had been an excruciating affair. Tom built igloos in his mashed potatoes as Paul spoke endlessly about presidential candidates and the coming election. He still couldn't figure what the guy did for a living.

It was a routine to which he was accustomed. Paul was the latest of his mom's long string of lovers. Tom learned to avoid any emotional bonds and walked that thin line between cordial distance and rudeness. He was polite on cue, shook their hands, greeted them in the mornings at breakfast (concealing any surprise), and maintained the charade of the obedient son. All the while he cradled a disdain, knowing they were merely passing through. It wasn't that he disliked Paul. The man seemed friendly enough; tall, broad-shouldered, with a pat of light gray hair, and a double chin. He drove a BMW, Tom's favorite automobile, so he couldn't be *all* bad. But Paul was a ship with a brief harbor, like his father. Like that cop before him. Or the biker guy with the Harley. Six months from now, the show would be over. His mom, P.T. Barnum, would show him the ambiguous sign—"THIS WAY TO THE EGRESS"—and Paul would march through, searching for the next exhibit, unaware that he had been given the exit.

"You built those things yourself?" the man asked from the dark.

"Yeah," Tom answered.

"What're they made of? Papier-mâché?"

Tom rolled his eyes. Papier-mâché? They never had a clue. "No. They're latex foam and . . . stuff. It's complicated."

"He bakes them in the kitchen oven." His mom laughed. "God, what a stench! I've learned never to go into his room when he's working. The mess!"

Maggie's auburn hair fell in wavy tresses past her shoulder blades. She wore too much makeup, and her spaghetti-strap blouse exposed ample cleavage. Polyester slacks clung tightly to her well-toned figure, which was tortured daily with sit-ups and butt crunches. At forty-one, she seemed frantic about the ravages of age and was eager to retrieve a stolen youth.

Tom's dad had split when he was nine. His memories of Robert DeFrank were fond, if a bit glorified. "Rob" was a wizard with electronics. He built Radio Shack gizmos and loved imported beer, sci-fi movies, and rock 'n' roll music. He had a favorite guitar he loved to strum on summer nights and enjoyed most of all a good jam with his friends in the garage. But his mom knew him only as a lazy lout who couldn't keep a job. Maggie's eleven-year marriage had been a prison sentence, and she'd paid her debt to society. A quick divorce settlement had extracted Rob from her life like a cancerous growth. He got a trucker's license and disappeared on the high roads.

Maggie, meanwhile, pursued a career in insurance. Three years ago, they returned to Chapinaw, New York, her hometown at the foot of the Catskills. Their last attempt at contact with Rob had been just before then. The letter was returned, unopened. There was no forwarding address.

Not a word in over three years. Tom missed his dad. It was from Rob that he got his passion for monster movies and the most important tool for his hobby—his first camera. The Keystone eight-millimeter couldn't hold a torch to his new Nikon, but the spring-driven box was one of his fondest possessions. His dad would be proud to know how it was put to use.

If Rob could only see his movies, Tom was certain the lumbering beasts would amaze him. His dad would appreciate them for what they were and not sneer at them like his mom. When she wasn't showing them off to impress her boyfriends, Tom knew Maggie abhorred his monsters. Perhaps they reminded her of Rob. Maybe she feared that too much of the deadbeat had rubbed off on him. Or perhaps it was something else entirely.

On screen, the tyrant lizard was fighting a Styracosaurus. Despite its bony frill, the fate of the horned dinosaur was the same—bloody T. rex jaws feasting on its carcass. As the final image left the screen, car headlights burst through the window.

Thank God, Tom thought.

"That's the guys. I gotta go."

He switched off the projector. "I'll clean up later."

Paul started clapping. Tom cringed at his overeager praise. "That was great, Tom," the man declared. "Academy Award winner."

"Thanks," he said, grabbing a hooded sweatshirt from the banister in the hall.

"Maybe some time we can—"

"Sure. Whatever." Tom felt very rude. He avoided eye contact with his mom as he made for the door.

CHAPTER 3

THE BELLICOSE ROCK VOCALS OF MEAT LOAF BLASTED from the speakers of the silver Trans Am in the driveway. Kevin Marshall's eyes bulged wide when he heard the payoff to Danny Kaufman's dirty joke.

"—so that you can carry them like a six-pack!" Danny repeated the punch line, demonstrating obscenely with his fingers. "Don't you get it?"

Kevin chuckled despite himself. "That is the sickest—"

"—a 'six-pack,' God damn it!"

"—most disgusting joke I ever heard." Kevin was a tall kid, a month shy of eighteen, wearing a denim vest over a plain white T-shirt. Long wavy locks of indigo-black hair made him a dead-ringer for Jim Morrison. He was sitting on the hood of his car—a Frankenstein construct of junked parts he'd rebuilt from the ground up. The chassis was a beaten relic bought dirt-cheap, the engine a transplant from a Nissan. He called it the Monstermobile.

Danny was the scarecrow standing on skinny denim-wrapped legs. Short once, he'd sprouted in the past year as though his entire body had been stretched in a taffy machine. His hair was the color of sun-dried straw. Below a hawk nose, he had a pale fringe that was desperately trying to become a moustache.

Tom appeared from the house, watching Danny snicker at his own joke. "Okay, what's so funny?"

Kevin sneered. "Danny just told the most demented—"

"It is not!" Danny protested. "It's an anatomical lesson. Tom, 'why do girls—' "

"DON'T YOU DARE say that joke to him!"

"Yeah, I forgot. 'Virgin ears'."

Tom feigned outrage. "Virgin *what*? Now you *gotta* tell me!"

Kevin slid off the hood of the car, grinning at Tom. "Drop it, man. You'll live longer. Can you grab your lantern from the garage?"

"The big tanker?"

"Yeah. We're gonna need it."

Tom went into the garage and pulled the camping lantern down from above his workbench. It was a trusty unit with a red chrome finish and shiny glass bell. He hadn't used it since the late spring, when the three of them went camping in Wurtsboro. He shook it, checking for oil. There was the reassuring sound of fluid swashing within.

"Wherever we're going, it's gonna be dark," he thought aloud, wondering what kind of crazy adventure they were in for. You could never tell with Kevin. The kid relished in foolhardy stunts and practical jokes, the kind that kept

Tom on the edge. They'd only been friends for a year, and it was one hell of a ride. A common interest in monster movies, and a personal tragedy, created an unlikely bond with the rogue teen. Kevin was adopted. Tom wondered if that gave life a diminished sense of value. He learned early on to be cautious and prepare for the unexpected. That's why he concealed a tiny flashlight in his side pocket as an extra light source. Just in case.

"Where to?" Tom asked as he rejoined them.

"Wait and see," Kevin said smugly.

"He's not saying a word, Tom," said Danny. "I already tried."

"Just trust me." His wily grin hardly put them at ease.

They climbed into the car, clamoring over soda cans and piles of cassette tapes. Kevin revved the engine and then peeled out of the driveway. The Monstermobile skidded slightly off the curb and hit a bump. Danny was thrown up into the cab light.

"Ouch! Think you can go any faster?"

"Like a bat outta HELLLL!"

The car jolted forward, a fighter craft launching into hyperspace.

CHAPTER 4

THE MONSTERMOBILE RACED ALONG A CLEAR STRAIGHT-away of country road. Tom's foot pressed impulsively against the floorboards, seeking the phantom brake pedal. He'd only just gotten his license earlier that summer (largely with Kevin's help), and his new instincts as a driver were kicking in strong. Kevin jammed another cassette into the tape deck. Meat Loaf gave way to Black Sabbath as twanging guitars blasted over the speakers.

Kevin glanced back at Danny. "Don't wrinkle my uniform, or I'll bust your ass."

"I won't." Danny brushed aside an orange bellman's shirt that hung, neatly pressed, over the side window. The hotel logo "Revele" was embroidered on the pocket.

The Revele was one of the many hotels of the Catskills, a resort renowned for its lakefront villas and golf facilities. Kevin spent the summer working as a bellhop. Good tips kept him in cash. The job also gave him access to the hotel's disco/nightclub, a converted ski lodge called the Chalet. It was a cool spot to hang out. Tom had been there twice, but he detested crowds and wasn't much for disco music.

Dan leaned forward. "So how was the big Labor Day weekend?"

"I made over two hundred in tips."

"Damn," said Tom. "Next year, I'm bell hopping." He'd spent the summer mowing lawns at the Concord.

"I'll set you up," Kevin offered. "But you gotta learn to 'hustle' to earn the big bucks. The celebrity guests on the weekends are always the biggest tippers. Joan Rivers gave me a *twenty* for carrying two bags! Oh yeah, and this weekend they had Silver Cross playing at the Chalet."

Dan's eyes bugged. "Cross was at the Chalet?"

"The rock band?" Tom asked, and received a *duh* look.

"That's right," Kevin continued. "I was doing a 'front' for them at one of the villas, and guess who shows up?" Kevin's eyes gleamed. "My old buddy Cliff Burke!"

Danny and Tom both scowled. Burke the Jerk. Kevin's former best friend and head of the rowdiest bunch in Chapinaw High. A bitter dispute had turned them into Cain and Abel.

"I was going in for the night shift, when I notice Burke's green Jaguar in the parking lot. I think 'what the hell is he doing at the Revele?' Then, I learn that Cross had just checked in. Sure enough, around six-thirty I get a 'front' for villa number six. I carry this tray all the way out there, knock on the door—and who do you suppose answers? Burke!"

"Son-of-a-bitch," said Danny.

"So first I think 'awww shit!' 'cause I'm all embarrassed,

him seeing me in my pumpkin suit. He's all surprised, and says 'what the hell do you want?' I push past him with the tray. Inside, it's dark. All the shades are drawn, and the lead singer, Jessie Boggs, comes out of the bathroom wearing a towel."

"Holy shit! You saw Jessie naked?"

"Hey calm down, you fag, and let me finish. So now it's Burke who's embarrassed 'cause I'm thinking something funny's goin' on. But then the guy tips me a measly two bucks, and Burke says 'You better get back to the desk before someone rings your bell.' The creep. I felt like punching him right there, but not with Mick Swagger behind me. Meanwhile, I notice Burke's blue duffle bag is on the bed, the one he carries around for 'business.' I figured they must be making an 'exchange'."

"A drug deal?"

"Damn straight. I think Burke's become the Chalet's 'supplier'! They got his buddy, Lenny Finch, spinning records there now. It must have given Burke the 'in' he needed."

"Yep," Danny surmised. "Bet he's rolling it in, big time."

"Not for long, though. He'll get what's coming to him in the end." Kevin gloated with a strange confidence.

He's up to something, Tom thought.

"Burke's going down, man," Kevin brooded aloud. "Just a matter of time." He stared into space with a satisfied grin that made Tom very uncomfortable.

He glanced out the window at the passing scenery and saw a familiar pillar of light wipe across the horizon. The

'Eye of the Dragon,' as he called it, was the beacon to the nearby airport, guiding planes to the safety of its runway. The light was an omnipresence in Chapinaw, a welcome celestial phenomenon. Tom could see it from his backyard at night, like the aurora borealis. Watching the soothing glow, he imagined he saw a pterodactyl glide ominously through its path.

Kevin steered the car off the main road, and the smooth blacktop gave way to a narrow dirt path barely two lanes in width. The overhead lamps had long since abandoned them. They drove now through pitch darkness. The bright headlights cut through the murk like a machete, illuminating the winnowy trunks of birch and maple that pressed closer and closer to the dusty path. As they passed a grove of malformed trees, the headlights cast eerie shadows over their bulbous knobs, giving each a startlingly human face.

Then, like a gasp after a held breath, the trees broke, and they turned onto Crohaven Road, which opened to reveal a stretch of lonely farmhouses, rambling hills, and planted fields kissed with moonlight. The car rose and fell with each hill, giving Danny ample occasions to hit his head.

As they reached the crest of an incline, the infamous Crohaven Estate loomed before them. It stood across the street from an ancient graveyard, which held the remains of some of the earliest residents of the town. Familiar names were carved on the headstones, with lineage to present generations. Just off the road, and beyond the black fence, granite crosses and slabs of icy marble flanked a small, gated mausoleum. A number of unmarked plots were the subject of local folktales. They contained the bodies of condemned witches or criminals that were hung off the ancient oak tree at the center. Or so it was told.

As Kevin drove the car slowly toward the manor entrance, the three boys savored the creepiness. Tall fencing of black enameled bars shielded the three-acre property from prying visitors. He switched off the headlights and pulled to a stop in front of the spiral ironwork of the black gates. Beyond it was a long cobblestone driveway hemmed by tall evergreens and lilac bushes. Standing sentry in the front lawn were two enormous weeping willows that spilled their foliage in ghostly shrouds. At the head of the drive was Crohaven Manor, a stark gothic-looking building that seemed like Poe's House of Usher uncannily resurrected. It stood dark and imposing, a chilling repository for bad dreams.

The property was veiled in a cloud of infamy and had the habit of attracting notorious occupants. Within its walls had lived a man named Jacob Tornau, leader of a blood cult that once held the region in a grip of terror. Tornau was gone now, vanished without a trace, but his legacy still plagued the region in goose bumps and hushed whispers. It was the kind of true-to-life campfire yarn that boys relished on windy nights. Tom had gathered some tidbits over the years, weeding truth from fanciful embellishment. All he knew for certain was that people had died in bloody rituals, and the killers were still *at large*. The fact that none of the murders had actually occurred at the mansion was conveniently ignored. Crohaven was the town's resident haunted house.

As they peered up at the triple-tiered, steeply gabled mansion, Tom noticed a light in the uppermost window. Framed within was a man's silhouette. It stood motionless, and for a moment, Tom felt an icy chill that the man was actually peering out at them. He crouched back in his seat and whispered to the others.

"Check it out! Is that Parrish?"

Danny glanced through his window up at the shadowy form. "Yeah, that's him, all right." He referred to the mysterious Stephen Parrish, groundskeeper and custodian of the Crohaven Estate. A most peculiar man. Seldom seen, Parrish was the town's Boo Radley, a scaffold on which to hang the darkest speculations.

They ducked down impulsively, peering over the dashboard, and watched the figure for any signs of life. It stood frozen like a gorgon's victim. Tom again felt the passing of eyes about him. Why didn't he move? Was he alive?

Rewarding their patience, the figure raised an arm and passed it over his chest. It made gestures in the air like a priest performing benediction. The arm was graceful, floating. Ethereal. The arm of a marionette, suspended on threads of mist, wavering with purpose.

Danny pressed between the front seats, intrigued. "Cool. Look at him go."

The figure rotated and took a step back, gesturing its arms in a backward stroke. It bent low, then pulled itself upright, raising a knee, and stepping forward. The boys were transfixed. All the Parrish stories they'd ever heard came alive in their minds.

Perhaps it was the legacy of Tornau, unjustly transposed, that made him such an enigma. Parrish was rumored to possess psychic powers. Tom had first heard the name in a radio broadcast three years ago. The report told of Parrish being sued on charges of inappropriate behavior toward a minor. His actions allegedly caused the death of a teenager named Josh Wilkens, son of a wealthy businessman. What held Tom's interest was the claim that Parrish was a "wizard" who had influenced the kid through witchcraft. He never saw the man, but he imagined a sinister Svengali with glowing eyes like Dracula.

"Weird shit," Kevin said, watching the shadow's gyrations.

"What's he doing?" Danny asked.

"Some kind of ritual, it looks like," answered Tom.

"He's casting a spell, I bet!"

"Naw. All that talk about witchcraft is bullshit," Kevin scoffed.

"Tell that to Josh Wilkens."

"That was a suicide."

"Yeah, but Parrish was involved. Remember the court case?"

"Sure, I remember. The judge threw it out!"

"That doesn't prove anything," Danny insisted. "He could've put a spell on the judge."

"What do you think he is, some freakin' Jedi? He's just a regular guy, Dan. I keep telling you. He's got a kid in school."

"Oh yeah. Julie," Tom nodded, remembering. "The warlock's daughter." He'd shared a class with her once, but she kept very much to herself. Julie was a skinny girl with short dark hair, and a pale, almost-sickly complexion. His one and only impression of her was that she looked cute, but sad and preoccupied.

They continued to watch for a time, until the figure withdrew from the window. Their gruesome curiosity sated, they decided to move on. Kevin still had his "adventure."

CHAPTER 5

KEVIN DROVE THE MONSTERMOBILE SLOWLY DOWN the road. He kept the headlights off, driving silently in the dark. The sight of Parrish had lent just the right air to the occasion, a weirdness that clung to their moods like the dew. The car filled with creepy night voices.

Tom strained his eyes to see ahead in the dim light. "How can you drive like this?"

"Sit tight. It isn't far now," Kevin answered, a delinquent grin on his face.

"Not far?" Tom glanced around. As far as the eyes could see, there were rolling hills, sparsely gathered with trees and bush. What could possibly be here?

With a sudden jerk of the wheel, Kevin steered a sharp left onto a small side road.

"Whoa!" Tom and Danny gripped their seats.

The terrain buckled up into steep hillside. Two rabbits darted off from the grass.

They reached a plateau, and Kevin steered right onto another path that widened into a flat clearing surrounded by hill and forest.

Bump! Bump! Tom squinted at the road surface ahead. They were driving over some abandoned railroad tracks imbedded into the road.

Railroad tracks?

A cliff face loomed in the shadows ahead, rising from the flat scrub ground, and just as they seemed about to collide with it, the car came to a halt. Kevin snapped on the brights.

"Ta-daaaahhh!" he shouted.

"Damn, Kevin. What the hell are we—" asked Danny.

"Guys, will you SHUT UP and look?" They stared ahead wide-eyed.

Carved into the face of the hill, a cavernous maw gaped before them. Its dimensions were large enough to engulf a locomotive. The dilapidated tracks exited the dark mouth like streams of drool.

Tom's jaw dropped. "Holy hole-in-the-wall, Batman, it's a—"

"Tunnel," Danny finished. "A freaking railroad tunnel."

It was a relic of an old railway system, long abandoned. There were many such train routes scattered around the Northeast, built during the early days of steam locomotion, before intercontinental systems made them redundant. They were never where you expected to find them.

The outer wall of the cave was striated with layers of slate that had chipped and weathered over the years, gathering into piles like confetti. The opening was almost concealed by the overgrowth of large evergreen trees. Ivy leaves and vines clung to the surface of the rock as though they were trying to heal the wound in the hillside.

They stepped out of the car, amazed by the discovery. The sounds of crickets immediately filled their ears. Somewhere in the distance, a whippoorwill cried out.

"How did you learn about this?" asked Tom.

"A friend of mine," Kevin answered as he reached back for Tom's lantern. "He was hiking up from Hackett Road, and he stumbled onto it. The other end is boarded shut."

"Holy shit," Danny said.

"This end's usually under water, but with the drought and all." Kevin pointed to the cracked mud patch at the base, evidence of a long puddle that usually gathered there; but with one of the hottest, driest summers on record, it had completely vanished, making the tunnel accessible for the first time in years. "I figure no one's been in there for quite a while."

He took Tom's lantern from the front seat and shook it, listening for that familiar *splish-splash*. Then he opened the glass dome, gave the wick a quick flash with the lighter from his car, and popped the lighter back into the dashboard. With a twist of the nozzle, the lantern glowed, illuminating a rascal smile on his face. "Wanna see what's inside?"

Tom and Danny both tensed. Danny's voice raised an octave. "*Now? At night?*"

Tom stared at the circle of blackness, nearly fifteen feet in diameter. He didn't want to let Kevin down, but the thought of entering that mouth of doom made his stomach do a backflip. He gave Kevin a dutiful look. "Kevin, I don't know . . . maybe we should—"

"There might be rats in there, Kev," Danny interjected. "Or worse."

"There could be holes and pits, and we wouldn't see 'em until—"

"What am I hearing?" Kevin shouted. "Are you guys wimping out on me? I go through all this trouble to bring you an adventure, and you ditch your nerve? Man, the squadron's grounded before the launch!" Frustrated, he tapped an imaginary headset. " 'Come in, Red Five. Are you prepared to make your run?' 'Negative, Blue-Leader. I have two chicken-shit engines that won't function. Over'."

Tom frowned. Using *Star Wars* lingo for coercion was a cheap shot, but it worked. He felt his machismo crumble.

Kevin plodded forward, shaking his head. "The hell with you two. I'm gonna check things out. Maybe find me some hidden treasure."

Tom and Danny looked to each other uncertainly, sighed in unison, then went to catch up to Kevin. "Okay, wait up. We're coming." Danny gave his patented "doomed to die" expression.

Cold air gushed from the entrance. It was damp and tinged with a mustiness that drenched their faces. They stepped between the tracks, using them as a guide. The rails were rusty and crusted over with age-old mildew, and the wooden crossbeams had crumbled into the ground beneath. Their footsteps made loud crunching noises on the gravel.

For several minutes, they plodded onward, bunched together behind Kevin—the lantern their only beacon against total blight. Its radiance barely penetrated for more than ten feet, striking against the darkness, which seemed almost a touchable thing. It caught in the striations of the walls, streaking tigerlike in the cracks and crevices.

"Ouch! Careful! There's water there."

"QUIT IT!"

"Looks like it goes on forever."

"Maybe it does."

"Colossal, man."

"It's like the goblin tunnels under the Misty Mountains."

" 'My precious-sss. Where ees my precious-sss'?"

They laughed and realized it was to relieve stress. Tom was unaware of the grin that sprawled across his face. Kevin seemed strangely confident and ambled along as though he was familiar with every chip in the wall. It made Tom suspicious.

"Have you been in here before, Kev?"

Kevin paused, hiding a smirk. "Well . . ."

"Uh-oh."

And then three things happened.

The light revealed an object ahead.

A white object with exposed teeth and empty staring cavities.

A human skull!

Tom gasped. "Shii—it!"

Danny's face froze like a zombie, and then he let out a tremulous whine and pushed his way backward. He collided with Tom and stumbled off the tracks, splashing into a puddle.

Kevin laughed at the top of his lungs! The laughter boomed and bounced about the stony surface like a ping pong ball, decimating the silence.

As Danny sloshed about in his wet sneakers, Tom went to examine the macabre display. There was something unconvincing about it. The skull lay amidst a pile of bones that were clearly not human. Probably deer or lamb shanks. A ragged shirt was draped around them, and the skull itself was too white. Only sunshine could bleach a bone so bright, and there would be precious little of that in a tunnel. As he picked it up to examine it, a seam could be discerned just below the cranial cap, clearly exposing the Monogram model kit. Tom smiled with accusation. "Kevin, you madman!"

"What?" he choked between laughs, like a cat coughing on canary feathers.

"Danny, it's a fake!"

"Whatcha mean 'fake'?"

"It's not only a fake, it's *my* fake. I lent it to Kevin last Halloween. *Here!*" He tossed the skull to Danny.

Danny glanced over the plastic cranium and leered at Kevin.

Kevin pointed a finger at Danny. "You shoulda . . . you shoulda seen your face! Uhhh . . . that was great!"

Danny glared, trying to repair his dignity. “You bastard!” He pounced on Kevin in mock anger, trying to wrestle him to the ground. Kevin fended him off, still laughing.

“You came in here alone just to set this whole thing up?”

“Yeah, but I came at *noon*! Only a jackass would come here at *night*, jackasses! But it was worth it just to see the look on your faces. And that sound you made! That was the funniest!”

Tom couldn’t help smiling, remembering Danny’s whine. This exasperated Danny to no end. Before Kevin could stop him, he snatched the lantern from the “barnstormer’s” grasp.

“Oh yeah? Well, I’m outta here. Maybe you jackasses can *feel* your way back.” He began to race back to the entrance.

Weak from laughter, Kevin chased after him. “Hey, beanpole. Wait up.”

As Tom watched them recede, the area grew dark. He remembered the mini-flashlight in his pocket, and pulled it out.

Always be prepared, he thought.

He was about to join them, when he heard something behind him.

Or *thought* he heard something.

It came from deeper within. A hissing whisper. Gaseous vapors rising from the stone, perhaps. Or was it just in his mind?

Tom pointed the light into the further recesses of the

tunnel, probing the darkness with his eyes. "Guys?" He looked back. They were fast retreating to the entrance, Kevin's laughter growing distant.

"Guys, wait up! I think I heard something." He listened ahead, but there was nothing. He stared and stared, inexplicably compelled with curiosity.

Something was there. It lured him.

The little hairs on the back of his neck began to rise.

He felt lightheaded with a mixture of fear and exhilaration. Faint dripping of water could be heard, echoing against the distant stone. The musty air was sweet and damp against his cheeks.

"Hello?" he called out. His voice echoed throughout the chamber and returned to him, unanswered. Yet something beckoned him onward. His feet, frozen in place, now began to move. He felt a yearning he could not resist, and an unquenchable need to discover. Greater than fear. Greater than the will to remain in the safe company of his friends, it called to him from the dark. Tom gave one more look toward the others, the light of the lantern now a dancing star in the distance, and then he took a hesitant step forward.

"Give me the damn light!" Kevin shouted.

"No! Keep away! Mine!" Danny fought him off, his anger replaced by a mischievous zeal.

"Stop being an idiot!" Kevin slipped on a mildew-slick rail and fell back. "Shit!" he scowled, rubbing his bruised palm. He leaped at Danny, but Danny tossed the skull at him.

Kevin snatched it from the air to prevent it from shattering.

"You bust that, I'm gonna bust your head!"

"You dare me?" Danny challenged and then gripped the lantern key, threatening to plunge them into darkness.

"Don't do it!"

With a click, the light vanished. *Everything* vanished. Except the vague gray circle of the entrance.

"You scumbag!" Kevin snarled.

"*Now* who's a jackass?"

"Suck moose!"

"I guess we should see the look on *your* face, right, Tom? Tom?" No reply. There were three ominous clicks on the lantern key as Danny learned how, unlike a flashlight, you can't relight a lantern once the flame has been extinguished.

"Ooops. Who has the lighter?"

"It's in the car, you idiot!"

"Hmm . . . folks, we have a problem."

"Where are you? I can't even *see* you. And where's Tom? Tom!"

Silence. Kevin felt his blood grow cold.

"Where did he go? He was right behind me."

"Great." He felt around in the dark, believing the kid was deliberately lurking behind to launch that inevitable *boo* retaliation.

Nothing. Kevin grew concerned. "Okay, Tom. Joke's over."

"He had a light, didn't he?"

"Then he's better off than we are. We gotta get to the car. Tom! Stay where you are! We'll come back for you!" He bumped into Danny. "Stay close."

"Got any more bright ideas?"

In the dark, he determined where Danny's head was. Slapped it.

"Ow!"

"Idiot."

They made their way toward the steel-gray sky.

The chill of the air began to penetrate Tom's shirt, and he rubbed his shoulders for warmth. He wasn't sure how far he had come. A hundred feet or a hundred miles. He thrust the little flashlight before him like a weapon and continued onward.

His breath was loud, and condensed into a vapor cloud. The summer never reached this part of the tunnel. He'd heard about mountain caves that held ice-sheets frozen since the Pleistocene era. That's what this chill felt like—prehistoric ice.

The *drip-drip-drip*ping was coming nearer.

Sparkles of moisture glistened on the rocks.

A splash of wetness struck him in the back of the neck, startling him. *Tom, you fool,* he thought, *what are you doing?* He wiped away the dampness, feeling a need to call again to his friends. They were probably looking for him by now. He spoke aloud to hear the sound of his voice.

"Hello?" The adventurous spirit in him waned. Yet he

was still seized by an irrational desire to forge ahead. He glanced up at the great arch of the ceiling, expecting to see stalactites dangling down as in some natural subterranean cavern.

A single cricket chirped. The dripping continued into some stagnant pool.

His light caught an object. A discarded leather satchel. It was caked with guano and nearly corroded. Tom kicked at it, and it let out a stench of bat shit and rotting paper.

A few steps more, he found a pottery urn and several jugs shattered against the sidewall. The objects rekindled his curiosity, and the light revealed something ahead that caused his eyes to gape in wonder.

Stones were piled in a circle, like a firepit a Boy Scout would build for a barbecue. Tom peered into the center. It was filled with white ashes and age-old charred wood. Nearby, he noticed additional firewood gathered into fagots.

Who would build such a firepit this deep in a tunnel? Vagrants, perhaps.

He dared to raise the light, and something reflected back.

Cryptic symbols were painted over the tunnel walls in patterns of yellow chalk. The emblems varied in complexity, from simple scribbling, to more elaborate tapestries of perverse line and curve.

"Oh-h . . . God," he whimpered, without realizing.

Tom was familiar with the mystical signs of black magic. His background in fantasy had versed him in such things. Rumors of witchcraft filtered through his thoughts, as did the visions of countless horror movies that now stabbed at his imagination. His first thought was of Jacob Tornau, and he began waving the light around nervously. *The man was never found.*

For the first time, the inadequate light of his pocket flashlight caught the objects off to the side. He gazed over, and blood pounded in his temples, bringing him to the final threshold of terror as he beheld what was sprawled across the floor. They looked like crumpled laundry, but there was something remotely human in their posture. His spine tightened, and he held his breath—ears keen and alert. He studied the shapes until satisfied they were not alive. Tom exhaled, realizing they were empty robes.

The vestments were crimson brown. They appeared woven of some coarse material. Tom could distinguish generous hoods on them, and long full sleeves, like the sacred vestments of a priest. But there was nothing sacred about the way they were strewn about, and it dawned on Tom the most disturbing of notions—that the owners were still present within them, but shriveled to some ungodly state of decay. A wicked temptation grew in him to lift the cloth of the nearest hood and peer within. But then he backed away, the very notion of touching—of prying into the robes—sent shivers throughout his being.

His ears began to hum. His breath labored, gasping at the brink of hyperventilation. He felt a mysterious awareness about him, and the alarming notion that he wasn't alone. Panic set in. He turned to leave, to race back to the safety of his friends, and the moonlight. As he turned, the blood rushed to his head, and a great sense of dizziness overcame him. The light dangled in his hand.

Pandemonium.

There was a flush of mental images through his head, and ethereal whisperings too fast to be heard, too quickly to be grasped. Flashes of light and murmurs of unidentifiable gibberish, rambling chaotic in an endless wave upon wave of visions, and cosmic voids, swirling and twisting, spiraling downward, rushing rushing rushing—and then it all stopped!

The cricket chirped.

The *drip-drip-drip*ping could be heard again.

Tom staggered on his feet, barely catching himself from a fall. His face damp, his head throbbing with an incredible ache, he had the uncanny suspicion that he'd fainted. Yet he knew he had never touched the ground.

He gripped the flashlight and made a mad headlong dash for the entrance.

Kevin raced his engine and rolled the Monstermobile as near to the tunnel mouth as he dared. He switched on his brights and shined them directly into the cave. Danny was beside it, staring within. He could barely make out a dancing star, coming toward them.

"I think I see him," he said. "Tom!"

After an endless moment, a response. "Yeah, I'm

coming! Shut the damn lights off! I can't see!" Kevin switched off the headlights and stepped out to join them. The prodigal friend emerged, moving with a seeming urgency.

"Holy shit! What the hell were you doing?" Kevin shouted. "Are you all right?"

Tom stopped, breathing heavily. "I'm fine. Let's get outta here!"

"Dammit, Tom, you—"

"Let's go! Now! I mean it!" He fought by them, seeking the safety of the car. He didn't want to give explanations. He just wanted to put as much distance between himself and the tunnel as he could.

When they had driven a while, Kevin shouted at Tom, "Don't you *ever* steal the payoff of a good joke like that! This was *my* horror show, and I had dibs on scaring someone to death."

Tom nodded without arguing. The ache in his head was still throbbing.

"Yeah, Tom," Danny added. "That was pretty stupid, going off alone. Coulda gotten hurt. You sure you're all right?"

There was a great pulsing at the back of his neck, like the ebb and flow of waves breaking against a rocky shore. He closed his eyes and shook it off. "I'm okay. Just a little dizzy."

Kevin glanced over. "So what'd you find in there? 'Cause you came out looking like you'd seen Bigfoot *and* the Loch Ness Monster."

"Right." Tom eyed him accusingly. "As if you don't know?"

"I never went in that far. Honest."

Tom considered telling them what he saw, but there was the dread that they would be enticed and insist on returning. "I didn't see anything. Just some garbage. Old beer cans and stuff."

The lie seemed to satisfy them, and they changed the subject. It was then that Tom became aware of the ringing in his ears. Remnants of a verse were playing in his mind. A familiar chant lost to memory like the words of a song. It was distant at first, a subconscious hum, but then it grew stronger in his brain. The lyrics took on a distinct rhythm. Tom focused his attention. He ignored the distracting voices of Kevin and Danny and pressed his fists against his knees, concentrating. He mumbled under his breath, playing the verse over his tongue for any sign of familiarity.

Then a single word burst out of his lips. "Fau'Charoth."

The other's looked at him. "What was that?" Kevin asked.

"Fow-ka-ROTH," he repeated, slowly enunciating each syllable.

"What the hell does that mean?"

He recited a full line from the mysterious litany. " *'Fau' Charoth . . . a Lammashta ra shagmuku tu'.*"

There was silence in the car. Kevin shook his head. "You lost me, kiddo."

"It's something that's playing through my head," Tom explained. "I thought maybe you could recognize it." He repeated the phrase, and they each passed it through volumes of stored sci-fi and fantasy memories.

Danny shrugged. "Nope. Sorry. Is it from *Lord of the Rings*?"

"No," Tom disagreed. "It's not Tolkien."

"Maybe it's Lovecraft. Or Robert E. Howard."

"I don't think so. Whatever it is, it's driving me crazy. It's playing back and forth in my head like a goddamn Gregorian chant. I've got a pounding headache." He rubbed his temples. "Fau'Charoth," he repeated. "Fau'Charoth. What the hell is Fau'Charoth?"

"Okay, you're definitely scaring me, now," Kevin said.

"Y'know, maybe you ran into some swamp gas," Danny offered. "They say old caves and mines develop these pockets of methane and shit. It coulda gone to your head and screwed you up for a bit."

Swamp gas, Tom thought. *Great.*

Kevin nodded in agreement. "Yeah, I bet that's all it is. You'll sleep it off. I think we'll call it quits, guys. Enough excitement for one night."

Tom didn't argue.

CHAPTER 6

As they neared Tom's home, it became apparent that Mrs. DeFrank's guest had not left. Franklyn's BMW was still parked in the driveway, despite the space he had cleared for him in the garage. The lights were out in the house. Tom cursed internally at his mom's indiscretion.

"Yep," Danny remarked, noting the Beamer. "Looks like Mom and Paul are tucked in for the night." He always knew the sore spots.

"Shut up, Dan!" Kevin scolded.

Tom didn't comment, though he appreciated Kevin's defense. His mom's social life wasn't a subject for discussion. Ever. He climbed out of the car with a nod. Kevin leaned over for a final look. "Hey, you sure you're all right? You look a little spaced. How many fingers am I holding up?"

"Eleven."

"Right. You're fine." Kevin smiled and clasped his hand warmly. "Chill out, man."

"I will. See you tomorrow. You too, Dan."

Tom watched as they pulled out of his driveway. He

was still a little dazed.

Across the street, Mrs. Wadowski, one of his neighbors, was out late, walking her little black terrier, Mitzi. The woman tugged on its leash, which had a retractable cartridge that allowed the dog to wander thirty feet. Mitzi had a particularly annoying bark, which often kept Tom up till all hours of the night.

Tonight, it was especially vocal. It just kept yapping and yapping at him.

"Mitzi, be quiet," the woman commanded, glancing at Tom apologetically.

Stupid dog, he thought as he turned toward the house.

Two hours later, he was still awake. He lay in bed, peering up at the bands of streetlight the blinds cast on his wall. Occasionally, a car would go by and the beams would send long wraiths of light up to the ceiling. He turned on his side, throwing off the bed sheet.

The words still echoed in his head. Blood was pounding in his temples like a great caffeine rush. He was aware of the silence. The sounds of it all—the ticking of his clock, the passage of air through his window. Every time he closed his eyes, slipping into a half-dream state, he had the uncanny feeling he was still there, back in that dark place! Those insidious emblems could burn their way through his walls. The decrepit ochre robes could suddenly appear as Nazgûl wraiths, and rise up to attack him. Any thought of sleep was banished. His nerves were taut as ironmongery.

He got up and did what he often did when he couldn't sleep. Hoping to exhaust himself, he sat at his desk, turned the small work lamp on, and reached for his sketchbook. It was encased in a black leather binder, engraved with his name, a confirmation gift from his grandpa. Inside was a large spiral-bound sketchpad of coarse-textured paper. A number of sketches already filled the pages, including some design drawings for "Primeval Kings." Beyond the dinosaur studies were a tableau of images that seemed coughed up from a demented mind. Snakes and tentacles undulating over skulls and bones. Fetid life springing from decay. Rock formations that hinted of feminine limbs and torsos in a landscape of twisted eroticism.

His mom was especially disturbed by these images. She didn't like him dabbling in such macabre subjects. Though hardly a model Catholic herself, she occasionally went to church and was frightened by things too obviously unholy. When Tom turned ten, she had him interviewed by a priest. It was in preparation for his first Holy Communion, but his conversation with the father was unusually deep, as though the man was analyzing him for signs of evil. He received a generous sprinkling of holy water that day. Later, as he began tampering with his stop-motion hobby, his mom sent him to a psychologist for further counseling. The shrink dismissed his unusual art subjects as those of a youthful mind struggling to establish an identity. He even encouraged it as a form of purgation. Purgation of *what* he never learned.

All of this made Tom self-conscious about his artwork.

He folded the more sinister sketches back into the pad, aware of their disturbing nature. He couldn't explain their origin and sometimes wondered at his own sanity. Yet he could no more suppress these hellish images than he could silence an urgent sneeze. They oozed from his fingers like pus onto the page, but once expelled from his subconscious they became his art, and he loved them as earnestly as any angel on the Sistine Chapel.

Tom removed the pad from its snug leather wrapping, flipped over to a blank page, then pulled several charcoal pencils from a canister.

For a moment he was at a loss, staring down at the virgin paper. Then the verse resumed in his head. It repeated again and again, and Tom knew instinctively what he had to do. He took his pencil and began not to draw but to *write*.

"Fau'Charoth," he began, in big scrawling letters at the bottom of the page. It was an odd spelling—an apostrophe after the *u*; *ch* pronounced as a *k*—but it felt strangely correct, though clearly of another language. His hands began to tremble. Then he transcribed the entire verse, like a steno-pool secretary recording dictation.

"Fau'Charoth a Lammashta ra shagmuku tu."

Staring at the phrase, Tom couldn't believe his eyes. What had he written? Where did it come from? The words could've been in his native tongue, so sure he was of structure and form. But he had no idea what they meant, or what their purpose was. They were emblazoned like chalkboard scribblings onto his subconscious. The words had trickled through his brain and spilled forth onto the page.

He looked down at the arcane verse, and in his mind saw a flash of wings, a horned monster face, and immediately—almost mechanically—he began to sketch it in the space above.

Joining the skulls and tentacles and dinosaurs, a new image took shape. It began with a human torso, but it grew a tail. Dinosaur legs sprouted from its hips, and sinuous, muscular arms from a barrel chest. Web-fingered wings rose from its back, and its lupine face snarled. His pencil strokes glided together, maneuvered in some way. *That's right,* he nodded, as spines were added to the crest of its skull. *Yes!* He nodded again as razor-sharp talons were attached to its heels.

Every line knew where to go. His own genius in all things monster blended with an otherworldly design that was unique to anything he had previously attempted. With every stroke, the pulsing at his temples began to ease. The phantasmagoric images jammed into his brain found their release. He got absorbed into the creation process, and it was sheer delight.

CHAPTER 7

THE CRISP MORNING AIR FELT GOOD ON TOM'S FACE AS he peddled his ten-speed bike to school. There was the first hint of a breeze in weeks. It refreshed his spirit, removing the last traces of sleepiness from his head. He wore a new pair of prewashed jeans, and a hunter green Polo shirt that gripped him at the shoulders. On his back was a knapsack filled with a tablet, several writing utensils, and his hastily prepared lunch. It also contained his sketch folder and the nearly completed monster drawing.

The BMW was gone from the driveway. His mom and "Paul" had left early, presumably to avoid any ungraceful encounters in the hallway, which was fine by him. It was that awkward period in his mom's relationship cycle, the flash before the fall, when her new beau would get accustomed to the game rules, just before things burned out like a meteorite in the upper atmosphere. Tom gave it two months, tops.

The peddling felt good on his legs.

He preferred biking to school whenever possible, before

the long winter months forced him to take the bus. The journey was beset with some steep hills that required him to practically stand on the pedals, bringing his speed down to a crawl. But his thighs were remarkably strong for a kid his height, and the blue Schwinn made him a flash on wheels. The main streets were busy with the early morning traffic, so he stuck to a series of side roads, avoiding the congestion of merciless rush-hour drivers.

Despite a mere five hours of sleep the night before, Tom felt strangely energized. He wanted to be alert for his first day as a junior and kicked his feet into the pedals as though he would traverse the boundaries of Chapinaw from one end to the other. An ambitious task. Chapinaw was one of the largest divisions of Sullivan County, a rural stretch of small hamlets and villages, all sharing the same township. It was a mixture of the old and new. A boom in construction had sent real estate skyrocketing, and rumors of a new rail line to New York City caused a migration of families into the new cookie-cutter house communities that specked the landscape. It seemed suburbia had dropped out of the sky onto an endless expanse of wood and farmland, filling the gaps with condos and shopping malls. Tom had reluctantly grown accustomed to the backwoods community. It was in his blood, after all. He was technically a 'townie,' having been born here, though he'd spent most of his life on the outskirts of Albany. Schenectady seemed like a metropolis by comparison. Tom's mom had roots in Chapinaw that went back two generations, so it wasn't surprising that, when all else failed, she chose to return here. It meant sucking up to her parents and coming to terms with the past. For Tom, it was like revisiting the locale of a previous incarnation, where the very ground you walked on knew you better than you knew yourself.

He skidded onto a road overhung with oak and maple trees. A half-mile later, it opened onto the verdant play fields behind Chapinaw High School. Wheeling his Schwinn through the faculty parking lot, he chained it to a long bike rack already flanked with other bicycles. Then he shouldered his bag, feeling a rush of excitement prick up his spine. First day of classes always had its mixture of thrill and apprehension. This one had the flavor of new beginnings.

Less than two minutes into a new school, and these kids were already looking for "stuff." "Forget homeroom and the locker banks. Just point me to the candy store 'cause I gotta get high." It meant demand was growing. Lunch money, allowances, and summer wages would lace his pockets in exchange for that little tickle on the cortex. Not that he needed the cash. His family was loaded. The petty change from the pill sales could barely put gas in his Jaguar. He had his sights, these days, on bigger territories, like the nearby community college. Plus, he had made a killing over the summer, landing some major accounts off the hotel circuit. No, it wasn't for the money that he kept his little shop open in the high school. It was for the power.

Burke was a November child, and his dad had deliberately delayed his entry into grade school a full year to give him an advantage. The gambit had paid off. He was nearly nine months older than his peers. With it came the swagger and confidence of a wolf among sheep. He had short-cropped cocoa-brown hair, gas-flame blue eyes, and perfect teeth that glowed phosphorescent white. With those eyes and that smile, he could charm the fig leaves off Eve in the Garden. Or so he liked to think. At five-nine, he wasn't the tallest of his group. That would be Al Gunthur, the brute behind him who silently watched from the corner. Gunthur was on the wrestling team. He stood six-foot-two, with a bulging chest, and a neck thick as a telephone pole. His crew cut made him look like an AWOL marine. Excellent grunt material, but his expression was dull and bovine.

Dumb as a yak. He did follow orders, though, to the letter.

Then there was Lenny Finch, Burke's right-hand man. Lenny had his back pressed to the wall, and was laughing at some private joke. He maintained an inner dialogue with himself, sometimes mumbling aloud in a way that made him look insane. His hair was dusty blond, and feather-cropped like Andy Gibb. He liked disco music and enjoyed hoofing it on the dance floor. The guy could move too. Like Baryshnikov on platform shoes. He'd spent so many nights at the Chalet that the Revele Hotel management gave him a job spinning records as a professional disc jockey.

Finch's DJ gig gave Burke clean entry into the hotel club scene. Wealthy out-of-towners were always looking for a quick high, and the rock bands practically ate the stuff!

A sophomore barged into the bathroom. He was dressed in denim and looked constipated.

"Hey Burke?" the stony asked. "Can you swing me an ounce of grass?"

Burke crushed the cigarette into the sink. "No grass, today. I'm totally sold out."

"No GRASS?" The kid was dumbstruck. "What d'ya mean? You can't swing me one joint?"

"Stockpiles are down. I'm expecting more any day now. I've got some dust, and a few 'zonkers' left over."

"Ahhh man. I need reefer today like nobody's business. Where am I gonna find some grass?"

Gunthur looked up. The kid was stepping out of line.

"Hey!" Burke leered. "I said, no grass today. Just pills

and dust. Now get out of here. Store's closed." The sophomore moaned a pisser and pushed his way out of the boys' room, followed closely by McBride and Plotnick. Burke stuffed the remains of his stash away, exasperated. Pot was his best sell, and to be short on supplies was going to cost him. That wiseass wouldn't be the first today to bitch about it. Others would complain.

What a waste.

He had lost his entire stock of marijuana over the weekend. It had mysteriously vanished from his car. Lifted. Enough pot to last through the end of October. He had just made a huge sale with the rock band Silver Cross at the Chalet. Jessie Boggs was a major pothead, and the others gorged on his grass like mules on alfalfa.

But Burke had been careless. After the delivery, he was coaxed into a little rendezvous with Lizzie, a member of the Cross entourage who was staying at the hotel. The girl was a college freshman and difficult to resist in her short black skirt. He'd dropped his bag off in the Jaguar and went up to her suite. It was a major fuck-up, screwing around with a groupie while a gross amount of contraband lay stashed in his car.

So there it was, sitting under his dashboard in an innocuous duffle bag. It might have contained a smelly pair of gym shorts and running shoes. Instead, it contained his ass in a sling. Then it was gone. Damn it! Another shipment wasn't due for weeks.

He didn't have to look far for a suspect. Angry as he

was, he was impressed that someone had the balls to pull off such a sting, and he wanted to shake the hand of the man responsible. Shake it and then break it.

CHAPTER 9

DANNY GAWKED AT THE NEW DRAWING IN TOM'S sketchbook.

"You drew that *last night*?" he asked.

"Yeah." Tom shrugged, taking a swig of his iced tea. "I guess Kevin's little scare trip inspired me."

Tom had the sketchbook open in his lap. He chomped on his sandwich with his left hand while the right diligently worked with a pencil. It was lunchtime, and they sat on the grassy hill below Senior Lane where the upperclassmen sat above surveying their exploits like the gods of Olympus. The courtyard was filled with students from the main dining room—cliques forming instantly, jocks with jocks, intellectual acrobats with other brains, and a band of stonies, wandering aimlessly, like oil floating to the top of a pond. The burnouts dressed in dilapidated denim, exposing knees and elbows in strategic tears. Rock band logos were embroidered on their backs.

Hanging in the shade of the underpass, Clifford Burke was making time with a cute blonde who looked like a pinup torn off a locker-room wall. She wore white shorts over a summer tan and a tight, clinging blouse that bulged provocatively. Tom thought for sure that Dan would make the usual lascivious remark about her.

But Danny hadn't noticed. He was still looking at the sketch.

What he saw was a creature part man and part dragon, with bat-fingered wings that unfolded from its shoulder blades like kites. A canine snout protruded from its face with dagger fangs. Horns spiraled from a bony brow above intensely savage eyes. Danny couldn't decide if he was fascinated or appalled. The creature had a fearsome, otherworldly grandeur that, like a tiger, was both majestic and terrible at once.

"Totally demented," he remarked. "How did you come up with it?"

"I couldn't sleep. I just got up and started sketching it," Tom said, applying little circlets to the creature's back with his pencil.

Danny shook his head in wonder. "You scare the bejesus out of me sometimes."

Al Gunthur and Lenny Finch entered the courtyard. Finch produced a Frisbee and tossed it. Burke took a few athletic leaps backward and snatched the flying disk from the air. He then hurled it underhand to Gunthur, who crushed it between his gigantic palms.

Tom watched, disgusted at their showmanship, and bagged the rest of his sandwich.

"Showoffs. They think they're hot shit," Danny complained.

"Well, they are," Tom complained. "Ya ever smell hot shit? It stinks."

Danny's eyes drifted back to the monster and noticed the funny inscription jotted at the bottom of the page.

It read: *FAU'CHAROTH A LAMMASHTA RA SHAGMUKU TU.*

"What's this?"

"It's that crazy verse I had in my head. Remember? It wouldn't go away."

"Fow-charrr," Dan struggled to pronounce it.

"Fow-ka-ROTH," Tom corrected. "That's its name, I decided."

"It would make a great fire-devil. You should bring it to the D&D club meeting after school. Spencer's starting a new dungeon."

"Naah."

Despite its many fantasy trappings, Tom had no interest in the game *Dungeons and Dragons.* He'd attended a session, once. It amounted to hours of map drawing, dice rolling, and squabbling over "experience points," chores more suited to a cartographer or an accountant. It seemed a dreadful waste of time.

"I'm gonna be sculpting, tonight," he said proudly, pointing to the sketch. "It's gonna be my new puppet." Tom knew it was the best thing he'd ever done, and was eager to bring it to life in his stop-motion world. The day was dragging, and all he could think of was getting home and immersing his fingers in plasticine.

There was a white blur as the Frisbee sliced the air onto the grass beside them. Tom looked up and froze like a hare before a stalking fox. Burke was heading their way. Danny noticeably tensed and seemed ready to bolt.

"Steady," Tom warned. Burke's approach became a cocky stride, flanked now by Gunthur and Finch.

Danny panicked. "That's it. I'm outta here. See you in science."

"If you run now, you'll be running all year."

"So what? Practice makes perfect." He grabbed his books and was *gone.* Burke came to the grassy spot, followed closely by the others. Tom felt the hair on his nape bristle. For a moment he regretted that he hadn't followed Danny's lead, but he held his ground, even as Burke's shadow loomed over him like the angel of death.

"Hey, it's Kevin's little sidekick, the mad scientist," Burke spoke in a mock-friendly voice as he bent to retrieve the Frisbee. "Dig up any corpses today, DeFrankenstein?"

"No, but he looks like one," said Gunthur.

Tom remained focused on his work, refusing to look up. *They can smell fear*, he thought.

"Hey, Burke," Lenny said. "Check out what he's drawing."

With a sweep of his hand, Burke snatched the sketchbook, holding it aloft.

"Lay off!" Tom yelled, grasping for his book.

"Whoa. Is this insane or what?"

"Scary shit, man. Like the Antichrist."

"You've got one twisted mind, DeFrank. Your mom

see this stuff?"

"Give it back!" Tom shouted.

"Looks kinda familiar, doesn't it?" Burke cocked his head quizzically.

"It looks like Principal Harding on a bad trip," Lenny laughed.

"No, it don't." Burke smiled with a sudden revelation. "It looks like Gunthur's dad! Yo, Gung-ho, he drew a picture of your old man!"

Gunthur, pretending to be insulted, pulled the sketchbook from Burke's grasp. When Tom grabbed for it, he gave him a powerful shove in the chest that sent him falling backward.

"Quit it, mesomorph!" Tom shouted.

"I should bust your face in." Gunthur flipped through the pages, deliberately bending them. "Are there any chicks in here?"

"Nope," said Lenny. "Just monsters and shit. I thought artists drew pictures of naked girls."

"Maybe he's a fag artist." Gunthur handed the pad back to Burke.

"Naw, I bet he's got a secret project somewhere in his basement," Burke added. "He's putting a chick together, piece by piece. A little 'Erector Set' of the T&A variety."

"Yeah? Erect *this*," said Lenny, cupping his hand obscenely.

"Give me the goddamn book!" shouted Tom, snatching for the sketchpad.

They played it for all it was worth, handing it off from one to the other. “Hey. It’s got wings. Maybe it can fly!” With a flamboyant back-sweep, Gunthur let the book sail from his grip. It soared past the grass and flopped open on the pavement.

“Son-of-a-bitch.” When Tom tried to go after it, Burke grabbed him. He snatched the pencil from Tom’s grasp and pointed it at his face.

“Listen to me, DeFrank,” he said with dead seriousness. “You tell your buddy Kevin to quit fucking with me and give back what belongs to me. ’Cause, if not, you and his other fag friends are gonna be hurting. You got that?”

A thousand replies went through Tom’s head. A thousand witty comebacks, defensive remarks, and deliberate threats that all melded together into one unified dragon snarl. But they all froze in his throat with the sane reasoning that he was hopelessly outmatched. He felt his shoulders sag in defeat and did the only sensible thing he could do.

He nodded his head.

With a painful snap, Burke broke the pencil in half and tossed the pieces at his feet. “Later for you, monster boy.” He left. The others followed. Snickering.

“Mad scientist. Gonna take over the world.”

Lenny sang, “Le-et’s do the time warp aga-*aaaain*!”

CHAPTER IO

TOM EXHALED TO SLOUGH OFF THE RUSH OF ANGER AND humiliation. *It could've gone worse*, he told himself, but there was certainly potential for that later.

What the hell was going on? Threats from Clifford Burke were not to be taken lightly. Evidently Kevin had pissed him off enough for Burke to set his sights on him and Danny. If so, it looked like the start of a miserable year.

Tom scowled in the direction they left as though the air there had turned foul, and then went to reclaim his sketch-book. At first glance, it wasn't where it had dropped, which worried him. But then he saw what had become of it.

A girl had it. Tom stopped. By the denim outfit she was wearing, he at first took her to be one of the stonies. But she was too pretty to be a strung-out pothead. She held the book to her eyes and was peering at it with fascination.

He stepped quietly to her side. A bit *too* quietly, for when she became aware of him she startled as though Tom had materialized out of the air. He found himself looking into the most intense brown eyes he had ever seen. Shyness got the best of him and his voice froze.

"Ummm . . . thanks. That's mine."

"Huh? Oh! I'm sorry. It was—"

"That's okay."

"—lying there, and I picked it up so that—"

"It was kind of *tossed*."

"I saw." She looked up. "That wasn't very nice of them."

He shrugged it off, smiling. "They like to give me grief. It's how they get their jollies."

She brushed dark bangs away from her forehead. Her face looked familiar, a face you might glance back at twice while passing in the halls. He couldn't place her, though.

"Are these your drawings?" She was studying the Fau'Charoth sketch again and perused some of his earlier works as well.

"Yeah, they're mine. Pretty weird, huh?" That was the usual response.

"Weird? Oh no, I think they're *wonderful*," she said.

His eyes brightened. "Really?"

With these words, the girl went from pretty to beautiful. People usually described his work as "strange" or "ugly." "Wonderful" from a beautiful girl meant an awful lot.

Her fingers reached into the back of the pad, and he braced when she flipped to the "forbidden sketches," but her brow arched deliciously with the sight of the vermin-infested bones, and female-limbed rock formations. "Wickedly erotic. A little twisted, but well executed."

As she studied his drawings, he took a moment to study

her. Dark chestnut hair fell to shoulders just below his own. They were small shoulders, delicate, yet graced with vigor. Her girlish curves were almost lost in the androgynous trappings. She was lithely built, her features delicate, with high, pronounced cheekbones, and a small nose that peaked elflike to a point. Her skin was like cream and had a golden glow against the flow of her hair. As he became aware of all this, he also became aware that he was *staring* at her.

She must have sensed his gaze, because she looked up and met his eyes for a moment. Then she was studying the cuffs of his shirt, seemingly.

Who was this girl? He considered uncomfortably that he might have met her once before, but forgot her name. She glanced at the leather binder, noticing the engraved signature.

"You're Tom DeFrank, aren't you?"

"Yeah, that's me."

"Hi. I'm Julie. I think we had a class together." She offered her hand. He shook it, remarking how small it seemed, and soft. Are girls' hands always so soft? And the nails were cut short, unlike—

"Where did you get the 'incantation'?" she inquired.

The question surprised him. "The what?" He watched as she pointed to the phrase below the new monster sketch. "That? Why do you call it an incantation?" The implication of the word disturbed him.

"Oh, it definitely is," she said with authority. "I'm not sure what kind, but I'm almost certain it's a spell."

He shrugged doubtfully. "I think you're probably mistaken."

Her voice got noticeably louder. "No, I'm *not.* '*Ra shagmuku tu.*' It looks to me like ancient Sumerian. That's a language usually associated with spells."

Tom was astonished. "How do you know all this?"

She shrugged. "I read a lot. So where'd it come from? 'Cause if it is a spell, you shouldn't be dabbling in that kind of magic. It's dangerous."

"It's not. I *don't.* To be honest, I'm not even sure where it came from. It just sort of zapped into my head."

"Zapped?"

"Kind of. My friends and I were goofing around over by Crohaven Road and—"

Her eyes sharpened on him. "Crohaven?"

"Yeah. By that creepy old mansion. You know, where that old witch guy lives."

Julie flinched as though stung by a hornet. Darkness fell over her features. "Oh. Yeah. *That guy.*" She handed the book back to him with a loud thump on his chest and began walking away.

Tom was mortified. *What did he say?* He gasped and remembered with terrible affirmation why she looked so familiar. The longer hair had thrown him off, and her body had filled out somewhat, no longer the pale wraith he spied from the distance. Julie was "the warlock's daughter." Tom crumbled under an avalanche of *faux pas.* "Oh, dammit. Good one, DeFrank."

He trotted after her and contritely touched her on the shoulder.

"Julie. Wait. I'm sorry. I didn't realize. You're Julie *Parrish*."

She turned to him, flushed. "He's not old. And he's not a *witch*, either! He's my father!"

"I didn't mean to upset you. I wasn't implying—"

"Sure, you were. You assume. You don't really know anything about him, but you just like to talk, like everybody else. Typical."

His face was on fire. "You're right. I'm sorry. I'm a total slug. I'm *worse* than a slug. I'm the crap off a slug's shoe."

Something in his tattered demeanor touched her. Her fury subsided. "Okay. Maybe I'm overreacting a little. I didn't mean to snap at you."

Tom released his breath. "I guess you get that a lot from people."

"Yeah," she nodded. "I should be used to it, but it still touches a nerve. Fortunately, most people don't seem to care much, anymore. That is, until *you* came along." She blinked. "But then most people don't draw monsters with devilish incantations under them."

"Touché." He was really beginning to like this girl and felt grateful for a second chance. "So, you don't *live* at Crohaven, do you?"

"No. With my mom in White Lake. They're split. My dad prefers to be alone, now, after everything that happened."

"I understand. This town's full of jerks. But why do

they say all those things about him?"

"My dad's got special talents," she explained. "If that makes him a 'witch,' then it's a shame. He's an artist, like you."

Tom raised his brows. "He's an artist? How do you mean?"

"He paints things. Very bizarre, beautiful things."

"Really? That's pretty cool. He sounds like an interesting man."

"He is. He's also one of the gentlest men you'll ever meet."

Tom sensed in Julie genuine admiration for her father. "I'd like to."

She glanced at him with a smirk. "I bet you would. I think he'd find that sketch of yours pretty interesting, as well. I'm biking there today, after school. Maybe I'll mention it to him."

"You're biking there, today?"

They both heard the bell ring. "Yeah. Well, I better run," she said. "I'll see you around." She began walking to the doors. About eighty percent of Tom's body wanted to walk after her. He wished he had a tracking device to stick on her shoulder. Spy glasses to watch her. High-tech telemetry to chart her movements and record her words. He wanted to know everything about this girl, but in another moment she would be gone. He needed a reason to connect further with her. Any reason at all.

"I got a bike," he blurted out.

She turned. “Hmm?”

“A brand new Schwinn. Ten-speed. Maybe I can come with you.”

“To meet my dad?” She seemed slightly troubled, as though it were a far greater demand than it might sound. “Well . . . I’m not sure. I barely know you.”

“There isn’t much more to know,” he persisted. “You get most of me in a glance.”

Tom stood there, palms wide as if to say “take me please.” She looked at him, and a bashful grin peeked through the clouds. “Okay. Meet me by the bike racks alongside the Social Studies building at 3:05 sharp. Bring your monster book!” She flew off like a sparrow. Tom watched her graceful form disappear into the building. For a moment he just stood in a daze, his head strangely light. *Son of a gun*, he thought. He glanced at his watch and bounded off in the other direction.

CHAPTER II

KEVIN HAD ALREADY SCORED 438,000 ON THE PINBALL machine. Two thousand more and he'd get another free ball. The pinball machine was one of the perks of Senior Lane, a lounge where seniors were able to spend their free periods loafing on sofas like the privileged class. Large windows and a sliding door led down a grassy slope to the courtyard. Years back, as an underclassman, Senior Lane had seemed to him like the pinnacle of coolness, the Valhalla of the grade years. Now it was just another place to idle away in wasteful thought.

Two girls, Sophie and Debbie, were admiring him from across the lane. He was keenly aware of their eyes on him, yet pretended not to notice. Debbie was cute but a little tall for him. Sophie was more his speed, a redhead. He'd hit on her a few times, but nothing beyond a brief flirtation. For now, he was keeping a safe distance, enjoying his reputation as the Shane of the senior corral. Sex was easy to come by, but it wasn't love. He'd already known love, and it hurt him too much.

He rammed the silver ball with his left paddle and sent it flying to the yellow pocket. The bells rang, adding an additional round, but Kev was tired of the game. He motioned to another senior to take over and sat in a corner.

Burke appeared from the hall. Upon spotting Kevin, he vaulted athletically over the guardrail of the lounge and sauntered toward him. Kevin sensed his approach, and a tingle went up his spine. *Here it comes*, he thought, playing it cool, even when Burke leaned over the bank of seats, gazing directly at him. "Ding ding!" he said. Kevin frowned and ignored him.

"Ding ding!" Burke repeated. "Hey, bellboy. That's your cue, isn't it?"

"Fuck off."

"I liked your monkey suit."

"Yeah? I'll get you one for Christmas."

"No, thanks. Scraping for tips ain't my style. So what's the bread like on a gig like that?"

Kevin turned to him. "Coulda done better with Cross. Boggs turned out to be a cheapskate. But then I guess he was all tapped out."

Burke smiled. "Too bad. I did pretty well by him."

"Looked like it." Kevin smirked, remembering the rock star all dripping in a towel.

The erotic insinuation went over Burke's head. "Market was up all summer. The Chalet's a goldmine. You could've been in on that, you know. Beats hauling bags."

"And share the action with you three stooges? I don't

think so."

"Like you're better off with those dweebs you're hanging out with, now? DeFrank and Kaufman? Man, what do you see in those guys?"

Kevin looked at him square. "They're real. And they don't sell dope."

"Right, like you never think about having a little sideline, moving a little stash at the hotel? You'd do ten times better than any loser bellhop."

"Pushing's your territory. Always was."

"That's right. Just remember that." He glanced around to see if others were listening. The girls had left, and there were few passersby. He leaned closer to Kevin, his demeanor deadly serious. "Okay, man, so what's this about? What's with the bug up your ass?"

Kevin eyeballed him with denial. "I don't know? What?"

"You know what I mean. I'm talkin' about you busting my balls."

"Are you high? 'Cause I don't like your altitude."

"You can hate me all you want," he said, shifting again to pure threat. "But when you start messing with my business, you're asking for trouble."

"What are you talking about?"

"I want my stuff back."

"What 'stuff'?" Kevin dodged him, indulging in the sight of Mr. Cool defrosting.

"Don't bust my chops, man. Just give it back, and I'll forget you ever took it."

"Are you accusing me of robbing you?"

"Listen, I know about the other night. You knew where I was parked, and you were the only one who could've pulled it off. So quit hassling me and give it back."

"What's this 'stuff' you're talking about? Describe it. Maybe we can go down to the sheriff and fill out a theft report."

"You're not going to make this easy for me, are you?"

"Well, you see, that's the thing. I figure if I make things any easier, you might just think you *own* this fuckin' town."

"It's about the girl. Isn't it?" Burke probed. "You're still upset over the girl?"

For the first time, Kevin felt his pulse rise. "Get outta here, Burke."

"Is this how you're gonna get even with me? With childish little pranks and thievery?"

"Get OUT!"

"'Cause I told you, man, what happened with Kathy wasn't my fault. You knew her as long as I did. She was sick. She was sick from the first day she came on to me."

Kevin trembled with rage. "Yeah, she was sick, all right, the day you looked at her! The day you contaminated her like a virus!" His voice was barely a whisper, but it echoed in Burke's ears like a mortar round.

Burke slammed his fist down on the alcove railing. "You're asking for major grief, man."

"Life's full of it, and so are you."

"Asshole."

"Cheap dime store pusher."

Burke scowled and walked off. Kevin wanted a piece of him. He wanted badly to reduce that strut of his to a painful crawl, but he kept his cool, out of respect for Kathy.

Kathy McGuire was long gone. Over a year later and the pain still lingered in his heart like a terrible vacuum. There were few things in his life he had truly loved. Kathy was one of them. Kevin first took notice of her in sophomore year, when he was still foolishly a member of Burke's "in" crowd. Though she shared his grade, she seemed younger, like a delicate flower that was just blooming. Kevin flirted with her innocently at first. She liked horses, so he brought her to the Monticello raceway. He remembered how dazzled she was, watching them gallop on the track below. They were too young to gamble, but Kevin had convinced another patron to drop ten bucks on a horse for them. They promptly lost the money, but the look in Kathy's eyes was precious as their horse, for a brief moment, rode the outside track and nearly stole the race. Later, they snuck into the stables where the horses were kept. Gunthur's dad worked the stalls and gave them a tour. They were able to stroke the finely trained animal as it cooled down after the run. Kathy wanted to "fly home" on him. She was a sweet, fragile kid with a sparkling disposition, and Kevin fell powerfully in love with her.

But she had a *thing* for Clifford Burke.

It was obvious whenever he was around. There was that friction between them, the kind of tension that masks a secret infatuation. They exchanged barbs and friendly insults like brother and sister. But eventually, Burke caught on to her crush and took advantage, hitting on her with all charms blazing. Kathy was overwhelmed. She had looked into the serpent's eyes and was hypnotized.

An "impromptu encounter" with Burke left her pregnant and suicidal. Apparently she was more fragile than anyone suspected. Learning the news, Kevin's vehemence at Burke was barely contained, but his first concern was for Kathy. He was determined to be her savior and confessed his love for her in a foolhardy display of affection. Sadly, it made matters worse. Kathy seemed wounded by his pronouncement of love, as though it was a betrayal of trust. It smelled of desire and sex, things she now abhorred.

In the end, to avoid family court, Burke rather ungraciously paid for an abortion, insinuating that it wasn't his child. It wrecked havoc on her sensitive disposition. After the pregnancy was terminated, Kathy suffered a mental breakdown and attempted suicide. Three razor slashes to the wrist. Her family had her committed to an institution in White Plains for treatment. Kevin was denied visitation, because of his role in what Mrs. McGuire called her "emotional impairment."

That's what his love did to the girl.

Burke, of course, denied all responsibility.

"It wasn't my fault," he'd claimed, "The girl had *issues*, man. I think the father screwed her up. That's what I think."

Kevin recognized the behavior of a sociopath. They'd

been enemies ever since. Dangerously so, with a malice cradled deep in the heart. Theirs was the kind of enmity with which cold wars were fought. Secretly, in little, clandestine acts of vengeance.

CHAPTER 12

A PAIR OF BLUE JAYS FLUTTERED FROM THE SIDE OF the road, alarmed by the swift passing of Tom and Julie on their bicycles. The late afternoon sun left patches of light on the road like fallen leaves. Tom kept his bike abreast of Julie's, but occasionally drifted back, allowing her to lead. It was partly out of chivalry and partly because he enjoyed keeping her in sight, watching the smooth grace of her body as she pedaled.

She slowed down, allowing him to pull alongside her. "He's not expecting company," she said breathlessly, "but I guess it'll be all right. I could show you his paintings, at any rate."

"Sounds good."

"But you have to promise me one thing. That no matter what you see or hear, you'll keep an 'open mind'."

"Hey, no problem. I've got the 'Mini Mart' of minds."

Julie cocked her head, baffled.

"The convenience store? Open twenty-four hours!" he explained.

She rolled her eyes, bemused. "Okay, 'Mini Mart,' how fast can you pedal?"

"Like a bat OUTTA HELLLL!" He shouted Kevin's battle-cry and launched into breakneck speed. She kept apace with him all the way, as the imposing structure of Crohaven Manor appeared on the horizon.

They came to a stop at the front gate. She went to the mailbox, and pulled open the flap. The box was empty.

"Does your dad ever get any mail?" Tom asked.

"Of course he does," she said with a furrowed brow. "He's not a ghost *everywhere.* He's even got a telephone. See?" She pointed to the wire that led from a pole to the rooftop. "Although, to be honest, I've never heard it ring. Not once."

They wheeled their bikes through the gate and parked them beside the Victorian gazebo that stood on the lawn in front of the building. Shaded within its circular structure was a comfortable set of wooden benches facing west to catch the sunset.

The mansion loomed massive before them. The front entrance had an extensive porch, four steps up from the ground. The largest wing of the building reached three stories above them.

"Spooky place," Tom remarked as he pulled the sketchbook from his bag.

"It has its creepy charm," Julie agreed. "I still get a chill now and then when I come here by myself. This building has a 'history,' you know. Some ugly business with the last owner."

"You mean Tornau," Tom declared.

"You know about that?"

"Of course? What's the fun living in Chapinaw if you don't know about Jacob Tornau?"

The Long Island town of Amityville had its haunted house; Salem, its witches; Loch Ness, its sea serpent. Chapinaw had the grisly Tornau affair. "He had some kind of satanic cult back in the sixties," Tom recounted. "There were ritual murders, and a baby was abducted."

"That's right," she added. "But did you know our entire town used to be called 'Crohaven'? They changed it to 'Chapinaw' because of what happened here."

"Yep," Tom replied. "Crohaven is on my birth certificate."

"Really? Me too." Julie sniffed in amusement. "It takes some explaining to people how I was born in one place and lived my entire life in another—without ever leaving. But I guess the town had its reasons. Nobody wants to live under the shadow of such infamy. A shame, 'cause now it's all everyone thinks about when they hear the name 'Crohaven.' It's like Sodom and Gomorrah is buried beneath the topsoil. Too bad, because it's really a beautiful place. The main building is over two hundred years old."

Tom nodded, distracted. "And nobody knows what happened to him?"

"Tornau? Nobody. My dad's done thorough research. Most people believe he escaped back to Europe. Some are even afraid he'll return."

"That's a chilling thought." He remembered what he found in the tunnel and considered for a moment mentioning it, but something restrained him.

"I think he's in Argentina having tea with Hitler and Jimmy Hoffa." Julie continued, "After his disappearance, the estate became a county acquisition. It was declared an historical site and is in a constant battle to retain its landmark status. People think it's a drain on the local economy. Occasionally, it's rented out to visiting dignitaries as sort of a glorified bed-and-breakfast, a way to recoup expenses."

"Why did your dad come here?" he diverted her.

Julie dwelled on it for a moment. "My dad has a passion for the occult, and he wanted to write a book on the whole bloody incident. It became his obsession for a while, and how could he resist such a great opportunity? To live within the very halls of the mystery? Besides, he needed the job. Evidently it was a difficult position to fill."

"Well, he's brave. That's for sure. I could never live alone in a place like this." He followed her to the front door. "How long have your parents been divorced?"

"Separated. For about ten years. My mom never officially divorced my dad. What about yours?"

He glowered. "My mom's *totally* divorced."

"Daddy?" Julie called as she opened the heavy redwood doors and peered inside. The doors squeaked appropriately on their hinges, and Tom felt like Jack entering the castle of the giant. "I don't see the station wagon, so he's most likely out doing his rounds in the garden. He won't be back for hours. Probably best this way."

He followed her into the main chamber. Inside it was like a museum. The town had lavished the place with an impressive store of exotic and domestic furnishings. Middle Eastern tapestries hung on the walls. Small pieces of statuary aligned the shelves above a mantled fireplace of massive gray marble. The sculptures suggested Turkish origin. The Persian rug Tom was standing on was woven with patterns of green and red, damasked in gold trim. From the threshold, Tom could distinguish three adjacent rooms, including the kitchen and dining room. A winding, intricately carved stairway rose from a marble floor. The banister was varnished a deep burgundy. The stairs led to a second level that overlooked the main chamber like a balcony.

"Everything seems so clean and untouched," remarked Tom.

"My dad doesn't use these rooms. They're mainly for display. He lives on the third floor. The town lets him have that because it's cheaper than giving him separate quarters off the grounds. The building has to be heated in the winter, anyway. It keeps the pipes from freezing."

They ascended the stairs directly to the third level. At the peak of the stairway were a few neatly framed samples of Parrish's work. They seemed at first like little more than splashes of color against fields of dark blue. But on closer inspection, Tom perceived an almost holographic depth and translucency, the result of overlaying pigments and varnish. Shapes could be discerned within them, like ghosts peering through a veil. In one of them, there was a cool violet orb with a resonating center of bright pink. Another had a volcanic explosion of red, expelling pseudopodia from its center. Julie waited patiently as he studied each one.

"They're thought-forms," she said. "What a thought looks like on the 'astral plane.' Every time you think of something, you create one."

Tom nodded without question. Thought-forms.

She pushed open a pair of cedar doors that led into Parrish's spacious study. The walls nearest them were taken up by a rustic brick fireplace that was curtained with chain-link drapes. It was joined to the gigantic chimney that scaled its way up the outside of the building. The mantle above the fire chamber was stacked with numerous volumes of occult and metaphysical lore. Tom glimpsed at the titles, among them *The Secret Doctrine* by H.P. Blavatsky and the *Tibetan Book of the Dead.* There were books by authors named Besant, Leadbeater, and Krishnamurti. Also, the Dhammapada, the Holy Kabbalah, and the King James Version of the Bible.

"Man, you weren't kidding about the occult," Tom commented. "Is it just for research, or does he practice?"

"He dabbles a little. It's complicated. My dad's kind of . . . *psychic,*" Julie offered, expecting a nonplussed reaction.

But Tom was quick to temper his response. "So that much of the legend is true."

“He can see auras and receives impressions when he touches things.”

“That’s cool.” Tom nodded. Julie smiled imperceptibly.

Two large windows faced the west, and the waning sunlight shined directly into the room, giving an orange glow to the interior. A lingering aroma of incense was in the air. There was an extensive library with even more books, a giant desk that Herman Melville would have been comfortable with, plus an easel, and an art table cluttered with paint tubes and brushes.

And then there were the *paintings.*

On nearly all the wall space were depictions of such bizarre and beautiful nature that Tom was instantly mesmerized. He felt himself pulled into several directions at once, absorbed by their gentle spectacle.

“Oh my God,” he said. His jaw loosened like a child in wonderment.

Julie snickered as he became totally enthralled. “What do you think?” she asked.

“They’re amazing!”

The first painting showed three rotund figures with squat little bodies. They were almond eyed, with broad Buddha-like faces. The figures were dressed in a homespun fabric that seemed to merge at places with their skin, and their heads were wreathed with flowers and twig. They exuded an aura of sagely benevolence, combined with a child’s innocence.

Other paintings revealed more of these angelic beings.

The child-people were at play in a landscape both surreal and natural. Colorful orchids and majestic trees sprang up from the moss-laden ground, amidst oddly shaped buildings that seemed sprouted from the ground rather than built. Contained within their architecture was an aura of perfection that challenged all of mankind's aloof designs to date. Tom knew he was gazing into another dimension, a world as rich and vivid as any he had traveled to in his flights of fantasy. His throat locked. Delight mingled with a strange melancholy. He felt a joy of discovery and a pain of yearning that what he saw could never be, yet *was*. For such beauty to spring from a human mind was remarkable. That it came from an individual held in contempt and suspicion by an entire community seemed the very epitome of injustice.

He shot a glance at Julie, marveling at the depth of Parrish's vision. His vocabulary seemed pitifully vulgar and insufficient to describe what he felt. "Where does he get these . . . ?"

"From beyond this plane of consciousness," she said. "He travels clairvoyantly to the *astral realm* and claims he's actually met these little people on a telepathic level. He claims they're 'dævas,' or nature spirits. You could also call them elves, brownies, fairies—"

"*Fairies?*"

"Hey, Mini Mart!" she chastised. "Open twenty-four hours, remember?"

He grinned, checking his skepticism. One final image stole his attention. The character depicted wasn't an elf or fairy but very human. A woman stared back from the canvas. Her skin was pale and shimmering, breaking through a black field like a candle glowing in darkness. She had blond hair that fell short below her ears and a youthful face of classic beauty. Long delicate fingers beckoned to him from her breast, and at her throat, a luminous orb. Her expression was solemn, and Tom sensed a great sorrow emanating from her eyes. There was also a peculiar sense of familiarity, as though he knew her from some distant encounter.

"Who is she?" he asked.

"I don't know," Julie answered. "My dad could never say. I always thought she was an angel. Isn't she beautiful?"

"Very." Tom moved on from the ghostly visage and got the prickly sensation that its eyes were traveling with him. He turned to the large picture windows, realizing it was the very place the man stood the night before, casting his "spell."

"So what's he doing when he stands by the window making those weird gestures?"

Her head bobbed with an accusing smile. "You were spying on him?"

"Spying? No! I—we just happened to be . . . I mean—"

"That's Tai Chi," she informed. "It's an Eastern meditative exercise he performs before he paints. It puts him in a creative mood, almost like a trance. He must have been painting last night, see?"

Nearby was the easel; Tom noticed a new canvas with a work-in-progress. Another otherworldly image was taking shape, a landscape emerging through swirling colors. The scent of turpentine rose from its surface, and he knew the paint would smear to the touch. He continued to explore the room and noticed a rectangular panel in the ceiling above with a knobbed strip or cord dangling down from it. "Where does that go?"

"Attic."

"Anything spooky up there?"

"You mean like dead bodies or ghosts? Sorry. This place has been thoroughly 'cleansed.' No spirits going 'bump'."

"Too bad." So much for haunted mansions.

CHAPTER 13

THEY HEARD A DOOR OPEN AND CLOSE BELOW, AND Julie blanched. She looked at Tom a bit sheepishly, as though they were about to be caught shoplifting.

"Hello?" called a voice. "Julie?"

Julie went into the hall to call down to her father.

"Yeah, Dad. It's me. I brought . . . a friend."

She looked back to Tom. "Okay. It's all right. Just remember what I said." She trotted down the steps, motioning for him to follow.

There was suddenly a peculiar churning in his midsection, a tingling from within. Tom hesitated as the sensation traveled up his spine to the nape of his neck. Was it "butterflies?" How strange it felt, as though some part of him dreaded the meeting of this mysterious person. He shook it off, berating himself for this childish fright. Anyone who could realize such beauty as he'd seen on these walls could not constitute a threat.

Yet his chest seized up like it was clamped in a vice. He placed a palm there, reflexively rubbing it, as he descended the stairs with arms wrapped snug around his sketchbook.

"Daddy, are you back there?" she called into the kitchen.

"I'm coming."

Parrish emerged with an uncanny, catlike grace. Tom's first impression of the man would always be the most lasting. It was the ease of his stride, the way his head seemed to hover weightlessly above his body, like that of a marionette suspended from a cord. Tom felt a tingle of excitement. Here at last was the infamous Stephen Parrish. He was younger than Tom imagined, mid-forties perhaps, and over six feet tall. His thin, lanky frame was covered in slightly soiled work clothes. Lines of introspection chiseled his clean-shaven face, the cheekbones pronounced like a bust of Lincoln. His hair might have been dark, but it was so mottled with silver as to conceal all pigment, and his hazel eyes were keen.

"Hi, Daddy," Julie said lovingly to her father, but she didn't greet the man with the traditional kiss or hug. There was no physical contact whatsoever. Rather they kept a cordial distance, respecting an unseen boundary, though the warmth between them was unmistakable.

"Hello, sweetheart," he replied gently in a soft, deep voice.

"Working the garden?"

"No, I went to Grumbach for some seed." His eyes shifted to Tom, and he seemed at first put off by the boy's presence.

"Daddy, this is a friend of mine."

"Hi," Tom interjected and immediately offered his

hand in greeting. "Tom DeFrank."

But Parrish hesitated, gazing at the boy's outstretched palm as though it was infested with germs. Finally, he grinned warmly and extended his hand politely in exchange. "Nice to meet you. I'm Stephen Parrish."

As their palms met, Tom felt a jarring sensation. A passionate flow of energy surged from his fingers into Parrish's grip. He noticed a shift in the man's expression. The congenial look in his eyes became one of puzzlement. A slight twitch developed over his cheek, and he whispered something under his breath.

Parrish's grip tightened, and then he snatched it away. As soon as their hands parted, the "spell" was broken, and Tom realized that less than five seconds had passed.

Julie sensed their peculiar exchange.

"Daddy?" she asked. But he continued to gaze at Tom with confusion.

Parrish regained his composure and cracked a crooked smile. "That's a strong grip you have."

Julie tried to dispel the awkwardness. "So . . . I took Tom upstairs to show him your paintings. You liked them, didn't you, Tom?"

"Yes!" he nodded, groping for enthusiasm. "Mr. Parrish, your paintings are the most incredible things I've ever seen."

"Thank you, Tom." The man was still distracted.

"Have you ever sold any?"

"Sold? No. Not many people have seen them."

"You mean you've never shown your work?"

The man seemed amused by the suggestion. "I doubt anyone would be interested."

Tom was shocked. It was like da Vinci locking away the Mona Lisa, saying "Who could care?"

"But of course they would be!" he insisted. "I'm sure any gallery in New York would be thrilled to have a showing of your paintings."

"See?" Julie supported him. "That's what I keep telling you, and Tom knows what he's talking about, because he's an artist too."

"Is that so?"

"Well . . . I'm trying to be."

Following her cue, Tom pulled out his sketchbook. He felt suddenly apprehensive, partially from an artist's anxiety in the face of a master. Partially from that *peculiar tingling* in his chest.

"Tom drew a sketch I thought you should see. He's into monsters and things."

He opened the book and handed it to Parrish.

"It's just a 'thumbnail' actually."

"There's something written at the bottom—" Julie began, but halted when she saw her father's reaction. There was a frigid expression on his face as his focus darted from the nightmare in graphite to the arcane verse scrawled below it. He looked up at Tom. His eyes were embers, capable of fire.

"*Where did you get this?*" Parrish asked.

"I'm not sure."

"What do you mean 'not sure'?"

"He said it 'zapped' into his head," Julie added.

"Zapped?"

Tom shrugged uncertainly as Parrish continued to peer at the words, dumbfounded.

"Does it mean anything?" asked Julie. "It looked to me like ancient Sumerian. When I first saw it, I thought it was an incantation."

He glanced at Julie. "I think you're right. I'm no authority on ancient languages, but it does look like Sumerian, or at least some derivative." Back to Tom, "You can't tell me anything more about it?"

"Well . . ."

"*Think.*"

Tom felt his throat lock. "I was out with friends, last night."

"You mentioned you were around *here*—" Julie added.

"Julie, please," Parrish interrupted. "Around Crohaven? You were driving around this area? Doing what?"

"Nothing. Just driving." He felt self-conscious, as though guilty of a despicable deed. What *were* they doing here? Just a foolish prank of Kevin's. The tunnel flashed through Tom's mind. It was on the tip of his tongue to mention it. But as before, the impulse was bundled up and chained within him, as though a part of his subconscious jealously guarded the memory, refusing its disclosure.

"We were just goofing around," he continued evasively. "And I suddenly started thinking up this weird phrase. It's probably just from some comic book, or horror novel I read, and couldn't remember."

The lie tasted bitter in his mouth.

"A comic book?" The man stared, obviously not buying his explanation.

Tom felt feel oppressed by the interrogation. "That's all I can remember. Honest."

Parrish responded by squinting at the boy, and his eyes seemed to glow in concentration as though he were reading Tom like a prayer scroll. The boy shifted his weight in a pronounced fidget.

Julie sensed his consternation, annoyed by her father's bizarre probing.

"Daddy, what is it?" she asked, aware of the deep intensity in his eyes. Parrish blinked with a dazed look, as though he had found more questions than answers. "Forgive me. It's not important." He smiled again. "This is incredible work, Tom. You have real style, the makings of a great artist."

"Thank you, sir."

"I was wondering . . . could I *borrow* this sketch?"

Julie was astonished. "Borrow?"

"I know somebody who would find it interesting. He's also into . . . monsters."

"Daddy, I don't know—"

"It's okay Julie," Tom reassured her. "Sure you can, Mr. Parrish. In fact, I'd be honored if you'd keep it."

Parrish grinned appreciatively. "Thank you, Tom." He

carefully tugged at the edges of the sketch. Tom heard the familiar rasp of the paper as the spiral edges tore free. He couldn't believe he was giving away the precious drawing, but he knew the image was so emblazoned in his brain that he would have no difficulty producing another. It was just a crude rendering. A better likeness would soon take form in clay.

Parrish closed the sketchbook and handed it back to Tom, cradling the drawing as though it was a Monet. "It'll be a valued part of my collection."

"It's getting late," Julie insisted. "We'd better be going home." Tom tried to meet her eyes, but she focused an icy stare on the banister.

"I guess so. It was a pleasure meeting you, sir." Out of impulse, Tom almost offered his hand in parting but caught himself in time. He wasn't ready to experience that again, so soon. Instead, he wandered to the door, hoping the distance he was placing did not seem purposeful.

"Me too," Parrish answered. "And thanks again for *this*."

"Any message for Mom?" Julie asked. But he wasn't looking at her. He was looking at the boy. A smile flickered on and off his face like a strobing neon sign. Julie tried to steal a final glance from him. "Dad? I'll come by next week if you need anything. Just call me."

Tom pushed the door open and went out. The cool air felt refreshing on his face. He glanced behind and saw Julie step closer to her father and whisper something to him. He couldn't hear the reply, but the man finally looked up to recognize her. He smiled and offered a gentle pat on her shoulder. It seemed a token gesture to Tom, substituting for a more familial exchange. She followed him out the door, and he couldn't tell if her spirits had lifted, or fallen to greater depths.

"That was strange," he commented. "Did that seem strange to you?"

"My dad can be *very* strange," she said as she straddled her bike.

CHAPTER 14

White Lake was a lakeside community near the center of Chapinaw. The lake itself was shaped like a maple seed, with two oval wings of water merging at a common stem. The shore was lined with docks harboring small motorboats, and there were a few patches of beach sand that accommodated the summer bathers. A stretch of moderately sized waterfront homes overlooked the lake's tranquil waters. Julie's was one such house adjacent to the shoreline. It was a small duplex, but it looked comfortable. She wheeled her bike into the driveway, a smile masking her sullen mood, and then turned to Tom.

He was still astride his Schwinn, an earnest look upon his face. They had been mostly silent for the remaining trip from Crohaven. Some attempts at brevity had fallen flat, and the lightheartedness that had accompanied the start of their journey was gone. He knew she was upset with her father and hoped the experience wouldn't color her feelings about him. The memory could put a strain on their budding friendship, and he didn't want to become a victim of Mr.

Parrish's odd demeanor. But he had no more cards to play. Every ace had been spent, and in a moment they would say goodnight. He would know in that moment whether they'd ever spend more time together, or whether he would become someone she politely said "hello" to in the hall before briskly walking on.

"Are you okay?" he asked.

She nodded, smiling. "Yeah. I'm sorry if things were awkward for you."

"It's nothing. Forget it."

"Thanks for riding with me. It was fun."

"Maybe we can do it again sometime." He cringed at how lame it sounded. "Or maybe just . . . I dunno, hang out."

She laughed. She actually laughed. But she didn't reply. His heart sank.

"Well . . . bye." He began wheeling his bike out of the driveway, offering a final nod. His prospects were fading fast, like the last speck of sun on the horizon. Going . . . going . . .

She called out to him again. "Tom?"

Not quite gone. He turned back. "Yeah?"

"Do you like tea?" she asked meekly.

"Tea?" He never drank tea. "Sure. I love tea."

They sat on the thick shag carpet of the lower den. The walls were covered in maple wood paneling, making it seem smaller and quaint, and there was a faded black-light poster of a unicorn on one side. Tom could smell fresh laundry from the room next door. Julie poured a green spice tea from a china pot decorated with Japanese artwork. The tiny ceramic teacup Tom held in his palm had no handle. The heat of the scalding liquid penetrated the porcelain but did not burn him. It was the simple logic of the Japanese; what was too hot to hold was too hot to *drink*. Julie kneeled beside him while Tom settled into a comfortable beanbag chair that squished under his weight. He could hear the lake outside splashing. Her bedroom was on the same level, just two doors down, facing the water.

Tom took a sip of the tea as they continued to discuss her father. "I didn't like the way he looked at me," he confessed. The memory of Parrish's probing gaze made him feel dirty. "I felt like I had done something wrong."

She sighed. "You didn't. I'm sorry he put you through that. He just gets curious about people. I'm sure he really liked you." She folded her palms over her knees, facing down, and Tom sensed her embarrassment. He decided to brush aside any lingering discomfort from the experience, and he had all the reason in the world to do so: she was sitting right there.

"I can't believe he's never shown his work," he commented, changing the focus of the conversation.

"He's shy," she said, moistening her lips with tea. "And he doesn't trust people anymore. Not that I blame him. People can be so cruel. It got really bad a few years ago. A man tried to run him out of town."

"I know. This town's filled with idiots," Tom dismissed

with a huff.

"They jump to so many conclusions. Like my father could really hurt anybody."

"Course not."

"It's no picnic being the daughter of the town 'bogeyman,' either. Especially after the whole 'Wilkens' thing."

Tom nodded in sympathy. He wanted to know more. He was aching for the truth, but it just seemed inappropriate at that moment to ask . . . about Josh Wilkens.

"It got me really depressed. I stopped eating for a long time and lost so much weight that I looked like a stick figure. They used to call me 'Witchy Woman' in school. Or 'Broomstick'."

"I'm 'DeFrankenstein'."

Julie snickered. "Hmm. So I guess you know what it's like. But worst of all, it drove a wedge between my parents. They used to be so close, even after the separation, and now they're like these friendly strangers. I hardly ever see him, anymore. I used to go there all the time to do housework for him, and occasionally I helped him with his studies—organized his notes. I even did research on my own to better understand what he's about. At least until my mom put a stop to it. She was a little freaked out about some of the things I was reading. Occult stuff. You're looking at the only sixteen-year-old *theosophist* in Chapinaw."

"Theosophist?"

"It's complicated. The trouble is I keep remembering what it was once like."

"Was he always, you know . . . psychic?"

"No. Believe it or not, my dad was once pretty normal. That was before the accident."

"What accident?" Tom leaned closer.

Julie took a deep breath and launched into her explanation. "It happened about eleven years ago. My dad was teaching art at the community college. He was already an incredible artist. He painted landscapes mostly and people, but nothing very imaginative. He helped support us by painting family portraits, and he did illustration work for print ads. All of that would change, though."

She crossed her legs and sat in a lotus position, as though to prepare herself. "Late one night in January, when I was five years old, my dad was coming home from work. There was a heavy snowfall, and the roads were pretty bad. He was driving along a lakefront when this car came barreling around a curve. It skidded into my dad's lane, ramming him *smash* through the guardrail, and his car plummeted into the lake."

Tom stared. "My God."

"He was knocked unconscious. The car filled instantly with the freezing waters. Someone called the police, but by the time paramedics arrived with divers in wetsuits, my dad had been submerged for over forty minutes. Now, supposedly you're brain-dead long before that but extreme cold can slow the metabolism and prolong your life. So paramedics rushed him to the hospital, hoping to revive him."

She sipped again from the tea. Tom sat on the edge of

his beanbag.

"It was after midnight when we got the call. I'll never forget the sound of the telephone ringing. It was late. I knew it was bad news. I was only five, but I knew. Just from the sound of it. Dad wasn't home yet, and my mom was worried. I heard her gasp on the phone, and I started crying. She took me out of bed, and we raced to the hospital where my dad was taken. But just as we got there he was pronounced 'dead'."

"I was too young to understand. I'd never had anyone die on me before—not even a pet. I just watched as they put him on a cart, with a sheet over his head. This orderly began wheeling him to the morgue. This is how I heard it, anyway."

She enlisted Tom's absolute attention. "About a minute and a half after he left the emergency room, my dad's arm started twitching, and he took in this loud gasp of air! I guess that orderly had quite a shock. They brought him back to the ER and found that all his vital signs had returned. He was alive!"

Tom shook his head in awe.

"They called it 'spontaneous resuscitation.' There was a big commotion about it, and it was in all the local papers. He remained asleep for hours, but his metabolism grew stronger and stronger. My mom and I stood beside the bed. She was too overwhelmed with tears to speak."

"We were there when his eyes opened. He just stared at the ceiling for a few moments, unaware of us, blinking confused as though he'd awoken in the middle of a dream. He bolted upright in bed. He had this look of shock and dismay on his face that gradually faded into . . . disappointment."

"Disappointment?"

"It was unmistakable in his eyes. You can imagine how my mom felt, seeing him return from the dead, after all we'd been through, disappointed to see her again. I think it broke her heart. She never quite got over it. I remember being a little frightened, seeing what seemed like a stranger staring out of my father's eyes. They did tests on him, and he was fine. The doctor assured us he would recover and live a normal life.

"But he was *far* from normal. Everything about him was different. His movements, his manner of speech, everything. He developed a peculiar second sight. Flashes of things when he touched a person or an object. He once petted our cat and knew she was pregnant months before she had kittens. Things like that frightened my mom. She was having great difficulty adjusting to it all. I was enthralled. To me, my daddy was *magic*. I used to play this game with him, watching TV. He would guess which Bugs Bunny cartoon would come on just by touching the set. It was *fun*.

"But his 'resurrection' affected him in so many ways. He grew distant and aloof, like he was afraid to touch people. He became totally preoccupied with the supernatural. It drove my mom up the walls. I guess it was inevitable that he abandon us. There was a huge cash settlement from the accident, and he used it to pursue his 'quest.' He moved out and spent some time in the city, before eventually taking the

Crohaven job. He was searching for cosmic truths, asking big questions, and apparently getting big *answers*. None of which included *us*."

Tom felt a familiar tingle in his heart. "Must have been tough for you."

She sighed. "It was. You see, with his 'cosmic awakening,' my father ceased to be my 'Dad.' He became this elusive mystic from another world. He's capable of some truly extraordinary things. But I could care less about all that. I just want him to be happy again. I mean . . . he's all alone in that *big* . . ." Her eyes welled up with tears, and her voice locked.

Tom instinctively drew closer to her. A tear ran liberally down her face. "I love my father very much, but I've always believed when he 'came back to life,' he didn't come back *all the way*."

She rubbed her eyes, self-conscious of the redness in her cheeks. "It seems I'm doing all the talking, here. So what's *your* story?"

"My story?" He fidgeted, uncomfortable with having the spotlight put on him. "Nothing as interesting, I'm afraid. My mom comes from Chapinaw, and she settled here with my dad for the first year of my life. We all moved to Schenectady, after some *incident* with my grandparents. But it didn't work out. My parents split up when I was nine. They were fighting all the time, by then. He moved away, and I got stuck with my mom."

"Stuck?"

"Yeah, *stuck*." He snickered at his own tactlessness. "We bounced around a few places while she struggled to make a living. Finally, we came back to Chapinaw about three years ago. She made up with her folks, who helped us out for a while. Then she got a job at a big insurance firm and is training now to become a regional manager. Plus she's with a new guy, so I hardly ever see her."

"And your dad?"

"My dad? He's . . ." His eyes drifted, studying the laces on his shoe. "He's a truck driver. Drives the big rigs out west. You know, greasy spoon diners, CB handles. The whole 'convoy' thing. He doesn't make his way east, much. I haven't spoken to him in a while, but he'll come around."

Julie dropped her eyes. She knew he was lying. "You must miss him."

"Kind of." The waves of the lake outside became very loud in the room.

"Well, don't you get lonely being by yourself so much?"

"Naw. I keep busy with my hobbies. I make 'monster movies'."

She leaned forward. "You make movies?"

He brightened. "I'm a stop-motion animator. I make creatures and bring them to life on film."

She beamed with interest. "Really?"

"Yeah. Dinosaurs and dragons and things. I build little puppets and animate them."

"Wow! That's incredible. You know, I always wanted to be an actress. Maybe I can be in one of your films. I could be the bimbo camp counselor, and your monster could eat me."

He laughed, enticed, and then attempted a Hollywood dialect. "Sorry, sweetheart. I only work with 'models'."

She rolled her eyes. "Typical."

"No, I mean *miniature* models. Usually ten inches or so."

"You mean I'm too *tall*?" She laughed in irony. "I always figured I was too short. But what about that Gap commercial with all the people running around? Wasn't that animated?"

"Sort of. It's called pixilation."

"So why couldn't you 'pixilate' me?"

"Well . . . maybe I could."

She pleaded. "*C'mon.* It would be fun!"

"You'd have to stand perfectly still for hours and hours. You see, with each frame of film, the model has to be moved—"

"I know, I know." She jumped to her feet, stiffening into a plastic mannequin. "In other words, one frame I'm like 'this,' and the next I'm like '*this*'." Her arm drastically repositioned itself.

"That's waaay too much." He approached, and she eyed him sidelong without moving.

"More like this." He boldly nudged her arm up a fraction. Julie barely stifled a smile. "Then your head," which he twisted slightly by gently taking her face in his hands. She held her doll-like expression, playing the obedient stop-motion model. "And your torso." Daringly, he placed his hands on her hips and shifted her weight. "Like so, for balance."

"Then I would take a frame of film." He squeezed an imaginary black bulb, attached to an invisible camera. "Click! Then I repeat the process." He quickly retraced every step on her body. This time, however, he was aware of touching her and began to blush. She could no longer refrain from smiling.

"Click," he said, with a second squeeze of the invisible bulb. "And so on and so forth."

"One more!" she teased. His face was red as he went through the motions again, touching her as though she were a very pretty, very *sexy* rubber-and-wire puppet. He gently posed her arm higher, until she appeared to be pointing. Her head was cocked, until a brush of hair fell enticingly over her brow. As his fingers touched her upper arm, he secretly marveled at how soft her skin was. Shyness got the best of him, and he stepped back.

"You forgot *balance*," she chided.

"Oh yes . . ." Another nudge of her hips. His hands felt like they belonged there. Her face was inches away from his. He could feel warmth radiating from her cheeks. He went back to the imaginary camera, and paused.

"Click," she said for him.

"And that would go on for hours. But enough for today."

She dropped her arms. "I guess even rubber puppets get tired."

He looked at his watch, feeling suddenly bashful. "I

should get going."

"Yeah. Can't wait to get back to your 'ten-inch models'."

He smirked and went for the door.

She wrote something down on a little pink square of paper and handed it to him.

"What's that?"

"My number, silly."

"Oh." He jotted down his own phone number for her.

She walked him to the stairs to the front entrance. As he was about to step out of the house, he turned to smile at her and found her face dangerously near his own.

"Goodnight," he said.

"Good night," she answered.

In the netherworld of Tom's mind, where dragons flew and trolls fought with dinosaurs, he pressed his lips against hers and kissed them passionately. But sadly, there was no such kiss in the real world.

CHAPTER 15

I SHOULD HAVE KISSED HER, HE THOUGHT, ALONE IN HIS bedroom.

Tom twisted aluminum wire together to form a frame for his sculpture. He was exhausted, weary from a long and full day. The bike ride from Crohaven to White Lake and back home again left his legs aching. His fingers felt like lead. He had wolfed down a macaroni-and-cheese dinner, barely saying a word to his mom, before retiring quietly to his room. It was nearing ten o'clock, and a good sleep would do wonders for him. But something compelled him to continue working. The wire would not be set aside. It willed itself into limbs and elbow joints, winding at the spine, projecting forth at the tail.

With a pair of pliers, he crimped the wire at the joints. It left tread marks where the pliers' teeth crushed the soft aluminum. Then he bent it into an upright stance. The wire skeleton was now ready for the application of plasticine. It looked like a stick-figure monkey about to perform on a stage. His tools were scattered about the desktop, where globs of green clay lay in an open Tupperware canister. Some of the lumps still held scaly details from a previous dinosaur sculpt. After the molding process, the clay from the figures was reclaimed, the body parts mangled together for reuse.

As he pressed his first lump of clay onto the form, fatigue suddenly caught up with him. He dropped the tool and pushed himself away from the desk. "Enough for tonight," he said in a weary voice, flopping heavily onto his bed. He then glanced over at the wall where Julie's little pink slip of paper was tacked up.

Tom closed his eyes and saw Julie's smile. It gave him a feeling that was warm, mushy, and altogether beguiling. The idea that he had been in her house, a room away from her bedroom, sent a shiver of excitement through his body. He remembered how she posed for him, her spry hips swaying over slender, denim-wrapped legs, and his cheeks blushed, recapturing the entire spectacle of gazing at her. Of *touching* her—

An electric grin radiated across his face. He realized that with his innocent animation charade, he had managed the most physical contact he'd ever had with a girl.

He gazed at the pink slip and felt the sudden urge to call her. *Should I?* There was her phone number. She obviously intended for him to call. But when? A week from now? Two days? This very night? Maybe she was waiting for him to call *right now.*

Sigh. In Tom's world, girls were an uncharted territory.

He stared up at his *One Million Years BC* poster; as though the fur-clad Miss Welch could give him badly needed insight into the female psyche. With enthusiasm in check, he decided to err on the side of caution. Don't blow it, he told himself. Play it cool.

I should have kissed her. Kevin would have.

The memory quickly took his grin away, and he sank into bed with sullen anxiety.

Tom was shy around girls the way zebra were shy around lions. A pretty face left him tongue-tied and clumsy, with the vocal capacity of Frankenstein's monster. Being an only child, with no sisters or close female friends, he grew up the solitary male and never developed adequate social skills. Young women were a complete enigma to him, like a novel in a foreign language he desperately wanted to read. He was in awe of the female body, for certain. With a healthy libido, well fed on swimsuit catalogs and a contraband *Playboy* or two, his hormones raged mercilessly like a stormy sea. Nor did his sexual ruminations depend solely on his shrine of under-the-mattress periodicals. Science-fiction was replete with nubile maidens, decked out in spandex and metallic corsets. Voluptuous babes were traditional fodder for dragons, space aliens, and monsters. In the realm of sci-fi fantasy, girls were either untouchable amazons, or they were on the *menu*. In real life, though, he knew them only through classroom acquaintance, admiring them from afar in ardent crushes, but rarely having the courage to pursue. His few attempts at dating had been dreadful affairs, and he'd suffered enough humiliation to quiver at the very notion. A date with Danny's younger sister Annette was an event they both wished to forget.

But Julie was different somehow. Speaking to her was so easy, like having a conversation with himself. The very thought of her dared him to contemplate, to hope, to wonder: *What would Julie Parrish look like in a cavegirl bikini?*

He crossed his arms behind his head, a playful smile returning to his face. To date a girl like Julie would be a welcome "glitch" in the continuity.

His eyes grew heavy. All he needed was a good night's sleep.

The wire armature beckoned to him.

All he needed . . .

He was back at the desk five minutes later, crushing lumps of clay onto the skeleton. Somehow, he knew he would be there for quite a while.

CHAPTER 16

THE SOUND OF A PHONE RINGING LATE AT NIGHT ALWAYS frightened Julie. Sirens didn't frighten her, nor did fire alarms, barking dogs, screeching tires or any other harbinger of doom. A telephone's ringing *did*, but only after eleven o'clock. She lay in bed, listening to the lake. She heard the phone ring in the hallway. Then she heard her mother answer it. Then she heard *nothing*.

That's how she knew it was her father.

Ellen Parrish whispered on the phone when her ex-husband was on the line. Her voice was filled with hushed sighs, her words barely penetrating the receiver as though fearful of a world listening. It always saddened Julie to listen to her mom's conversations with her father. There was a mixture of resentment and guilt in her voice. They were once so close, she thought. But the "scandal" had thrust them all into the public eye. Fending off the gossip and accusations had taken its toll on her mom. She withdrew completely from the man and in some ways from part of herself. Yet she never completely severed the bond of their marriage. Divorce papers lay in a drawer, unsigned. The gold band she still wore on her finger was a link in a chain that could not be broken. Julie was but another link.

Her curiosity got the best of her. She left her bed and stood by the stairway, listening. Her mom met her halfway. She was wearing an oversized pink robe, and the dim light in the hall cast dark circles under her eyes. Slivers of gray already streaked her dark hair to the roots. It made her appear old, and tired. Exhausted, the way she always was after speaking with him. It drained her spirit.

"Julie? It's your father. He wants to speak to you."

"To me?" Julie questioned with her eyes and climbed the stairs to the living room telephone.

"Daddy?" she said meekly into the receiver.

"Hello, Sprite. How's my little girl?" His voice sounded miles away. The name "Sprite" caught her off-guard. He hadn't called her that in years. She sat on the sofa as her mom withdrew into the kitchen.

"I'm fine, Daddy. It was nice to see you today. I'm sorry I surprised you with Tom like that. I just wasn't thinking. When he offered his hand to you, I almost—"

"Julie, it's okay." She heard him take a long deep breath before continuing. "No harm done. I called because I was wondering . . . well . . . how much do you know about Tom DeFrank?"

The question piqued her concerns. "Not much. I just met him. He's nice."

"Yes, he is. And very polite. Is he from around here?"

"Originally. He moved back recently from Schenectady."

"Do you think you'll be seeing him again?"

"Well . . . I guess so. Why? Is something wrong?"

There was pause over the line. "No. I'm just curious about him."

He was being evasive, but she knew something was on his mind. Julie probed deeper. "You responded so strangely when you shook his hand. Did you 'sense' something about him?"

Another pause. He was uncertain how to proceed. It bothered Julie to imagine her dad uncertain about *anything*.

"I received an odd impression," he confessed at last.

Julie frowned into the receiver. It's what she feared the most. "What kind of an 'impression'?"

"I can't say for sure what it was. Something peculiar, and it gave me a bit of a start."

"Peculiar? In what way?"

Again, an excruciating silence.

"Daddy, are you going to tell me what this is about?"

She heard him shuffle over the line, and he modified his tone to put her at ease. "I'm sure it's nothing. Just an odd vibration. I may be imagining things."

"You think Tom is in some kind of trouble? Is that what you sensed?"

"I don't know."

"Dad, please promise me that whatever it might be, you won't get involved." It was a firm request, spoken with uncharacteristic authority.

"Oh no, I promise. Nothing like that." He made an attempt at levity, sounding like the inquisitive parental figure. "So are you and he just friends, or is he—"

She rolled her eyes. "Just friends. I don't know, I just *met* him."

"Well . . . I like him, and I hope you two can have a good time together."

"Oh, Daddy . . . Thanks. I think."

"But Julie . . . ?"

"Yes?"

"Let me know if he speaks of any more 'peculiarities'."

He said goodnight. She listened to the silence on the receiver, before placing it onto its base. "Julie?" The sound of her mother's voice startled her. She hadn't noticed, but Ellen had stood in the threshold of the kitchen and was watching her curiously. "Something wrong, Julie?"

Julie felt a knot in her stomach and sank against the back of the sofa.

"I don't know," she answered.

"Was it about the boy?" her mom asked.

Julie looked up and met her mother's eyes.

CHAPTER 17

"I SHOULD BURN IT." STEPHEN PARRISH SAID AS HE hung up his seldom-used telephone. The monster sketch lay on the back cushion of his armchair, its sinister verse blazing with challenge. It challenged him to take it in hand again and decipher its mysterious message. He crinkled his brows. Obsession could be a danger when you lived alone. There was no one to distract you from your inner thoughts. You sail the current of your mind's river, only to discover too late that you've floated off course. The vaguest hint of suspicion in his daughter's voice was enough to alert him that he had already drifted far out to sea.

But the sketch mocked him with intrigue.

He picked it up from his armchair. It hardly left his hand all evening.

"Julie's right. I should purge every thought of it from my mind." He recalled her severity over the phone. She alluded to the disaster from the last time he pursued his clairvoyant instincts. "I won't put her through that, again. She's been through enough pain."

But even as he chastised himself, his eyes scanned every syllable of the verse. There was significance to it. He was certain.

Incense caressed his nostrils; the fumes rising from a brass tray where the embers of aromatic plant matter burned. He walked about his study, stopping before the big picture windows, his shadow flickering in the light of several candles. Whenever possible, he lit the room with simple candlelight. Along with the fragrance of the incense, it cleansed the area of disharmonious energies. Firelight was pure. It was an aura of energy visible to the naked eye. One could focus upon the dancing flame and distinguish the spectrum of colors within.

But life had an aura as well. It too had a spectrum that could be perceived and broken down. To the clairvoyant, the colors within the aura are the expression of feelings. Passions are a rainbow, enveloping the body in an ever-changing chromatic dispersion. Each shade distinguished an emotion. Deep red signified anger. A blue cloud, serenity. Rose was the color of generosity; and yellow, strong intellect. Then there were the endless in-between shades, the merging from light to dark, like the smearing of oil pigments. How rarely an emotion was clearly drawn. How often the solid becomes the plaid, a flashing tapestry of mood and melancholy, reflecting the kaleidoscope of the heart. Of what hue was enlightenment? What color was love?

Parrish had developed his spectral vision through meditative practice. He seldom found use for it except as an exercise. A clairvoyant toy. One could learn at a glance the mood of a person, or his spiritual state of being. Earlier that afternoon, against his better judgment, he had examined Tom DeFrank spectrally, using his psychic vision to penetrate the boy's aloofness. What appeared in his orb was both puzzling and disturbing.

Tom's aura was an indistinct haze of colors; typical for an angst-ridden teen, but hovering within the orb was a mist of lilac purple. It spidered its way across his ghostly veil like fungus over ripe fruit. Its essence felt malign, a powerfully negative field of energy. The region was speckled with flashes of ultra-red, a color of the lower spectrum attributed to those who dabbled in black magic. The mist seemed to thrive on Tom's energy, but it was clearly separate from it. This was baffling to Parrish. Nothing in Tom's demeanor suggested a source for such an emanation. He had perceived winter in a field of green.

So where had it come from?

It troubled Parrish on a deep level. He liked Tom. He saw a glint of himself in the boy's eyes and wished him no harm. He liked that Julie liked him, something that any father could perceive without the benefit of clairvoyance.

He considered that he might have misinterpreted the boy's orb, or perhaps it was simply an emotional configuration he had not ever encountered. Kids Tom's age experienced a plethora of conflicting passions. With a single touch, their traumas could transmit to his psyche and fill the open vessel of his consciousness. Once before, he had gotten lost in the private pains of a troubled youth, with tragic consequences.

It was the curse of the psychic not to be able to ignore a soul in peril. Many succumbed to a Savior complex, unable to extract themselves from the plights of others.

Parrish had been psychic for eleven years now. It was a journey that began the night of his tragic accident. The night he "died."

In Parrish's former years, there had been little speculation into life, death, or afterlife—these were things best left to the mystics. He focused on the here and now, seldom venturing beyond the borders of his experience. As an artist, he was a cipher. His paintings depicted images from a mundane existence. His youth had been spent in relative comfort. He had a family, like other families, a home like other homes. His loving wife cooked his meals and made love to him once a week. His little girl promised to wear pigtails and cradle plastic babes in her arms. Each day was lived without reflection on his role as artist, husband, and father.

But then a twist of fate sent his car to the bottom of a lake. The accident itself was a complete blur. Tires slipping on icy roads. Bright headlights blinding him. A sudden and violent crash. Beyond that, all was darkness. It should have ended there, his consciousness snuffed out like a candle, but it didn't.

Instead, he awoke with a jolt in a hospital room.

Upon awakening, Parrish felt immediately displaced. His body was strange to him, like he'd been crushed and squeezed into a tiny vessel, and there was a dim recollection of some extraordinary event that was being snatched away. Parrish struggled to reclaim the memory, but it disintegrated like a mist in sunlight. Once it faded, there was a terrible sense of loss, and he fell back into his bed, feeling barren, and isolated.

He wasn't even aware of the wife and child by his side.

The look of despair on his face had frightened poor Ellen. He could see her gladness at his revival quickly replaced by worry. He could *sense* it.

In fact, he could sense *everything* she felt. As she touched him, his mind filled with her thoughts. He received flashes of her frantic trip, driving on treacherous roads to the hospital, and the lingering hours of distress in the waiting room. And it didn't end with his wife. From that morning, every doctor, nurse, and intern became intimate with him. As each made contact, the turmoil of their lives flooded his consciousness, turning his mind into a thoroughfare.

His clairvoyance shattered the boundaries of his senses and tore away the veil that separated him from others. He was flung into a strange new world of intruding perceptions.

Parrish was haunted to distraction by this bombardment. He began to have peculiar visions—memory flashes that belonged to another time and place. To identify the source of these images, he underwent psychotherapy, hypnosis, even regimens of biofeedback and acupuncture, but nothing could release him from his obsession. There remained an impenetrable barrier to which his mind was closed. With persistence he attacked it, throwing himself like raging waters against a dike. But the barrier held. Troubled and lost, driven almost to madness, he withdrew into himself as the world he knew collapsed about him. He could no longer teach. He could no longer relate to wife and child, or function in his world.

One night, as the artistic rhymes of Parrish's heart were challenging his reason and intellect, the portcullis opened. He awoke from sleep with an image so crisp and clear that he was compelled to capture it. In a half stupor, he went to his art table and pushed brush against canvas.

He began painting his vision.

His sleepy fingers fumbled, smearing pigments together, splashing turpentine and lacquers until the room smelled of pungent odors. As his brush moved across the canvas, a solemn face appeared: a beautiful young woman with large, doleful eyes. Who was this woman? Why did she look so sad? Even now, Parrish stared at the ghostly portrait in his study and wondered at it.

She was the first to breach the veil, but many more would follow. From his subconscious, other visions emerged to be painted, his supply of art board barely containing them. Each was a reminiscence of a time he'd spent on the "other side," encounters with beings he could never have imagined. The pieces came together like a mosaic and soon depicted in exquisite detail the glorious tableau of his near-death experience.

He was *channeling* the spirit world through his art!

Upon completion of one, he moved on to the next, their purpose served, the message delivered. It was an odd form of communication, a picture window to the beyond. Today, the paintings were mounted on his walls or gathered dust in corners where no one could see them, as though their very innocence was too much for the average soul to bear.

With the awakening of his psychic abilities came an unquenchable thirst for knowledge. He needed to explore, to chart for himself this bizarre new territory. The quest led him down avenues of research into the hidden realms of the occult.

Tension with his wife began almost immediately. Ellen couldn't understand the transformation in her husband. His plunge into icy waters had been for her an unholy baptism, the emerging man no longer the one she married, nor the father of her child. It frightened her. She was suspicious of the strange beings he depicted in his paintings. Were they angels or devils? The 'ghost woman' in particular offered a threat. The pale beauty made her jealous, and though Parrish insisted he had no knowledge of her, it created a rift in their relationship.

But the change was hardest on his daughter. Julie was so young at the time of the accident, and it saddened Parrish most of all that it had deprived her of a good father. As his clairvoyance developed, he became physically awkward around her, afraid to touch her in even the most casual way. He feared the sadness and disappointment she hid so effectively would flood into him, and he would experience his failure as a parent *through her eyes.*

He glanced again at the sketch. Its mystery beckoned to him. All art contained a message. What was it trying to tell him?

"I promised Julie I would not get involved this time." The welfare of this boy could not—*would* not—become his concern. He wasn't a social worker. The boy had parents. He had friends, relatives, teachers, counselors, and the entire institution of society to assist him. Whatever earthly difficulties Tom DeFrank was fated to endure, they would have to be dealt with by traditional means.

But what about *unearthly* difficulties? He considered again the "spider" in the boy's aura. It was clearly of supernatural origin. What did it mean, and how would it affect the boy? Was Tom in any danger? If so, then how could he turn away?

The "parasite" in Tom's orb was disquieting, but nothing proved as disturbing as the impression he'd received with the boy's handshake. As their flesh made contact, there was a fierce exchange of energy. A shocking picture projected cinematically into his mind.

Parrish sat in his armchair, focused his inner sight, and sought to recapture the image in its entirety. He relaxed his brows, softening the lids over his eyes, and put a finger to his temple. Short controlled gasps created a mental energy screen that filled with pictures. For a moment, he saw a darkened space; rugged stone walls lit by firelight, and robed figures swaying in ritual.

He saw a man with a gray goatee, raising his arms in blasphemous prayer, and a sinister torrent of bright purple fire that seemed to rise up at his command.

Then he saw a terrified woman, bound and prostrate, thrust headlong into the flames!

The energy screen went blank. Parrish gasped and settled with a sigh into his chair. He was dismayed at the limitations of his second sight. It was like gathering the tattered threads of a tapestry.

But from his vision, he was able to establish several things. The image was from the past, not the future. The event occurred somewhere nearby, within the last two decades.

And the man in his vision was the Reverend Jacob Tornau.

Parrish felt a shiver, uncertain if it was from fear or excitement. It was that name, and its shroud of infamy that first drew him to this estate. He now lived in the last known residence of the dreaded necromancer. It was a convenient arrangement for him, given his interest in the story. In an example of unique synergy, Stephen had first approached the town's chamber of commerce to do research into the Crohaven affairs. When he learned the caretaker position was available, he'd eagerly accepted. The job offered gainful employment and a place of residence while giving him unlimited access to Tornau's property. It was his intention to learn the nature of the wizard's magic and hopefully write the definitive volume on the subject. Dwelling within these walls, he forced himself to enter the mind of a madman, to contemplate murders, blood rites, and hideous ties to ancient powers. There were times when he feared for his sanity, as the abyss he stared into began to stare back. After he'd spent the better part of three years deciphering every shred of the events, the trail went cold. All leads were exhausted. In disgust, Parrish was forced to abandon his quest and put his thoughts and talents to more wholesome pursuits. But always the mystery of Tornau was on his mind, as though the man's fate was inexplicably tied to his own.

And then, from out of the blue, a vision that at last offered a key! Where did it originate? Julie's young artist friend and his drawing of a monster.

What possible tie could Tom have with the Tornau phenomenon?

"Maybe Humphrey can help me," he mused aloud, thinking of his old friend, a scholar of the magical arts. "He'll be pleased to hear from me, after so long. I'm sure he'll have some insight."

The fire was set in his mind. There seemed to be no alternative for him. With rekindled fervor, he went to a cabinet and removed from the lowest draw a file bursting with note pages and newspaper clippings. Withdrawing a microfilm printout from a local newspaper, he reread the banner headline.

SHOOTOUT WITH DEMON CULT AT FARM; MISSING CHILD RECOVERED

A barn on Liberty Road was the location for a violent and bloody confrontation between local police officers, and an alleged "devil cult" of the reverend Jacob Tornau. In a shootout that occurred just after midnight, Sheriff Kurtis Kronin and two deputies opened fire on Tornau and his cult worshippers as they were engaged in an allegedly satanic ritual.

Four members of the cult were killed in the shootout while five others, including Tornau, managed to escape. The exchange of gunfire also killed Officer Scott Foster and wounded both the sheriff and Deputy Brian Davies. Both are reported in stable condition at Sullivan County General Hospital.

The officers rescued an infant child that was intended for use in an apparent blood sacrifice. The child was abducted the previous day from a shopping plaza. An unrevealed source alerted the sheriff to the location. The infant, whose name has been withheld from the records, is reported in good health and has been returned to its parents. The barn was owned by farmer Terence Whateley, one of the cult members who, along with his wife, Lavinia, were slain. A full investigation is in progress to determine the full nature of Tornau's activities. Known associate of Tornau, Sarah Halloway is believed to be one of the accomplices. The FBI has issued an All Points Bulletin to neighboring counties, in an effort to apprehend the fugitives. The massacre leaves some to speculate that Tornau and his followers may be responsible for the recent accounts of missing persons in the vicinity, including the disappearances of several young women. The incident was described by officials as the "most vicious account of criminal activity in Crohaven's history."

Parrish returned the article to its folder and went to the big window to peer out into the night. The window was open, and the voices of the crickets could be heard. He saw fireflies gathering in the lawn below, flickering on and off, even as his thoughts flickered between apprehension and objective.

CHAPTER 18

THE DREAM BEGAN AS A NIGHTMARE.

Tom was asleep at last, having mercifully passed out from exhaustion. After an additional three hours of work, the rough shape of the demon was taking form in plasticine. It now stood on his work desk like an eerie sentinel, the warmth of his fingertips still present in the oily surface. Tom had collapsed on his bed without undressing. If his fingers hadn't literally begun dropping tools, he would still be at the table sculpting away.

He slept soundly at first, but then his eyes began twitching beneath his lids. His muscles tightened as the peaceful images in his head were torched and swept aside. He kicked out convulsively, and if not for the natural inhibitions of his sleep, he would have flung himself off the bed. But then his struggles ceased, and his body settled into deathlike stillness.

Dark.

At first, he thought he'd awoken, so clear were his thoughts. But had he done so, had his eyes been open, he would have seen the shine of the streetlights, casting shadows off the monsters on his shelves. But here was a veil blacker than char off incinerated oak.

I'm blind, *he thought. Panic seized him. He instinctively reached for his eyes, to snatch away whatever was obscuring his vision, but his hands did not respond. He was overcome immediately with a surge of claustrophobia, like an amputee awakening for the first time to his missing limbs. His entire body was paralyzed!*

But then he realized . . . he had no body.

He was as formless as a fogbank, devoid of shape, yet conscious and alert. And there was something different about him. His very essence felt strange, as though he was cloaked in an alien skin. The dark closed in on him. Such suffocating blackness, like the space between stars.

The stars! If he could just see the stars.

He cried out, but heard nothing. The silence engulfed him.

He knew this place. It lingered in his memory like an evil deed. He knew what he would see were a shred of light to be cast on the walls about him. The idiot markings in yellow chalk. The vile symbols of necromancy. He was back in the tunnel! With that revelation, Tom struggled to force himself awake.

There were things out there, waiting for him. He could feel their sinister hands clutching at him. The spirits that dwelled within those vacant robes.

No.

He felt them cling to his consciousness, groping at him, dragging him into an abyss. He knew their touch. It was ghastly familiar, like a horrific memory buried deep in the subconscious.

No!

If he could see the stars. One pinpoint of light to shatter the darkness!

Just one star, *he begged. He prayed,* please, please, *lashing out against his blindness with his fingers, hoping to shred the black wall before him, because his first thought was for—*

Light!

And then, a sound. "Fau'Charoth."

It broke the silence. A voice! Barely a whisper, but he heard it.

"Fau'Charoth a Lammashta ra shagmuku tu."

It was the verse, a welcome friend in the smothering silence. He embraced it.

"Fau'Charoth ud kalama shagmuku tu.

Aga mass ssaratu. Ia mass ssaratu.

Fau'Charoth kur amda lu amesh namaritum."

With each phrase, he felt his will get stronger, and mass was restored to his shapeless limbs. The incantation repeated.

"Fau'Charoth a Lammashta ra shagmuku tu.

Fau'Charoth ud kalama shagmuku tu.

Aga mass ssaratu. Ia mass ssaratu.

Fau'Charoth kur amda lu amesh namaritum."

Tom willed himself free. The shackles were breaking.

The spell repeated endlessly over in his head, until it was just a high-pitched vibration, resonating on a frequency higher than sound. There was a flash of colors against the darkness. Vibrant bursts of yellow, red, and green.

His consciousness pulled free. He catapulted out of the tunnel.

Then he was outside.

The shining stars graced the sky. The moon was a sliver on the horizon. He felt a wave of unfathomable relief and a joy of freedom that lifted him like a feather into the darkness.

Unfettered by gravity, he willed his shapeless body into the night air, soaring with the speed and agility of a falcon. He reached a height far above the treetops, and soared still higher until the land below was shrouded over with mist and cloud. He dove in swift descent, piercing the white canopy, and soaring with incalculable speed over the countryside.

Trees, houses swooped past, a blur of images.

He circled above a street, recognized it as his own, and below the tree line, he could make out the roof of his house.

Mrs. Wadowski was an early riser, for those who considered three-thirty in the morning early and not late. She was at an age when sleep came difficultly. Since her husband died two years ago, she found herself keeping strange hours, sleeping in mostly during the early daylight, rising to walk her dog, Mitzi, in the dead of night. It put her at odds with her neighbors. She complained often of their lawn mowing at ten in the morning, and they retaliated with complaints of Mitzi barking at late hours, waking them from sleep.

The old woman followed slowly behind her terrier. It took tiny steps, sniffing at the sidewalk, perhaps catching a whiff of a squirrel that had scampered by earlier. It stopped to take a whiz on a mailbox.

Mitzi had a high-pitched bark—an angry yap filled as much with frustration as with canine savagery. Tiny dogs had more than their share of arrogance. It was as though they recalled their wolf-hood—the true nature buried deep in their genes. A few thousand years was hardly enough to breed out the wild instinct. It had been merely stuffed into a tiny package, incapable of expressing its fierceness and ferocity. Mitzi would never hunt caribou, or terrorize the frozen steppes. She had to content herself with being as "annoying" as possible.

Something caught her attention. The terrier raised her snout with a sharp jolt. Her tiny black nose twitched excitedly. She cocked her head, ears lifting in a comical expression of canine interest, as she gazed up at the sky and then into the bushes ahead.

Then she did something Mrs. Wadowski had seldom heard. She growled.

Tom soared above the grove of well-clipped hedges. He felt like a kite that had lost its mast and floated past a picket fence. A fluttering breeze took him higher. He heard the yapping. It was an irritating sound, familiar to his sleeping mind. It broke the serenity of his dream.

It made him angry.

"Mitzi! Stop it!" Mrs. Wadowski scolded the dog. It was prone to barking fits, but these were not the angry yaps she was used to. This time, the dog was barking out of fear, the way a watchdog barks at an intruder. It made the old woman nervous. She looked about, trying to see what upset the dog. The streetlamps did an ample job illuminating the sidewalk, but the shadows were dark and deep. Anything might lurk there.

She pulled at Mitzi's leash, self-conscious of the noise, as Mitzi continued to leap up, barking at the nothingness in the sky and then the street ahead. It circled around the woman, growling and snarling. Now it was in the other direction, facing the path behind them. Mrs. Wadowski probed the street with her failing eyesight. But there was nothing. She felt her blood pressure rise.

"Mitzi!" she yelled, but to no avail. The dog was in frenzy.

Tom circled invisibly above the dog. The little animal sensed his presence, and its yapping assaulted him. He landed in the bushes nearby. The dog pattered to the hedge, snarling and yapping some more. He wanted to silence it. He wanted to return to his peaceful, undisturbed flight. The dog wouldn't let him. The dog wouldn't stop. The dog would never stop. Stupid dog! Stop barking! He glared at the terrier. It snarled.

Mrs. Wadowski watched as *something* came out of the bushes. It looked like a patch of shadow darker than the rest. In an instant it was on Mitzi, and the dog yelped in terror as it was crushed flat to the sidewalk. The amorphous shape gripped at it like a bird of prey seizing a rodent.

Then she saw Mitzi lifted into the air! Paralyzed with fear, she felt the leash spool unwind its contents into the sky, whirring like a fishing reel. The leash pulled taut, jerking her hand upward as the handle was snatched from her grasp. Spool, leash, and yelping terrier vanished into the night.

Tom awoke with a jolt. Consciousness seemed to crash back into his body from a great height. Disoriented, he sat upright and glanced about his room.

"What the—" He shook his head, feeling a slight chill from the morning air. His mind went blank for a moment. He couldn't recall what had happened, but he felt elated. Then his memory sharpened, and the joy of flight returned to him. He smiled, amazed. Flabbergasted.

It was only a dream, of course. But what a dream!

He looked at his desk, at the clay figure that stood in its rigid posture, and wondered.

Then he heard Mrs. Wadowski screaming down the street.

CHAPTER 19

PARRISH DROVE HIS PLYMOUTH STATION WAGON OFF THE exit of the Henry Hudson Parkway and onto Bleecker Street. Morning sunshine, passing through the windshield, made the dashboard hot to the touch. The old engine grumbled on long journeys. He seldom made the trip to New York City these days, but he was seeking answers that would not be found in the quaint bookstores and libraries of Sullivan County. So Parrish decided to pay a visit to a unique old bookshop in downtown Manhattan, whose proprietor was a very unique man named Humphrey Culhane.

Memories of Culhane brought a smile to Parrish's face as he followed the twisting roads of Greenwich Village toward Washington Square Park. He first met the eccentric scholar early in his "wandering" phase, the first two years of his clairvoyance, when he spent time alone to engage his preternatural pursuits. The man was immediately intrigued by his unique "crossing over" episode and offered him valuable insight into his psychic abilities. Culhane employed him part-time as an assistant in his Occult bookstore, and he became a fast friend. He introduced Parrish to a mystical study group that met weekly in the village, and he served as a mentor of sorts on his spiritual journey. With the man's guidance, he developed his astral senses and practiced the great disciplines of mind and spirit. Regimens of meditation, exercise, and diet transformed his body. Contemplation sharpened his soul, and what remained of the old Stephen Parrish became a pale apparition within.

The summer lingered in the tree-lined streets of Washington Square Park. A new semester had begun, and students from the nearby NYU campus gathered on the grass and benches, watching a band of street musicians perform in front of the fountain. Parrish walked past the youthful crowd, enjoying the academic atmosphere of his old haunts. The sights brought a rush of contentment to his heart. He made a left onto Sullivan Street.

The bookstore was at the center of the block, flanked by an antique shop and an exotic jewelry boutique. The name ORPHEUS was boldly carved upon a wooden sign that dangled from chains above the entrance. The window was filled with religious curios. A jeweled scimitar hung above a statuette of Buddha while the Hindu god Shiva danced majestically upon a bronze platform. The shop was an attraction for tourists, renowned for its occult volumes, sacred texts, and black-magic *grimoires*.

Parrish stepped through the front entrance, ringing a set of Chinese chimes that hung over the door. The store seemed larger from within and gave off a vital pulse of energy. It brought a feeling of elation and well-being to Parrish as he glanced over the familiar shelves. The air was sweet with incense, and Japanese pipe music played delicately from a sound system. Statues of ancient gods and goddesses filled a glass case, and gothic prints were framed on distant walls.

Elegantly displayed with distinction were two masterfully rendered paintings. They were his own, produced early in his "revitalized" period. One was a woman emanating colorful rays of light from her seven *chakras*, the energy centers of the spirit. The other showed a sagely cherub-like figure, such as the ones in his study. They were a parting gift to Culhane, ten years ago, when he moved back to Chapinaw.

Humphrey Culhane slumped over his countertop, completing a sale to a woman with thick rimmed glasses. Before him were two volumes that were coverless, and the worse for wear. Undoubtedly, that didn't lessen their value, for the woman seemed positively delighted with them. Culhane grinned at her reverent glee. He was a burly bear of a man in his early fifties, with thick arms and a generous paunch. Red sideburns wrapped around his cheeks like the paws of some wild beast. His hair was shaggy and slightly orange where it wasn't peppered with gray, and he wore a moustache that faded into his chin. His presence was strong and formidable. Yet that strength was tempered with a humor that glistened from his eyes. He was a Viking

Santa Claus—cup of mead in one hand, Christmas bells in the other.

The woman made the purchase. Culhane handed the books to an assistant for processing. It was when he passed from beyond the countertop that he noticed Parrish standing quietly by the Sufi section. Culhane's fleshy cheeks lifted into a grin so broad that his sideburns stood up like bristles on a brush. He let out a bullroar of a laugh.

"Hah! Stephen!"

They exchanged a hardy embrace, a surge of warmth passing between them.

"It's good to see you, hump!" Parrish said sincerely.

He held Parrish at arm's length. "My God. Look at you! Thin as a rail! What have you been eating?"

"Macrobiotics."

"That gerbil shit? No wonder. Still painting, I hope."

"Yes. When I have time."

"Time? What else have you got, taking care of that old relic of a house you live in? Did you happen to notice?" He pointed to the paintings above with a proud wink. "Got another offer for them last week. That's the third in a year, but I'm not selling. *Those* are an investment."

Parrish smiled humbling. "Thanks, but I've done better since then."

"Really? Well, when you're tired of playing Siddhartha, we'll talk about having a show. One call and I can get you both a gallery *and* a sponsor. That's if I don't sponsor you *myself*."

"You're generous to a fault, as always."

"How's Ellen?"

"Doing fine. She's still in Chapinaw."

"It's a damn shame what you did," Culhane chastised him. "Wrecking that perfect family of yours to pursue ghosts. Ellen's a terrific lady. She deserved better. And little Julie?"

"She just turned sixteen, a young woman now," he said with a glint of fatherly pride. "She's seeing boys."

"*Boys?* My God, Stephen. Are you gonna allow that?"

He lifted his palms. "It's out of my hands, I'm afraid." They laughed, and Parrish wondered how long it had been since he'd shared in laughter of any kind. Culhane had provided him with a generous amount, during those early days of soul-searching. Listening to the robust chortles of his friend, he felt the stubborn pull of his own humanity, drawing him back to a life of love and friendship.

"It's about this one boy that I called," Parrish shifted the subject.

"Ahhh yes. The great mystery. I hardly expected you'd indulge in a mere social visit." Culhane instructed his assistant to tend to the store as he guided Parrish to the back study.

The room was quaint and cluttered with old volumes of all kinds. Culhane lit a pipe, and the sweet aroma of tobacco filled the room. Parrish opened his leather attaché case and removed the monster sketch, passing his eyes over it one more time before handing it to his friend.

"Julie paid me a visit. She brought with her a young man named Tom DeFrank. The kid's an artist with a penchant for monsters. He had this in his sketchbook."

The man sharpened his gaze on the creature. He twisted the pipe in his mouth, chewing on the stem, and laughed. "It looks like a gargoyle I once saw in Venice. I like the countenance of the face in particular. Very frightening." His eyes drifted then to the inscription below. "What's this down here?" He held it up to the reading light for closer inspection. "Did the boy write this?"

"Yes. It's what drew my attention immediately."

"It looks like part of an incantation."

"I thought so as well. I hoped you might be able to identify it."

Parrish's confidence in the man was well founded. Humphrey Culhane was a savant of tremendous erudition. A mystic from childhood, he joined a seminary in his late teens, but he found the rigors of the Catholic Church repressing. He broadened his focus into occult theology and comparative religion and traveled to many parts of the world observing traditional forms of worship. He studied voodoo under a Jamaican *houngan* and published a book on Rada, the traditional white magic of the Caribbean. A historian by nature, with no desire to become a wizard, Culhane rarely practiced magic himself, although he was well versed in its technique. He was an honorary member of several covens and contributed regularly to various publications. As a bookseller, he specialized in obtaining rare occult manuscripts. His sources were legendary. He boasted that if it existed in writing anywhere on this plane of consciousness (or any other) he could find it, deliver it, and charge it to MasterCard.

Culhane placed the paper on his desk, and with a pencil began counting the syllables of each word, marking them with little scratches. The structure of the verse held some significance, like the stanzas of a sonnet.

"Hmm. Interesting."

"You've found something?"

"It's rather what I *haven't* found. Parts of the verse appear to be missing. Like they were squeezed together. Introverted. Are you familiar with that term?"

" 'Introversion'? It's the conjunction of words of power into an abbreviated form, a way of concentrating the energy."

Culhane nodded. "It was a common device used for creating mantras in magical rituals. Did the boy mention where this came from?"

"He claimed he doesn't know," Parrish replied. "Although I suspect he's withholding. All he told Julie was that it somehow 'zapped into his head'."

"Zapped? Is that how he put it?"

"Apparently he was in the Crohaven area when it happened."

"Hmm. It could be an 'ætheric fragment'."

"What's that?"

"Theoretically, the performance of magic can create psychic impressions—*remnants* within the æther, which can be transferred to a sensitive person."

"So you're saying that Tom might have stumbled onto a location where some powerful ritual was performed. This fragment was imprinted on his mind and then passed onto me."

"Essentially. It may have awakened some latent psychic ability in the boy."

Parrish dwelled on this. He gazed deeply at Culhane. "When I shook the boy's hand, I received a vivid impression—a sorcerer engaged in some kind of occult ceremony. I'm almost certain it was the Reverend Jacob Tornau."

Culhane's eyes flared with interest, and he chuckled. "The Necromancer of Crohaven? Of course. I should have figured. Still looking to finish that book of yours?"

"And why not." Parrish grinned, hiding his true objective. "I've invested so much time already. It would be a shame to completely abandon it, especially if there's a new lead."

"Yes . . . except you didn't come all the way here for the sake of a book." Culhane pierced his denial, "It's really the boy you're concerned with."

Parrish dropped his shoulders in surrender.

"It's a thorny path, Stephen," Culhane said. "You've walked it before."

"I know," he relinquished. "I vowed never to do so again. But there was a strange emanation in Tom's aura. An unhealthy glow, like something had attached itself to him." Parrish described the malign, spidery energy that clung to Tom's orb in his spectral examination.

Culhane listened to the description, sensing Parrish's

reticence to evoke it, and he knew the man was deeply conflicted. He leaned back in his chair, supporting his head with his palms. "Tornau dealt with some truly malevolent forces," he began. "Very little is known of his magic. I assume nothing new has turned up at the mansion?"

Parrish shook his head. "The place was emptied out years ago. If he kept any records, they were lost. Most of his belongings were confiscated, or burned by local zealots. They wanted to destroy every trace of the man. I did as much inquiry as I could but very little remains, except speculation and rumor. Until now."

"Could you tell from the vision where it took place?"

"I can tell where it *didn't*. It wasn't in the barn."

Culhane raised his brows.

All the known blood rites of the Tornau cult were performed in a large barn on the property of Terence Whateley, a mere mile and a half from Crohaven Manor. But the locale depicted in Parrish's vision was a dark space with rugged stone and concrete walls. "It might have been a wine cellar. Or a mine, perhaps. But definitely a different location."

Culhane tapped his pipe again, ejecting some glowing coals into a tray. "So we're talking about an entirely new ritual site, and possibly a new cycle as well. Well, the man was prolific."

In his early years, Jacob Tornau had been a magician, skilled in theatrical wizardry. He traveled in popular circles, won friends in Hollywood, and gained the kind of prestige and distinction afforded by those with wealth. His quest for visceral appeasement was legendary. Tornau was a notorious hedonist and party to a number of Hollywood scandals. He was rarely seen without a new young starlet on his arm, and jokes were made that he ate them. But it was for his reputation as an occult scientist that he was most renowned. Under the tutelage of famed "antichrist" Aleister Crowley, he studied "magick" at Oxford University, then traveled extensively to enrich his knowledge of the black arts. He set up a Gnostic temple in Padua, Italy, for a period, before returning to the United States, where he relocated to the tiny town of Crohaven, and purchased the estate. The community welcomed the renowned socialite, but his celebrity soon gave way to paranoia.

It was around the mid-'50s that the aging "reverend" set up a ministry of unspecified denomination. The congregation was small, roughly two dozen locals, but they were devout and highly secretive in their activities. The town heard less and less of Tornau, who isolated himself within the dark walls of Crohaven Manor, seldom venturing into public. He took a young lover, the beautiful Sarah Halloway, a highbred actress who abandoned a successful career on Broadway to become his constant companion. She became Tornau's only contact with the outside world. With her charms, Sarah helped curb the growing speculation about his group, but in time she too went into seclusion, her appearances in the town less frequent. People spoke of strange goings-on at the Crohaven Estate. Strange lights, unusual sounds, and weird vocalizations were reported coming from within the mansion. Soon thereafter, in 1965, there began the disappearances of young women, and suspicions began to fester.

"Those were horrible times," Culhane mused in morbid fascination. "Four women captured and slaughtered. The abduction of the baby and big showdown at the farm."

"And then he vanished," added Parrish. "Just like that."

An anonymous informant led the police to the ritual site, where the cult was confronted at gunpoint. During the crossfire with the sheriff, Tornau escaped with five of his group. What followed was one of the biggest manhunts in Northeastern history. A nationwide search, organized by local and federal authorities, was engaged. Rewards of up to one hundred thousand dollars were offered for information leading to an arrest. Despite it all, Tornau was never captured. He and his devil cult simply disappeared without a trace.

The remains of four women were exhumed on the property. One was identified as Georgia Hendricks, a schoolteacher who disappeared from her trip home from a soccer game. Three others, Jane Sheffield, Stacey Willis, and Doreen Lamont, were young girls in their teens and twenties. They each vanished a month apart from neighboring communities. Dental records were required to identify them. The bodies had been dismembered and—from the looks of the remains—charred in a fire. *Roasted.* It was commonly believed that they were *cannibalized*, a hardly farfetched conclusion given Tornau's sexual proclivities, but to Parrish it portended something far more diabolical.

Culhane folded his burly arms and leaned back. "Four sacrifices in as many months following the phases of the moon. The last sacrifice an infant child." His eyes sharpened. "They may have been attempting an 'anthropomantic cycle'."

Anthropomancy, the blackest form of magic, used the energy released from human souls at the moment of death. After the slaying, the flesh and entrails were consumed in fire, accompanied by chants and talismanic ritual. Women and children were the most frequent victims; their life forces rich in spiritual innocence, but infants were by far the most potent.

Parrish nodded, his pulse racing. "A ritual like that would have unleashed a colossal amount of supernatural power."

"It could tear a rift into the very fabric of our dimension. Sounds like they were trying to create an Asmodai-fueled portal."

Stephan's eyes glinted. "A what?"

"It's a form of dimensional travel, first described by Hermes Trismegistus. It required a cycle of blood sacrifices to create a vortex into the dark realm, or what you might call *Hell*."

"Using the torture and death of innocents." Parrish said in disgust. "I can't imagine a more diabolical enterprise,"

"Well that's the idea," Culhane responded. "Remember that it's the emanations of the mind that create the magic. The more vile the deed, the more potent the energy.

Blasphemy and sacrilege are deliberate in black rituals. Upending the crucifix, violating the Host. To spit in the eye of God is to harness a terrible force. Satanists are the anarchists of the spiritual world. They tap into the darkness of the human soul, milking it like sap from a tree. Human sacrifice is their most potent fuel source—their nuclear energy, if you will. They would've needed *seven* to complete an anthropomantic cycle."

"It seems they completed four at least," Parrish said.

"Oh, I suspect as many as *six*."

"Why do you say six?"

"Because of the infant. From what we know, the child would have completed the cycle. It was the *final* rite that was interrupted in the barn."

Parrish crinkled his brow. "So there were two additional murders at the farm. And a possible third somewhere else, if my vision is correct."

"It would have been extremely frustrating for him," said Culhane. "Having to abandon the process, so close to completion."

"Then perhaps he didn't," Parrish said. "After his escape, everyone assumes Tornau fled abroad to avoid capture. But what if he managed to stay in Crohaven and performed the seventh ritual?"

"You would have yourself one nasty little hellhole right in your backyard."

Culhane took up the drawing anew. "Your only clue lies somewhere in this fragment. We now know that a trace exists on an ætheric level. It seems Tornau left footprints: a web of psychic remnants that has lain dormant in the region. Then something came along to trigger it awake. With your 'faculties,' you may be able to follow the trail. Start with the last known location of magical activity, and take up the search from there. Have you been to the ritual site?"

"I made an attempt years ago," Parrish informed. "Whateley's brother Sam owns it now. He wouldn't let me near the place. I imagine it's been thoroughly cleansed."

"True, but there are some things you can't clean with a mop and wash bucket. My guess is there are other visions trapped in the æther that are newly activated, waiting to be revealed. You have to try to get in there."

"That may prove difficult."

"I thought you had 'connections' with the local law enforcement. Couldn't you make it an official investigation? After all, we are talking about unsolved *murders*."

Parrish agreed, but his eyes wandered to an unpleasant time and place.

CHAPTER 20

FIVE O'CLOCK ON A THURSDAY EVENING.

Tom pressed another globule of soft plasticine onto his monster figure. The clay stole the warmth of his fingertips and became increasingly malleable. With skilled hands, he rounded it smooth until it merged into the underlying form. He then took a tool with a wire-loop head and began scraping off wide curling ribbons of clay, creating contours from the rugged chaos. The arms bulged with sinewy biceps, branching out from a pseudo-human chest that protruded forward at the sternum. The feet were fiercely clawed.

A work lamp burned brightly above his scalp, and he was experiencing the first pangs of a headache. But, as the creature took shape with uncanny precision, he became impressed with his progress. He didn't work from the usual reference. No atlas of anatomy was required. The original sketch would have been his only guide, and he had given that to Mr. Parrish. There was no need to produce another. Every detail was memorized. In his mind's eye, the creature was as real and complete as anything he had seen in a zoo. His fingers were treading a known path, pioneered once before in a half-forgotten dream. Somewhere beneath the greasy mass of clay, like one of Michelangelo's angels, Fau'Charoth lay waiting to be exposed.

It was now 6:25 PM.

Another lump of clay. Another curl of plasticine.

His mom called from the hallway. "Tom! Are you coming to dinner?"

"I'll be right there!"

"Now!"

"I'm coming!"

His hands were aching. He was hungry too, and dinner was waiting. One more lump around the shoulder. Just a few more touches to the spine. He picked up a rounded wooden tool and glided it around the deltoid, merging it into the shoulder blade.

His mom called again, what seemed a minute later. "Tom. I'm leaving. Your dinner is wrapped in the fridge. Turn the front light on before you go to sleep."

"Fine!"

Oblivious to her, he focused on the creature's jawbone, which needed reshaping. Layers of petal-like scales came off its cheeks in jagged spires. The lips were encrusted with mosaic tiles.

Finally, Tom leaned back in his chair, dangling a pointed tool and letting it drop noisily to the desk. His fingers felt hot from the insulating layer of clay. He studied his handiwork with satisfaction.

The figure's pose was not particularly dynamic. Its stance was rigid, arms falling stalwartly to its sides like a British sentry. Tom longed to bend it into a menacing crouch, thrusting back its elbows with that Harryhausen flair. But that would have to wait. The neutral pose lent itself best to the mold making, which would commence soon after he completed the sculpture. The clay figure would be imbedded in plaster, the mold impression then used to cast a duplicate in flexible rubber. There was so much work to do, and he had barely begun.

The phone rang.

He ignored it. His mom would get it eventually.

It rang again. "Mom?" he called. Did she leave already? He couldn't remember. He stepped across the hall into his mother's room and plucked the receiver from its base.

"Hello?"

"Hey!" said a whispery voice. It was Julie!

His eyes widened, and a smile streaked across his face. "Hey!"

"What's going on? I hope I didn't wake you."

"Wake me? Of course you didn't. It's only—" He looked at the alarm clock on his mom's night table. The digits read 10:23 PM. It was like ice water in his face. He had lost over five hours! "What the . . . How did it get so late? I have to eat dinner yet!"

There was a loud giggle over the line. "Do you normally just forget to eat?"

"I don't know what happened. I was sculpting my

creature, and time just slipped away."

"Boy, if I hadn't called, you might have starved to death. We could patent a new diet. 'Doc DeFrank's sculpt away the flab. Be a new person in a week. Or *something*'." She giggled at her own joke. He liked the way it sounded. He also liked her using the term "we."

Tom pulled his legs under him, sitting on his mom's bed. It had only been a few days, and he and Julie were already remarkably close. For the past week they had spent each lunch sitting at the edge of Senior Lane, swapping snacks, and chatting up a storm. Boy, was Danny ever impressed, seeing him with his pretty little companion. And not just *any* girl, but the daughter of the infamous Parrish himself! Danny called them a "perfect match," and Tom wondered long after if it was a hidden chide.

"Your friend Danny is strange," she remarked.

"Tell me about it."

"He stares at me like he's never seen a girl before."

Tom snickered. "Oh, he's seen *plenty* of girls. They're plastered all over his bedroom wall."

She giggled again. "Ugh! Gross! I think he drooled on my sneaker."

Tom sank his face into the pillow, laughing, as she continued.

"So, as I mentioned yesterday, my mom and I were supposed to go to Boston tomorrow night to visit my Aunt Mishy, but there was a change of plans, so she postponed. You know what that means? That means I've got nowhere to go on a Friday night. Isn't that a shame?"

"Uh-huh?"

There was a pause, and Tom snapped to attention like an actor who'd missed his cue. "Oh! Wait! Julie . . . would you like it if we did something, like go to a movie?"

She snickered. " 'Uh-huh,' I thought you'd never ask. I was afraid I'd have to carry this entire operation myself!"

He sank against the bed board and moaned. "Don't laugh. This isn't easy for me."

"I guess you don't ask girls out too often."

"Never. How did I do?"

"Not too bad. We grade on a curve."

"So dinner and a movie then? The mall, afterward?"

He could hear her smile. "Deal."

"Speaking of dinner, I should be eating mine."

"Mm. You should. I'll see you at lunch. Goodnight, Tommy." Followed by a smack.

"Goodnight, Julie." Her line clicked first. At last, he lowered the phone to the base and hung up, ignoring for the moment that she had called him "Tommy," and that the smack he had heard was her kissing him over the phone. All he wanted to think about was his dinner waiting in the fridge, and how hungry he was.

CHAPTER 21

The Galleria shopping mall bustled with teenagers. It was the first Friday night of the new school year. Hordes of weary students looked forward to a chance to hang out in the plaza and cut loose. The combined voices of hundreds of teens, herding their way though shops and eateries, sounded like a unified sigh of relief. Though the mall was a fair distance from Chapinaw; it was the best hangout the county had to offer. Kids made the pilgrimage every weekend, filling the parking lot with their parents' borrowed autos, and dilapidated "first wheels."

Tom and Julie sat in a booth at Bubble's, a diner that fancied itself an authentic replica of a 1950s malt shop. The decorum was a nightmare of art deco. Everything was slick and glossy with Formica, brass, and shiny blue vinyl. Brown fizzy seltzer from chocolate-syrup egg creams overflowed from tall soda glasses. *Life* ads for Edsels and Peppermint Patties adorned the walls while Dion and the Belmonts doo-wopped from a jukebox.

Julie contentedly munched the last few bites of her

cheeseburger and fries while Tom nibbled birdlike at his grilled cheese. God, she could eat fast! He had to force himself to gnaw at the crust of his sandwich, taking an occasional sip from his vanilla shake. His stomach felt like a big knot.

Julie wore a pretty white blouse and a faded denim skirt. It was the first time he had seen her legs. They had a tan glow from the summer. Tom wore new jeans that felt stiff and a polo shirt with a slightly upturned collar. For a brief moment, he had actually considered wearing a tie! As it was, he felt tightly wound and fidgeted with his napkin until it was crushed into an oblong ball in his palm. Being on a formal "date" made things considerably different between them. There was that uncomfortable feeling he was neglecting some critical dating *ethic*.

They'd gone to an early showing of *The Elephant Man* at the mall's triplex. It was *her* choice. He expected her to choose a "chick flick," and it thrilled him that she shared an interest in the grotesque. Directed by David Lynch, the movie was a biography of the severely deformed John Merrick of Victorian England. Tom was drawn into the stylish black-and-white photography and horrific character makeup.

"Are you going to eat that?" she asked, pointing to his pickle.

"No. Help yourself."

"I eat like a pig. I hope you don't mind." Two bites, and the pickle was gone.

"That's all right." He smiled. "People say I eat like a

dinosaur."

"Oh, really? How does a dinosaur eat?"

"Are you asking me to show you?"

She beamed at him. "Yes."

He glanced for watching eyes and then demonstrated a reptilian chomp on his sandwich. His neck cocked back and then darted forward cobra-like at the grilled cheese in his hands. Monster jaws snapped onto the crust, and with a flip of his head the morsel was tossed to the back of his throat as he swallowed. Julie was chewing a French fry at that moment, and her silent laughter nearly made her choke. A tear of mirth formed in her eyes.

She reached for a napkin. "I see what you mean. You could be the antithesis of tonight's film. Everyone treats you like this regular guy, and meanwhile you're struggling to prove you're this hideous creature."

He distorted his face like John Merrick. "I'm not a man! I AM an ANEEE-MAL!"

She grabbed his hand tightly. "Wasn't John Hurt great in that role?"

"His performance was incredible."

"I loved Anthony Hopkins. He's one of my favorites."

"He's okay," he baited her deliberately.

"*Okay?* Are you crazy? The man's brilliant!"

Tom shrugged. "He's a human playing a human. What's so difficult about that?"

She looked like a puppy about to pounce on a ball. "Well, what's he supposed to play? A lamppost?"

Tom smiled. Leading her into familiar territory gave him an edge. "It's just that I like an actor who can play something different. 'Transcend his physical limitations.' Take Willis O'Brien, f'r instance."

"Willis O'*who*?"

"Willis O'Brien. He was the guy who invented stop-motion animation. When you watch King Kong climb the Empire State Building, you're watching him in his greatest role."

She rolled her eyes in playful opposition.

He leaned over the table toward her. "You see, every time he animated Kong, he had to step out of his human form to become that giant ape. Just like I do whenever I animate. Animators are the most versatile of actors."

"I think you've got monsters on the brain," she teased. "So you're saying that when animating your puppets, you're acting?"

"That's right. Now, I may not be Anthony Hopkins, but I've played a few good roles in my day. I've been a Cyclops, an ape, a troll, three billy goats, a pterodactyl, a couple of dragons, and a whole bunch o' dinosaurs. You see, you take a model, and you move it a little each frame—"

"I remember." Her eyes sparkled, smiling at the obvious joy in his voice. She wondered if there was anything in her life about which she felt so passionate.

"So now you got this body," he continued, "and you have to behave for it. You gotta act out its movements and think its thoughts. How does a dinosaur walk? What's it feeling when it chases its prey? You gotta learn how to snap your jaws, and swoosh your tail, and *eat* like a dinosaur."

He took another ferocious chomp out of his sandwich, barely swallowing, and continued with strong bravado in his voice. "Julie, animators are the greatest actors in the world! I can be a dragon! I can fly high above the clouds with my great dragon wings, stare down at the countryside and roar!"

She was impressed. "Wow."

"I dream about it."

"What?"

He looked puzzled, as though startled by his own words. "Oh . . . nothing. I've been having these dreams." The experience of the flight dreams came back to him, and he reflected on it for a moment. The first was already a distant memory. He had since been to a mountain river and recalled the sparkle of moonlight on the wet stones.

"Have you ever dreamed you were flying?" he asked.

"I think so. Flight dreams are pretty common, actually." She smirked. "I read they have a *sexual* connotation."

"No, seriously. Have you ever had a dream that was so real that you thought you were awake? You could hear sounds around you, and feel things, and have a strong awareness of space and speed?"

She studied him, trying to understand his perspective. A tingle of dread touched her spine. Peculiar.

He leaned closer, as though offering the secret of Atlantis. "I've been having these dreams, and it's so real that when I wake up, I have this definite sense of having been somewhere."

He didn't notice her smile had faded.

"How long's this been going on?" she asked.

"A few nights now. Just out of nowhere. The first time, I was out in the neighborhood, soaring above the houses and trees. I think I attacked my neighbor's dog!"

She blinked. "You *attacked a dog*?"

"It barks all the time. Keeps me up at night."

He described flying off with the annoying little beast, only to drop it some distance away in the bushes. The look of terror in its eyes was hilarious. Maybe "Mitzi" would think twice before yapping in the future.

"When I awoke, I heard Mrs. Wadowski screaming down the street. I don't know. I guess I sound wacko, but it felt as real to me as being here with you, now."

"Well, surprise, Tom!" she argued playfully "We're not really here. This is *all* a dream!" Her own skepticism was alarming. There was too much conviction in his eyes to simply dismiss it all. Julie sat deep into her bench.

"I guess you could be astral-projecting. Your spirit could be floating out of your body while you sleep. I've read in fact that all dreams are a form of astral travel, but we don't usually retain the memories or learn to control the process."

His eyes danced with excitement. "Wouldn't that be great? If we *could* learn to control it and fly places and do things?"

"Yeah," she answered, masking a feeling of uneasiness.

She wanted to probe him for more. It seemed significant, somehow, but the waitress came by to drop off the check.

Tom snatched it up before Julie could glance at it and reached for his wallet. *This* much he knew how to do. He put down some cash with a generous tip as they rose from their booth and headed for the mall complex.

For an instant, Tom's arm brushed across the gentle curve of her back. She tensed ever so slightly under his touch. It felt like forbidden fruit.

As they passed the video arcade, Tom reached into his pocket, checking for change. "You wanna drop a few quarters?"

"You go. I gotta go to the 'ladies.' Meet you there in a flash."

She whisked away to the twin doors. He watched her, then strolled into the game room.

Inside the arcade, there were three corridors of high-tech machines, a vast array of colorful monitors that glowed in the dim light. The air was thick with electronic explosions and screeching cars. Pac-Men gorged themselves on beeping amoebic ghosts. At least three kids stood by every game. One played, the others watched, catching a vicarious thrill off the same quarter.

His quarter clunked into a slot for *Galaxian*. The game activated with a series of musical beeps. A fighter craft hovered at the lowest level of the screen. Rodent-like *dagon*s rained down. Tom flexed his trigger finger, blasting them with little shafts of light.

An electronic hornet dived in a graceful arc toward his fighter. He barely dodged its torpedoes before laying waste to the blue bug. He pressed the trigger continuously. Three more red insects were insinuated.

There was some loud laughter. He glanced around and saw four figures enter the arcade. They were Al Gunthur—*shit!*—"Reef" Demarco, Lenny Finch, and—

Hell and Blood! Clifford Burke.

Dammit! Not now. Not tonight.

They were heading in his direction.

Tom buried his face in the monitor, feeling like the proverbial cat in the tree. He tried to look oblivious to their presence. It didn't do any good.

"Well lookit what we got here. Tom DeFrank." It was Burke's voice in his ear.

"The mad monster maker himself."

"What's he doing out? I thought he worked the 'graveyard shift'."

He tried to ignore them as a yellow wasp peeled off for the kill. He fired and missed.

"Not doing too good, DeFrank." Demarco leaned over the machine. "That yellow one is the worst of 'em all."

"He has trouble shooting bugs," Burke quipped. "It's like killing his own."

Tom kept silent. Nothing he could say would match their "cool." He would be shot down like one of the flying insects.

Three of them came from the left corner, dropping pixels of firepower.

Boom! His second fighter fell prey to a bug-eyed *dagon*.

His last fighter appeared. Finch and Gunthur peered over his shoulder like awed spectators. His score was low, as though he cared. He wanted to finish and get away from them, without making it obvious that he was running. Where was Julie? She was probably looking for him by now, but if he saw her, they would see her too.

"Y'know, DeFrank's a real artist," Burke remarked. "He drew a picture of Gung Ho's old man, and I swear to God it looked just like 'im."

"No shit?"

Gunthur grunted.

"The dweeb's got a lot of guts. What do you think of that, Al?"

"I think I should twist his head off."

"DeFrank's all right. He just chose the wrong friends, that's all."

"Yeah, like Kevin Marshall."

"Someone's gonna have to bust that dude's ass."

Burke leaned closer to Tom's ear. "You hear that, Tom-Boy? Your friend Marshall is walking on thin ice."

"Why don't *you* tell him that?" he muttered under his breath.

"What?"

"What did he say?" Lenny Finch asked.

Boom! The last fighter bit the dust. Tom frowned to hide his sigh of relief. The three moaned in gross disappointment as though a hero had been slain. But as Tom stepped away, Burke gripped his shoulder.

"That was my fault, DeFrank. I distracted you. Here. Have another quarter on me."

"I gotta go."

"I insist."

Before Tom refused, Burke clunked another quarter into the slot. The musical bleeps played again. Tom stared down at the screen and at Burke's reflection in it. He took the joystick in his hand and began firing aimlessly.

"I saw you with some girl today," Burke asked. "Build her yourself?"

"That was that Parrish chick," Finch offered.

"Oh, yeah! Julie Parrish. Man, that chick filled out. Put some meat on her bones."

Heat burned around Tom's neck.

"Little sparrow tits, but a nice ass. I could go for a piece of that action."

"Yeah, but she's weird. Her father's that dude who works at the mansion."

"They have an old cemetery there," Burke pointed out. "That's convenient. He provides the bodies, and Tom can put 'em together. You two should seriously date, man. Young Frankenstein and Dracula's daughter." They laughed.

"Just make sure you don't end up like Josh and blow your skull off."

"Yeah," Lenny mimicked a radio ad. " 'Need a new brain stem? Gee Wilkens'!"

Julie entered the arcade and glanced around for Tom. He wasn't by the entrance, or near the pinball machines. She wandered to just beyond the front row, and peered around the crowded bodies engaged in video warfare.

There he was. He was playing a game at the far end, drawing a small crowd around him. *Must be pretty good*, she thought as she made her way. Then she stopped. One of the "crowd" was Clifford Burke, and that meant trouble. From their body language she knew they were taunting him. She considered how best to support Tom without adding to his humiliation. It was a delicate affair. She decided to duck out of sight. Too late.

"Hey!" Burke spotted her from the distance. "Is that who I think it is?"

"Speak of the devil!"

Burke grabbed Tom by the shoulder. "DeFrank, it's her! It's Julie Parrish! Now's your big chance." Finch and Gunthur were squealing with delight.

"Lay off," Tom's voice was like a growl. He begged fate not to bring her into this.

"Hey, where'd she go?"

A quick glance revealed that she was nowhere in sight.

"Took off on her broom. Woooooo-oooo!"

"I bet when you screw her, she turns into a bat!"

"One way to find out. Lenny, go get her."

"No!" Tom was angry now. He pushed himself away from Burke and collided with Gunthur's chest. "Get out of my way!"

"Come on, DeFrank. Where're your balls? She's waiting for you!"

"Shove it, Burke!"

He walked to the next corridor. They followed, herding him against the back wall. Tom's fists were tight. He felt an insane itch to use them. Julie could be watching, and it wasn't the time to turn coward, but getting beaten to a crimson smear would hardly serve to impress her.

"Better go after her, DeFrank. If you don't put your brand on her, she's on the market."

"Suppertime!" Lenny chimed in.

"Stay away from her," Tom hissed between clenched teeth.

The crowd turned to observe a confrontation better than the pixilated light shows on the screens. "Jeez, the guy's turning into a monster himself."

"Unbelie-eeeeeeevable."

"Gonna take a swing at me, DeFrank?"

Kids waited for Tom to make a move. But there were three of them, and Burke seldom took his own punches. It was undignified for a leader to do so—and other vain excuses. Tom backed into a corner. His fist felt like steel, but it weighed like lead.

There was a fire door behind him.

Numbers clicked in sequence. *Ting ting ting.*

There seemed like no other choice.

He pressed the lower latch on the door and pushed his way backward through it, hoping not to trigger the alarm.

God was with him. He didn't.

It was Burke, 10. DeFrank, 0.

"Just trying to help the guy," Burke shrugged. "Kid's got an attitude problem."

"Yeah, real Zippo-personality kind of a dude."

The back of the complex was lit with a single arc lamp that bathed the area in a cool blue glow. A few steps off a platform found him amidst the garbage dumpsters, overflowing with cardboard boxes. A rat darted from behind the wheels. He had never wandered behind the mall before. It all seemed so desolate and strangely tranquil in the blue light.

Humiliation crawled and stuck to his ego like sticky sap. He had thought retreat was the wiser move but now reconsidered. It might have been better to defend his manhood, take his blows, and stand up afterward like Paul Newman in *Cool Hand Luke.* Better than the pounding he would surely give himself in the morning.

What he feared most was that he was now a target. The Burke clan would not let up on him. They had tasted the flesh of his pride and would come back for more.

Now Julie was involved as well. Some date he turned out to be, leaving her alone in the lion's den.

Tom came through the parking lot, listening to the lonely crackle of his sneakers on the gravel as he approached the front entrance. He considered going in again, but uncertainty weighed on him like an anchor. The loud bustle seemed very uninviting.

He stared up at the sky, wishing he could sprout wings and fly away.

Julie appeared as if by magic from the dark. Tom looked up at her with surprise.

"Hi," she said in a voice filled ironically with apology. "I came out through the diner exit. I figured you would catch up to me eventually out here."

"Good move." They started walking to his mom's car.

"I'm sorry. I didn't mean to leave you so long. There was a line in the—"

"Did they hurt you?" he asked in a rattled voice.

"Who? Them? No. They're idiots. You shouldn't let them get to you."

He pulled in a deep breath and let it out slowly. "It's not easy, sometimes. After a while, you start believing what they say about you."

"I know." She gazed at him solemnly. They leaned on the hood of the car.

Tom remained flustered. He stared at the sky, his nerves still vibrating with unspent anger. "I should've just punched the guy in the jaw."

"What? Macho bullshit? That doesn't impress me. What *you* did impresses me much more." There was authority in her voice, and he took strength from it. "You showed mastery over them by walking away. I'm proud of you, Tom."

Before he could respond, she had her arms around him in a hug.

He was frozen for a moment; unable to grasp that this beautiful warm body was pressed so closely to his. Slowly, he raised his hands and put them gently on her back. He traced the delicate outline of her shoulder blades through her blouse, felt the straps of her bra beneath the cloth, and indulged in touching her.

"I'm into hugging, you know," she revealed.

He held her closer, letting his first hand join his second around her back as she moaned in satisfaction and continued. "I read this article once. It said a person needs to be hugged at least once a day just to survive."

"Really?"

"Uh-huh. And twice to be healthy and happy. *Three* times to be 'totally rejuvenated to face the world.' Or something to that effect."

"So where does that leave me?" he mused. "That leaves me dead and buried ages ago."

She let out a short sniff of laughter, and he could tell she was smiling. "Awww. I guess we both deserve more hugs in our lives."

She loosened her embrace and gazed up at him with a little smirk, and then, somewhat hesitantly, kissed him. It was experimental—a quick smack on the lips that left him aching for more.

"You're my best buddy, now. You know that?"

Tom smiled as they entered the car, feeling content, and befuddled. Always wanted to be somebody's "best buddy," he thought to himself.

CHAPTER 22

I AM DREAMING, *TOM'S MIND TOLD HIS SLEEPING SELF.*

Yet that very self was awake. Where a moment before, he was lost in a sea of scattered images, his mind was now brought to sharpened awareness. He was staring at the ceiling of his room, crisp and vivid in the dark, his mind strangely alert *and focused.*

His body sank heavily into his bed like a slab of concrete. A prickly sensation traveled up the length of his arms, plucking at the hairs of his chest. The tingle converged from all corners. It joined together at a point above his navel, where it concentrated into a ball of energy.

He felt light, floating upward like a cobweb lifted by a breeze. There was a humming that vibrated just at the borders of perception, before raising to a pitch higher than the range of his ears. It was the verse of the spell, throbbing subliminally through his brain.

The ball of energy began to tug upward—a zeppelin straining against its moorings. It pulled at his solar plexus.

I am dreaming, *he reminded himself.*

It pulled harder. He lifted higher, his body a feather, and then—

Snap!

A burst of colorful orbs—red, green, yellow—like a cathedral window.

He was a helium balloon rising to the ceiling and passing through it.

Then he was outside, soaring high above the landscape.

He passed over houses, cushioned by the wind, trailing along currents like a kid sledding down an icy slope. Elation brought him still higher, as though ecstasy was the fuel of his wings. Adrenaline soared through his veins, energizing a body he'd left far behind. Off in the distance, as he gained altitude, he could see White Lake. It bent like a boomerang around a populated shore.

I am dreaming!

The faster he thought, the faster he traveled. Quickly, he left the familiar borders of his town and traveled to the densely forested regions. The woods below him were aglow, shimmering with a phosphorescent halo, as maples and pine trees mingled their fiery energy fields, radiating an aura of life-essence.

He swooped into the glowing trees. Black limbs encrusted with living embers blurred past. The leaves and branches made no contact with him. He was as immaterial as an idea.

An owl left its hollow in search of food. Tom followed it, sharing in the hunt. It flew skillfully, but it was no match for Tom's dream wings. He soon overtook it, skirting the tips of its tail feathers. It never responded to his presence, unaware of the game of tag it played.

Following the owl brought him out of the woods, into a rolling field that loomed for many acres. Familiarity drew him to the ground. He settled to the earth, a mere wraith, and looked about. A whippoorwill cried out in the distance. A rabbit darted out of the brush, a flickering halo of infrared emanating from its fur. It stopped and glanced up as though sensing Tom's presence. Its eyes were like livid coals!

Insects leaped out of the grass, the chorus of crickets in full session. Another owl hooted from the treetops.

He became the wind, soaring above the night terrain with incredible speed. Rapture filled him like a great inhalation of breath. Looming before him was a hayfield, newly cut. Rectangular bales were scattered about. A big red tractor was parked in the grass. Tom dove for it, catching its details in crystal clarity. Fenders were rusting at the edges. Tires were crusted with mud and straw. Whoosh! He soared past it.

Over the hill, the edifice of Crohaven Manor and the cemetery appeared. He fell adrift on a current of air, drawn to the estate like a magnet.

Below him, the graves expanded in all directions. He dropped to ground level and soared past them.

The headstones were crisply discerned by his night vision. He could read the names engraved in the granite.

STANLEY BISHOP

Whoosh!

JUSTIN AND EMILY WALLACE

Whoosh!

And then he stopped. Stopped and stared. A wind passed through him.

The name on the stone was FREDERICK BURKE.

Burke!

Bitter contempt and loathing churned his sleeping stomach. He became aware of a rising fury that seemed separate and apart from him. It was as though he was no longer alone, and the new presence shared his anger. A red blaze blinded his view, concentrating with intense rage. Suddenly, it exploded at the stone with the force of a thunderbolt.

The headstone shattered into fragments!

The impact startled him. He was aloft again, high above the graves.

The stark shape of Crohaven Mansion loomed before him. He stealthily approached it.

Nearing the building brought sudden apprehension as the rustic gables of the mansion grew defined. A febrile energy radiated from within. Icy needles of dread assailed him. He glided about the structure, an immaterial falcon seeking to perch, yet sensing danger.

Boldly, he drew close again, defying its barrier.

As he passed around the highest peak of the building, he noticed a figure standing there. A man surrounded by an orb of white light. Tom soared toward the figure just as it turned to face him.

It was Parrish, gazing at him like a hawk!

And Tom woke up!

He was sitting upright in bed; his arms thrust out before him as though shielding himself from the man's piercing eyes. The vista of Crohaven was gone. He blinked, disoriented, and lay back against his pillow, his heart beating madly.

Jesus! This was too much!

Dumbfounded, he pushed the covers off and got out of bed. The blood rushed to his head, and he felt light and dizzy. A whirl of vertigo caused his vision to spin, and he rubbed his arms, grateful to feel his own flesh.

"What the hell is going on?" he asked himself.

Miles away, sitting in his study, Stephen Parrish gripped the soft arms of his chair. He rose to his feet and stepped to the window that overlooked the cemetery. An exercise in lucid dreaming had resulted in his wandering outside of his body, traveling to the rooftop where he could survey the property in tranquil thought. But the brief sojourn from his physical body had been disturbed. By what exactly, he wasn't sure. Nocturnal encounters in the dream state were fairly common. Astral entities flourished in the sleep world. Spirits of the dead, disembodied travelers clad in empyreal raiment, and thought-form phantoms, the figments of a sleeping mind. He could dispel them at will.

But here was a phenomenon he'd never experienced. It was a sinister wave of energy that tainted the æther. It possessed enormous emotional force.

And it scared the hell out of him.

CHAPTER 23

SHERIFF KURT KRONIN MADE A LOUD RUMBLING IN the back of his throat when his secretary Elyse informed him that Parrish was waiting to see him. "What the hell is Stephen doing here?"

"Something about the Crohaven murders," she answered. "He's been checking the old records."

"Oh Christ." Kronin frowned and reached for a mint from his pocket. Since he quit smoking, he'd developed a fondness for mints. They helped take away the bitter taste in his mouth, like the one he was experiencing now just thinking about Parrish and Crohaven. The sheriff was a thread shy of sixty years old, and the job showed in his face. Dark hair had given way to gray, his moustache almost entirely silver. His face was wide and had a wealth of creases that delineated his years in law enforcement like bands on a tree stump. Yet admittedly many of those creases could be traced to a brief period over fifteen years ago.

The year the girls started vanishing.

Kronin had three daughters of his own, and there

wasn't a night he didn't worry about them. It was strange that one needed to worry in such a small and affable town. Chapinaw was a community like none he'd ever known. He had lived here most of his life and was around to see the changes. He'd taken part in the vote that forever renamed the town from the tainted Crohaven to the friendlier Indian moniker. Over the years, the people had joined together to make it a safe haven. The churches filled on Sundays, and active, concerned citizens attended town meetings.

Fear can do that to a place.

He could still recall, like it was yesterday, that accursed fall when the Tornau affair was exposed. It stabbed into the very heart of the community, leaving folks shaken that such evil could dwell within their very midst. He had led the raid on the farm that killed one of his deputies and seriously wounded another. They managed to save the abducted child, and slew six cult members in the process, but the devil himself, Tornau, escaped with five of his minions.

They remained at large, and though there was never another incident, terror continued to fester for years. Parents were stricken with dread and uncertainty, until it seemed the town would die from its own paranoia.

But as the years wore on, people fell into peaceful forgetfulness. The old tales of witchcraft in the "big house" died down, or settled into regional folklore. Rarely if ever was the name Jacob Tornau spoken aloud in public. In such cases, short memory could be blissful, and Sheriff Kronin preferred to foster that oblivion.

But he knew all of that would come to an end the moment he entered the room and gazed upon the gaunt visage of Stephen Parrish.

Parrish exchanged a cool but familiar glance with the sheriff.

"Been a long time, Stephen," Kronin said in blank greeting.

"It's good to see you, Kurt." He took the sheriff's hand and perceived instantly that the man was suffering from a peptic ulcer. He was also experiencing some tension in his marriage and drank way too much caffeine.

"I'm sorry we've been out of touch," Kronin continued, oblivious to the psychic's impromptu examination. "I could've used you with that Hawkins incident last year."

"From what I read, you solved it well enough without me."

"Yes, we did. Forty-seven man-hours later. You might have accomplished the same thing in an afternoon."

"But . . ." Parrish quoted, " 'the department has no knowledge of soothsayers and has never and will never employ the use of psychics in its investigations.' Or so I recall you saying. For the record."

The sheriff noticeably tensed, hearing his own words spoken back to him. It was apparent they'd reached the end of their cordial chitchat. "So what brings you here, Stephen?" he asked dryly, shuffling into the big chair behind his desk. "Certainly nothing for my benefit, I hope."

"To the contrary," Parrish smiled. "I think it's good news. I've continued my research into the Tornau affair, and I've got some new leads."

"Leads?" Kronin looked doubtful. "You mean 'hunches'?"

"Educated hunches, and they've lead me to some new theories."

"Hot on the trail, are you?" Kronin quipped.

"There's been an upsurge of psychic activity in the region," Parrish explained. "A dormant web of impressions has been reawakened. It's like plucking a single string on a guitar, causing the rest to vibrate. If I backtrack over the crime scenes, I may be able to follow its path."

Kronin leaned back in his chair with a characteristic groan and folded his arms behind his head. "Sounds to me like you're getting lost on another one of your 'ghost hunts'."

Parrish was piqued by his dismissive tone. "As I recall, Kurt, some of my 'ghost hunts' proved fortuitous." He pointed to the wall behind Kronin's head.

Framed on the wall was a newspaper clipping from the *Times Herald-Record*: HERO SHERIFF LOCATES MISSING GIRL. Kronin was shown clutching the frightened six-year-old, smiling triumphantly. "Yeah." Kronin shifted uncomfortably. "But I thought we had an agreement about that."

Wandering in the woods during a summer clambake, a little girl, Leann Gibney, had gotten lost. The clarion call went out, and for two days the entire county searched. Every available man volunteered, combing the countryside for the missing child. But by the eve of the second day, all hope had faded.

Hearing the news, Parrish offered the sheriff the services of his keenly honed second-sight. Kronin initially laughed him off as a crackpot, but there was such conviction in his eyes that the police officer consented.

Armed only with a piece of the child's clothing and a vague description of her appearance, Parrish clairvoyantly located the six-year-old. She had managed to wander clear through to the next county and finally took shelter in an abandoned building deep in the woods. The girl was severely dehydrated, but unharmed.

The article made no mention of Parrish's efforts and offered no explanation for how the sheriff determined the child's location. Having authorized the psychic in secret, Kronin garnered full acclaim for the rescue. It got him an accommodation and further cemented his reputation as a hero cop. In the ensuing years, there were other such cases in which Stephen employed his talents. He became the sheriff's glorified bloodhound, sniffing out stolen vehicles, criminal hideouts, and even a small plane that had crashed into the mountains. When news of his assistance was leaked, though, Kronin made an official statement to the press, denying all rumors of psychic detective work. If the local law enforcement was deemed to use "supernatural methods" in its operations, he feared it would lead to public outrage. Chapinaw was justifiably sensitive to such matters.

The sheriff reached for another mint, having impatiently crunched down on the one he was sucking. "Well, you wouldn't have come this far if you didn't need something from me, so out with it."

"I need to examine the farm," Parrish said directly. "And I know the owner won't casually let me on his property. It'll take a search warrant."

"Damn straight it will, but I can't just walk into City Hall and request a warrant because you have a *hunch*. I need a better reason to—"

"You need a reason? Here it is. The murder investigation at the Whateley farm was never officially closed. You exhumed four bodies at the site. There may be others: a total of six."

"Six?" Kronin's eyes flared. "How did you come up with that?"

"Like I said, new research. He was engaged in a particular ceremony, requiring a sequence of blood rites that would end with the sacrifice of an infant."

"Damn." Kronin gazed at him sullenly. "You got the whole thing figured out?"

"I'm close. We may be able to solve the mystery at last."

"It's like you're walking over my grave, Stephen. I'd rather you drop it."

"Why?"

"Because people get nervous about witchcraft around here. You know that better than anyone. I'm surprised you would even attempt something like this again."

Parrish felt his blood rise. "All I need to do is walk in and out. You can send your deputy with me, if you like.

Nobody will be the wiser. It's important."

"Important to whom? You act like somebody's life is at stake."

"There might be," Parrish said, and regretted it. Kronin was already probing him. The last thing he wanted to mention was the boy. Parrish sighed. "Get a warrant, Kurt. Tell the judge you have reason to believe a further search on the Whateley premises will unearth at least two additional victims."

"Based upon the speculation of the town warlock?" he barked. "Are you out of your mind? There's still shit on my face from the last time you stuck your psychic nose out. Jesus, Stephen, why do you insist on digging up this old business?"

"Because I want to learn the truth."

"You want the truth? Here it is. Tornau was a madman and a murderer. He killed girls, chopped them up, and *barbecued* them. What more do you need to know? His recipes? No one's heard from that devil cult in fifteen years. The FBI took his name off the ten-most-wanted list a decade ago, and if they don't care about him, why should I."

"It's his legacy I'm more concerned with, Kurt. The town needs closure. Think of the families of those victims! It would benefit the community to put those remaining souls to rest. Don't you agree?"

The sheriff leaned forward, challenging him fiercely. "Of course I do! I'd like nothing better than to catch the bastard and put him in a grave where he belongs. The guy escaped on my watch! I lost two of my best officers that night and took a bullet myself." He tapped his shoulder. There was fire in his eyes as he remembered. "There hasn't been a night since that I haven't seen the man in my sleep. I had to raise three daughters with that fear. But that was fifteen years ago, and what good would it do to bring it all back, now? Tornau's gone, and the town has finally learned to sleep at night. I won't be the one to raise old nightmares."

Parrish knew he was losing ground and felt desperate. "Kurt . . . please. I need to get into that barn."

"Leave it be, Stephen. I'm warning you. You go snooping around with your 'voodoo eyes,' and people will start asking questions again. Do I have to say it, Stephen? Do I have to remind you what happened to Josh?"

"No."

"Wilkens still has it in for you, and if he hears wind of this he'll get on your ass for good this time. The man's on a rampage. He blew his stack last weekend because some bozo was wearing a hat in church. A freakin' hat! His wife is sick, probably dying, and he's just looking to vent his rage. I can't protect you anymore."

"When have you *ever* protected me, Kurt?" he said, which caused the sheriff to squint. But Parrish knew that arguing further would prove futile. It was hard to argue with the truth.

CHAPTER 24

THE SKY-BLUE FLIER WAS TACKED HIGH ON THE SCHOOL'S bulletin board. Julie noticed it while exchanging books in her locker. She drew near curiously. The paper contained a logo featuring the harlequin faces of comedy and tragedy, and below it was an announcement:

> "Chapinaw Drama Club presents *Dark Victory.* Production of the dramatic play begins September 23 and will be performed October 27–30 in the high-school auditorium. Tech crew positions are available. Auditions for eleven roles will be held in the chorus room on Monday, September 20, at 4:00."

The drama club's annual presentations were a special event, and Julie had toyed with the idea of getting involved. Perhaps it was all the talk about "acting" with Tom, or perhaps she had greasepaint in her veins, but she felt a strong pull to the theater. The spring musical was a lavish production, requiring the collaboration of the music and chorus departments. Julie remembered how much she enjoyed

Brigadoon the previous year. The fall drama productions were smaller, but well suited to budding thespians. They were a great way to make friends, as the cast and crew spent long hours together building sets and staging the scenes. Rehearsals were usually held after class, but sometimes they went late, requiring group trips to the pizzeria. It all seemed like so much fun. The idea of competing for a role excited her. It would be nice for once to be involved in something other than a rumor.

She reread the bulletin, and smiled.

"I'm going to try out for the dramatic play in school," she announced later to Tom as they walked down Main Street toward the tall gray edifice of St. Peter's Catholic Church.

"Really?"

"They're doing *Dark Victory.* Wasn't that a movie with Joan Crawford?"

"Bette Davis," he corrected. "And Humphrey Bogart."

"I doubt I'll get the lead. But any part will do for starters. Do you think I'm silly? Wanting to be an actress?"

"Sure, of course you are," he quipped.

"Very funny. This could be my big chance. Who knows? Maybe I'll get discovered!"

"Yeah, I'm sure all the big Hollywood agents will be there."

"Don't laugh! It'll be fun. Let's hope so, 'cause if I get a part, you're gonna be there for *every* performance!" She stabbed him in the ribs, then had a flash of inspiration.

"Hey, why don't you try out with me?"

"Naw."

"C'mon!"

"I told you. I only do monsters."

"Oh-h. You *are* a monster."

He clawed at her, snarling.

"Eeeek! I'm scared!" She cringed like a B-movie bimbo and trotted ahead, enticing him to chase. Tom felt his heart flutter. He wanted to kiss her so badly.

Looking back, she nearly collided with a man coming out of the church's side entrance.

Julie startled. The man was tall and grim as a cigar-store Indian. He wore a tan fedora with a dark band over a head of white hair. His chest was like a barrel, and his huge hands had thick sausages for fingers. His large moon of a face creased with wrinkles at the eyes. As they sharpened on Julie, they took on a contemptuous stare that chilled her to the bone.

Julie was frozen, a doe caught in the headlights. Tom could only watch, uncertain.

The two confronted one another for a heartbeat. Neither seemed to know what to do.

In an effort to be friendly, Julie squeaked out a greeting. "Hi, Mr. Wilkens." It was a peace offering, filled with fear and condolence, and Tom waited for the man's response.

Silence. "I'm praying for Mrs. Wilkens," she said. "I hope she gets better soon." Wilkens glared in return, as though Julie were a vile object in his path. He lowered his eyes and continued on his way past them.

He very conspicuously made the sign of the cross as he went, banishing an unholy presence.

Tom could hear the slightest of gasps from Julie, as though the man had spit in her face. She looked at the ground, deeply offended, as he faded into the distance.

Tom went to her side. "What was that about?" he asked, but she was too dumbstruck to answer. He could see her trembling.

"Julie?" he whispered to her. "Was that *Gee* Wilkens? The guy on the radio?"

"Just forget it."

They walked on, the encounter lingering like a foul stench.

Though Tom sensed her discomfort, he couldn't curb his curiosity any longer. He had to know. "Julie . . . was that his father? Was that *Josh* Wilkens's dad?"

Julie's eyes flared. "What do you really know about the Josh Wilkens thing?"

Tom stepped back from the fire in her voice and shrugged innocently. "Just the stories I heard. I'm sorry. I didn't mean to upset you."

She began walking again at a brisk pace. Tom struggled to keep up.

She stopped with a sigh and faced him as though confronting an indignity. "You want to know about monsters, Tom? *Real* monsters? 'Cause you could never know a monster as terrible as Gerard Wilkens."

CHAPTER 25

BRIGHT CLUSTERS OF ORANGE AND CHERRY RED LEAVES blew about like whirling dervishes as Parrish revved up the motor of the portable weed trimmer. He had finished mowing the grass in the statuary garden for what he hoped would be the last time for the year, and was now engaged in cutting down the dry milkweed and vines from the edges of the fence. Some reseeding of the lawn was required due to the summer drought. The leaf piles and grass cuttings would have to be collected for composting. It was a considerable amount of work for one man, but he preferred to work alone. One summer, over three years ago, the town had provided him with an assistant.

Josh Wilkens.

The whirring gears of the weed trimmer always reminded him of the boy. Josh especially enjoyed attacking the outgrowth with its spinning cord. He was a good worker, and seemed to enjoy the rugged outdoor labor.

Josh was the son of Gerard Wilkens, or *Gee* Wilkens as he was known from the banal ad slogan. The family owned the three branches of G. Wilkens Home Appliance Centers in Sullivan County. The catchphrase was posted on billboards along the highway, and Gerard's own voice could still be heard in his radio commercials everyday on WVOS:

"Need a new freezer/washer/dryer? *Gee Wilkens!*"

In a small town, it's easy to become a celebrity. Most everybody knew Gerard Wilkens from his famous fedora and deep guttural voice on the airwaves. A run for public office had put a face to the name. For months, his campaign posters plastered the town. He was a religious man, strictly pious, and regularly attended St. Peter's Roman Catholic Church, where he served as a lector. His enthusiastic Sunday readings, bursting with fire and brimstone, were more suited to a Baptist rally than a solemn Catholic mass. He gave generous tithes every week to the collection plate, and once a year donated brand-new appliances to the charity auction. He was also a volunteer fireman, and his wife Connie belonged to the Ladies' Auxiliary. His only son Josh attended the Catholic Youth Organization and played shortstop on the ball team. They were a model family, risen to prosperity through hard work and keen investment. But this idyllic façade hid an ugly interior, and like the corrosive force of seawater on a ship's hull, it was telling on the boy.

At Wilkens's request, the town had hired Josh to provide grounds assistance for the Crohaven Estate during the laborious summer months. Wilkens felt the minimum-wage job would help build his son's character, although some speculated that Josh's real purpose was to scout out the landscape. It was no secret that Wilkens was interested in buying the property. Whatever his intent, the boy worked closely with Parrish for four months. Long afternoons were spent dumping mowed grass into piles, trimming hedges, or repainting the black finish on the wrought-iron fence. Since they were both on the town payroll, Parrish never considered himself Josh's 'boss,' but rather a worldlier equal. He took Josh into his confidence, engaging in conversations, and eventually showed the boy his paintings. Josh was impressed with the artistry, but the imagery was somewhat lost on him. He was kept unaware of Parrish's more exotic talents.

But Josh clearly had troubling issues. With every handshake, Parrish was jolted with a flash of internal pain and received glimpses of the boy's private anguish. He was acutely claustrophobic, for one thing, and steered clear of the basement, the closets, and even the work shed in the yard. Darkness and confined spaces held a grip of terror on him. He also suffered from a deeply penetrating sense of shame. His mom was sickly, and his father subjected him to harsh discipline and stabbing condemnation. He snapped shut during any discussion about his home life as if to hide some horrible truth.

By the end of the summer, the boy had grown strangely despondent. He showed up for work earlier each day, and left increasingly later, until one night he seemed reluctant to leave at all. Parrish found him resting under a marble bust of Pericles in the garden, reading a book long after the sun had reached twilight. It was as though he would sleep there if he could.

"The grass won't grow any faster if you watch it," he'd joked.

"I can wait," Josh answered dryly. It didn't take a psychic to realize the boy was afraid to go home. Parrish sat with him, trying to draw him out, but Josh was too private a person to acknowledge his pain. When all else failed, Parrish insisted he go to a relative or friend. Someplace he felt safe. Josh grimaced at the suggestion, and left.

Parrish regretted he couldn't prevent the boy from going back to what was obviously a severe state of abuse. The summer was ending, and Josh's employment would soon come to a close. Action needed to be taken. To get past his outer defenses and address the boy's trauma, Parrish decided to engage in something he would regret for the rest of his life.

He would examine the boy psychically.

There was nothing more he could learn from a quick handshake. A longer, sustained contact was required. At first, he considered revealing his clairvoyant abilities as a subject of trivia and demonstrating them with a cold parlor reading. But this seemed insincere, and with his strict Catholic upbringing, Josh would likely be put off by such a display of "sorcery." He would have to be clandestine and distract the boy with labor.

The next day it rained, so he invented indoor chores to keep the boy busy. Josh was scraping paint off a windowsill, preparing to refinish it. His back was turned when Parrish stepped casually beside him, brushing away the flakes—"Here, let me help you with that"—and then he gripped Josh's arm firmly, flooding himself with painful images.

Josh flinched. His aura flickered with bright shades of red. Anger, fear, and toxic shame passed into the man's psyche in an emphatic stream of energy. Parrish was overwhelmed with the rush of raw emotion. He was witness to unbearable castigation, the words of the father like daggers of contempt. He felt like a yoked animal, cruelly whipped by its master. With eyes closed, he experienced darkness and near suffocation and felt himself trapped in complete blackness, his arms restrained about him. It was like being in a coffin. He could feel his own fingers clawing desperately at the cloth and wood, pulling at the velvet lining.

Let me out! Let me out! Please, Dad!

Was he buried alive?

The words echoed in his mind until he shuddered aloud, his expression labored and contorted. Too late, he realized his grip on the boy had lingered too long.

Josh pulled free of his hold and looked away uncomfortably. "What are you doing?"

Parrish blanched, still shaken. He backed away, embarrassed. "Nothing. I was just—"

"I gotta go, Mr. Parrish."

"Josh . . ." Parrish pleaded. "You don't understand. I'm psychic. I was simply reading you."

"You're *what*? I'm not into—I don't do that shit."

"Josh. It's all right. I know what you're going through. You can talk to me."

"No. Get away from me!" Josh fled the building, startled and confused. He never returned.

Later, Parrish sat in his armchair, processing an assortment of images. The vision of the father was so frightening. His jaw went rigid as he visited the darker side of Gerard Wilkens, a volatile manic-depressant, prone to violent acts of abuse. Wilkens persecuted the boy at every turn, verbally, physically, and emotionally.

Disparaging such a well-respected man was an unenviable task, but Parrish could not ignore Josh's plight. Having acquired the knowledge through psychic means, there was no legal course he could take, so he reported his findings privately to Kurt Kronin. The sheriff scowled at the charges, but agreed to visit the Wilkens home and investigate.

The result was a disaster. In a conference with the sheriff, Josh denied all the accusations. He dismissed Parrish's claims, referring to him as a "lunatic" and a "queer." It was a savage blow to his testimony, and left Kronin powerless against further action.

"Did you touch the boy?" Kronin interrogated him later. The question made Parrish feel unclean. He knew the insinuation would lead to something tragic.

Two days later, Josh was dead. The boy took Wilkens's shotgun, and in an act of defiance and self-destruction, put the barrel in his mouth. He shot himself in front of his father.

The news shocked the community and devastated Parrish. For days he suffered in seclusion. He also endured terrible accusations from the father, who personally blamed him for his son's suicide. Anonymous phone calls threatened him in the middle of the night. A burning cross was placed on his front lawn. But Wilkens never faced him directly. He never looked Parrish in the eyes. Except in open court.

Wilkens transformed his grief into a civil lawsuit. Parrish was charged with inappropriate behavior toward a minor. The high-profile case filled the local media. Wilkens determined that Josh was a delicate soul, diabolically influenced. Brainwashing and mesmerism were among the charges, as well as sexual impropriety. Kurt Kronin was summoned to testify on Parrish's alleged "psychic" abilities and address his involvement with police investigations. It became a great embarrassment for the department, and crushed what remained of their tenuous alliance. In the years to come, Kronin openly avoided him.

Ultimately, the case was dismissed, but the black cat was out of the bag. Parrish was now the target of gossip and hearsay. "Witch!" the rumors went. "Sorcerer!" He withdrew himself from the public eye and became a recluse. But the onslaught continued.

Not content with the court's ruling, Wilkens then went to City Hall, demanding that Parrish be fired from his job at Crohaven. But his own religious zealousness worked against him. Wilkens rooted his attack in scripture and raved too strongly about Parrish's "satanic" practices. Strange as it seemed, to dismiss Parrish on such charges would have been prejudicial. You can't fire a man for his religious beliefs, however unorthodox. Opting to avoid litigation, the council voted to retain him. Although Parrish was relieved with the decision, he was perplexed that his psychic abilities could be classed as some kind of "religion."

To this day, Wilkens had an ongoing crusade to challenge the landmark status of Crohaven Manor. He sought to buy the property outright. Uproot the evil and salt the earth. Parrish had become his great white whale.

The turn of the season would always haunt him, thinking about Josh. He preferred to work alone now as penance for the role he unwittingly played in the boy's demise. In an attempt to help him, he inadvertently destroyed an entire family, and he vowed never again to use his "curse" to benefit another person's welfare.

With Tom DeFrank, it was proving a difficult vow to keep.

It was near twilight, and the sun blazed red on the horizon. The pungent smell of fermenting grass filled his nostrils as he passed the compost heap. Parrish carried the weed trimmer across the road to the private cemetery, where a row of headstones was overgrown with clumps of ivory vine.

He frowned with dismay. One of the stones had been damaged and overturned. Vandals. Troublesome teens occasionally stole into the graveyard for mischief. It angered him that kids would desecrate a grave. They usually came armed with cans of spray paint. This one, apparently, brought a sledgehammer. Parrish put the trimmer down and went to examine the shattered grave marker.

One large chunk of stone retained the letters BUR, but the rest had been demolished. "Frederick Burke," he recalled, was the name. He bent to pick up one of the shards of the headstone.

And dropped it, startled.

The stone gave off a pulse of psychic heat. He stared at it uncertainly and put his palm over another chunk. The negative vibrations were unmistakable, and vaguely familiar. He knew it was no vandal that had attacked this stone, but something of unearthly origin. His blood grew cold, and he gazed at the stone shards as though they would burst into flames.

CHAPTER 26

CONNIE WILKENS WAS SITTING UPRIGHT IN HER BED, dressed in a white cotton nightgown buttoned tight to her neck. Her pale arms lay limp beside her. Nadia, the Guatemalan nurse lifted a spoon to her mouth, trying to feed her a clear chicken broth. Some of the briny fluid dripped down the side of her mouth like spittle. The nurse frowned and wiped it away with a cloth. She had another patient to tend to that evening, and she was conscious of the time.

"Mrs. Wilkens, you must eat." Nadia insisted, offering another spoonful of the broth.

But the woman's lips wouldn't part to accept it. She became more and more withdrawn each day. Her once beautiful tresses of long hair were now streaked with gray, and her face had a pasty yellow complexion with blue shadows around her eyes and temples. Cerebral cancer had taken its toll on her, but the true affliction was one of spirit. The family physician came by once a week to check on her, but she was beyond all treatment at this point and released to home care. With each morning, she seemed to diminish further, wasting away like an orchid in dry sand. The nurse knew her employment at the Wilkens home would not be for much longer. Even the sickest of her patients could sustain themselves for extended periods, if there was a will to survive. But Connie Wilkens was making her own deathbed.

Mr. Wilkens returned from work, entering through the bedroom door, his face dark and weary as he stared at his wife. Heaviness pervaded the air. In public, Wilkens was a cordial and articulate man, the consummate salesman. But at home he was as grim as a requiem, his eyes stern and downcast. Nadia was grateful that he was absent for most of the hours she spent there. It would have been unbearable otherwise.

He removed his fedora and held it by the brim. "How's she doing today?"

"Not too well, Mr. Wilkens. She won't eat."

Wilkens peered at his wife. Creases angled in from the corners of his eyes. "She knows it's his birthday, soon. Josh would have been nineteen."

"Yes, sir." Nadia put the soup bowl on the night table and the spoon beside it. "You can try for yourself, if you like. It'll stay warm for a bit longer."

"She doesn't need food. She needs *prayer*." He pulled out of his pocket a familiar chain of black-and-gold rosary beads. Nadia frowned. She herself was Catholic and prayed often to the Lady of Guadeloupe, but there was something oppressive and suffocating about this man's devotion. It was bleak and devoid of hope. The room was filled with religious icons. A Blessed Mother statue stood on a dresser, wreathed in cheap rosary beads. Tacked to the wall behind her was a collage of Mary images from Fátima and Lourdes. The Holy Mother's visage graced every inch of wall space as though she was some celebrity pinup adored by an adolescent. Nadia wondered if the priests at St. Peter's were aware of his fanaticism. Had it always been so, or had the man descended into this state only recently? She gathered her things, eager to leave the room even as he crossed himself and began to recite. On the way home, she would stop by the church and say a prayer of her own to the Blessed Mother for Connie and Gerard Wilkens. But not in this room.

Gerard gently sat down beside his wife on the bed. She barely seemed aware of him. So little of her resembled the woman he married. The cancer first took her five years ago. It began as a headache about which she barely complained. Connie never complained about anything. She tolerated the pain as best she could, smothering it with aspirin, but when her vision started to blur, they decided to go for tests. They visited three clinics and consulted a variety of specialists. The prognosis was grim: metastasized cerebral cancer. It would mean the slow deterioration of her cognitive functions, followed by dementia, pain, and paralysis. The physicians gave her a less than thirty-percent chance of recovery, and so they were surprised when with radio and chemotherapy, she went into a seemingly miraculous recovery. Wilkens knew it wasn't the medicine that caused the remission. He was convinced it was the rosary, recited as often as eight times daily, that saved his wife.

But now, even that miracle was being stolen from them.

He took his wife's hand and held it as he rotated the beads with his left fingers, whispering the verses under his breath. Connie responded to the sound of his voice and joined his prayer with a breathy whisper.

"Hail Mary, full of grace."

"Hail Mary . . ." Connie repeated weakly.

"The Lord is with thee." Wilkens said the rosary often. He knew the prayers so well that he could recite them in his head while driving. He wore a ring with little globules that he rotated on his index finger, allowing him to keep track of the verses. Sometimes he recited them with both arms outstretched in a crucifixion pose, until the weight of his arms was unbearable. In time, as his shoulders grew stronger, he stuffed cans into his sleeves to increase the exertion. He deliberately put sharp pebbles in his shoes, and sipped his coffee scalding hot, offering the pain up to God. It was called *arrepentimiento.* Devotion through suffering. For Gerard, faith equaled sacrifice.

Wilkens had always been a devout man. His first wish had been to enter the seminary, but his family was poor, and he was forced to work at an early age. Soon after, he entered the army, and a tour of duty in Korea removed any aspirations of the cloth. He had become tainted by a wretched world. Too defiled for the Holy Order. But marrying Connie and raising a child had brought new hope for him. He could redeem himself as a father and offer his son to the priesthood. Josh was to be his salvation.

Instead, he burned in the flames of Hell, the fate of all suicides.

Because of the witch-man and his influence.

Gerard flinched at the thought. He balled the rosary beads tightly into the palm of his hand and crushed them until the metal crucifix bit into his flesh.

"Hail holy queen, mother of mercy . . ." he began the final verse.

"Holy . . . holy holy . . ." she stammered now. She was seldom able to complete the prayers anymore, as though her mind was being snatched away, bit by bit, by the devil. A tear formed in Wilkens's eye.

"Don't, sweetheart. Don't let him take you. Get thee behind me, P-p . . . *Satan*." He'd almost said *Parrish*, as though the two were synonymous. In some dark place of his mind, he blamed the psychic for his wife's illness.

It was shortly after Josh's suicide that her cancer returned with a vengeance. The shock of losing her son weakened her system, putting her into a severe depression. Some small seed of the tumor might have still have existed in her brain, but her grief had surely caused it to sprout.

Because of Parrish.

Wilkens had just passed his daughter on the street. She was happy and alive while his own boy suffered for redemption. Was it the devil's retribution? Was Satan stronger than God? Sometimes he wanted to lash out at the Holy Father, demanding an explanation. Why wasn't *he* smitten down? He was unworthy and deserved punishment. Why Josh? Why his boy? Wilkens had made every effort to ensure that Josh grew up to be a morally disciplined and God-fearing man. He seldom spared the rod, and his words were severe. On occasion, he experienced a moment of agonizing clarity, when he heard the boy crying and his own bitter words like poison in his head.

Had he been too harsh?

No! He couldn't allow doubt to creep in. To do so would be to question the very bedrock of his faith. Chastised and rigorously punished all his life, the man had long ago retreated into shame. Only the rigors and sacrifice of the church had brought him solace. It was in the expurgation of the confessional, the sacrament of penance, that he found his peace; a peace he could share with his boy.

But the church, Wilkens decided, was too hallowed a place to confess their sins. Even the curtained stalls of the confessional were not private enough, so to spare himself and his son from terrible humiliation, he built a plywood chamber in his basement. He painted it black throughout, stapled a black velour curtain to the interior, and added a door to preserve the dark. He stood it upright and put a small stool inside.

Christ himself would hear their confessions.

Josh was made to sit in it, for hours at a time. He confessed his sins to the darkness. Often, Wilkens would use it himself, for a day or more until absolution was achieved. It

CHAPTER 27

JULIE OPENED A BAG OF COCKTAIL PRETZELS AND poured half its contents into a bowl. She then raced out of the kitchen to place it in front of Tom.

Tom sat awkwardly in Julie's living room. "Can I help you in there?" he asked.

"No! Just relax and watch your movie." She returned to the kitchen to continue helping her mom cook.

"You're gonna miss the best part," he called after her.

"I'm coming."

Tom returned his attention to the movie playing on the television. It was one of his all-time favorites, the Harryhausen sci-fi thriller *Twenty Million Miles to Earth.* He had suggested catching the late afternoon showing, and Julie used it as an excuse to invite him over for dinner. Now she was busy preparing chicken breasts and yams with her mom, enjoying her chance at domesticity. Julie's mom seemed to approve of him. It was the second time they'd met, and she was being especially nice. He could hear them whispering from the other room, and was beginning to feel like a pampered suitor.

Julie returned and dropped in the sofa beside him.

"Dinner won't be ready for an hour. If you get hungry I have some fresh pears in the fridge."

"I'm fine." He reached for a pretzel.

She pulled her feet onto the edge of the coffee table until her legs formed an arch. His eyes darted at them with quick little peeks, and she smiled to herself, knowing she was being a deliberate tease. Tom liked to look at her legs. She wore a pink T-shirt, tucked into the waist of her khaki shorts. Her calves were especially nice from that angle.

Tom folded his arms across his chest and stared at the television screen. The room was immaculate and attractively furnished in earthen shades of orange and brown. A handsome cherry cabinet held a stereo, and glass shelves were filled with ceramic bric-a-bracs, mostly owls. Mrs. Parrish was fond of owls.

Along a far wall, an exquisitely rendered portrait of Jesus hung above a contemporary fireplace. The face of Christ glowed through layers of varnish and pigment that gave it a rich almost holographic effect. Tom recognized the style of the painting. The masterful blends of color could only have come from the hand of Stephen Parrish.

"Your father painted that?" He pointed to the image.

"Years ago," she whispered, grabbing a handful of pretzels. "It was a gift to my mom. Sometimes, when she's alone, I catch her praying to it. I think she believes Jesus really lives in that painting."

"Maybe he does," Tom smiled.

He studied the portrait, and for a moment imagined he saw Parrish's eyes staring out from it. Then he was distracted by the otherworldly voice of the monster on screen.

Twenty Million Miles to Earth was about a strange Venusian creature brought back to Earth on an American space mission. It escapes and goes on a rampage across the countryside of Italy. The creature, known affectionately as the "Ymir," was one of Ray Harryhausen's most popular characters. It was a hybrid of man and dragon, with a catlike face and long forked tail. The Ymir's iconic stance and unusual stride were the stop-motion artist's trademark—head and neck hunched forward, arms and elbows held rigidly back. In its movements, Harryhausen had established not only a character, but also an entire library of idiosyncrasies. It was a language that every animator learned to speak fluently. Tom purposefully spiced his own creatures with that Ymirian flair.

Onscreen, the Ymir stalked the fields of a peasant farm, terrorizing a herd of sheep. It took quick steps like a bird, the long tail undulating in a serpentine curve. Raising its head, it let out another earth-rattling shriek. Tom froze in his seat. He felt the old magic pumping in his veins. As it approached a bleating lamb, Julie reached over and gripped his arm tightly. A smile broke across his face.

The Ymir plodded cautiously toward a barn, driven on by the cacophonous music of the soundtrack. Harsh light glistened off its bumpy hide. As it entered the barn doors, a trio of plow-horses began to scream and rear in frenzy.

Julie gasped. "Is it going to get the horses?"

"No. Shhh."

She watched the monster with interest, but was especially amazed by Tom's *response* to it. He was being literally *pulled* toward the set. She felt the taut excitement in his frame, and the profound scrutiny he gave to every nuance. His posture underwent a metamorphosis, mimicking the creature perfectly, absorbing its very essence into him. She half expected his face to pucker up into scales.

Commercial break.

With the movie gone, Tom relaxed, dropping his shoulders. Then he noticed Julie's unabashed stare and the startled smirk on her face. He turned a shade of red. "What?"

"*What?*" Julie asked. "What was all *that* about?"

"That? Oh. I was practicing."

A laugh exploded from her lips. "Practicing?"

"Don't laugh. That's how I get poses for my creatures. I study animals and copy their movements until I can duplicate them."

"Okay. Let me watch you *practice*."

He shook his head self-consciously. "I don't think so."

She poked at him playfully, then folded her arms. "Come on, Stanislavsky. Mr. 'Greatest Actor in the World,' let me see you perform."

"Okay-y."

Tom rose reluctantly to his feet. He cracked his joints, trying to relax. Julie watched him expectantly. He tuned her out and withdrew into deep concentration, seeing the creature in his mind. Space-monster from Venus. Human-gargoyle-dinosaur. Immediately his whole demeanor changed. His spine curved, head thrust forward like a lizard. Shoulders raised, elbows back, fingers curled into claws. His movement took on a staccato rhythm, like a dancer under photographic strobe. Then, with dashing speed, he took three birdlike steps across the room, turning with a twist of his torso. His eyes were hooded with reptilian menace, and his lips raised from teeth that, for all the world, should have been fangs.

Julie felt spiders creep up her back, startled by the transformation. She remembered his dream about becoming a dragon. Flying above his house. Attacking a dog.

And then he relaxed, smiling a bit, and was Tom DeFrank, diminutive young filmmaker once more. Julie sat frozen for a moment, uncertain how to respond, and then fell into rapt, gleeful applause, hoping to hide her brief alarm.

"I also do a great 'Mighty Joe Young'," he offered, pleased with himself. "Care to see?"

"No, that's okay," she said with a snicker. "I prefer you human."

CHAPTER 28

Miss Delmonte sat in the auditorium several rows back from the stage. She adjusted her glasses and made some notes in the loose-leaf binder as she listened intently to the student auditioning on stage. Legs crossed, her foot dangled and wagged impatiently. It would be the third play she directed for the school. Casting was always the most difficult part, selecting from among the many students who tried out each year for the theatrical productions. Only a few could be chosen. The rest would leave, disappointed, and perhaps even crushed from the experience. The girl on stage was attempting to read from the audition pages. Sadly, "read" was about the extent of it. She fumbled a bit and failed to make eye contact with the boy who fed her lines. Delmonte stifled a frown. Getting a performance out of a "cold reading" demonstrated one's ability to find character and improvise: skills essential for a thespian. Whatever dreams the young girl had, she was not going to be an actress.

"Thank you, Cindy," Delmonte said formally. "Okay,

next."

Another girl, Janine Meadows, walked center stage. Out of habit, she brushed a hand through her long blond hair. "Hi, Mary," she said with confidence.

"Take it from line three, Janine," Delmonte answered.

Backstage, Julie felt her heartbeat rise. She was excited to be trying out for the play. The thought of losing herself, of temporarily becoming a different person in the eyes of her peers, intrigued her. She re-sorted the pages and glanced again at the opening line. There were only four female roles in the play, and she had her heart set on the second lead. To play the lead would have been far more than she could handle.

Besides, Janine Meadows was auditioning, and she was sure to take the lead. She played Anne Frank the previous year and was already in good with the director. Julie watched her perform, half-hiding behind a scrim curtain, as the girl shifted her weight from leg to leg, her cute little butt swinging from side to side like a pendulum. Janine's hips bulged with what looked like an inch too much cushion. Her jawline seemed a little wide, and she had a red spot on her forehead that was about to erupt into a fresh zit. Julie noticed these things because they were flaws in an otherwise god-awful perfect physiognomy, what with her carefully coifed hair and "babe from Hell" body.

There she was, hamming it up on stage, her perky breasts beckoning forth through an angora sweater (as though Miss Delmonte would be impressed). Julie barely felt her own bosom poking through her blouse. She finally managed to put on some weight over the summer, but her body still felt skinny and scraggly, her jeans hanging loosely off her hips. A bout of depression, two years before, had brought her dangerously close to anorexia. Julie cringed as she recalled the sickly pale stick figure that stared back from the mirror. Her mom put her on a diet of protein milk shakes with raw eggs and bananas, and insisted she spend time in the sun. She took to bike riding and gained some muscle tone in her limbs. She now had color in her skin, a pleasing shoulder-length hair cut, and a trim, girlish physique her classmates might even envy. If only her breasts would blossom, like Janine, perhaps guys would notice her more, and at the very least be nice to her.

It wasn't about being popular. It was about being less *unpopular.*

But then she smiled, reminding herself that there was already a guy in her life who noticed her just fine. Tom genuinely enjoyed *looking* at her. She could feel his eyes when her back was turned, stealing glances as though he was pilfering sweets. At times, she felt like an organism under a microscope, but his admiring gaze gratified her.

Boys, she thought, as a blush came to her cheeks.

She could tell girls were new to his life, even more mysterious than those bizarre creatures he to build. Experience-wise, Tom was fresh out of the box, a late bloomer at sixteen. He fumbled with their kisses like a boy taking his first rim-shot at a basket. She found it endearing. Julie was starting to realize just how much she liked Tom DeFrank. He had an awkward charm, and a dark, ironic sense of humor that brought her out of her shell. She was glad they had met so early in the school year. It took away so much pressure, worrying what guys thought, and whether she would be spending her weekends alone. There were things she could look forward to now. Halloween parties. Christmas gifts. The Junior Prom.

Her cue came to audition. Janine stepped aside as she made her way to the stage.

Julie glanced and couldn't take her eyes off that huge potential-zit on the girl's face.

About to erupt. Like Mount Vesuvius.

Once at center stage, she nodded to Miss Delmonte, and gave the reading of her life.

Off-stage, Janine observed her performance and sighed with disapproval. Her friend Suzanne Goldfarb joined her in the wings. "Oh, no. It's 'Samantha'." She smirked to Suzanne while twitching her nose like Elizabeth Montgomery in *Bewitched*. "*Tinkle-tinkle-tink*."

"Yeah, really," Suzanne agreed. "I hope she doesn't put a 'spell' on them."

CHAPTER 29

"OH-HHH SHII-IT!" KEVIN SHOUTED, HIS FACE TWISTED in dismay.

Tom followed him into the student parking lot as he fell into a wounded trot to his car. The sky was a brilliant azure blue with clusters of white cotton gathered at the horizon. The lingering summer sun was warm on their backs, and they were going for a quick ride to the mall. Tom couldn't imagine anything ruining such a beautiful afternoon.

And then he saw.

"Damn," Tom cursed aloud. Kevin fell silent.

The Monstermobile had an obscene cobweb of splintered glass sprawled across the windshield, with a hole in the center the size of a cannonball. The interior of the car was pebbled with little fragments of blue safety glass. Lying on the front seat was a large rock that had been hurled through the windshield in a petty act of vandalism. Kevin circled the car with a look of crazed irony, checking for other damage. Tom's nerves peaked, expecting another volcanic eruption from Kevin.

But Kevin remained quiet, searching the gas tank for signs of tampering. "Well," he said at last. "If you're gonna do something, do it right."

"You think it was Burke?" Tom asked.

"That's a stupid question. Of *course*." He pulled sections of the fractured windshield away from the driver's side. He opened the front door and brushed the glass off the seat. "The bastard's pushing it, big time. Get in."

"What are we gonna do?"

"Find a new windshield. What do you think? Ben'll have one. Just get in."

Tom wondered if what he was getting into was more than just a vandalized auto.

"Okay, hand me the lug nuts." Kevin reached back with his open palm, snatching the nuts from Tom as he adjusted the tire onto the rim of the Monstermobile. The silver car was elevated on the rack in Ben Cooper's auto garage. Their leisurely trip to the mall had been replaced by an afternoon of car maintenance. They'd completed an oil change, and now the tires were being rotated. Kevin was an engine junkie, and the Monstermobile was his drug of choice. One hand on the transmission and he was lost for hours, tinkering and rebuilding. It was at Cooper's that Kevin first acquired the Japanese jalopy he transformed into his souped-up chariot. Barely anything remained of the original vehicle. He had recently installed new brakes and suspension coils, and was considering adding pinstripes to the chassis.

"Would make it slick, don't you think?" he asked.

"Sure, I guess." Tom shrugged.

"What if we went a shade darker? Midnight blue?"

"Sounds cool." Tom peeked at his watch. The windshield was replaced an hour ago, and they were still at it. He was skeptical that they would find an exact window match for the Trans Am, and so was surprised when Mr. Cooper directed them to the heaps of vehicular rubble out back. Sure enough, there was the monster's bride, a mate of the exact make and model. In some creepy part of his mind, he imagined the crippled car hadn't been there moments before.

"Told you Ben would come through." Kevin smiled as he removed the windshield off the wrecked auto. "And if I'd needed a new exhaust, he'd have had one here waiting for me. Guaranteed."

"Where does he get all this stuff?"

"Thin air!"

If Tom was surprised, Kevin wasn't. Cooper's Garage and Auto Salvage was a veritable treasure trove of used parts. Abandoned autos were stacked in columns ten feet tall behind the building, awaiting compression or dismantling. Tires and seat cushions gathered in mountains of black rubber and springy foam. It reminded Tom of the fabled elephant graveyard, where the bones of thousands of pachyderms gathered in ivory clusters. Kevin's love for mechanics inspired Ben to take him on as a pseudo-apprentice, training him in the venerated wisdom of the grease monkey.

In exchange for a few weekly hours of garage labor, Kevin had full use of the tools and facilities.

Tom watched as Kevin used a power-driver to bolt the tire secure. The pneumonic gun sounded like a jackhammer as it rotated the nuts tightly into place.

"When you're ready for your first set of wheels, Ben and I can set you up." Kevin pointed to a lime green LTD parked along the side of the building. "That Ford over there just needs a tune-up. Plus some better tires we could find in the back. Ben would probably let it go for two hundred."

"Really?" Tom eyed the vehicle like it was the Millennium Falcon.

"It would make one hell of a cruise machine. You could take Julie for the ride of her life." He jerked the lever of the platform, and the Monstermobile slowly lowered on the hydraulic pylons.

"I gotta show you something before we go," Kevin said as he wandered to the small bathroom to wash his hands. Tom glanced at his watch, again. Five-thirty. Most of the afternoon was lost. Already he could feel that pull on his skin to return to his own workshop, where *it* waited for him. It. *His* Monstermobile. If he got home by six, he could do his homework, call Julie, and still put in three or four hours of work until midnight.

Kevin came out, wiping his hands on a dirty towel, and went to a metal locker where he kept his personal tools. "I hear Burke's been giving you a hard time."

Tom nodded. "Yeah. So what else is new?"

"I thought I should fill you in. I've got something of his. I've been keeping it here, because my folks at home get a little snoopy." He zipped through the dial of the combination lock, glancing to see that Mr. Cooper hadn't returned. "Promise you won't say anything to anyone, okay?"

"Okay."

"Swear."

"I *swear.*"

Opening the rusty locker door, he pulled out a blue duffle bag.

"What is it?" asked Tom.

Kevin opened the bag and pried it apart just enough to expose its contents.

"What the—" Tom cringed back. Inside was a large plastic bag with a greenish, oregano-like substance. Even he could recognize it as marijuana.

"Take a look. But don't touch it. I don't want your fingerprints on it."

He gave Kevin an incredulous stare. "Pot?"

"No shit, Sherlock! But look how much. Like more grass than you mowed in a week. Must be worth about five hundred, easy."

"Are you kidding me? What are you doing with it?" Tom asked in a whisper, getting increasingly uncomfortable. He glanced nervously around the garage as though expecting narks to burst out of the ground like the Children of the Hydra's Teeth.

"Will you relax? I swiped it from Burke."

"You *swiped* it?"

"I counted the biggest 'coup' on him, yet."

Counting "coup" was an Indian tradition. An Indian brave would humiliate an enemy by tapping him with a stick, or stealing an item of clothing. It demonstrated superiority.

"Remember my little encounter with Burke at the hotel? Well, afterward, I felt like a little mischief, so I snuck out to the lot where his Jaguar was parked. Now, once before, I had locked my keys in the car and went down to maintenance for help. This guy Clarence came out with this flat metal bar he uses to jimmy locks open. So I went back to Clarence's workstation and kind of borrowed his jimmy bar. It took me three seconds to get Burke's car door open. Man, it was the most intense moment of my life! I tried to think of some stunt I could pull on him, like hotwire and re-park it somewhere, or jam his tape deck. But then I looked under the dashboard, and there's the same bag from the hotel room! Not covered up or anything! The guy thinks he lives a charmed life. So I snatched it. Maybe six month's worth of stash!"

"Oh shit! No wonder he's so pissed." It all began to make sense, now. Burke's rage. His accusation. Tom didn't know whether to be angry or impressed. "He suspects it's you."

"Sure he does. That's why he smashed my windshield, but what can he do about it?"

He can bust my *ass*, Tom wanted to say. Being Sancho Panza to his Don Quixote was becoming an increasingly risky assignment. "So what are you going to do with it?"

"Haven't decided. It's enough right now just to let him wonder if I have it. Make him sweat. I can always turn it in to the sheriff." He shoved the bag back into the locker. "Until then, don't say a word. You got me? And don't tell Danny, whatever you do. The guy should sleep in a crib, he's so immature."

Tom wanted to argue, but it would be pointless. He watched Kevin return the "goods" to the locker as a dark look passed over his friend's face.

He knew Kevin was thinking of Kathy McGuire again.

CHAPTER 30

THE AIR WAS CHILLY AS THE HOUR WENT PAST MIDNIGHT. The door to the DeFrank garage was slightly ajar to allow for a breeze. It served to dissipate some of the fumes that accumulated from the brazing. It also helped Tom to stay awake. He was busy at his workbench, acetylene torch in hand, looking every bit like a junior Hephaestus in the foundry of the gods.

A tiny steel ball began to glow cherry-red under the flame of the torch. Tom held the gas nozzle steady to ensure precise heat on the bearing, which lay beside a steel rod on a shard of brick. When it was bright orange, he carefully applied the shaft of silver solder, letting a drop of metal melt from its tip. The molten solder spread magnetically over the fiery surface of the bead, joining it to the rod in an indestructible bond.

With a snap, Tom extinguished the flame and lifted the glowing hybrid of ball and rod with pliers. It looked like a minuscule planet Mars on a stick. He dunked it into a bowl of water, which fizzed and hissed violently. When it was cool, Tom held it to his eyes. The weld was perfect. It would need cleaning and polishing, but another "bone" of his creature was completed.

The "armature" had been under construction for several days. The rest of it lay in an open mold section on the workbench. Much of the torso was already completed. It was an intricate configuration of joints, all of steel and iron.

Beside the mold were the crushed remains of his Fau'Charoth sculpture. Having completed the clay form, he'd wasted no time capturing its likeness in plaster. The three mold sections, divided and set apart on the bench, looked like eggshells from which something monstrous had hatched. The sculpture had been reduced to piles of clay rubble, agonizingly torn out of the mold bit by bit, leaving a negative impression. This part was always difficult for Tom. He felt like a back alley abortion doctor, tearing a fetus out of a womb. For now, Fau'Charoth was gone, but its soul would be reborn from the crusty shell in foam latex. Tom worked feverishly to reach that stage.

He polished the ball-rod assembly on an electric wire brush, removing the soot. The surface of his workbench was speckled with pixie-dust; piles of silvery metal shavings that gathered at the base of his vise. Occasionally, when brazing, they would ignite under the torch flame into dancing little sparks.

The workbench was well stocked with tools his father had left behind. There was an industrial drill press standing beside a sturdy red vice, an anvil for pounding metal, and various wrenches, screwdrivers, and hammers. Little jars contained nails and casehardened screws in assorted sizes. Tom often thought of his dad when he worked here. Occasionally, he'd find some old gadget concocted of Radio Shack gizmos and try to imagine its purpose. The push of a button might send him to the moon.

Taking an Allen wrench off the tool board, he attached the new ankle joint to the armature. The shin-ball was sandwiched between two metal plates, its tension determined by the tightness of an Allen screw. When properly secured, they formed a ball-and-socket joint, the classic mechanical device that made so much of stop-motion possible. He'd deciphered its construction from a magazine photo of the original King Kong armature. Many hours of painstaking experimentation had yielded the ideal puppet skeleton.

Tom wiped his brow; unaware of the greasy smear he was placing there. His hands were covered with grime, and the denim apron he was wearing did little to protect his clothing.

It was late. He was fighting off a headache, and his neck was stiff. It had been over seven hours since he'd eaten anything. Tom was used to working into the night, but never before had he felt this compelled. It wrecked havoc on his body. There was an urgency about this project that pressed him to outrageous limits.

But there was a reason for it all, a secret he kept subliminally to himself. Outwardly, he was still just an animator building a model, but deep down, he knew there was something more. The puppet was his magic lamp, and inside there was a genie. A genie that promised flights of fancy on a magic carpet.

The dreams had persisted. Every night, they grew stronger and more visceral. He would soar over landscapes and observe the heavens from an eagle's point of view.

He was *flying*!

Hush! he scolded himself, as though even to *think* such things threatened to banish the magic away. He kept up a front of healthy denial that anything uncanny was happening. They were just dreams. Extraordinary, exhilarating fabrications of his subconscious.

Weren't they?

He wondered if it was a common phenomenon for artists to acquire the attributes of their creations. Do sculptors in Florence, carving angels in a chapel, soar to the heavens with holy wings? Did Ray Harryhausen ever have a flight dream? If anyone could relate to his situation, it had to be Ray. Perhaps his harpies and homunculi had taken *him* into the clouds. Tom smiled at the thought of the god of stop-motion becoming a pterodactyl. There was nothing about it in his book *Film Fantasy Scrapbook.* The man was tightlipped, but even Harryhausen couldn't keep *that* a secret. No, he decided. The experience was uniquely his own, and he guarded it now with a jealous fervor. No one would take it from him.

He went to shut the garage door. A head rush made him dizzy on his feet, and the cold air gripped him.

And then the shivers began.

His core temperature dropped, and he jolted with a painful, stabbing chill. He braced himself as the shiver passed over him in spasms.

What the hell is this about? He sat in a chair and curled himself into a ball, allowing his body heat to restore. Tom wasn't used to physical ailments. His constitution was strong, and he seldom got sick.

Another shiver. He trembled. Was if from hunger? Could his body simply need rest?

But there was still so much work to do! That tail wasn't going to finish itself!

"Enough!" he said aloud, rising shakily to his feet. It could wait another day. But even then, he felt compelled to continue. He was so close to completion.

If he could just stay another hour.

"No!" he scolded himself. Again, a stabbing chill, like icicles shot from a crossbow. This time he clutched and bent over like a wounded soldier. What was happening to him? With great effort, he resisted the pull of the model and turned off the lights as he left the garage. Part of him still remained behind.

CHAPTER 31

It was ten-thirty, the following Saturday morning. Julie pulled into Tom's driveway on her bicycle. She wheeled it to the open garage entrance and lowered the kickstand.

"Hey, Buddy," she said with an exuberant smile.

"Julie!" Tom looked up in surprise. He was soldering again, the torch flame blazing. "I'll be right with you."

Julie took off her jacket and laid it on her bicycle saddle. Her hair was tied back in a ponytail, and she wore a white cotton sweater. A pink vinyl sales kit with a silver metal snap lay in her bike basket.

Tom extinguished the torch and set it aside, turning to her at last. He met her with a warm kiss, but when they embraced he was careful not to lay hands on her. They would leave sooty fingerprints on the cotton.

"I was in the neighborhood," she said, "so I thought I'd drop by. How are you today?"

He rubbed his eyes. "Is it 'today' already, because last I looked, it was 'yesterday'."

"Oh God! Did you work all night, again?"

"Yes, Mom."

"Huh! I wish I *were* your mom. I would make sure you got some sleep. And you've got soot all over your face. You look like a raccoon!"

He grinned unabashedly as she began rubbing motherly fingers over his cheeks and nose, smearing away the grime. It was good to see her. He felt tired. Three hours of flopping restlessly on his bed, and he was back to work by 5:00 AM.

"Wow!" she exclaimed, wandering about the garage like a seven-year-old in a museum. "This is neat! What are you working on?"

He showed her the armature, which stood now on the workbench like the skeletal remains of a famished robot. She smiled, amazed. "Cool. Is this what puppets look like inside?"

"This is what *Fau'Charoth* looks like. But soon it'll look more like my sketch."

"Hmm. I like it better like *that*," she teased. "I'm selling magazines to raise money for the play." She had landed a part in *Dark Victory*. Not the second lead, as she'd hoped, but a nice role with a few pages of dialogue. It didn't matter, though. To her it was *Hamlet*. "I have a sales kit and everything." Julie lifted the vinyl package out of the bike basket and showed it off proudly. "I was wondering if you'd like to join me."

His shoulders sank heavily. "I don't think I'd be very good company. I'm about to collapse. It's just that I'm trying to get this thing done so that I can begin the foam-rubber process." He went to the vice and pried free the new piece.

"Yowch!" He dropped it, shaking his hand. The metal was still hot. He forgot to quench it.

Julie sped to his side. "Awww. You burned yourself. Where does it hurt?" She took his hand and examined it. She was about to "kiss it better," but reconsidered when she saw how filthy it was. She kissed him on the cheek instead.

"Put some ice on it. Do you think we can get together later tonight?"

"Definitely. I'll take a nap, a shower, and be a new man."

"In the meantime, I'll practice my spiel on you. You can be my first customer." She stepped back and put on a toothy grin like a plastic android. "Good afternoon, sir. My name's Julie, and I'm selling magazine subscriptions to raise funds for Chapinaw High School's production of *Dark Victory*."

"Sold!" he said jubilantly. "I'll take ten subscriptions to *Mademoiselle*."

"Stop!" she giggled. "But seriously, there's one called *Fantastic Films* you might like. Just buy anything. We're trying to raise money for a new lighting console."

"Deal."

She beamed and kissed him, delighted. "Pretty good sales pitch, huh?"

"Citizens of Chapinaw, beware." He smiled and kissed her again.

Julie peddled along enthusiastically, having made a few good sales. Initially, she had been shy. It was all so strange and new to her, pounding on doors, asking people to shell out bucks to support the arts, but with each house she grew bolder and modified her sales tactics. A lady on Tom's street had been kind enough to renew a subscription to *Woman's Day.* On Bischoff Street, a gallant old man had fallen for her charms. He bought subscriptions to *TV Guide* and *Newsweek*, and offered marriage to his grandson.

She was disappointed that Tom hadn't joined her. It worried her how worn out he looked, and she hoped he'd taken her advice to eat and sleep. She knew how obsessive he was with his hobby, but there was something about it that troubled her. Particularly since it was *that* creature upon which he was working. The creature in which her father had taken such a strange interest.

The creature, she reminded herself, that had brought them together in the first place.

Maybe she was jealous. Imagine that! Jealous already. Over a monster puppet.

I guess that makes us a couple, she mused.

It was two o'clock. She had traveled to the rural parts of town, not far from Crohaven, and decided to pay her father a visit. The Kawasaki fell into a long, leisurely dive down the wooded hill.

Parrish dropped a crate of wood pilings to greet Julie as she rode into the front yard. He was surprised by her sudden visit.

"Hello, Sprite."

"Hi, Daddy."

She hit the kickstand on her bike and approached him, experiencing the usual awkwardness as they drew close. He brushed a friendly hand over her shoulder and fell just short of hugging her. Shrugging off his aloofness, she smiled broadly. "I'm selling magazines door-to-door for the drama club. Are there any magazines you'd like to buy?"

"How about I buy one for you?"

"Oh, okay. It's a deal."

A crooked grin appeared on his face, with sudden inspiration. "So they have you going from house to house like an Avon Lady?"

"Yeah. Can you believe it? I'm getting the knack of it, though. I've sold eleven subscriptions, so far."

"Have you been through this area much?"

"No, but I was hoping to get beyond Liberty and Latham before sunset."

There was a crafty gleam in his eyes. "How would you like some company?"

Her face lit up. "Really? That would be great!" She couldn't believe he was volunteering to assist her.

Parrish drove the station wagon to the crest of the hill, with Julie beside him, clutching the sales kit in her lap. They had made two stops along the way, and her coffers were filled with the proceeds from two additional subscriptions. Parrish had sat patiently in the car on each occasion, allowing her to complete her sales. It was nice to have him with her, but her enthusiasm had dampened, somewhat, now that she knew his generous offer had an ulterior motive. So much for fatherly support.

The Whateley farm appeared in the distance like an Andrew Wyeth painting come to life. It was nestled on a hill facing the west. Kansas fields of yellow straw spread for acres in all directions, bordered by remnants of wooden fence posts and barbed wire. The aroma of crisp honeysuckle and hay filled the air. The house was a square white two-story that had not known a paint job in decades. Behind it was a massive barn dominating the horizon. Its walls were shingled with hand-shaved boards that had aged to a charcoal gray. Adjoining its side was a tall cylindrical grain silo, rusty-brown in color, and numerous pens and corrals filled with hogs. An ancient red tractor was parked in front.

Julie looked about suspiciously. "So this is the place?"

Parrish nodded forebodingly. "This is the last known site of Tornau's magical activity. The cult held their rituals here before they were scattered in the big raid. What happened after that is anyone's guess, but I have reason to believe that they had one more go at it."

She stared at him, an odd mingling of wariness and puzzlement in her eyes. "So what do you need me for?"

Parrish smiled awkwardly. "I was hoping to probe the area for psychic flashes. Something recently triggered a new wave of energy in the area."

"What something?" she probed.

"I'm not sure, yet. I figured . . . if you could distract the Whateleys with your sales pitch, I might try to see what I can perceive from the location."

"Oh-h. So now I'm your 'decoy'." She pouted. He glanced at her apologetically as though reading her mind.

"I can't exactly go up to them and ask to scan 'vibration impressions' left there over fifteen years ago."

She resigned, "I guess not."

Parrish grinned. "You'll make some detective a good 'sidekick,' Sprite."

Julie smiled in spite of herself.

Parrish parked along the side of the road, out of view of the house, but not conspicuously so. "Just go about your normal business," he reassured her.

"I feel like a desperado," she said.

"You're not doing anything wrong. I'm just going to stay here, maybe step outside and see what I can pick up. That's all."

Knowing her father, that would *not* be all, but Julie agreed and exited the car. "Don't get your hands caught in the cookie jar."

She approached the front entrance to the house, holding the sales kit in front as though it were part of a uniform. Several cats appeared from the grass and began flanking her approach. She winced at the sound of a barking dog. A golden retriever raced toward her from behind the house, announcing her presence with a series of yelps. She hesitated, watching the dog approach, but continued on courageously, concealing her fear from the animal.

A silver-haired woman appeared at the front door,

shouting at the dog. "Katie! Stop that!" The dog became immediately docile and sniffed at Julie's feet.

"Don't worry, dear," the woman assured her. "She won't hurt you."

"Hi," Julie said pleasantly. "Mrs. Whateley?"

"Yes." Katie ran to her side, and the woman patted her head affectionately. "Katie here is just a big ol' fuzzy-bear. Ain't cha, Katie?"

"My name is Julie. I'm raising funds for Chapinaw High's dramatic production, and—"

"Well ain't you the prettiest thing! Come inside, dear, and tell me all about it. My, but don't you look like my granddaughter, Margaret Anne."

Parrish watched with satisfaction as Julie entered the house with Mrs. Whateley. He quietly stepped out of the wagon, casually leaning on the side of the door as though sunning himself. In fact, he was in deep concentration, breathing slowly, inhaling not only the atmosphere and various smells of the farm, but its ætheric essence. He probed deeply with his feelings, like a hound sniffing for a scent, hoping to hone in on even the faintest presence of a necromantic event.

The ætheric canvas came alive with a sudden surge. His eyes snapped shut, feeling the familiar sensation of footsteps on his consciousness. It was fleeting and faint, like ghostly fingers poking him from behind, but Humphrey was right. The area was alive with psychic activity. Parrish reached out with his mind, but the images were too weak to clarify.

He sighed and glanced over to the large imposing building a short walk away. Here at the periphery, the signal was too vague. As he assumed, he needed to get closer to the nucleus. The true investigation could only be performed from *within* the barn. He avoided mentioning it to Julie for fear of concerning her, but with the perfect opportunity upon him, he began a stealthy approach to the barn entrance.

The area surrounding the barn was caked with dried mud imbedded with deep tire tracks. Parrish could hear the voices of the hogs, squealing noisily in their pens. He approached the bordering wooden fence and quickly ducked behind it. His footfalls were silent as a veil of mist passing through the grass. He stopped to listen, and peered about. The main entrance had two large doors on cast iron hinges that creaked silently in the breeze. Above the entrance was a colorful hex sign with roosters and obscure symbols.

In the pigpen, filthy, sprawling hogs grunted indifferently to his presence, except for a few younger ones who trotted to the edge of the fence to see if he carried food. Hog urine mingled with the stench of fresh manure and old pig slop.

A dog barked. Moments later, Katie darted about the side of the barn, snarling at Parrish as he gazed directly into its eyes. She seemed dubious but continued to growl, held at bay by his intense gaze. Then Parrish offered his hand out to the dog, sweeping the air gracefully with his fingers. The snarling stopped instantly. Katie cocked her head quizzically, then whimpered in a submissive manner. Parrish smiled and gently patted the dog on her head as she whined and grinned with a mouthful of glistening teeth.

There was a side entrance to the barn, out of view of the house, and he crept toward it. It was unlatched. Quickly, he stole through and entered the barn, followed closely by the dog. It was dark, but his eyes soon adjusted. The scent of straw and stale air greeted his nostrils. He closed his eyes and began to take in its essence.

Julie sat in a comfortably padded kitchen chair. The maple dining table was draped with a handmade tablecloth. The kitchen looked quaint and old fashioned, the walls covered in floral paper and decorated with hanging pots and cast-iron pans. There was a circular hex sign above the stove and a Currier and Ives painting over the sink. The room smelled of herbs and spices.

Lancey poured hot water into her teacup from a copper kettle. Steam billowed from the spout. She spoke on about her granddaughter Margaret Anne, who recently graduated from a school in North Carolina. Julie listened courteously, sensing an eager joy in the woman to be speaking to her. *She must be lonely*, she thought.

"Tell me now, Julie. Do I know your mother? Does she go to St. John's Methodist?"

"No, Ma'am. St. Peter's. She's Catholic."

"Call me Lancey, dear. Now let me see some of those magazines."

CHAPTER 32

SUNLIGHT PENETRATED THROUGH TINY CRACKS IN THE barn's high-angled ceiling. Heavy beams crisscrossed like crucifixes to support the main frame above a hayloft. Amid these beams were nests of starlings and a flock of wild pigeons that cooed from the upper perch. One of them fluttered noisily out a window. There were large pigsties on either side, with hogs slumped lazily in straw and filth. One monstrous boar snorted at him, pressing its snout through the wooden rails of the corral. The stench of hog feces was thick. Parrish crept silently toward the center.

As he did so, a wave of psychic vibrations penetrated him like wind through a portcullis. He tightened his brows and slowly lifted his outstretched fingers into the air. Katie looked up at him and whined softly.

"You sense it too. Don't you, girl?" he said to the dog. Katie gave off a low bark.

Parrish methodically moved his hands about, probing the dim veil with his eyes closed. He passed his fingers over the wood supports of the loft and along a section of the wall, absorbing the vague impressions buried within. The wood had been scraped and sanded to remove symbols that were painted there, but Parrish could still see them in his mind's eye.

Ceremonial sigils.

Flash images entered him from the wood. He reached out with his clairvoyance, collecting the memories like particles of dust floating in the breeze. They gathered together, forming a tapestry on the inner screen of his mind.

"A goat. They've killed a goat," he spoke aloud in a whispering voice, scanning swiftly through a series of events. "And a dog. They slit its throat." Katie whined sympathetically. She raised her ears, perplexed, as Parrish dropped to his knees and raked the old straw and clay with his outstretched fingers. There was blood here. Deep within the ground. Human blood. "There's a fire. No . . . yes! They've built a ritual pyre . . . right here. I see them! There are twelve. Eight men. Four women. Tornau is with them!"

The hogs snorted, and some of the piglets squealed.

He crinkled his nose and sniffed. "I smell flesh burning."

The images went wild, like film at high speed. An assault of ghastly pictures flooded his brain in a frantic stream of information. Fleeting glimpses from a sequence of unhallowed rites, each leaving its fragments in the æther. Parrish clutched his head, struggling to filter through the impressions. Human victims cried out in a cacophony of wailing voices.

In his mind, one of the rites materialized like a Grand

Guignol performance. A chain of dangling lamps lit the chamber. Symbols were painted on the walls in bright yellow. Largest was a sinister double pentagram, embossed over with wavy slashes and overlapping curves. Parrish committed the symbol to memory. At the center of the chamber, imbedded in the concrete floor, was a circle of stones. A fire was blazing within.

He saw the gathering of Tornau's cult, dressed in dark robes, the hoods down about their shoulders so that he could see their faces. They were townsfolk of different walks of life, young and old. Some of the faces Parrish recognized from his research. There was Stan Halberton, a dairy farmer who had lost his livestock to an infectious blight. He saw also the Whateleys, Terence and Lavinia, who lent their property for the rituals, perhaps hoping for a bumper crop. Superstition was strong in the rural northeast, where remnants of pagan ceremony often colored daily traditions. Hex signs adorned the entrances to barns, camouflaged as decorative emblems, and the slaughtering of livestock vaguely took on the semblance of sacrifice. The purposes behind these traditions were lost in time, but there existed always an unspoken acknowledgement of unexplainable forces at work. Farm folk of this nature were easy to sway. Promises of a better harvest, the sparing of flocks and herds from afflictions. These were the lures that bound their souls to service.

There was another among them, her pretty face a sharp contrast to the haggard features of the farmers. Parrish determined it was Tornau's consort, Sarah Halloway. Sarah the harlot. Sarah the succubi, as she was sometimes referred. A stage actress and daughter of a wealthy textiles magnate, she had abandoned a cosmopolitan lifestyle and was universally scorned for her affiliation with the cult. Parrish had seen her only once before. The papers had reproduced her theatrical headshot, showing her beautiful smiling face and long flowing hair. Perceived now, with short-cropped tresses and sullen expression, he recognized her immediately from another source.

Sarah was the face in his ghostly portrait!

Parrish stood puzzled with this revelation. Sarah Halloway was dead, a ghost reaching out to him. But how and why? He focused again on the vision, searching for answers. The group gathered in a circle around the fire.

And there was the man himself, Jacob Tornau. Parrish's heart drilled in his chest as he perceived that terrible face, with its stark features and bristling goatee. Tornau fed cracked bones into the fire, altering the color of the flame. The worshippers uttered phrases under their breath, awakening dread spirits to their presence. Parrish could perceive a grotesque negativity that violated his inner being. He knew he was in close proximity to a force utterly malign and wholly outside the experience of modern man.

Slabs of wood formed a crude altar on which a candle was lit. One of the cultists carried a large clay urn to the altar and began to splash the surfaces with its contents. Blood poured over the edges in crimson streams, the blood of a human victim sacrificed in an earlier rite. Tornau stroked the air with his outstretched finger, sketching the five corners of a pentagram across his body. He recited a phrase aloud:

"Zi Dingir Anna Kanpa! Zi Dingir Kia Kanpa!
Utuk xul, ta ardata! Kutulu, ta attalakla!"

The fire in the stone circle was blazing high. Parrish heard a muffled cry.

Two men carried a human form wrapped in white cloth. It fought against their grasp. The rest of the cult parted to allow their passage to the altar.

The figure was brought before the wood slab and laid upon its bloodstained surface. The face was revealed as the cloth was pulled away. It was a young woman, stripped naked, bruised and beaten by her captors.

Parrish held his breath, and his emotion momentarily blurred the vision within his head.

The girl was perhaps seventeen, only slightly older than Julie. She had vibrant magenta hair, artificially dyed, and a face that was heavily made up. Her lipstick was smeared about her mouth, and streams of black mascara ran liberally with her tears. Her eyes went wide with terror as she gazed around. The ropes that bound her wrists and ankles bit deep into her flesh, leaving red welts and bruises. She peered helplessly at Tornau and cried out from beneath the strip of tape that cruelly gagged her.

Tornau glanced back empty and passionless. He rubbed his index finger across the wood slab, coating the tip with the crimson fluid, and then smoothed it over the bare white flesh of the girl's midsection, painting crude symbols on her belly.

Another urn was placed beside the altar, below her head.

The girl was breathing heavily, exhausted from struggling. The other worshippers began to chant until their voices united in unholy song. The vibrations echoed throughout the barn.

From his transient viewpoint, Parrish saw the girl's frightened eyes, her tragically youthful face, and he wanted to identify her name from his research. If only he could remember her name, he could be present for her. But she didn't match the description of any of the reported dead, and he knew he was witnessing one of the unknowns, a prostitute or street urchin. She would die unaccounted for in the newspapers. No one would miss her or mourn her passing.

Shadow images, he reminded himself. Long in the past.

A curved dagger was withdrawn from Tornau's robe. It shined in the stark lamplight. Tornau grabbed the girl's hair and pulled her head flat to the wood surface, stretching her neck. He placed the blade to the girl's throat, and with the smooth, precise stroke of a butcher, deftly sliced it from ear to ear. There was a terrible gurgling as the girl choked, her eyes registering a moment of terror, before going lifeless and glassy. Hacking through gristle and bone, Tornau then cut the head free until it dangled from his hand like a trophy. Blood gushed from the neck stump, spilling into the waiting urn. The body convulsed under the grip of the ropes, draining its fluid in a red fountain, and then lay still.

Parrish recoiled. He dropped to the palms of his hands, breathing heavily.

Katie nudged against his arm, whimpering with concern. She let off a shrill bark that banished the monstrous image from his mind. The trance broken, Parrish lowered a shaking hand to the dog's head, gratefully stroking it.

"Horrible . . . horrible," he shuttered in sympathetic terror for the poor girl, dying alone in this grisly manner! Trembling from the morbid flashes, Parrish forced himself to chase after the remaining fragments. Scattered images, out of sequence. Fully six sacrifices, each ending in ritual dismemberment, the organs and limbs burned in the fire. His nostrils twitched to the phantom scent of burning flesh. He saw the faces of the victims and matched them to the names in the documents: Lamont, Hendricks, Sheffield, Willis. Contorted with terror, they bore little resemblance to the smiling portraits in the papers. There was a second unknown, a black woman from the city streets. She died anonymously with the others. Six of the seven cycles were accounted for.

Another ritual filled his mind. "They've built another fire," he recited aloud. The group was poised as before in front of the flames. Sarah was conspicuously tense and distracted, her eyes darting to the barn entrance as her hands were crossed in supplication. From her position, she seemed to gaze directly at Parrish.

Does she see me even now? he wondered.

The purple fire raged like a hungry beast, awaiting another meal. With each summoning, it had grown successively larger, fed with the essence of human sadism and torment.

Tornau pulled out a small wooden object. Parrish could not perceive it clearly. It looked like an idol. The sorcerer recited an invocation.

"Fau'Charoth a Lammashta ra shagmuku tu.

Fau'Charoth ud kalama shagmuku tu.

Aga mass ssaratu. Alakti limda.

Fau'Charoth kur amda lu amesh musha tu!"

It was Tom's spell! Parrish pressed a finger to his temple to sharpen his perception.

Tornau motioned, and a wrapped bundle was brought to him. From within came the wailing of an infant.

"The baby," Parrish whispered aloud.

Tornau removed the child from the folds of cloth. The baby was naked, its male genitalia clearly exposed. The roar of the fire was evidence to the child's potency. It seemed to pulsate like a living thing eager to be fed.

The flames reared up, flailing toward the child with pseudopodia of glowing energy.

Parrish noticed Sarah Halloway turn away. She seemed sympathetic for the child, and also—*expectant.* She was peering at the barn doors in desperate anticipation.

The child was raised before the flaming pit, and the fire burst into magnificent color, as though the very nearness of the child triggered an atomic reaction. It escalated into a cyclone of pale purple light, spiraling from the depths of another world. This sacrifice would not require the blade. The baby would be tossed headlong into the flames and unleash a tremendous power. Parrish felt helpless. Tendrils of impotence raced through his soul. He wanted to cry out. But then fate intervened.

With a loud crash, the front doors flew open.

"Freeze!" shouted Sheriff Kurt Kronin.

Kronin and his two deputies stormed the barn, guns drawn. The cultists all froze in place. The officers seemed momentarily stunned by the bizarre spectacle, but they held firm, firearms aimed rigidly at the group.

Still bearing the child, Tornau turned from the conflagration, exposed in all his satanic glory. He grinned at the officers in defiance—and *tossed* the baby into the air toward the sheriff.

Kronin dropped his weapon and caught the child in his arms as he rolled to the ground. The distraction was enough for the cultists to draw firearms concealed in their robes.

Gunshots ensued, and the room fell into chaos. Kronin shielded the child. A bullet tore into his shoulder. His deputies leapt behind whatever sparse cover the barn provided.

Denied focus, the raging purple fire extinguished with a loud snap. Docile tongues of yellow flame replaced the roaring purple torrent in the firepit.

Parrish reflexively ducked as hallucinatory muzzle flares burst around him. Under the cover of gunfire, Tornau withdrew with Sarah and four others out a back door while the remaining cult members held their ground. They managed to take down the two deputies before the last of them fell. Then a horrible silence, except for groans from the wounded policemen. And the wailing of the child in Kronin's bleeding arms.

The child. Who was this little boy? Parrish could never find out. To protect the family, the child's name was withheld from the public, the records sealed by a court order. He wondered where the child was today.

A gravelly voice shattered his concentration, jolting him to the present.

"Okay, mister," it demanded. "Now, you're gonna stand up, turn around slowly, and tell me what you're doin' in my barn."

As the psychic impressions fled his mind, Parrish found himself facing a pitchfork poised threateningly at his chest. Disoriented, he was for a moment uncertain if the man before him was real or another phantom from the past.

It was Sam Whateley, the grizzled old pig keeper, and brother to Terence, one of those just slain in his vision. Whateley was a lean man in his late sixties, with leathery tan skin and tight, sinewy forearms. He had a face speckled with week-old beard growth, and the scent of whiskey was on his breath. There was fear in the farmer's eyes, a terrible fear of the uncanny, as though he too had witnessed the hideous shadow shows.

"If'n you got a tongue in your head, you'll answer me," the man warned.

Parrish took a moment to breathe, still shaky from his

clairvoyant time travel. He held his palms out to put the man at ease. "Mr. Whateley . . ." He searched for an explanation, but there were no easy ones. His trance state had him crawling across the barn floor, so he was soiled with clay and straw. Surely he looked like a madman. "I know this looks strange, but I promise you I mean no harm."

Whateley spat and pressed him back with the pitchfork. "Like hell you don't. I been standin' right here, watchin' you. Sniffin' around the floor like some kind of animal."

He continued to press Parrish back with the fork until they were out of the barn and into the sunlight. Their eyes locked together, and Parrish perceived a depth to the man's fears—a dark secret he had buried deep in his own mind.

"Please. You're certainly aware of what transpired here before you acquired this farm. You know about Jacob Tornau, don't you?"

Whateley's face whitened with mention of the name.

"Who are you? What do you care about that?"

"I'm a . . . I'm a psychic investigator."

"Yer *what*?"

This wasn't doing at all. Parrish thought of an explanation to which the man could relate. "I'm a spiritualist. I have *visions*. I can read the past with certain abilities that I have. Certain gifts."

"The past is gone, mister. The dead are asleep. Who are you to go wakin' 'em?" Something glimmered in his eye. "Yeah . . . yeah, I reckon I remember you now. You're that Stephen Parrish from Crohaven. Came by here years ago, askin' to look about. You got all them mystical powers. Regular Merlin the Magician was what I heard. Well, what kind of Satan's brew are you mixing?"

"Nothing like that, I assure you."

"We'll see what Sheriff Kronin thinks about that."

Katie trotted behind Parrish and gave out a bark as though in his defense.

Whateley glared. "I see you bewitched my dog."

Lancey was considering a subscription to *Family Circle* when the back door opened, and the men entered the kitchen. Parrish was still pushed forward by the man's pitchfork.

Lancey blanched. "Good Lord!"

Julie's eyes widened, and she shot a look of surprise to her father. His own were filled with apology. The old woman scolded her husband.

"Samuel! You get that dirty old thing out of my kitchen. What's got over you?"

"We got here the witch Stephen Parrish," he answered coldly. "I caught him casting a hex on the barn."

"What nonsense! You're scarin' Julie. We got company, and you're acting like a damn fool!"

"Don't argue with me, woman!"

Julie went to her father's side. Whateley glared at her. "This here ain't no schoolgirl selling magazines. This here's the witch's helper. His demon-spawn daughter, I reckon!"

His words stung Julie. Lancey was outraged and embarrassed.

"Samuel! Have you gone mad?" But for all her sass, the woman had no sway over the man. Whateley reached for the kitchen telephone and began dialing.

"I'll get the sheriff up here, and if'n we can't lock you up for casting spells, then we can get you for trespassin', at least. This here's private property, and damned if I'm gonna let no 'witch' come trampin' through and put a curse on it."

As Whateley dialed the phone, Parrish subtly pressed himself toward the pitchfork as it dangled before his chest. He felt the dirty metal prongs against his ribs and instantly received a collection of images. The man's secret was revealed to him, and he decided to use it to advantage. He looked into the farmer's eyes, making one last attempt to reason with him.

"You know something, don't you, Mr. Whateley? The bodies they discovered. It wasn't *all* of them. There were more. Two more you found. What happened to them?"

Lancey gazed at her husband in question. "Sam? What's he talking about?"

Whateley froze amidst dialing, as though Parrish was shining a harsh light on him, and then pressed the receiver back down. Clearly, he was reluctant to discuss the matter. The sinister heritage of the farm held dominion over him, and he was loath to reveal its secrets. "Now you see here." The man pointed a taut finger at Parrish. "You take your spells and evil eyes, and git off my property right quick, or I'll have the sheriff on your tail faster than spit. If'n I find you here again, I'll take my shotgun and send you to the devil. Folks up here don't like your sort. We're God-fearin' Christians and want nothing to do with witches! Now GIT!"

Parrish led Julie out the door, without dropping his eyes from Whateley.

They were walking up the driveway, when Julie stopped. "My sales kit!"

Suddenly, as though reading her mind, Whateley stepped out of the house, and with an angry fling, tossed the pink vinyl sales kit onto the front lawn. It landed with a thud on a muddy patch, spilling its contents. Then he reentered the house, slamming the door behind him.

Julie gasped as though she'd been struck a blow. She gazed down at the sales kit with eyes wide as saucers, too humiliated to move. Her father bent to retrieve its contents for her.

Julie sat cross-armed in her seat, staring into nothingness as Parrish drove off. She could still hear the accusations of that crazy farmer. *Demon-spawn daughter!* The words burned like a cattle brand and affected her in a deep and pernicious way. Parrish looked about as guilty as a father possibly could, lacking the means to comfort her.

Finally, she spoke, her words laced with accusation. "You lied to me. You said you were going to stay near the car."

"I'm sorry," he said. "I was lured in! The visions were too strong."

She sank back into her seat. "Well . . . I hope you found

what you were looking for."

Parrish sighed. "No. Nothing to take me further. They never returned to this location." He deliberately avoided telling her the gruesome details. He would spare her that horror if he could. "I have to find out where they went. It's vitally important."

"Vitally?" She was losing patience and shifted uncomfortably on her seat. "You make it all sound so crucial. Why does it matter so much? It ended so many years ago."

"I need to learn the truth."

"But you're *obsessed* with it." She realized she was shouting and stared out the window, lowering her voice. "You alienate people with these ridiculous quests of yours. You *scare* people. No wonder Mom gets so nervous speaking with you."

He brooded on this. She felt a stab of remorse. "Daddy . . . let it go."

"Julie . . . how can I make you understand that this isn't just some obsessive tryst on my part? There's an evil, pervasive force active in Chapinaw. I sensed it in Tom's vision, and it's growing stronger."

Julie cocked her head at him. "Tom's 'vision'?"

His breath locked, having let the truth slip. Now he would have to tell her everything.

He glanced over as he drove, enlisting her full attention. "When I shook Tom's hand, I received a powerful image. It showed Jacob Tornau and his cult engaged in a blood rite."

"What?"

"Tom's vision is a psychic remnant of an anthropomantic ceremony. That's a human sacrifice. They release very potent energies that can leave a vestigial imprint in the æther. A memory impression. I suspect the one depicted is the last of seven in a cycle. That's three more murders, Julie, uninvestigated. Mr. Culhane and I think that Tom stumbled onto the remains of the last ceremony, and absorbed the impression. It's a long shot, but I think the image might lead me to Tornau's final ritual site. Perhaps Tornau himself."

"This is all fine for the history books," she argued, "but why the urgency?"

The luminous purple specter crept into Parrish's mind. He hesitated.

"Dad, speak to me."

"I perceived something bizarre in Tom's aura, an aberration in the color pattern. It felt powerfully malign. I fear it may be some kind of *contaminant* in his astral orb. Something he picked up from his exposure to the site."

"A contaminant?" The words resonated ominously on her.

"Think of it like radiation after a bomb blast. But I haven't been able to determine its nature, or why it adhered itself to Tom. What about him was it drawn to? Is Tom unique in some way, with some strange tie to the events? I can't imagine—unless . . ."

He pulled the car abruptly to the roadside, staring blankly.

"Daddy?"

"How old is Tom? About sixteen, right?"

"I believe so."

"You say he's from Schenectady. But he didn't always live there?"

"No. The family moved there when he was an infant, after some 'incident.' But he says he was born in . . . oh my God." Julie tensed in her seat. "The baby."

Parrish pounded the steering wheel with his palm as the truth snapped into place like the tumblers in a lock. "It was *Tom*! Tom was the baby they tried to sacrifice to the fire."

Julie's heart was ramming in her chest. "Do you think he knows?"

"I doubt he could remember, except perhaps on some subliminal level. Whether he was ever told, I couldn't say."

"Daddy, this thing you saw, do you think it could be affecting him in some way? Could Tom be in any danger?"

"I don't know, sweetheart. We're dealing with such ancient, diabolical forces that there's always the potential for danger. The greatest is psychological. We'll keep an eye on him."

She studied him. "This is what you've been after all along. Why didn't you tell me?"

He sighed heavily. "Because I didn't want to worry you. And I promised I wouldn't get involved." Julie fell silent, a tear falling silently down her cheek. Every breath seemed to fan coals in her chest. He glanced at her. "You're fond of this boy, aren't you?"

". . . yes."

"Then help me to help him. I need to learn all that I can on this matter."

"What do you need me to do?"

"We need to learn exactly where it was that he first perceived the spell."

"But he told us everything he remembers."

"Julie, he's *lying*."

Her voice raised. "You have no right to say that!"

"He's withholding the truth. He may not even be aware of it."

"I don't want to interrogate him." She sulked, recalling Tom's every word on the matter. "He said he was out with friends that night. Maybe Danny Kaufman was with him. I could speak to Danny on Monday."

"That's a start."

Something else occurred to her, which she decided needed mentioning. A tingle of apprehension plagued her. "Dad? One more thing. You asked me to tell you if Tom mentions anything 'peculiar.' Well, he kinda said . . . I think he might be . . . Dad, I think Tom's *astral-projecting*."

She had hoped to dismiss it as nothing out of the ordinary. People had flight dreams all the time. It was perfectly normal. Commonplace. Even sexual.

But her dad's prolonged silence suggested otherwise.

CHAPTER 33

"SO YOU SUSPECT THAT TOM DEFRANK WAS THE BABY spared from the fire?" Humphrey Culhane said to Parrish, his generous frame sinking deep into the armchair behind his desk. Fumes of freshly lit tobacco emanated from his pipe, which he chewed on from the corner of his mouth. In his lap was a sketch Parrish had made from his vision in the barn. It showed the peculiar symbol he had seen scrawled on the wall. Culhane studied it, but continued to cast a speculative eye on Parrish. "An interesting development, I must admit. And he grows up drawing monsters. Remarkable transference. Jungian, to say the least."

It was a bright Sunday afternoon in Greenwich Village, and the streets outside were filled with trinket shoppers and brunch-goers. Parrish had taken full advantage of the light traffic on the highway to get to the bookstore as quickly as possible. Culhane listened to the full account of the Whateley barn. He could sense how deeply concerned Parrish was for the boy, and how torturing it was for him to express it. As intrigued as he was with the information, his first goal was to put the man at ease. They were treading a dangerous path.

"When Tornau lifted the child to the fire," Parrish described, "the flames reacted to his presence. It flickered toward the baby like it was tasting his essence. I suspect it left an imprint in the boy's aura. More recently, Tom stumbled onto a ritual site, and something lingering in the æther was drawn to the magical residue. I suspect this accounts for the strange emanation I perceived in his aura, and the new psychic activity in the area."

"A reasonable theory," Culhane agreed. "But let's not jump to conclusions. I think what you saw in his aura might simply have been the emanations of some very frightening primal memories. I sincerely doubt it's something that could cause any significant damage, beyond a bad dream or two."

"Julie mentioned dreams," Parrish recalled. "She claims he's astral-projecting."

"As boys often do." Culhane grimaced. "Never underestimate the imagination of a teenager. I dreamt I flew once to Louisiana to be with this beautiful Cajun girl. It was so real I thought for sure it would end in a paternity suit."

"But this dark energy I felt?"

Culhane laughed. "I'd be cautious about sensing 'dark energies' in your Julie's boyfriends, Stephen. Don't all fathers suspect Satan in their daughters' suitors?"

Parrish chuckled aloud. Was he just being overly paternal? It was reassuring to hear the man dismiss his suspicions so rambunctiously. "So I shouldn't be worried about Tom?"

Culhane shook his head reassuringly. "No, I doubt he's in any imminent danger. I think Tom DeFrank's role in this affair has been played out. Lord knows he paid his dues as a child and needn't be troubled any further with ghosts and goblins. He served as a messenger to you, and delivered a package, so let's let him go on his way. He's got enough to worry about just being a young man, pleasing your daughter. And you have more pressing business."

"That's some comfort, at least."

"I'm sure." Culhane smiled warmly.

"But there's still the issue of this 'hellhole.' The feeling gets stronger every day."

Parrish hooked his thumbs into his pants pockets, and quietly padded about the study like a solemn tiger. He gazed out the door, and into the shop.

A young couple entered, and were studying the curios on the shelves. The girl pointed to the Shiva statue while the man explained it. They were students. Young. Impressionable. No longer afraid, like the earth-tiller of the Bronze Age, this generation was drawn to the mystical out of wonderment and curiosity. Unfettered by the traditions of their parents' religion, they were willing to explore, to find out for themselves. There was so much good in that.

And so much danger.

For such a quest exposes one to a great many influences. So many forces that would attract a person's soul, shouting "Hear me! Hearken to my call! For I know!" For every spirit who wished to guide and nourish, there was one who would deceive and destroy. It could be a perilous road. Parrish returned his attention to the study.

"I'll continue my investigation as best I can. It's frustrating, like trying to restore a shattered mosaic. For every tile I fit into place, another three fall loose. I felt I was very close to unraveling this mystery, but it seems I've reached another dead end. Yet I'm being plagued by a lingering dread. Something's wrong in Chapinaw, Humphrey. We need to learn where that seventh ritual took place. If it didn't occur in the barn, then where? *Where?* If only."

"If only what?"

Parrish frowned in uncharacteristic agitation. "If only this misbegotten *talent* of mine were more reliable. There are endless holes and gaps in what I perceive. It's like trying to gather honey with a vented spoon."

"Flame and air," Culhane agreed. "That's what we're dealing with. But don't lose hope. Something will turn up. The universe has a way of regurgitating secrets."

"What about the symbol?" Parrish inquired. "Can you get anything from that at all?"

Culhane dropped his eyes back to his lap and reexamined the drawing. He had a flash of recognition. "It might be *Voc Caru*."

"Voc Caru?"

"This looks like a symbol used by a very old pagan religion called the Voc Caru. It originated in the Mesopotamian basin, chiefly Sumer, but scattered to Assyria, Egypt, and parts of India. It was a widespread demon cult, almost a plague. The Zoroastrians essentially wiped them out, but they were a tenacious group, and variations have popped up throughout history."

"So you're saying Tornau based his magic upon this ancient Sumerian cult?"

"It's an educated guess. For one thing, Tom's spell fragment is in Sumer. And I believe there are Voc Caru spells preserved in the *Dæmonolatreia*. It's a notorious demonology tome compiled by Remigius in 1595."

"A *grimoire*? Do you own a copy?"

"No. It's a rare volume. The catalogs list only twelve copies, and I'm fairly certain Tornau purchased one."

"Destroyed, for certain."

"I may be able to track another one down. It'll take time."

"Do what you can. I'll pay whatever it costs."

Culhane smiled, doubtful of his friend's dwindling resources. "A volume like that would do well in my collection. But I'd be willing to *loan* it to you for . . . let's say, three of your best paintings. When all this ugly business is behind us, we'll discuss your *gallery opening*."

Parrish nodded in gratitude, and for the first time in weeks he felt some control in the situation.

CHAPTER 34

JULIE FELT A LITTLE PUT OFF BY EVERYONE AS SHE wandered out of the high-school auditorium. Miss Delmonte had released her from rehearsal, deciding to focus on scenes with the principals. She was beginning to understand what it meant to be a bit player. Meanwhile, Tom was well on his way home to finish prepping his new monster for the mold. One more day, he kept saying to her. It was almost done. Lonely and dismissed, she found herself with a free afternoon and nowhere to go.

The halls were vacant. Only a few students remained in the building. Making her way for the exit, she saw Danny Kaufman by the water fountain and realized it was a perfect opportunity to fulfill her "mission" for her dad. If only she could learn what she needed without it getting back to Tom. She'd hate him to think she was prying. It would take some finagling. "Hey, Danny," Julie announced as she approached.

Danny smiled back at her, wiping his mouth. "What's happening, Julie?" His eyes swept up and down her body like a brush applying whitewash.

"Nothing. I'm bored. No rehearsal today."

"Where's Tom?"

"Home. Making monsters."

Danny gave her a commiserating look as though he sensed her dejection. "Figures. That guy needs to get his priorities straight."

Good subject, she thought, *but not the right one.* "What are you doing here so late?"

"I'm heading for a D&D meeting. Spencer has a kick-ass dungeon. I play a mage. Last week I reanimated some corpses to do battle with a stone troll. Ya interested? I'm sure he could put you in as an elf maiden, or something."

"No, thanks. I have enough magic in my life, you know, with my *dad* and all."

"So what's your dad up to these days?" he asked with sudden interest. *Perr-fect*, she thought, as the conversation shifted to her advantage.

"If you mean is he conjuring zombies out of the cemetery, I hate to disappoint you."

"I'd love to chat with him, wizard to wizard," Danny said. "I could use the 'experience points'."

Julie dismissed his smug attempt at humor and went in for the kill. "Is that why you were spying on him a few weeks ago? For 'experience points'?" She deliberately laced her question with accusation, hoping to elicit a guilty response.

Danny paled, as though caught shoplifting. "Tom told you about that?"

"I think it's rude of you to make fun at his expense," she chastised.

"We weren't *spying* on him," his voice raised an octave. "Not deliberately."

"Sure you weren't."

"Julie . . . we just happened to be in the area and he caught our attention."

"What were you doing there at all?" she demanded. Her words seemed cruel, but they were part of a strategy; to force him into a confession by choosing the lesser of two evils.

"It was Kevin's idea, the *maniac.* He took us on this little expedition near the cemetery. You see, there's this tunnel."

"Tunnel?" She cocked her head, curious.

"It's an abandoned railroad tunnel just down the road. It's hidden behind some trees."

"I know it." She remembered it now. A large dank hole in the hillside, a quarter mile from the estate.

"Kevin had this practical joke all prepared, but it got out of hand when Tom went off wandering."

"Tom got lost in the tunnel?"

"Only for a little while. He looked pretty messed up, though, afterward. He started reciting this weird gibberish in the car, like he was speaking in *tongues.* Gave me the creeps."

Julie struggled to conceal her reaction. Had she just heard right? Did Danny just reveal the origin of the magic spell? "You mean the spell he wrote down on that sketch? Is that the one?"

"Yeah, that's it. Although I think he just made it up to

get back at Kevin. He's great at inventing things like that. But we weren't spying on your father. Honest."

She feigned remorse. "I'm sorry. I guess I am feeling a little rejected. Tom's been . . . distracted."

He rolled his eyes. "Tell me about it. I'm seriously gonna have a talk with him. I mean . . . with a girlfriend like you . . ."

She blushed. "Thanks." Julie could feel his eyes on her chest again.

"Well, I better go," he said. "Dungeon's a-waitin'."

"Have fun. Don't get swallowed by a giant worm."

Julie stood silently as Danny rushed off and considered the implications of what she'd heard. Tom had wandered into the tunnel and came out quoting magical phrases. *Why hadn't he mentioned any of this?* His secrecy bothered her. Maybe he just felt foolish about getting lost. She knew she had made a significant discovery and decided to call her father immediately.

CHAPTER 35

THE SUN WAS A BRIGHT ORANGE ORB NEARING THE horizon by the time Julie could join Parrish. Armed with a pair of large flashlights, they drove up to the concealed tunnel entrance.

"Humphrey was right," he remarked excitedly as he pulled the car into the gravelly clearing that overlooked the hillside. "It was right in my backyard the whole time. I would never have guessed. But now it makes perfect sense."

"What do you mean?" Julie asked as she tested the flashlights they'd taken from the mansion work shed.

"After his escape from the Whateley farm, no one dared imagine Tornau would remain in the Crohaven area. The whole region was too closely watched. But he *needed* to perform the final ritual somewhere in the vicinity of the last. This was the safest place he could find." His eyes scanned the setting sun with concern. "Come on. We don't have much time."

Julie followed her father into the tunnel, feeling an icy chill as the cavernous maw swallowed them.

A distant dripping of water echoed through the bitter silence as their flashlight beams passed over the firepit. Parrish felt his nape bristle when he saw the remains. His flash beam wavered over the decrepit robes on the floor, crumpled and decayed, and he knew he was looking at the end of the mystery. But it wasn't what he expected to find.

"My God," he said aloud. "This is it."

Julie shivered. The frigid air caused her to clutch herself, and she was glad for the woolly sweater she had put on beneath her denim jacket. She cringed at the haunting display.

He scanned the walls, revealing the faded scribbles of yellow-and-white chalk on the slate and concrete. Arcane symbols like the ones he perceived in the barn, but they were hastily scrawled, written with a desperate hand. He reached into his pocket and removed the small notepad, sketching the images on paper.

Disturbed by the sinister emblems, Julie turned away and focused her attention on the circle of stone chips. Inside, she could see the ashen remains of a fire. Crushed and charred fragments of wood were nestled in a pile of white ash. Her father joined her, holding his hand out toward the circle as though tasting the air with his fingers.

"There was a fire like the one in the barn . . . right here," Parrish said cryptically as he probed above the surface, growing more and more perplexed.

"Incredible. Can you feel this?" he asked.

"What?"

"An intense pulse of astral energy radiating from within."

She questioned him with her eyes, but Parrish was silent, focused again on his psychic examination. He moved his fingers deliberately through the ash and soot of the pyre. His brows crinkled with concentration. Once again, clairvoyant fragments rushed into his mind from the æther, filling his inner eye with visions from the past.

"They stood here with him. The remaining five."

Flashes from an earlier time. Figures of shadow.

He glimpsed the man again, Jacob Tornau. So cold were his eyes, so completely devoid of humanity. *Was there a soul in those eyes?*

Julie saw her father's entire frame suddenly snap rigid, as though jolted by electric force.

"Daddy?"

"Uhhgh. They've . . . called . . . forth . . . the flame!" His voice was jagged and tremulous. His eyes rolled up into their sockets as his mind catapulted back in time.

Parrish wrestled with the phantom energies. He saw them resurrect the fire. He saw it roar immediately into a purple torrent. Tornau recited the Fau'Charoth spell verse, holding up the carved idol of the doglike creature. Again, the necromancer prepared for a sacrifice, only this time there was no child. The hapless victim was one of their own, taken in surprise, restrained and stripped of her robe. Parrish could see her face clearly.

"Sarah Halloway," he uttered between clenched teeth.

"Who?"

"The final victim. Tornau's associate. He's sacrificing his own lover."

His hands clenched into fists so tight that the nails dug into his palm. Julie bit her lip in concern, watching him struggle with the image stream.

He watched as Sarah cried out for mercy. It began to make sense now—how the sheriff was able to zero in so swiftly to save the child. An anonymous phone call placed by a guilt-ridden cult member. She betrayed him, a repentant act with dire consequences. Parrish knew it was the terrible price she paid for a moment of mercy. Again, he was repulsed, an uneasy spectator witnessing the vile deeds first hand. Julie watched him reel unsteadily on his feet.

He flinched as they hurled the luckless woman into the flames, expecting to see her body flail in agony on the burning pile of timber. But with a flash, she was gone! Vanished! As though she'd fallen through a crack in space.

The response to the sacrifice was immediate. A glowing nucleus was revealed within the flame. White hot, like magnesium fire, it burned on the psychic's inner eye.

"They've created an Asmodai-driven portal. Bright. Extreme brightness. What in God's name were they trying to do?"

Parrish snatched his hand back from the ash as if it had been scorched. Julie was startled. Immediately, the image vanished.

"Daddy? What is it?"

"It's warm!" he said with alarm, looking at his fingers.

"Like there are live coals here."

"What? How is that possible?"

"Embers of hellfire. Rekindled after all these years."

As he continued to examine the firepit, Julie approached the crumpled robes. They were collapsed in decaying heaps like old laundry, the cloth desiccated from years of intermittent dampness and drought. They stank of guano, which crusted over the surface in white gobs. Overcome by curiosity, she pointed her foot toward the nearest one. Her toe lingered just beyond the cloth when Parrish gestured forbiddingly.

"Don't touch those." The firmness in his voice caused her to immediately pull back.

He approached the first robe and brought his palm across the fabric. His mind again traveled to the past as his senses awoke to the bitter spectacle. His eyes glazed over into a distant stare.

He watched as Tornau and his followers stood before the vortex, which glowed like a supernova. Whether they intended to enter or waited for something to emerge was unclear. A throbbing hum filled his clairsentient ears. He could feel another presence in the chamber, incorporeal but alert. It lingered like a terrible phantom, filled with hunger.

A shrill sound pierced the monotonous drone.

A bright shaft of plasmic energy shot out of the vortex, striking one of the cult members.

Tornau's eyes gaped with alarm.

Parrish watched as the cult-member was consumed by electric fire. The man shrieked in agony and collapsed onto the ground. The empty robe smoked with fetid vapors.

The circle of worshippers fell back, shocked and bewildered.

Another shaft, like a thunderbolt, shot out of the vortex. It ricocheted off the wall, exploding into the rock.

Parrish gripped his head. "Lightning from the vortex! Everything—crazy!"

The robed figures fell into panic as the vortex spit tongues of fire at them. Each found its mark, devouring the cult members, crushing them to the earth. Their wails of terror and pain rose above the roaring winds.

Tornau stood transfixed with horror.

He raised his hands once more, in a vain effort to contain the fire, and cried out with the incantation, his voice filled now with pleading and fear.

"Fau'Charoth! Fau'Charoth!"

The verse went uncompleted. A shaft of fire struck him directly in the chest, knocking him to the ground. The wooden idol fell beside the firepit, enveloped in flames.

He screamed, even as his body seared and melted beneath his robe.

With a final flash, the purple torrent extinguished like a candle. The humming winds ceased, and the remaining tongues of yellow fire flickered and faded within the firepit.

Dark and silence resumed.

A *drip-drip-drip*ping of nearby water was heard.

The stillness of past and present merged as the stone walls revealed the last of Jacob Tornau and his cult.

"There's no more," Parrish said with grim finality. "This is where they met their end."

"How?"

"Something went terribly wrong."

Parrish gazed about the chamber as though viewing it in a new light. He focused his astral vision to view the firepit. The stones took on an alien glow, and from within the ashes he could discern an unholy purple luminescence. Wisps of the colored light spiraled outward like smoke. He was gazing at a split in the fabric of this dimension. Tornau had succeeded in piercing the barrier between this world and the next. The doorway was held ajar by negative essences that seeped through and smoldered like coke. So long as the embers burned, the gate to the dark realm was open!

Julie was worried. The eeriness was getting to her. She waved the flashlight about as though every shadow held a threat. "Daddy, let's get out of here."

Parrish nodded to her without turning his gaze. It had shifted to another object on the ground, a small black shape that was charred to a crisp. He bent to retrieve it and found it to be the burnt remains of a wooden figure, the one Tornau had held to the flame. Turning it over in his hands under the flash beam, he recognized the carved features of an animal with pointed ears and what appeared to be wings. The snarling grimace was wolflike in countenance, brittle with white ash, and even as he studied it, most of the face crumbled to dust.

There were a few screeches from above, and the flutter

of wings.

The sound startled Parrish, causing him to drop the charred icon. It crashed to the ground, disintegrating into a cloud of soot.

Julie quaked, "What was that?"

Parrish's eyes flared with concern. "The time? Quickly."

Julie checked her watch. "It's 5:44. Why?"

"Sunset! We have to leave now!"

He grabbed her hand, racing for the exit. In the distance, the blue circle had dimmed to gray, with an orange fire at the base. The sun had just passed below the horizon. As they ran, Julie could hear more screeching, and then the loud flapping of hundreds of tiny wings. Her heart pounded. A dense, seemingly endless flock of dark shapes fluttered past them. All around her, she began to see them.

Bats. Thousands of them. Fluttering into the twilight sky.

Parrish could feel them glancing off his back in a tornado of cascading bodies. As they neared the entrance, he grabbed Julie and pressed them both to the ground. Crushed to the damp earth, Parrish and Julie waited for the juggernaut of wings to pass. It seemed a very long time.

CHAPTER 36

TOM PEERED STEADILY INTO THE BOWL OF THE HOBART cake mixer as it rotated with a loud whirring. He clenched a stopwatch in his hand, glancing at it peripherally as though the contents in the spinning bowl would vanish if he withdrew his eyes from it. The foaming latex was reaching its peak, frothing to a thickening mass like whipped cream. Fumes of ammonia tickled his nostrils as they evaporated from the mixture.

It was early on a Tuesday morning. The garage workshop had practically been his home for two days.

Six minutes. One more to go.

The fluffy batter increased in volume, threatening to spill over the top of the bowl. The ammonia was bringing tears to his eyes. It was a natural component of the raw latex rubber which, when properly mixed with other chemicals, yielded a dense, frothy foam. This foam, injected into the creature mold and cured in the kitchen oven, would become the spongy flesh of his stop-motion monster.

Tom was poised, ready to pounce on the machine as

soon as the stopwatch reached seven. In his hand was the final component, part D, the gelling agent. Tricky stuff, that part D. It was the catalyst that would trigger a chemical reaction, turning the foam into a gelled mass. If everything had been precisely measured, and the humidity of the room was just right, then Tom would have just three minutes to add the catalyst, mix it thoroughly, and inject it into the mold.

This was the process of casting a foam-latex model. It was a skill not so much learned as rewarded. One had to go through a trial by fire, adapting formulas like a chemist, often failing. Sometimes the gel would kick off too soon, and the foam would become a thick lump in the mixing bowl. Other times it would miscarry, collapsing in the mold during the baking process. Too many attempts had ended in disaster. Malformed shapes had been pulled from molds like stillborn fetuses. Yet at long last he mastered the process. Like Bellerophon with the golden bridle, he had conquered Pegasus.

Tom braced himself and looked at the watch. Ten seconds to go. Let no phone ring, let no dog bark, let no cloud pass over the sun! Three . . . two . . . one . . . BLAST OFF!

In went the gel with little squirts of his vile. His left hand madly spun a spatula through the goop, feeding the colored gelling agent into the beaters. The white foam slowly turned a bluish gray as the tinted fluid was evenly distributed.

Don't trap any air in it, he reminded himself.

Damn! Rubber smeared on his jeans.

Screw it!

He tossed the empty bowl. Reached for the plunger.

Hurry up, hurry up!

Plunger in place, he inserted the spout of the gun into the entry hole of his mold and put all his weight onto the plunger. *Now push!*

With controlled pressure, the thick grayish foam oozed into the mold, filling the negative space around the armature contained within. He sighed with satisfaction when streams of rubber gushed out of the escape holes. It meant the mold was completely filled.

He removed the gun, hands covered with the sticky latex. Moments later, the exposed puddles of foam solidified into a solid mass of wet, compressible rubber. Every excess lump and spillage now had the feel of a poached egg. He crushed them with his fingers, testing how well the foam congealed.

A perfect gel. All that remained was to load the mold into the oven for a slow seven-hour bake. He gently lifted the mold, groaning under its weight, and carried it out the garage and into the waiting kitchen oven. There, it would sit on the lowest rack, curing in the heat. He checked his watch. Eight o'clock in the morning. Time to head for school. And what an unbearably long day it promised to be.

CHAPTER 37

HOURS LATER, THE FINAL BELL SENT TOM RACING DOWN the hall toward the exit. The mold had baked all day, and by now the rubber would be perfectly cured. He had just enough time to drop his books off, say goodnight to Julie at the bike racks, and—

"Watch yer back!" Danny appeared from out of nowhere, playfully snatching a textbook from under his arm.

"Hey!" Tom grasped at it. Missed.

"Whatcha got?"

"Quit fooling around. I need that!" Tom snapped. He grabbed the book back from the thief and stuffed it away.

"Chill out, man," said Dan, dejected.

"Sorry," Tom apologized in a huff, heading for the doors. "I'm in a hurry."

"I know." Dan had to run to keep up. "Rushing home again to another monster from Hell."

Tom beamed at him. "Not just another monster. Fau'Charoth!"

"Whatever."

"Not *whatever.* It's my masterpiece. I've been working on it for weeks, now."

"Yeah. Julie must be thrilled," Dan muttered to himself.

Tom overheard. "What was that?"

"I spoke to her yesterday, and she's feeling a little . . . put off."

"What are you talking about?"

"Wake up, man! If *I* were dating a foxy chick like Julie, I wouldn't be spending my evenings at home making monsters."

This caused Tom to stop abruptly. "I make plenty of time for Julie."

"That's not the impression *I* got. She seemed pretty dejected."

"But she . . . that's ridiculous. Julie and I are doing just fine."

"Yeah? So how far have you gotten with her?"

"With what?"

Dan rolled his eyes. " 'With what?' With *you know.*"

The intrusive question took him by surprise. "Pretty far," he answered evasively.

"Details?"

"We go to movies together. We're *kissing.* Sort of."

"That's cool. During the movie, have you reached over yet to . . ."

"What?"

"You know." He made a suggestive grasping motion with his right hand.

Tom frowned at him, irritated. "No. It's way too soon

for that."

"Too soon? Tom, it's been weeks. It's not too soon."

"Maybe for sleazos like you, but Julie and I are different."

"Ohhh, the classic cop-out. We're 'different'."

"I don't want to talk about it." Tom trudged along, eyes downcast.

"Tom," Dan raised his voice deliberately, knowing how much it would infuriate him. "If you haven't touched her titties by now, you're blowin' it!"

"Will you lower your voice? What *is* it with you?" He always did this. He always knew what buttons to push. Flustered, Tom continued to the side exit, with Dan padding beside him like a hound.

"I'm just saying you gotta stay ahead of the game and get *serious*. Forget Fow-ka-who-chee. Julie needs your full attention right now, or you'll lose her."

"Right," Tom scoffed impatiently. "Listen to 'Fonzie,' over here. Voice of experience."

"Better than *you've* got."

"Yeah? So when did *you* acquire all this carnal knowledge?"

Challenged, Danny beamed with pride. "Okay, I wasn't going to tell you this yet, but . . ." He herded Tom around a bank of lockers to disclose his triumph. "Marie Sandiego, over the summer."

"Who the hell's Marie Sandiego?"

"She was this friend of my sister. Stayed over a couple of times. One night, when Annette's asleep, she crept down to my room, and next thing I know she's all over me! You shoulda seen the boobs on this chick!"

Tom gawked as though the kid were suddenly a giant. "You *did it* with her?"

"Yep." He smiled unabashedly. "We did the deed."

"God, Dan! Thanks for telling me." Tom lurched forward, feeling betrayed.

Noting his dismay, Dan downplayed the achievement. "Only once, though. Then she had a fight with my sister, so she never comes around anymore. Man, it totally broke my heart."

The news bothered Tom. He had always assumed Danny was *behind* him in sexual accomplishment. The buddy who'd ambled along beside him had stolen secretly ahead, winning the race. "Y'know, it isn't cool to hold out on your friends. How come you never mentioned any of this before?"

"Well, for one thing you never seem *interested*."

"Of course I'm interested! It's just that . . . shit."

Kevin appeared behind them. "What's going on?"

Tom scowled. "Dan's lecturing me about girls."

"Oh, well that's freakin' preposterous!"

"He says he made it this summer, with some girl named—"

"Shut up, Ace!" Dan interjected. "I'm just telling him he's gotta get serious with Julie soon, or he'll blow it."

"Dan," Kevin contradicted, for which Tom was immediately grateful. "The guy's only sixteen, for Christ's sake.

Tom, don't let this freakazoid rush you into anything. Give it time. You'll know when you're ready. And when you're ready . . . be careful."

Tom smiled at his older friend. Kevin smirked slyly. "Be careful her dad doesn't read your mind! He's got that second sight thing, you know. Talk about a guy's worst nightmare."

Dan chuckled. "You believe in the hereafter? 'Cause you know what *I'm* here after."

With Tom distracted, Kevin slipped something into his jacket pocket.

As they left the side entrance, he saw Julie in the distance waiting by the bikes. A wave of masculine pride coursed through him. *See? That's my girl.*

"Gotta go, guys." He nodded to them and went off to join her.

As he approached, his hands slipped casually into his pockets, and his fingers discovered a small packet inside. He pulled it out and found it was a little square envelope. A condom.

Kevin! He turned back and saw them grinning like raccoons.

Tom quickly stashed the prophylactic into his jeans, hoping Julie didn't notice. His cheeks burned just having it there.

"What's that?" she asked immediately.

"Nothing."

She aimed a shy kiss on his cheek. He turned her head

and took it on the lips instead, savoring the sweet taste of cherry-flavored lip gloss. He hoped the guys were still watching.

"I'm not going to keep you," she said. "I know you have that 'thing' in the oven."

Remembering Danny's words, he turned to her. "No . . . it's all right . . . I've got time."

"Oh, don't start turning all chivalrous on me," she chided. "You're about to rip out of your skin to get home."

"Yeah, but . . ." he said as he hauled his bike from out of the long tangle of wheels and chains. "Julie . . ."

He didn't have to say anything more. The warmth of her smile told him that she understood. "Go on. Get outta here," she said. "I've got rehearsals in five minutes, or I'd come over and be your hunchbacked assistant. I do a great Igor impression." She humped her spine and waddled like the bell ringer of Notre Dame. " 'Saa-anctuary! Saa-anctuary'!"

Tom laughed out loud, delighted. "That's 'Quasimodo.' Thanks, but I'll spare you that horror. Some things a man has to face alone."

"Yes-s, m-maaas-ster."

He chuckled again and appreciated how easy it was to be with her. She looked really cute, and at that moment he just wanted to smother her with hugs and wet kisses.

"I'll call you later and tell you how it came out."

She straightened her back and brightened. "Really? Maybe we can celebrate the new arrival and pass out cigars!" She giggled and switched to a baritone. " 'Congratulations, Mr. DeFrank. It's a monster'." They lingered close for a moment, and he was suddenly reluctant to leave. "Well . . . see ya," he said. Then he was off with a blur down the road. Julie watched him, smiling, catching fire from his enthusiasm. Life with a mad scientist. She was glad to see him in such bright spirits. And she wanted most of all to banish from her thoughts the dire concerns of her father.

Tom's legs ached with the speed of his peddling. To save time, he went the direct route, rather than the back roads. He could feel himself drawn to the house as though the mold had sent out a tractor beam and was pulling him toward it. Had he ceased his pedaling, the bike might well have continued on its way, caught up in the gravity stream.

Seven hours of anxious waiting. It had been like—*gasp!*—getting to the top of this hill!

He smiled, thinking of Julie again. Maybe Dan wasn't a complete jackass after all. Julie deserved more attention from him. She'd been so patient. It might've been nice to have her there tonight, and that really *was* a great hunchback impression, but opening a mold was such a stressful time. Too many things could go wrong. Air bubbles, collapsed body sections, broken joints. Any one of them could plunge him into a fit of whimpering despair. But if it all went well, and Fau'Charoth was released from its plaster womb, it would be smooth sailing from this point on. The model would be finished and ready to perform in a matter of days.

He wondered how that would change things.

There was the sound of an approaching auto. The car stole directly behind him and honked. Tom turned, expecting to see Kevin in the Monstermobile.

But it wasn't Kevin. It was a green Jaguar, Clifford Burke at the wheel. The front bumper was edging dangerously close to him.

Damn!

Tom increased his peddling. What was this about? Tom swerved his bike far to the right, hoping the jag would pass, but Burke kept his sports car in a deliberate position behind him. Tom could feel the cold stare of eyes behind him. He increased his pace, sensing a vengeful mischief in Burke's pursuit. The Jaguar kept up to him with shark-like persistence.

He reached the crest of another hill, fearful that Burke might force him into a blind turn—and perhaps an approaching auto. They entered a straightaway. The Jaguar veered alongside him. Burke honked again.

"Hey, DeFrank! Quit hogging the road!" he yelled out with a laugh.

With a hard push of his legs, Tom launched into a forward thrust. But the car sped up to overtake him. He pedaled with all his might—for his life, perhaps, and realized he was actually mortally afraid.

Burke's horn blasted as the Jaguar slipped beside him. Without warning, he veered into Tom's path, sideswiping the biker off the road. His front wheel fell into a ditch, causing him to plunge headlong down an incline of rocks, bottles, and part of a chain-link fence. Tom saw all of this in a blur as his bike tumbled, tossing him. For a second, he was airborne, and then he crashed painfully to the ground in a heap.

The Jaguar screeched its tires, soaring away to the sound of Burke's laughter.

Tom rose painfully and crawled from the ditch. He rubbed his knee, which was badly scraped. Mud was smeared over his torn pant leg. No bones were broken, at least, but the pain was agonizing. The bike had suffered a grimmer fate, the tire frame bent out of shape. He wheeled it back to the road, walking beside it with a limp. It would be a long walk home.

"Tom!" shrieked his mom as he entered the house. "For God's sake, will you get that thing out of my oven?"

Oh, brother. She was home early. Just what he needed.

He ran up the steps to the kitchen. His knee ached and burned, sending icy tingles up his leg. His left palm was also scraped, with an ugly black-and-blue bruise. Wheeling the bike home had been slow and excruciating. He was returning from a battle, and the barracks held no succor.

Maggie appeared, gesticulating impatiently. "I've been waiting to put a chicken in, and now the whole place stinks like burnt rubber! How long is that thing gonna be in there?"

"It's done!"

"You better open a window and put up a fan."

"Okay!"

"Paul's coming in two hours! What am I gonna do with you?"

A gust of warm air hit his face as he opened the oven door. There was an acrid stench of cooked latex. He pressed a finger to a residue patch of rubber along the edge of the mold and sighed gratefully. It sprang back to his touch, a thorough cure. His throat locked, and a tear of relief clouded his eyes.

His mother watched as he wrapped the mold up with moist towels and carried it out of the oven. "You've got a mess to clean up, young man. I want you to scrub that oven—"

"I will."

"—and sweep the floor. You've got plaster chips everywhere."

"Okay! I'll get to it!" he said as he hauled it past her.

She noticed his bloody pants for the first time. "And what happened to your leg?"

The door to his bedroom swung shut with a crash behind him. His heart pounded in his chest, making his head feel light. He gently lowered the mold onto the floor and knelt beside it. His knee exploded with pain as he put weight on it.

Bastard! he thought.

The plaster was still warm to the touch. Taking pliers, he began cutting the wire straps that bound the mold together. He inserted a large screwdriver between the hard sections and pried upward.

Bastard Burke!

Heat vented from between the gray-white shells, and the rasping sound of stretching rubber could be heard. Carefully, he applied more pressure, biting at his lower lip, fearful of tearing the model within. The heat of the plaster was starting to sting his fingers.

His mom too. Never noticing. Never caring.

And Dan with his crazy criticisms. What the hell does he know about anything?

He wiped sweat from his brow, trembling. Was it fear he felt?

No. It was anger. He was tired of the abuse. Tired of the harassment. Tired of being different, and not good enough, and not *bold* enough. He noticed the red-blue cobblestone bruise on his palm. It was like a brand of dishonor.

He felt the anger build, forming like a cherrystone of rage in his stomach.

"Why can't they all just get off my case!?" he asked.

The screwdriver worked around the edges of the mold until the rubber gave way. He could feel the section loosen beneath his grasp. With a deep breath, he lifted it away.

From the shelf above, Gothmaug watched. Chrysophylax watched. Gwangi, Cyclops, Styracosaurus—they *all* watched as the shells of the stone "womb" were removed, revealing the newborn creature within.

Halfway imbedded in the plaster, the model Fau'Charoth gazed up at its creator. Its features were perfectly formed, capturing the essence of the sculpture in flexible rubber tissue.

A smile broke Tom's face as he passed his fingers over the warm, scaly flesh. Carefully, he tugged at the limbs until they pulled free from the mold, and then he held the new model in his hands. He tore away the webs of rubber flack along the edges and dumped them on a pile like synthetic afterbirth. He felt a shutter of excitement as he stood it on his desktop and adjusted its posture. The joints bent perfectly, with mechanical precision.

It seemed eager for life.

PART 2

CHAPTER 38

FAU'CHAROTH STOOD POISED ON A CLIFF TOP WITH wings outstretched like sails on a cutter ship. Its claws drew close to its chest, legs flexing in a crouch, as it prepared to launch.

Tom squeezed the black bellows—*click!*—exposing another frame of film. He then peered through the lens of the Nikon Super-8. Framed within the camera's aperture was the fully completed articulated model. The light of the clamp lamps shined brightly on the creature's mosaic hide. Erect on its dinosaur legs, the puppet stood ten inches tall. Its lupine jaws held a snarling fury of epoxy fangs. The thin, bat-like wings were webbed with a skin of textured latex, stretched over fingers of wire. They were frozen in mid-flap, ready to fly.

Animating a flying creature was a most difficult process. Three strands of fish line extended up from the puppet's hips and shoulders to an elaborate aerial-brace rig. The transparent threads were secured to a rotating disc that could be tilted, raised, and lowered on a series of joints and calibration rods. The entire apparatus was attached to a small trolley that traveled across a scaffold above. The rig suspended the puppet like a marionette and provided three axes of movement that allowed the monster to dangle in simulated flight. With each exposure, Tom checked to see that the fish lines were not reflecting the light. If so, he would hand paint them invisible. It was all very time consuming, but well worth it. Through the camera lens, Fau'Charoth was soaring, its wings flapping in single-frame increments across the backdrop of the sky. The camera panned along as though capturing the flight of an eagle across the badlands.

Many increments later, Fau'Charoth made its descent. Tom lowered the puppet to the ground surface of the set. Reaching below the tabletop, he passed two wing-nutted screw tie-downs up through predrilled holes. Each screw entered a threaded socket in the souls of the puppet's feet. With a few twists of the wing nut, Fau'Charoth's legs were anchored secure to the tabletop. Tom removed the wires and rig, grateful to be free of the aerial brace. He gripped the torso, feeling the warm foam-rubber flesh, and bent it slightly forward to simulate momentum. Then he adjusted the tail, the legs, the jaws. And—

Click!

For the past two weeks, Tom had been animating almost every free moment he could steal. It was showing in his face, tired eyes from lack of sleep. Twice he had dozed off in class, and he knew his grades would plummet if he didn't start hitting the books. Yet his energy was strangely renewed when he stepped before the camera, as though animation was an elixir that rejuvenated him. Life had changed for him in the past six weeks. It was filled with glitches—unusual experiences he had never encountered. His relationship with Julie was a strange and wonderful thing, but it challenged him at every turn. And the flight dreams—well, they were a phenomenon beyond compare. He was grateful for every chance to escape to his hobby, where things were under his control and progressed at a single-frame pace.

He glanced through the lens. A mysterious world in there.

The set was of alien topography. Jagged cliffs mangled a sky of swirling clouds. Twisted trees festooned the landscape. Aluminum foil, crumpled over wire and sprayed with brown acrylic matte, resembled actual tree bark. One tree was formed like a deer antler with twisting curls that came to thick points. Some of them had tufts of lichen for foliage, but most were barren. It was an infertile world Tom was constructing, built on a foundation of decay.

The backdrop was hand-painted on a new stretch of butcher paper. It covered most of his back wall. The set was larger than previous film sets, and it seemed to be growing. Each day, he had added to its terrain, expanding the borders of his "netherworld," as though his nocturnal excursions had discovered new territories. He put a new tree here, a scrag of rock there, tapping into some nightmare realm of his subconscious. The mountains created a stark landscape for Fau'Charoth to romp through.

The puppet's screen test was going remarkably well. The armature held the fine gradations accurately, with no drift. The ankle joints were flexible yet strong enough to support the model's weight even in mid-step. He had surpassed himself.

Tom considered the puppet's stance. How should it walk? Should it skulk or take quick steps? Where was its center of gravity, and what effect did wings have on its balance? He studied its grotesque physique and projected himself into it. In his mind, he shape-shifted into Fau'Charoth. Part hell-hound. Part Ymir. Part Tom DeFrank.

Step by step, the model duplicated his moves. He squeezed the black bulb. *Click!* Another millisecond recorded. The cycle repeated endlessly over, again and again.

It took truckloads of patience. That's what people said. Twisting the joints, placing and displacing tie-downs on the feet for long, laborious hours—it seemed like self-inflicted torture. But they failed to see beyond the mechanics of the process. Tom had learned to pinpoint his concentration and edit those peripheral steps from his mind.

Satori. That's what the Japanese called it. Absolute focus.

One hour, one minute, one second. All the same.

He wasn't just manipulating a puppet. He was manipulating time as well.

The creature prowled the set restlessly. It needed an adversary, something to test its mettle. To sink its teeth into!

Tom wondered if the notion was his own or Fau'Charoth's.

Few of his models were camera-worthy. Rigor mortis had set into many of them. Foam-latex tended to stiffen in time or disintegrate. Such was the fate of the rubber-people.

But there was his favorite—Gothmaug the undefeated. Tom had been reluctant to bring the dragon into the fray. Gothmaug was his gladiator champion. It had earned its laurels and deserved a peaceful retirement. But the gauntlet had been tossed, and the challenge had to be met. Like a seasoned combat veteran, the dragon was brought down from the top shelf and placed in proximity to the Fau'Charoth model. Damned if Tom couldn't *feel* the hatred between them, like rival tigers in territorial dispute.

In the netherworld, many clicks and exposures into Tom's mind, the monsters squared off. Talons and claws were curled into blades, while wings fluttered, and teeth dripped malice. Fau'Charoth roared a challenge, and the dragon hissed in response. The creatures fell into a grip of death, clawing savagely at one another. The earth beneath their feet was trampled as their titan fury was unleashed.

Hours later, Tom exposed the final frames of film. He stared down at the puppets that had completed their action. One lay crushed in defeat.

Gothmaug, the ever victorious, had fallen.

The dragon's ravaged body was streaked with theatrical blood. Chunks of sponge had been torn from the base of its neck, where Fau'Charoth had sunk its teeth. Tom's

CHAPTER 39

It was nearly three o'clock on a Saturday afternoon, and surely the mailman had made his rounds by now. Tom returned from a lengthy, distracting walk to the convenience store. He chugged the rest of his chocolate milk and dumped the bottle in a trash can. The latest issue of *Spider-Man* was under his arm. It was the best he could do to get away from home, where he watched the road for the mail truck like a sailor's wife gazing out to sea. As he neared his driveway, his heart leapt. The red flag of the mailbox was up! He ran and flipped open the silver door. His roll of animation film was due from processing. For a full week he'd waited, and now he hoped to see—

Yes!

Among the pile of letters and weekly magazines was a familiar green envelope from Mystic Color Lab. Tom snatched it out, spilling a cascade of envelopes to the ground. With a quick tear, he lifted the adhesive flap and pulled out the new plastic film cylinder. He snapped off the blue cover, unspooled a long trail of white leader, and held aloft the Super-8 footage.

There it was! Bright against the sky stretched a sequence of tiny film frames, the first ever of Fau'Charoth. Tom beamed with excitement. He couldn't wait to put the reel on the projector and see his monster come to life at last.

Bending to retrieve the spilled mail from the grass, he then saw the address of one letter, and immediately his mood darkened. It was a letter from the Kenneth Brown Detective Agency, a private investigator his mom had hired to pursue his neglectful father. Tom frowned. He knew what it meant. The hunt was over. They had found his dad.

Despite her seething opinion of Rob DeFrank, Maggie relentlessly pursued him for child support, armed with court orders and a petty vengeance. His father had fallen off the grid over three years ago. His vagabond lifestyle made him an elusive target, difficult to pinpoint. And with good reason. Once before, Maggie had him tracked down by Social Services and hauled before a judge in North Carolina. He was forced to sign over almost forty percent of his weekly earnings. A few checks were coldly sent to them like blackmail payments, before he disappeared once more. Three years later, Maggie sent the hounds out again.

The letter burned in Tom's hand. He knew better than to open it, but did so anyway. Inside were an invoice of expenses and a brief description of Mr. Robert DeFrank's whereabouts and activity. Neither the freeway cowboy of Tom's dreams, nor the enterprising electronics wizard, Rob had apparently relocated to Florida and was living in a trailer park in Pompano Beach. He worked completely off the books, doing odd jobs at a construction site for a low wage. The sleuth tracked him down through a DWI police charge, driving drunk on I-95. Rob had sunk to a new low.

Overwhelmed with emotion, Tom slammed the mailbox shut and stashed the envelope under his arm. His hands trembled and tension jaunted up his spine, but he resisted it, refusing to let it upset him.

Refused. Like an ice cube refusing to melt in the sun.

Damn her petty vendetta! Why couldn't she just leave the man alone? Divorcing him wasn't enough. Did she have to smother his remaining embers of dignity? Was it any wonder he hid in every backwoods shack in the country?

Tom walked back up the driveway to the front door. Paul Franklyn's Beamer was parked outside the garage. Just what he needed. The man was becoming a fixture, staying over almost every weekend. His best efforts to avoid him were tedious, and it further increased the tension with his mom. Tom felt like the unwelcome tenant in a boardinghouse.

As he entered the house, he could hear Maggie giggling flirtatiously with her date. Tom wandered into the kitchen and saw her straddling Paul in one of the chairs. Her pelvis ground provocatively against his as she caressed his neck and spoke in a cutesy voice. It made Tom's skin crawl. When she saw him, she shifted uncomfortably to her feet. Paul's eyes dropped, noticeably embarrassed.

"Hi, honey," she said. "I didn't hear you come in." Tom handed her the mail with a blank expression, his eyes brushing past Paul as though he was a fly on the fruit bowl. She glanced at the detective envelope, saw that it was open, and gave him a studied look.

"Looks like they finally nailed your father," she remarked, scanning the contents. "Florida now. And he's hitting the bottle again."

A hundred words welled up in his throat. He felt his neck flush, but his rage quickly dissipated. It was a tired argument, and he was in no mood for it, especially in front of Paul.

"Leave him alone," he responded in a tired, breathy voice and then turned away without further word, heading for his room.

Maggie frowned and chased after him. "Tom, I had to find him. This was the only way."

"You had to hunt him down like a dog? Why can't you just leave him alone to die in his hellhole? It's what you want, isn't it?"

"He's got responsibilities, Tom."

"Not to me, he doesn't. I don't need his money, and neither do you. I don't need anything from the guy, so just get off his case! He's my father! You keep pushing him away from me, so he'll never come back!"

"I'm not pushing—*Here!*" She tossed the letter at him, angrily. "Did you read it? He's a bum, Tom! He's not even a truck driver anymore. He's just a lazy drunken bum living in a trailer in south Florida. And he's not coming back, ever! He doesn't care a stitch about you!"

"I don't give a damn!" His eyes were tearing now. "I just want him to live his life without feeling ashamed of himself. You make him feel like a criminal! Like he's Jacob Tornau or some—"

Tom stopped. His mother had gasped, her face blanched with distant horror. *What did he say?* For a moment she seemed like a cripple who had stumbled off her crutches; then she regained her composure. "Okay . . . okay. We'll discuss this another time. It's Saturday. Are you going out with Judy tonight?"

Tom paused, stunned by the shift in subject. He scowled. "It's 'Julie,' Mom. And . . . yeah."

"You can have the car."

He nodded, feeling a strange vibe from his mom that piqued his curiosity. Then he went to his room. As he entered, he glanced back through the threshold. She was still standing in the hall, gazing vacantly.

CHAPTER 40

THE SKY WAS MISTY, BUT THE FOG PARTED IN PLACES TO reveal the stars.

Julie and Tom went for an evening drive in his mom's Chrysler, passing down some of the side roads until cornfields surrounded them. A couple of miles farther put them onto a broad industrial thoroughfare. A sign read "Sullivan County Airport." Julie gave him an anticipatory grin.

"Are you taking me to Paris?"

"No, but I think you'll like where we're going." He smiled, struggling to get past his glumness. The letter about his dad had sent him spiraling into a dark hole of bitterness. He knew Julie already sensed his sullen mood and tried to cheer himself for her sake. She was dressed casually in a soft flannel shirt, jeans, and a zip-up hooded sweat jacket. Just having her beside him was a balm to his battered spirit. He gazed out to the bright lights of the airfield ahead.

The airport was used mainly for small craft by recreational aviators, but commercial airlines like Allegheny provided shuttle services to the larger airports. Frequent flights to JFK, Newark, and Albany helped connect Sullivan County to the rest of the world.

Just beyond the main gates was a side road hidden by trees. It opened at the crest of the hill, revealing a small park. It was a picnic area overlooking the runway, a popular spot during the summer, especially for the big air show, when flying acrobats and the famous Blue Angels air troupe performed for the crowds. But in fall, it was seemingly forgotten.

A bright, rotating beacon stood above the trees as Tom drove into the glen. Julie stared with wonder through the windshield as the big beacon tower, standing at the center, came into view. It was over a hundred feet tall, composed of red metal scaffolding that brought to mind the Eiffel Tower. Atop the lofty structure was a glowing star, transforming the tower into a lighthouse that guided planes safely to the airstrip.

"Oh God. It's so beautiful," she exclaimed, producing a contagious smile that spread quickly to Tom's face.

"I call it the 'Eye of the Dragon'," Tom informed her.

"Of course."

"I can see it from my backyard, especially when it's misty out."

Julie held her breath. She had known of the airport beacon before this, and sometimes, when riding down the border roads of Chapinaw, she had seen it skirting the horizon at nightfall, another celestial body shining in the heavens. But she had never thought to visit it. It was like visiting the sun! "What a wonderful idea, coming here."

Tom beamed proudly as though he had built the luminous tower himself. "It's one of my favorite places."

He drove the car around the tower, hearing the mechanical grind of motors coming from within, and parked near some picnic tables. They stepped out. With the headlights off, the area became magical. The air was misty, and the beacon reflected off the fog, casting a vaudeville spot on the surrounding trees. Julie craned her neck to observe the tower.

She walked through the grass, her hands buried in her pockets. Ribbons of white mist draped around her legs, like wraiths clinging to her soul. They wandered silently through the fog. Tom passed a hand through the nook of her elbow, locking their arms together. She drew closer to him, and it felt very comfortable.

"I've never been up here with anyone else," he said, taking a refreshing breath of air.

As they walked, a bat darted through the sky. Julie flinched. She'd come to hate the jittery creatures since her experience in the tunnel. She wished to forget all about spells, blood rites, and devil cults. Right now was all she wanted to think about, being alone with Tom in this place. She pulled closer to him.

They sat on a grassy slope overlooking the field and watched a passing airplane take to the sky. The runway was lit with many parallel orbs of light that loomed far into the distance. It reminded Tom of the landing strip from *Close Encounters of the Third Kind*. He peered up at the sky, hoping to see a shooting star, or some other cosmic display that would add to the mood. The grass was alive with night sounds. An occasional firefly blinked on and off like a tiny supernova in a galaxy of green. The crickets were chirping the final movement of their summer concerto.

"I love the crickets," he said distantly.

"Definitely."

"When I was in Schenectady, I used to sit out on the front porch and just listen to the sound of the crickets for hours. It just reassured me, somehow. I knew they would be there every summer, without fail, regardless of anything that would happen. Never changing. The same song. *Pleep pleep pleep.*"

She glanced over at him, encouraging him to continue.

"Well, everything changed. My parents split up. We moved. Nothing's the same as it was. And now, every once in a while, I have to come to a place like this, forget everything, and just listen until it all goes away. I could never imagine what eternity must be like, but listening to the crickets makes it easier, somehow. There's that promise . . . Whatever might happen in life, however I might screw up, and long after I'm dead and done with it all, the crickets will continue to play."

She rolled over onto her side to smile at him. "It's funny," she said. "You can never judge a person by what's going on outside. It seems he's got a one-track mind, just monster movies and dinosaurs, and all along on the inside, he's contemplating crickets and eternity."

Tom smiled. "I guess it would surprise some people to know that about me. Maybe they wouldn't think I was such a weirdo."

"You're not a weirdo. You're just . . . I don't know, different."

"Yeah, well maybe if I weren't so different people like Cliff Burke would lay off me."

"Clifford Burke has a lot of growing up to do."

"I know. I just wish he'd have found somewhere else to do it."

"But then *we* would never have met."

Tom stopped to think about that. She was right. If Burke and the others hadn't harassed him and tossed the sketchbook, he would never have met Julie.

"That *is* weird. Not that I'm gonna send him a thank-you card for it. I'm sure he would bust a gut to learn he had brought something nice into my life."

"True, but he *was* instrumental in our destiny. Maybe we were *meant* to meet that day."

He eyed her sidelong. "How do you mean?"

"I believe things happen for a reason. That we're all part of a big cosmic circle of energy, and we draw things to ourselves. Things that we need. Even *people* we need. It's all part of a pattern. You may not notice it now, but later you'll see it and realize it's all connected and has a purpose. Clifford Burke. You. Me. Even your monster. It all has a connection."

Tom tightened the corners of his lips and quoted *Star Wars*. " 'Hokey religions and ancient weapons are no match for a good blaster at your side, kid'."

"Hmm?"

"I don't see myself as being guided by some sort of destiny. It makes me uncomfortable thinking about it."

"Why?"

"'Cause I like being in control. Too many times in my life I was forced to . . ." He paused. A security device kicked on. "I just don't like it. I rather have all the cards on the table and decide for myself. I don't like someone else telling me how to live my life."

"That's very existential of you."

"Existential? I've never been sure what that means."

"It means being totally free and responsible for one's acts."

He nodded. "Yep. That's it. You got it."

"I don't believe in existentialism," she countered. "The idea of carrying the entire load scares me."

"But do we have a choice? I mean, I prefer being alone rather than have to depend on someone else for my salvation. It's all right here." He held up his hand. "I live or die by this."

"Don't you ever pray?"

"No. I don't really believe in God."

Julie was abashed by his agnosticism. It was outrageous for her to doubt the existence of higher powers. So much of her life had been filled with evidence of the supernatural. Her research had revealed the existence of angels and guide spirits. She believed in the saints, and dævas, and in her own father's ability to reach out and communicate with them.

"I believe in something," he explained. "I'm just not sure what it is, and I don't trust it to be there for me."

"Why? What's made you so doubtful?"

"I don't know. Anger, I guess."

"Anger? About what?"

"I don't know."

"It's about your father, isn't it?" Julie ventured.

He stared at the sky, suddenly quiet. She softened her voice, trying not to pry. "You avoid talking about him. That's how I can tell. You don't have to if you don't want to. But it might help if you do."

The silence persisted. Julie knew she had touched a nerve. Perhaps *the* nerve.

His eyes studiously fixed on a star, formulating his thoughts.

"He's a total loser!" Tom shouted in an angry, taut voice. "Just a lazy drunken bum, like my mom always said. I don't give a damn about him anymore."

Her eyes gazed deeply into him, penetrating his shield.

He drew in a deep breath and reluctantly began. "When I was young, I was very fond of my dad. He was sort of an overgrown kid. Very creative. Always making things in the basement. Once, he built a two-way radio from scratch, and I could speak to him from my bedroom to the garage. Goofy stuff like that. He liked science-fiction almost as much as I did. When my parents split up, I wanted to stay with him. That would've been so cool. But my mom sued for sole custody. It hurt him, and it made me furious. So I cried, I complained, I even ran away to a friend's house and spent the night. It was my way of protesting. I was *determined* to stay with my father. In the end, though, the courts granted her sole custody. Nothing I did had any effect on their decision. I was just this piece of property to them."

"Maybe they thought it was best for you."

"It doesn't matter. I felt like a puppet."

"A puppet," she repeated, noting the irony. "And now you're the puppet-master. Now, you make your own little worlds and you have complete control over them."

Tom raised a brow at her analogy. "Interesting. I never thought of it like that. Well, anyway, my dad disappeared off the face of the Earth, and I just wanted to think he'd come back, one day. That he cared enough." His throat locked, and he fought back the tears. "I just wanted to hear from him one more time. But maybe it's best, now, if I don't."

He wiped the moisture from his eyes, and she snuggled close. "I guess it's hard to figure parents out, when they've done such a lousy job of it themselves. You're lucky, at least, that your father's still around."

"My father's a ghost, remember?"

He reflected on this, and then his mind drifted for a while. He crinkled his brow and remembered something disturbing. "She freaked out today."

"Who did?"

"My mom. This afternoon, in the living room, and it

reminded me of the time I ran away as a kid. When I came home the next day I assumed she'd be angry, but she totally lost it, broke down crying, like I had died or something."

"Well of course. She's your *mom*."

"I know. But she had this look of terror on her face when I came home. Today, I made a sarcastic reference to Jacob Tornau, and she went totally white on me. She had that same look."

"Really?" Julie shifted uncomfortably with the name. "Why do you think?"

"I have no idea."

She looked at his face and confirmed with certainty. *He doesn't know. She never told him.* It was too deep a subject to get into, and Julie felt suddenly overwhelmed. She shook her head, brushing it all away. "Let's not think about it any-more. Let's just sit here and be alive for a while." She put her head on his shoulder.

They sat quietly, allowing silence to heal the mood like a salve. Over the airfield, another small plane took to the air. Julie tried to imagine they were both on it, leaving behind the disappointments of parental love. She drew her face up to his and pressed her lips onto his own, giving him a tender kiss.

With gentle uncertainty, Tom returned the kiss. His inhibitions began to melt, and he took her delicately into his arms and pressed her onto the grass, gazing down at her soft velvet eyes. His body relaxed and found confidence in the desire she expressed. He placed a delicate kiss on her forehead and drew a line of kisses past her eyelid, her brow, the bridge of her nose, exploring the beautiful contours of her face, before they settled gently again on her lips. She lay there silently in his arms, feeling warm and safe under him. Tom savored the moment, listening to the crickets, wanting it to last for eternity.

CHAPTER 41

After an hour of sleep, Tom awoke in bed and found himself staring blankly at his bedroom ceiling. A few feet away, on the tabletop, his Fau'Charoth model stood in suspended animation, one claw locked forward in a grasping pose. A glance at the glowing digits of his clock revealed it was only one-thirty in the morning. Restless, his mind filled with bleak thoughts as he reflected drearily on his dad. The PI report about Rob's dismal life caused him to wallow in shame and disappointment.

Since Rob made his departure, over seven years back, Tom envisioned him in the best possible light, as a free spirit with a spark of genius. Fantasy? Perhaps, but it was a consolation to the neglect he felt. He was, after all, his father's son, and so often goes the child after the man. He wanted to believe they were kindred spirits, each harnessing a secret fire that would take them to great heights in life.

The report shattered it all. It painted a dreary picture of a hopeless white trash drunk, scraping a living as a gofer.

How could his father be such a total screw-up?

Where was that passion he remembered? That unbridled creativity? To fall into such an abysmal hole, running away from responsibility—running away from him—made Tom fiercely angry. He wished he could see his dad. He wished he could simply catch a glimpse of the man and prove everything wrong. Brooding in bitterness, he eventually faded back to sleep.

In his dreams, he was a little kid again, fishing with his dad in a rowboat. The small skiff floated just off the shore in a long, narrow lake, surrounded by lily pads and cattails. Rob was teaching him how to hook a worm for bait. Following his dad's example, Tom needled the sharp fishhook through the slippery worm and accidentally pierced his thumb. He cried out and looked up to his father, who was no longer there.

His dad was standing on the shore, watching the boat drift away.

The lake had become an ocean, and a gale wind was blowing.

The little boat began to toss about in the waves. Tom yelled to his dad, reaching out with his bleeding hand. Rob stood with arms folded, watching. His figure grew smaller and smaller as the boat was cast out to sea, taking his son away.

And then he vanished, leaving the boy alone in the violent waves.

Tom thrashed about in bed. Then he lay heavy and still beneath the covers.

Snap!

Even as he dreamed, he was elsewhere.

His embittered heart took control, piloting his journey many miles from home.

The dream took him into the clouds, high above the suburban streets and grassy farmlands of his home. With the speed of thought, he traveled south along the eastern coast. Far below, the lights of great cities flashed by like constellations. Mountains flattened, and forests transformed into groves of palm trees. The continent stretched out into a massive peninsula, where the ocean crashed against sandy shores.

It was last call, 2:00 AM. Rob DeFrank stepped out of the Pink Flamingo pub, inhaling the thick humid air. The trees were swaying in the breeze, and he could make out a canopy of the gathering black clouds. Looking skyward gave him a rush, and he teetered slightly as he entered the street. With his lanky physique and unsteady gait, Rob looked like a scarecrow tethered to a pole. He was dressed in old jeans and a faded T-shirt. His long dark hair was pulled back into a ponytail, and his hairline had retreated at the corners. A thin wisp of a moustache shadowed his upper lip, and the stubble on his cheeks and neck had come in thick. He was still sipping his third and final Corona and squashed the lime into the bottle before heading on his way. The citrus flavor at the rim tasted like the tropics. Three beers were normally his limit, and tonight he'd thrown in two tequila shots for good measure. Too much alcohol, even for him, but hell, it was Saturday night.

As he stumbled onward, he noticed immediately the electric charge in the air. The winds were picking up. It was October, and the hurricane season was over, but there was always the threat of a tornado. He had been in Pompano Beach for three months and already knew what a twister was like.

Rob made a right off the thoroughfare and headed home along the maze of deserted side roads. The street ran parallel to a canal, and he knew if he followed the aqueduct for a mile or so, he would reach the ocean. Streetlamps sparsely lighted the road. Milky luminescence spilled over the pavement. The squalid trailer parks were nestled in groves of palm and wild orange trees. Abandoned autos and piles of trash lined the curbs, creating a shantytown appearance. The uncollected garbage was beginning to stink.

Florida was a dump. There were too many cars, and the heat and humidity were almost unbearable in the summer. He missed the seasonal climes of North Carolina, where as an electrician he had wired over a hundred new condos. But the job market fell through, and he was forced to head south to Florida, where there was a construction boom and plenty of cheap-labor opportunities.

He trudged along distractedly, sipping occasionally at the bottle. The walk seemed endless, though he'd made it almost every night since he lost his wheels. A recent DWI charge suspended his driver's license. His Chevy Nova was impounded until he could pay the fines. Fortunately, most of his needs were local. He could bum a ride from fellow workers to the construction site, and the Pink Flamingo was a mere quarter mile from the spaghetti box he called home. He could get by for a month without a car.

What a stupid mistake, that DWI. A minor infraction, but enough to get his name into the system. Enough for his ex-wife's SS officers to track him down and charge him with delinquent fatherhood. He was still on the lam from the last time it happened.

Maggie. Just the thought of her kept his suitcase half-packed. He was barely making enough to feed himself, and yet if she had her way, half of it would go to Tom's college fund. It made it impossible for him to earn any kind of a living. Three times, he'd relocated to escape the court orders, forced to work odd jobs off the books. The tax-free cash was finally adding up. He was saving for a move to Mexico, where he would finally be free, but now he had to get his car out of hock. Thinking about it made Rob irritable. It was a waste of a good high.

He downed the last quarter of the Corona and tossed the bottle into the ditch. Nature called with a vengeance. He unzipped his fly and ejected a yellow stream of urine at the base of a telephone pole. Then he glanced around to get his bearings. The scenery was strange.

Nothing looked familiar.

Damn. He'd taken a wrong turn. These side streets all looked the same at night.

He continued onward, searching for an identifiable landmark.

There was an unearthly quiet.

It was dead silent, as though time itself was holding its breath. Not the tiniest click of a cricket or whine of a mosquito. Strange how the silence itself could become a distinctive sound. Moisture fell on his cheeks, and he wiped droplets away with his hand. If it turned into a downpour, he was screwed.

Damn it! How did he get so lost?

Something made the hairs bristle on his nape. Startled, he cast a backward glance. The road was empty and desolate. Another streetlight hummed above and cast a broad spot on the broken pavement. Rob probed the shadows, inexplicably aroused.

Did he hear something?

His mind snapped alert, all trace of intoxicants banished. Suddenly, he felt alone and exposed. A chill in the wind ripped through him, and he clutched himself, trembling with inexplicable fear.

"Who's there?" he asked aloud. No response.

After listening intently for several seconds, he decided he hadn't actually heard anything.

Just imagination, he thought.

Then he chuckled, amused at his timidity. Back muscles all bunched up into knots. Jittery like a schoolgirl. Rob was used to being alone, and certainly not afraid of the dark. That extra tequila shot must be affecting his nerves.

He continued onward, and then stopped in mid-stride.

Did something just move near that bus stop?

He listened for footsteps. The white shelter was empty, but he studied every corner, searching for concealed figures waiting in ambush. "Who's there?!"

Heroin addicts would brain you for your wallet.

Rob jabbed a hand into his jacket pocket, feigning a grip on a firearm. "I have a *gun*, motherfucker!" His keys jingled loudly against some change. He brandished his phantom pistol past the bus stop and found the shelter empty. The lock on his spine softened. Another breeze whooshed past him, bringing a drizzle of rain against his neck.

The stark street lighting created voids of blackness. Armies of phantoms could lurk there, cloaked in darkness.

Just ahead, he blinked at the sight of a green bungalow with a chain link fence. A familiar sight at last—enough for him to gauge his location. A right at the intersection ahead would take him home. He neared the bungalow.

A savage body flung itself at the chain link fence. Rob cowered back in fright. A German shepherd was contained just beyond it. The dog snarled and leapt viciously at the metal lattice.

Rob cursed aloud, putting a hand to his chest as he breathed heavily. He slowly backed away, gazing at the dog. Its ears lay flat on its head, and the long fangs gleamed in streetlight as it snapped at him. Suddenly there were other dogs barking as well. A smaller mutt let off a high-pitched yap from inside a nearby trailer, and a large deep-throated

Dane bellowed in the distance. It was a unified canine alarm.

Rob walked trembling down the street, heart hammering, nerves lacerated to shreds. So close, now. He knew where he was. A tire swing dangling from a tree was definitely familiar. Another right turn, and then a left. The dogs continued to bark. It was creepy as hell. He'd read how dogs became agitated before the coming of an earthquake. Was the same true of tornadoes? Rob looked to the sky in fear of a cyclone suddenly stomping down on the trailer complex.

The rain started to come down.

There was a breathy exhale, like the hiss of an awakening dragon.

Again, his head snapped back, scanning the vicinity. Some primordial instinct alerted him to a presence. His eyes struggled to focus.

Behind him, bushes and trees billowed in the wind. The waving of branch and leaf seemed to follow a deliberate path, as if an invisible ogre was skulking through the brush. Rob squinted. His hazy eyesight labored to pierce the dimness.

Prickly sensations at the back of his neck.

Something was following him.

There was a crash. He glanced back just in time to see a garbage can roll out into the street, its contents spilling messily. Then another trash canister was *hurled upward* and flung aside right before his eyes! He gasped in disbelief.

More debris took to the air in a whirlwind. A big-wheel tricycle was upturned and tossed. Hedges and palm branches were pressed aside by an unseen hand.

He peered deeply into the space less than twenty feet away, and his eyes discerned an anomaly in the air pattern. There was a shimmering, transparent cloud that bristled with angry energy. Droplets of water bounced off its surface, outlining a grotesque shape, and it was heading straight for him!

His legs catapulted him away in mortal terror. Filthy yards blurred past him. He whimpered aloud and began to cry out in a hoarse voice.

"Help me! Somebody help me!"

At last his trailer came into view. He could feel the stalker coming from behind and heard loud breathing and a throaty snarl.

He was racing to his front door when something struck him savagely in the side. Slammed away from the trailer, he hit the ground on his back. Instinctively, he shielded his face, peering in terror at his attacker. A pair of large canine jaws was snarling ferociously with a wet gurgle. At first, he thought it was the German shepherd, somehow free of the fence. But the streetlight cast a terrifying silhouette above him, and he knew he was being threatened by something monstrous and preternatural. He pressed into the grass, away from the razor fangs that slathered inches away. Yellow eyes gleamed at him with an eerie bestial recognition.

Rob screamed.

In that instant, his assailant fell back. It shook its head and vanished with a bright flash of lightning.

The sky opened with a furious downpour of rain. Rob crawled beneath his trailer and remained there for some time, sheltered from the drenching downpour, too horrified to move.

Tom jolted awake, aghast at the vividness of his dream. For a flash, it seemed his ephemeral dream-shape had actually solidified into flesh and bone! He sat up in bed, feeling very unlike himself, and recognized that in that instant of materialization, he—it—was no longer Tom DeFrank.

CHAPTER 42

THE HIGH-SCHOOL LIBRARY HAD LITTLE TO OFFER ABOUT "magical flight dreams." Tom combed through the card catalog, cross-referencing everything from self-hypnosis to the writings of J.M. Barrie. Most of the "supernatural" material consisted of books on the Salem witch trials and the Inquisition. Little to help him there. Julie said that astral projections were common, and he'd had plenty of them by now, but never like this! Never with the clarity and visceral detail he experienced last night. Never with the tactile sensations of flesh!

He actually dreamed he was Fau'Charoth!

In his vision, he traveled to Florida, somehow pinpointing the exact location of his father. Cloaked in an invisible ghost shape, he stalked Rob to his trailer. It was mere curiosity, a desire to see the man after years of absence. A chance to deny ugly rumors and restore his paternal faith. But the man looked so pathetic. Wandering in a drunken stupor, pissing in the street! The miserable sight of him provoked Tom into a fit of rage. Rob sensed his presence.

His cowardly flight triggered a predator's response. In an animal fury, he transformed into a monster and attacked his dad.

Tom remembered the terror in his father's eyes. He recalled the furious roar, the sharp fangs inches away from Rob's throat. The image pressed brutally against his mind. The encounter only lasted for an instant, but in that brief moment Tom felt awake and physically real. His ire had manifested into physical form.

Was it true? Did he really travel to south Florida and take on a monster shape?

Tom wandered to the back of the library to conceal his bewilderment.

These dreams! What was causing them? Was it all the result of that ridiculous incantation? Or did he pick something else up in that tunnel? Some kind of supernatural virus? The suggestion seemed logical on one level, and totally insane on another. He wanted a better explanation, one that made sense.

Simple answers were often the best. He'd gone to sleep angry with his dad and conceived an ugly nightmare. Case closed. All this mystical mumbo jumbo was twisting his brain. And yet he still wasn't satisfied. With the remaining minutes left to the library period, he continued his search.

Checking the religion section one more time, he found a book with a damaged spine hidden between volumes. It was called simply *The Occult*, by Colin Wilson, and was an overview of paranormal subjects. He glanced through the

CHAPTER 43

THAT WAS HER LOCKER, KEVIN THOUGHT TO HIMSELF as he combed the bank of cabinets in the high-school "B" section. Locker B-33. He'd spent many an afternoon chatting with Kathy McGuire in front of it. Sometimes, when she wasn't around, he'd sneak by and drop letters and objects through the cracks in the door. She always seemed to enjoy it.

That was her math classroom.

He passed the room on his way to the boy's lavatory. Kathy was everywhere in this building. It was as if her spirit haunted the halls. He had to remind himself that she wasn't dead, just locked away in an institution somewhere in Westchester, where he was forbidden to see her. *He* was the only ghost in these halls, and he walked them like a specter with a mission of vengeance. Everything felt like epilogue since she left. His whole world revolved around her, so deep was his love. But then he reminded himself that Kathy had never loved him the same way. The child she aborted was not his. It was Cliff Burke's. The sociopath. The drug dealer.

The murderer, for he was convinced that Kathy would surely have borne the child if Burke had taken responsibility for it. Kevin swallowed the bitterness in his throat. He himself was an orphan raised by a couple incapable of childbearing. A young girl, perhaps Kathy's age, had given him up for adoption. Kevin never found out who his real mother was, but in his mind, he imagined her in a similar situation, young and innocent, prematurely pregnant. He imagined her sacrificing her youth to bring a new life into the world. *His* life.

It should have been my baby, Kathy. They would have raised it together. His heart was an empty vessel now, and it could only be filled with ice.

And purpose.

Kevin watched from just beyond the bathroom for Zack McBride to exit. He'd been waiting for an opportunity like this for a while, and now was his chance. The freshman was doing business with the almighty drug lord himself. Burke always "opened shop" in that bathroom at this hour. Time was running out. Come on, where was that kid?

He'd long considered what action to take after the creep smashed his windshield. It demanded retribution. Burke probably expected some kind of attack on his Jaguar, or some other puerile response, but Kevin was tired of the childish tit for tat. The bastard deserved more than a petty act of vengeance. He deserved to be put out of commission. Aborted.

Zack exited the bathroom, nonchalant, hands buried in

his jeans pockets. Then he sprinted off. Kevin had to hurry to catch up to him. The kid could move fast! He scurried through the hallway like a squirrel with a mouthful of stolen nuts.

"McBride! Wait up!" He tapped the boy on the shoulder.

Zack turned, startled. He nearly bumped into a girl passing him.

"Did you just square a deal in there?" Kevin whispered.

The boy looked at him suspiciously, wondering if Kevin was a nark. "What's it to you?"

Kevin let his eyelids droop like a stone. "I need stuff, man. I gotta get straight." A convincing performance, he felt.

"Go buy your own!" Zack continued on his way.

"Hey!" He stepped in front of the freshman, looking desperate.

"Get away from me, loser!"

"You gotta help me, man. I need a fix. Burke and me don't see eye to eye.

C'mon, whatcha got? I'll give you double what you paid for it."

"You got a screw loose? Get lost!"

"Okay twenty bucks! I'll give you a twenty, cash, right now!"

The boy hesitated, considering the offer. That was a lot of money for a little dope, Kevin knew, but it would be worth it. The boy wandered to a bank of lockers in the hall corner.

"You better not be vice," he warned.

"That would be entrapment. I'd be just as guilty."

"All I got is some 'dust' and some 'ludes.' But it's my entire stash."

"You can buy more. Let me have it."

The boy pulled out a couple of small Ziploc bags from his pants pocket, glancing around nervously. Kevin carefully took the bags from him. He avoided touching the surface, keeping his fingers to the edges, hoping Zack wouldn't notice. He dropped them in his book bag and handed the kid his money.

"Now I got nothing for the weekend," Zack complained.

"Next time you go to the store, pick up a little extra for me. I'll make it worth your while." His heart was beginning to race with excitement. He loved a good sting.

"Meet me here again on Monday," Zack said, and then he was off, squirreling his way down the hall.

"Nice doing business with you, kid." Kevin smiled. The drugs in his book bag would be added to the blue duffle bag at home, the one containing the stash of marijuana. He was building a nuclear device, and Burke's ass was its target.

CHAPTER 44

"HOLY MARY, MOTHER OF GOD. HOLY-MARY-Mother-God. Holy . . . ho . . . Holy-Mary-Mother-God," Connie Wilkens stammered, huddled in a corner of her bedroom. With what strength she had left, she'd fled from the comforts of her bed and crawled across the floor. Her legs were now curled up around her. She gripped them tightly and shivered in deranged fear as she recited a litany that had gotten "stuck" in her throat like a broken record. "Huh-huh-holy . . . holy holy holy . . ."

Nadia stood beside Father MacClair, frightened and uncertain what to do. The nurse watched as the old priest comforted the woman, attempting to get her to rise. He gripped her shoulders, pulling gently, but Connie resisted his grasp, cowering. He placed a soothing hand on the side of her head, drawing her close, until her rantings became a gentle whisper.

"Holy Mary, Mother of God, Holy Mary, Mother of God . . . pray for us . . . p-p-pray for us . . . ss-ss-sinners . . . pray for us sinners . . . Holy Mary, Mother . . ."

"How long has she been like this?" the father asked the nurse.

"On and off for weeks," Nadia answered, "but this evening it just got so much worse. I didn't know whom to call. I couldn't find Mr. Wilkens at his job."

"We need to get her back into bed. Then I want you to call an ambulance."

"The doctor released her into home care, Father. They've already done what they can for her. Mr. Wilkens insisted—"

"I don't care what Mr. Wilkens insisted. We'll take her to the infirmary," the priest maintained. "I want her out of here. Away from all *this*." He gestured uncomfortably to the makeshift shrine of Holy Virgin cutouts on the wall. MacClair was familiar with Wilkens's obsession. Since Josh's death, Gerard had haunted the church like a vengeful seraph, often alienating his fellow parishioners with self-righteous retorts. For the highly devout, there was a thin line between devotion and dementia, and Wilkens had passed over it a long time ago. Enduring it day to day had clearly contributed to the poor woman's illness. Connie was deteriorating rapidly, and the priest knew he would be required soon to give last rites. But his mission, first and foremost, was to grant solace and peace. These were not things he could give her in this household. He gripped Connie's arm again firmly and attempted to lift her. This time she struggled fiercely.

"No! No! Holy-Mary-Mother-of-God!"

"Come on, Connie. Only a few steps to your bed."

Just then, Gerard Wilkens burst into the room. He

glared when he saw the priest and turned to the nurse. "What's *he* doing here?"

"I tried to reach you, Mr. Wilkens," Nadia replied fearfully. "I didn't know who else to call. You said you didn't want the doctor."

"I'm here to help, Gerard," the priest implored. He knew how stubborn the man could be. MacClair had warned the clergy about his fanaticism, and it put him at odds with the man. But he had to consider the woman's well-being.

"We don't need your help," Wilkens snapped. "Leave us alone!"

The loud voices startled Connie, who seemed to withdraw deeper into herself. "Holy-Mary-Mother-of-God, Holy-Mary-Mother-of-God . . ."

MacClair confronted Wilkens. "Gerard, be reasonable."

"Get out of my house!"

"Holy-Mary-Mother-of-God, Holy-Mary-Mother-of-God . . ."

"She needs to be administered to. I insist you call an ambulance—"

"No!"

"Gerard—"

"Holy-Mary-Mother-of-God, Holy . . . holy . . . holy . . . *Wgah'nagl fhtagn!*"

Both men turned to the delirious woman, whose litany had suddenly changed. Connie was staring into space, her phlegm-filled voice charged with a new force.

"Aga mass ssaratu! Fau'Charoth a Lammashta ra

shagmuku tu. Fau'Charoth ud kalama shagmuku tu!"

MacClair and Wilkens were equally mortified. It seemed at first like more of her stammering, but then she repeated the peculiar verse, word, and syllable.

"Aga mass ssaratu! Fau'Charoth a Lammashta ra shagmuku tu. Fau'Charoth ud kalama shagmuku tu! Wgah'nagl fhtagn! Aga mass ssaratu! Fau'Charoth!"

"*¡La madre santa del dios!*" Nadia crossed herself fearfully. "*¿Cuál es ése?* What *is* that?"

Wilkens's ire gave way to panic as he listened to his wife's demented ravings. "No! He's getting to her."

"Gerard," the priest implored.

"He's getting to her the way he got to Josh!"

"Wgah'nagl fhtagn! Fau'Charoth a Lammashta ra shagmuku tu."

Suddenly, Connie's throat locked, and she fell choking to her side. Her eyes rolled up in pain. Gerard grabbed her and began shaking her forcefully. MacClair pulled at his arm, but he pushed him away violently. He reached into his coat pocket and pulled out a small bottle of holy water, which he immediately uncapped and began dousing on his wife.

"Gerard, no!"

"I banish the devil from thee!"

"Nadia! Call an ambulance!"

The nurse rushed from the bedroom.

"I banish the devil from thee!" Wilkens shouted, oblivious to the priest's protest. "I banish the devil from thee! I banish the devil from thee!"

CHAPTER 45

JULIE SCRUBBED AND RINSED HER CHEEKS AND FOREhead, then reached for a towel. The sink was cluttered with cosmetic pencils, powder brushes, and eye-shadow palettes. She glanced repeatedly at a *Seventeen* magazine article, demonstrating the proper use of eye makeup. "THE EYES HAVE IT!" read a caption in bold letters. She studied her clean face in the mirror. With a soft sponge applicator, she smoothed a powdery gray eye shadow around her orbs, accentuating their contours. Then she thickened her lashes with mascara, reddened her lips with rouge, and stepped back to survey the damage.

"Yikes!" She squirmed at her raccoon-eyed reflection. Was it too much? She wanted to look sexy for her boyfriend, but not *too* sexy.

This was going to be a special evening. Her mom was away for the weekend, leaving her alone for the first time since she met Tom. And though Ellen gave her the prerequisite "No boys" speech, she lived in the modern world and knew her daughter was reaching an important age. She trusted Julie to use good judgment and make the best decision for herself. Right now, even Julie didn't know what that was. She and Tom were going out for the usual dinner and a movie, but she intended the evening to end here. At her place, alone. It would be the most time they'd spent together since the "eye of the dragon," where their romance had reached its bloom.

Tom was already waiting in the living room. She panicked a little over the makeup. Her hand reached for a cotton ball, but she restrained the impulse to wipe her face completely clean. A few dabs removed the excess vamp effect. *It's just makeup*, she decided, an experiment in glamour that she hoped would turn up the heat on their relationship.

Recently, there were too many distractions. He'd been animating almost incessantly. It worried her. She felt sidelined and needed to win back his attention the only way a girl could.

A delicious smirk worked across her lips. "If this doesn't do it, nothing will. He's into science-fiction, and you always wanted to be an actress," she giggled. "Tonight's performance: *Sex 'Droid from Planet XXX*." She fluffed her hair one more time, sprayed on a mist of perfume, and bent to put on her shoes, the *dangerous* ones.

Sitting in the living room, Tom thumbed through a girl's magazine from a pile under the coffee table. Articles about boyfriends, fashion, and exercise gave way to an ad showing breasts. Tom gawked and quickly stashed it away, embarrassed. You simply didn't expect to see naked boobs in a magazine like *Mademoiselle.* He fidgeted restlessly, glancing at the stairs where Julie had disappeared, wondering what she was doing or for that matter what she was *thinking.*

It was Saturday night, and Mrs. Parrish was visiting Julie's aunt. Julie had the place to herself. There had been a hint of naughtiness in her voice when she had invited him over.

His hand reached into a pocket, fingering the little square envelope Kevin had given him. He was carrying it like a good-luck charm, always prepared. The prophylactic burned in his pocket with radioactive heat. It served as both incentive and warning. Was he ready to use it?

Danny had done it, already. Why shouldn't he?

They were old enough. They loved each other, right? Why did he feel so giddy and nervous? He wished the night were already a distant memory, filled with delicious and satisfying recollections.

Julie returned with the telltale *clip-clap* of heels. She was wearing pumps! They made her legs look long and shapely. Her dress was black, with thin straps that exposed the creamy nakedness of her shoulders. Below the hemline, dark hose caressed the contours of her calves. As she caught his wide-eyed gaze, she broke into laughter. "What are you looking at?"

"Wow."

"Do you like it?"

Tom swallowed. "God, yeah. You look incredible!"

She blushed bashfully. Her hair was neatly coifed and fell loosely to her shoulders. It shimmered in the pale light. Little pearl earrings dangled from her ears, and a single golden star was chained about her neck. There was an intoxicating aroma of fresh lilac perfume. The dark mystery of her eyes was boldly enhanced with mascara, making them large and piercing. Her lips glistened with red gloss. A little eye paint, some alluring choices of wardrobe, and Julie was transformed from pretty to *gorgeous.* It made him feel light on his feet. Suddenly, he seemed underdressed in his jeans and sport shirt.

"Are you sure we're just going to a movie?" he asked as she flung a black sweater over her bare shoulders and headed with him to the door.

All the way to the mall and back, his heart trembled. He watched as she walked self-consciously on her heels through the shopping plaza. She seemed to enjoy the glances she was receiving from other boys (coupled with the angry leers from their dates). All the while, Tom endured the staggering challenge of her nearness. The smell of her perfume caressed his nose, and her breathy voice tingled like a feather in his ears. Throughout the movie, he held her hand, or kept a warm arm around her shoulders. He had never felt so powerfully aroused.

The evening ended in Julie's bedroom.

Her windows swung slightly out toward White Lake.

The waves, only a short walk down the hill, could be heard splashing along the shore. The Moody Blues were crooning "Nights in White Satin" on Julie's stereo. A moment ago, they were giggling. Now they just listened to the music, and each other breathing. Julie was lying sideways on her bed. Tom fidgeted in a wicker chair—sinking into the cushion as he tried to summon light conversation. "So where did your mom go?"

"Boston. If she knew you were here, she'd *kill* me," Julie confessed with a naughty grin.

"You mean she didn't expect I'd sneak over and take advantage of you?" he asked with a rascally leer he wasn't sure he could live up to.

"No. She trusts you too much."

"Really?"

"So do I. What about your mom?"

"She's out with Paul, again. I'll be home before she gets back. Probably tomorrow."

"She lent you the car. Doesn't she care where you'll be?"

"She couldn't be bothered to care."

Julie smiled. "Don't be bitter with her. She needs love too, you know. I wish my mom would get out more often. It's lonely being a divorced parent."

"I guess." He kept dropping his gaze. Every time his eyes wandered, they landed on the graceful, feminine slope of her hips. He knew he had to make a move. Showtime, as Kevin would say. But if he made his approach—if they did what he was *thinking* they would do—he knew everything was going to change. There would be no more carefree bike rides and innocent trips to the mall. They would no longer be kids. He felt like a man about to dive off a cliff into unknown terrors and ecstasies. She waited for him, gazing now with strong affirmation. He felt a tremor in his knees and knew he was stalling.

"Ouch," she said, rising up from the bed. "This sweater is very itchy. Do you mind if I take it off?"

He smiled, tongue-tied. "No. Here. Let me help you."

He went to her side, and as he gently held the woolen garment, she pulled her arms out of the sleeves, exposing once again those luxurious white shoulders. She stood alluringly before him. The message in her eyes was starkly sexual. "I was thinking . . . Maybe—"

"Yeah?"

"Maybe . . . we could . . ." She put her arms around his neck. And then he was kissing her. Her soft lips were smothered against his. The taste of her lip gloss was like nectar.

His apprehension melted away instantly, and Tom fell into her embrace. Her quick tongue met with his own, and the kiss was long and lingering.

The lamps went out as if by magic, and they were together in the dark of her bedroom. The soft glow of the moon filtered through the window. She pulled the straps of her dress down off her shoulders, reached back to unzip, then let the dress fall down to her ankles. Soon she was revealed in silk panties and bra, the broad bands of her nylons black across her thighs. A halo of blue moonlight caressed her ghostly form. She kissed him again, pressing forcefully against his mouth until his face was pushed back. Her arms embraced him, and her leg rose up against his hip. He reached down and gripped it firmly, the flesh of his palm abrasive against the nylon. Then he kissed the smoothness under her chin, the long silky neckline below her ear. Her skin was like fresh cream.

His body trembled. He wanted her so badly.

Kevin's gift was in his pocket. Before he knew it, he was reaching for it.

Julie poked at the buttons on his shirt and slipped it off him. Bare-chested now, the touch of her fingers on his skin was electrifying. He ventured down her sides, to the swell of her hips, and soft cushions of her butt. Their bodies drew closer. The insatiable aroma of her perfume filled his senses.

His fingers traveled up and down her with intense physical awareness, and he was powerfully aroused.

Then suddenly—a *peculiar churning* below his ribcage.

It felt strange, like an engine had kicked into gear.

Her hands went to the top of his jeans. He stifled a gasp and went rigid to her touch. His mind filled with conflicts. Desire and fear in a tug-of-war. There was vacuum pressure in his midsection. The sensation distracted from his passion.

Was this normal? This churning, like a tornado in his belly?

It pulsed now, a throb of energy that seized up from his

abdomen in waves of desire. But the waves were siphoned off into a void. With every breath, it got stronger.

She tugged at his belt, searched for the buckle with exploring hands, and ever so slowly began unfastening it.

Pleasure transformed into uncertainty? *What's going on?*

Julie was oblivious to his mood shift. The strap of his belt was pulled through the buckle. She found his belly with her mouth. The touch of her lips kindled an alarming jolt of energy.

Snap! Suddenly he was outside his body, watching!

An alien viewpoint filled his vision, and he was looking down at himself. He saw Julie on her knees, caressing his midriff. His own body stood listless, as if in a trance. An intruding presence was in the room, and it had *stolen his eyes.* He felt its ravenous desire, a voracious *hunger* for the girl, and had the terrible dread that it would pounce on her delicate form and rip her to shreds!

"No!" With a gasp, he was back in his body. He grabbed her, and the vision fled. The torrent of energy receded from his midsection.

Startled by his firm grip, she gazed up into his eyes, sensing his turmoil.

"No?"

"Julie . . . We can't."

Her eyes registered a million emotions at once—yearning, rejection, and shame. "Did I do something wrong?"

"*No.*"

"I just wanted to . . . please you."

"I know."

"But I thought we were . . . I thought you wanted . . ."

"I *do.* I want to . . . really badly. But not now. Not . . . just yet."

She seemed baffled, and utterly embarrassed.

At that moment, he felt abominable. The fragile look in her eyes caused him to enfold her in his arms, hoping to repair the damage. Was he insane? Julie was about to fulfill every boy's adolescent fantasy. And, because of some sick, crazy hallucination, he was saying no?

He held her tight, still famished for the touch of her skin.

"Julie. Something wasn't right. I just think we should wait."

"Okay," she said vacantly. He felt her tremble a little, her disappointment melting into relief.

"Seemed like a good idea at the time," she joked, as though part of her agreed they were doing the right thing. He nodded with a forced smile. Then he got dressed, kissed her one more time, and left her for the night, chastising himself fiercely all the way home.

CHAPTER 46

Fau'Charoth flapped its great bat wings, catching a thermal of warm air that lifted it high above the countryside. Its keen yellow eyes blazed with a fury.

No longer the wraith of its previous flights, it was now clothed in living flesh, giving it mass and substance. Never had it worn such a shape as this. It was a good shape. The limbs were lengthy and strong, and the clawed fingers could grasp. The jaws were equipped with massive fangs for slashing. With this form it was free of limitations and more capable of destruction than in any of its previous incarnations. The leathery wings stretched outward as it glided swiftly, slicing through the thick October air. Fog brought a chill to its newly formed body.

It was alive.

Alive and voraciously hungry!

The desire was overwhelming. There was a terrible emptiness at its core. Passion was aroused in its host, and the wild, unfettered emotion spread like a contagion. Filling it with hunger. Tormenting it with need! A thirst for blood tingled in its jaws. Bestial savagery flared in its chest. Driven to distraction, it sped through the air in a rapacious frenzy.

An enticing scent reached its nostrils, and it soared toward a familiar structure below. A large barn appeared in the distance, surrounded by acres of grassy field. A tall rusty-brown silo stood beside it. The building throbbed with a memory its primitive mind could not identify. But something lured it like a magnet. Fau'Charoth snarled and dove into a steep descent.

It felt a terrible urge to kill.

The hairs bristled on Katie's neck as the golden retriever raised her head from the throw rug and sniffed the air, alert. Her shaggy ears pricked up, and there was a penetrating glint in her eyes.

The dog's movement was enough to arouse Sam Whateley. The old farmer lay beside his wife, caught in a limbo between sleep and awareness. Sleep was hard enough to come by for a man his age, but it was more than just insomnia that kept him awake. Whateley was tense these days. There was apprehension in his stride. Lancey had noted his mood change and dutifully questioned him to no avail. A shadow had pervaded his senses. He found he was glancing about himself, looking into the dark corners while tending chores on the farm, as though there were hidden eyes on him.

The old man sat up in bed, inexplicably disturbed. In the dark of the bedroom, eerie thoughts entered his mind—thoughts that reached to the very depths of his fears. Whateley wasn't an especially superstitious man. Before coming to Chapinaw, he had believed in Christ risen from the dead, celebrated it every Easter with his wife. Beyond that, his boots were firmly planted in the muddy earth, and he had no time for ghost stories. But inheriting this farm from his brother had changed things. The hills had tales to them—hearsay of witches that stretched way back to colonial times. The immigrants who settled this area had brought with them a Puritan paranoia that quickly routed out all forms of devilry. Yet the roots of evil penetrated deep into the earth and could not easily be extracted. Generations later, they sprouted through the topsoil, and the shroud of necromancy returned. It was a legacy Whateley bought into when he acquired this property. Now he clutched his Bible tightly and recited from it chapter and verse.

Terence had been an evil man. There was no love lost for his brother, gone now these fifteen years, shot dead in the barn—he and his wife—by the sheriff and his deputies. The man was wicked to the core. He aligned himself with the wizard, Tornau, and met a terrible end. Whateley imagined them burning together for all eternity. But some part of him dreaded that Hell could not contain such evil, and even now his brother's soul walked the Earth! It took a long time before Whateley could wander comfortably after dark. Now, years later, the dread was returning.

It began when he found the "witch" conjuring in his barn.

He'd found Parrish on his knees in a trance, disturbing

things that lay quiet in the ground. It chilled him to the bone that the man would somehow awaken Terence from his unholy slumber. He regretted he'd allowed Parrish to leave with little more than an idle threat. Better it would've been to have him arrested for trespassing, locked away from decent society.

Katie twitched her neck and whimpered.

Better it might've been to shoot the man dead where he stood and bury him up on the hilltop, where . . .

. . . where he unearthed the bones years ago as he tilled the soil on the northern border. Whateley knew they were the bones of a human being, slaughtered for some devilish purpose. The police had located the first four, but two more graves he found, the bodies scorched and dismembered. He remembered they were blackened with soot, the femurs cracked and charred, as from a hasty cremation. Against better judgment, he never reported his findings. The property was already tainted with evil history, and he didn't want to rekindle the memories in people's minds. There was a farm to run and livestock to bring to market. But he never planted in that soil again and had been uneasy ever since, gazing up at that blasted heath. To this day, there was something queer and unholy about the growths on that fearsome hillside. Even the weeds looked sparse and malformed.

He lay awake, listening to the sounds of his wife breathing. A moth tapped against the window. He slowly perceived a rhythmic throbbing, like the repetitive beating of a drum. His own fingers on the bed frame.

Something wasn't right.

He glanced at the dog. Katie stood rigid by the entrance to the door like a stone lion in front of a library.

"Whatcha got, girl?" he whispered. Katie sniffed, testing the air. Then she snarled.

Lancey woke with a start. "Luvva Jesus! What's got into the dog? Old Man?" Whateley was already dressed and putting on his boots. He opened the closet and withdrew his shotgun. He gripped it so tightly the veins in his arms bulged.

"Samuel!" Lancey shouted. "Where ya goin'?"

Katie raced from the room, yelping and barking in frenzy.

"Something's goin' after the hogs. They're hollerin'."

They could hear them squealing in terror. The normal grunting was replaced with a high-pitched shrieking. The color drained from Lancey's face as she gazed into her husband's eyes. Her skin was like parchment. He could see the blue lines of age scribbled in her features. "Sam! Don't go out there!"

He gave her a stern look and left the room before she could stop him. Before she could see how he was *shaking*. In the kitchen, he snatched up a flashlight, checking it for power.

He nearly tripped over Katie as the dog bolted to the front door ahead of him. He hesitated, even as Katie scratched the screen with her forepaws.

The front door creaked open, and Katie disappeared

into the night air, barking ferociously.

Lancey grabbed him firmly. "Don't go out there!" Whateley faced the terror in her eyes.

"Confound you, woman! Let me go! Something's got at the hogs!"

He pulled free of her and stepped into the dark, following after the dog. The shotgun was ready in his right hand, the flashlight shining in his left. The chill wind bit through his nightshirt, and his jaw muscles clamped tightly shut.

Outside, there were crashes and splintering sounds. And that ululant snorting of the hogs. Never had hogs made such a sound, more of a scream than a squeal. A tremulous shriek was cut short, and he knew a massacre was underway in the pen. His blood ran cold, and he pumped his shotgun, hearing the chamber clunk into position. It reassured him.

Something howled.

It was a sound unlike anything he had ever heard. Long and guttural, high-pitched like a banshee's wail, it gnawed its way deep into Whateley's gut.

The screaming stopped. The air was cool and heavy with silence.

Whateley heard the crunch of grass beneath his feet as he approached the barn. The moon provided enough light to see by, and enough shadows to shield a thousand horrors.

Something darted by him, nearly freezing his heart. He practically got a shot off when he realized it was the dog.

"Katie!"

The dog halted long enough to turn to her master. Her

eyes were timorous, and she whimpered nervously before racing back to the sanctuary of the house. "Fool dog!" Whateley cursed. "Go on wit' you!"

But Katie's frantic retreat crushed his boldness. The dog had never before been timid. His old heart was pounding now, and he knew it would serve him right if he fell dead from a stroke right there. But something in his ancient frame told him to go on. His legs were heavy as he proceeded.

Fool. Old fool.

The flash beam became a beacon in the mist.

A few pigs could be heard snorting and squealing as he neared the pen. A portion of the rails had been shattered *outward.* Splinters of wood littered the stiff mud below. He quivered and glanced about nervously. Then he shined the light into the pen.

What he saw caused him to utter a gasp of disgust.

"Uhhhhgh . . . Christ!"

Four of his prize hogs lay dead. Torn savagely apart. Pieces of carcass lie strewn about the pen, with clouds of mist rising from the glistening entrails. The survivors were huddled behind the slop-trough, which had been upturned. Whateley rested on the fence railing then quickly withdrew his palm from the wood. It was greased with thick blood. He promptly wiped the stickiness on his overalls.

A young pig lay in a corner, stiffened in death, yet still trembling. The carcass was unscathed, but the eyes were wide as the moon—dead of fright. Whateley felt bile rise up in his throat and cursed aloud in anger. But his voice rattled as he trembled. His knees were weak, until he had to hold himself from falling.

Something long and slimy caught his eye. It passed out through the smashed wall of the pen and snaked around the side of the barn. At first his mind played tricks on him, and he imagined it to be some dreadful serpent, slithering back to the bowels of Hell. He followed the glistening green thing with the flash beam, edging around the corner of the barn. There was a grunting snort.

His largest sow was standing along the barn's wall, staring blankly at him. It had wandered stupidly from the pen. Whateley saw the gaping wound in its belly. The "serpent" was its intestines, which had snagged along the splintered railing. A full eighteen feet had stretched and unraveled along the ground as the sow marched zombie-like to its death.

His own bowels churned at the sight. He raised his barrel to the hapless creature, and shot it dead with a single round.

The shot broke the silence like a thunderbolt.

Lancey's silhouette was standing in the doorway of the house, calling for him. "Samuel! Samuel!"

She seemed miles away. His knees trembled, and he felt rooted to the spot, unable to move. He feared he would collapse to the ground, knowing that if he did so, he would succumb to his terror and cry like a weeping child. Slowly, he forced life into his legs and began to walk toward the light of his front door. He prayed he would make it back to the house. Before whatever took the hogs came for him as well. He retraced his steps, forbidding himself to run. He heard more nervous squeals from the hogs and dared to look back.

And for some crazy reason, he looked *up* toward the roof.

As he did so, he saw a tremendous shape rise from the top of the barn, unfolding its wings against the night sky. It gave off a hideous wail, like the cry of a thousand spirits lost to wandering. The flying shadow ascended into the air, circling the sky above the farm, before vanishing into the night.

CHAPTER 47

THE SUNDAY MORNING SKY WAS THICK WITH FOG AS Tom drove the hill up Latham Road.

He couldn't recall ever taking this route. Everything beyond the Crohaven Estate was new territory, but the landscape seemed hauntingly familiar. He recognized the rotted fence posts along the road and the endless fields of straw, having seen it all previously . . . in his dream.

The night before, he once again left the boundaries of his sleeping body and soared away.

But this dream was no pleasant moon voyage. This dream was a gory nightmare. Like the attack on his father, it was unbelievably tangible, the image—the *sensations*—still crisp in his head.

As Tom drove up the crest of the hill, his heart beat in anticipation. He had to verify the image. He had to know if what he'd seen in his crazy zoetrope of a brain bore any element of reality. The road ahead smelled of insanity, but there was no turning back. The visions were uncannily vivid, much more so than before. Visions of a farm he had visited during his "travels" the previous night. As surely as he drove this car, he had traveled to that farm.

The evening began as paradise.

He had been with Julie. Her feminine charms cast a powerful spell over him, and as their desires flared, they became passionately physical. So close they were to having sex.

But at the height of his passion, a strange energy blazed in his midsection. It was a primal eruption strangely detached, like a sinister voyeur that fed off his lust. It hurled him into confusion and caused him to withdraw from their lovemaking. Poor Julie was left baffled and disappointed.

At home, he experienced a terrible onslaught of regret and self-abasement. In a fit of unbearable loneliness, a great fire raged in his solar plexus.

And then: *Snap!*

He went aloft again in his dreams. The frightening memory now haunted him. He remembered the pigs.

Bloody pigs. Squealing in terror.

He saw them tramping before him in a pen. Heard the squealing and hollering, splashing through mud as they pressed against one another in terror.

Whoosh! He fell like judgment from the sky!

A hog crushed beneath him, and with a quick swipe, its throat tore out. Blood splashed out in dark fountains. The smell of gore assaulted Tom's nostrils. The crimson fluid was hot on his skin. He heard a bellow from his own jaws.

Another hog savaged. Spilled entrails, with steam

rising out of them. A pink carcass quivered in death. His fangs gleamed red, tearing through the porcine hide!

A partridge fluttered from the side of the road.

Startled, Tom snapped back to the present and found himself once again in the car, traveling the country road, looking for something.

"It was just a dream. Just a dream!" he repeated to himself like a mantra.

The fog cleared.

Blue-gray clouds draped the horizon like brushstrokes in a dreary watercolor. Houses were sparse in this area. He scanned the sprawling fields, trying to match the landscape to what he saw in his sleep. It had been dark, but the moon was out. He recalled a large blackish barn, and a—

The car came to a screeching halt.

—a towering red-brown silo surrounded by weathered rails of wind-beaten fencing. A small white house that hadn't been painted for years and what appeared to be—his knuckles whitened as he gripped the steering wheel—a spacious animal pen!

Tom gazed at the Whateley farm as though it were a mirage. His breath intensified, and he could feel blood pounding in his temples. Even from this distance, his suspicions were confirmed. There was no desire to go closer. Indeed, he felt the grave urgency to steer the car around and leave at maximum speed, the way a criminal flees the scene of a crime.

CHAPTER 48

SHERIFF KRONIN SAVORED THE COOL GLASS OF WATER Lancey poured for him. As soon as he had drunk his fill, he popped another mint into his mouth and began to chomp on it. He needed it to wash away the flavor of bile that had risen to his mouth at the sight of the carnage. No trip to the Whateley farm could ever be pleasant for him. From the moment he got the call, Kronin's gut told him to fear the worst. Lancey's description over the phone had been disturbing enough, but nothing could have prepared him for what he saw.

Six hogs were mutilated. Torn to shreds by something big and mean. By what, he couldn't say. There was something monstrous in the way the carcasses were strewn about, randomly tossed after disembowelment. Only one corpse showed signs of being devoured. Whatever killed those hogs did so out of sheer delight. His first assumption, before witnessing the carnage for himself, was that some marauding pranksters had gone on a killing spree. Perhaps they had selected the location because of its history, and wanted to strike terror into the community. But these hogs weren't shot or stabbed with conventional weapons. They were gutted and torn up right in the pen, surrounding by over a dozen fully grown animals. This made Kronin doubt a human killer. You don't climb into a sty and attack a hog with its friends watching you. Some of those boars were the size of Saint Bernards—mean mothers with tusks and fangs that could rip you to pieces. A man would have a tough time keeping them at bay, unless they were *afraid of him.*

"And you didn't see anything?" he asked the old woman.

"Nothing, 'cept what's out there," Lancey answered. "But Sam swears he saw . . . well, I can't rightly say *what* he saw. And Katie came runnin' in like she'd seen a ghost."

"Whatever it was, it had to be big," Kronin remarked. "And mighty powerful. Have you ever had any trouble like this before?"

"We had a coyote early on in the year, attackin' the chickens. But it never went after the pigs. The boars would give it a run, for sure, if it tried to get to the littl'ins."

"What about a bear?"

She looked doubtful. "Never seen one around here. Figurin' it was a bear?"

"I don't know. I didn't see any tracks."

That was the thing. No tracks. Nothing unusual in the mud surrounding the barn. As though whatever it was had appeared and vanished within the confines of the pen. The ground was soft. Anything else would have left prints of some kind. No prints anywhere.

Except for those strange markings he found in the pen itself. Sort of three-toed scrapings, like a bird's. But they were trampled over with the hoof prints, and Kronin figured his eyes were playing tricks on him. Hell, he was chasing ghosts just being near that barn. The phantom pain in his shoulder began to ache again.

"Tell 'im about the witch," Whateley called from the porch. He sat with a bottle of whiskey in his hand, staring bleary eyed at the hilltop. There was a slight tremor in his wrist, but Kronin assumed it was due to the alcohol.

Lancey scowled and turned to the sheriff. "We had us a 'visit,' a few weeks back from that Mr. Parrish. The one from Crohaven? Sam claims he was in the barn chanting spells."

"What?" The sheriff resisted the impulse to curse. This was trouble of a different sort. What was Stephen up to?

"Raisin' the dead. That's what he was doin'," the old farmer snorted derisively.

"He hasn't slept at all," Lancey said, dismissing his husband's drunken ravings. Kronin nodded and decided to join the man on the porch. He didn't look up when the sheriff approached him.

"Sam, I'm gonna send some men over here to clean up the mess. We'll get that vet over from Grumbach to do a postmortem on the carcasses. Then we'll have folks from the forensics labs at Cornell University come over and investigate the crime scene. Maybe we'll get some idea what we're dealing with."

"I figure ya ain't gonna find anything," Whateley grumbled.

"Now, we don't know that. These guys don't miss a trick. They can take samples from the wounds, tooth measurements from the gashes, saliva drippings. With all their fancy equipment, I'm sure something will come up."

Whateley scoffed. "Whatever that thing was, it left no marks what yer gonna identify. You see . . . there ain't no book what's ever been written gonna put a name to that thing, 'ceptin' maybe Revelations."

Kronin didn't know how to respond to this. These old coots could get sorrowfully lost in their superstitions. He'd seen it all before. Any cloud that passed before the moon became a harbinger for the Second Coming, or one of the "seven signs" recorded in the final book of the Bible. Triple sixes. Antichrists. Beasts of the Apocalypse. It got so that he couldn't hold a twenty-minute conversation with them without being reminded of Judgment Day.

Maybe Whateley was crazy, after all. Maybe he had taken an axe to his own hogs, haunted by some insane recollection of his brother. Or maybe it was just the whiskey talking.

"Well," he concluded. "We'll have them take a look anyhow." He nodded to the man, and to Lancey, and went on his way back to the patrol car.

The morning sun had peeked through the clouds and washed the surrounding terrain with a golden glow. He could smell the sweet scent of rotting apples gathered at the base of the fruit trees on the lawn. If he focused his nose to it, he could also catch the scent of blood coming from the barn. He glanced again at the foreboding gray structure.

Something caught his eye. "What the . . . ?"

He quickly reached into the front seat of his car and pulled out a pair of binoculars. He held them to his eyes and gazed at the sloping roof of the barn. The flavor of bile rose again in his throat. His mouth fell open in morbid fascination.

"God . . . damn," he said in a whisper to himself.

From below, it was skewed from view and easily missed. It didn't surprise him that he had overlooked it. Besides, he was preoccupied with the slaughter in the pen. He had searched for tracks in the mud, scrapings on the wood, even fur samples that might have caught along the fence. He presumed naturally that the perpetrator had been earthbound.

He had never thought to look *up*!

There it was, along the slanting roof, clearly visible in the noon light.

Blood.

Long stains of blood and gore, and globs of meaty tissue that had dropped onto the roof. The gnawed corpse of a piglet was stuck on the tiles!

The sheriff scratched his head in disbelief.

Whatever it was, it had ended its gory onslaught *up there.*

The patrol car pulled along the side of Crohaven Road, where Parrish was leaving the cemetery. Kronin gazed out at Stephen with the tired eyes of law enforcement.

"I should arrest you for trespassing," he said, too unnerved for a confrontation.

Parrish understood the nature of his visit almost immediately. It didn't take a psychic to predict what was coming. The sheriff stepped out of the car.

"I warned you not to go snooping around the Whateley place," he continued. "You got old Sam ranting on about the end of the world."

Parrish turned to him defensively. "I would have preferred to follow proper procedure, but you left me no choice. I didn't intend any harm."

"Do you know anything about a hog massacre?"

This took Parrish by surprise. "A what?"

"Something went after his livestock last night. Something big! He has six hogs that look like they passed through a meat grinder. I found one of the little ones high up on the roof!"

"I don't know anything about it," Parrish said, dumbfounded. "Did you say the *roof*?"

Kronin cleared his throat and nodded. He was aching for a cigarette. "Damnedest thing I ever saw. And you *know* I've seen some weird shit at that place."

"I don't know what to tell you." It disturbed him on an intuitive level. A livestock massacre at the Whateley barn? What was he missing?

"I'm sending in the troops on this one," Kronin said. "We're having the carcasses examined to see what the hell we're dealing with. A large animal, a bear, most likely. Maybe more than one. But Whateley seems to think it was something else. Something from 'Hell's abyss.' I guess he figured *you'd* know something about that."

"I don't."

"Well, you better keep your eyes open. Whatever it was, it may still be lurking about this area." The sheriff reached into his pocket and pulled out another mint, wishing again that it was a Marlboro. He stuffed it into his mouth and glanced at the psychic. "So, you went in and did your little investigation, after all. Did you find anything?"

Parrish sighed and delivered the news like a eulogy. "There were two more sacrifices at the barn, as I suspected. A teenaged girl and a black woman. You'll find the remains buried on the property. Speak to Whateley about it. He knows. And there was one more, as well."

"Another one?"

"Sarah Halloway."

Kronin raised his brows. "He killed Sarah too? Christ."

"Retribution of some sort, my guess. It was Sarah who made the call, wasn't it? The one alerting you to the ritual."

"That's right," Kronin answered, revealing details he'd kept to himself for years. His voice echoed into the past as though he were experiencing a psychic flashback as vividly as Parrish had. "The call came in only a half hour before. She demanded immunity first, and then told us everything. She must have become maternally sympathetic at the last moment. Murdering moms and schoolgirls was all right in her book, but she found a conscience over the baby. There were only two squad cars in the vicinity, and the state troopers would never get there in time, so we rushed in to save the child. When we got there, we saw things . . ." He looked suddenly pained. "You can't imagine."

"I saw. I *can* imagine."

"Sarah insisted we round her up with the others to avoid suspicion. She failed to warn us the cult was *armed*. Stupid bitch. When she fled the scene with the others she became a fugitive. We couldn't help her. I guess Tornau caught on to her and killed her."

"Evidently."

"Can you locate her remains? She still has family."

Parrish recalled the image of the woman thrust bodily into the vortex. "There *are* no remains. She's *lost*."

Kronin lowered his eyes in grim finality, then clenched his jaw. "Maybe someday I'll cry, but not today. She got what was coming to her. Murdering bitch. She made "Squeaky" Fromme look like an amateur."

"Don't judge her too harshly, Kurt. Tornau's influence was all consuming. It's a wonder she found the strength in the end to defy him. She helped save that child, and paid with her life."

"Yeah. The only reward in that entire ordeal was returning the baby to its parents. The look in the mom's eyes . . . I'll never forget it. They moved away pretty quickly after that."

"The DeFranks?"

Kronin's eyes flared. "That was classified. *How do you know that?*"

Parrish grinned. "I got lost on another of my ghost hunts." He considered sharing his discovery of the tunnel, but that would lead to a formal investigation. Detectives would invade the site, unequipped for the potential hazards. It would have to remain a mystery a while longer, until he and Humphrey Culhane could do a thorough examination. They were meddling with terrible powers, but he saw no other way.

Something was active in that tunnel. Something dangerous.

Kronin surrendered with a frown. "Promise me you'll steer clear of the Whateley farm from now on, Stephen. It's my haunt." He returned to the car with a shuffling gait.

Parrish offered a final comment. "When I was *reading* the barn, I witnessed your heroic moment during the big raid. Nice catch." It sounded glib, but he meant it with respect.

The sheriff eyed him curiously.

"You took a bullet to save that baby. It was very brave of you."

Kronin nodded, shaking off the compliment with a shrug, and then rubbed his shoulder. "Still hurts on a rainy day."

CHAPTER 49

Tom was glad to be back home. It was still early, barely 10:00 AM. Though his mom had still not returned from the night before, he shut the bedroom door, seeking privacy as though his very thoughts could leak out and be heard. His nerves were raw, and trembling.

The image was true! The farm was exactly as he envisioned it! It had been too fantastic to believe at first, but he was convinced now that the rampage at the hog farm actually occurred!

Glitch! Another shift in the continuity.

Tom fell heavily onto his bed. He examined his train of thought and found it to be preposterous. Absurd! "This is crazy!" he said aloud. "I've seen too many horror movies!" There was an internal boundary in the mind that could distinguish illusion from reality. That boundary had become significantly blurred.

It just wasn't possible. It defied sanity. It defied *science*!

But madness prevailed. It was real! All these years he labored, conceiving dragons, vivifying them for the world.

He had found the speckled egg and nourished it with his own warmth. Now the egg hatched—the emerging creature too magnificent for him to behold.

He played over the images again and again, revisiting the horrible carnage. Soon, he was able to distinguish not only the details, but the very passions he felt. There was such a glorious feeling of power! An intense primordial savagery. It tapped within him the hunger of a predator. He now understood that hunger for what it was: the purest form of lust. It was being projected somehow into his dreams. And from there outward! Into the world!

Crazy! Crazy! He gripped his head in bewilderment.

The phenomenon was outrageous. It defied even the logic of astral projection. From what he'd learned, AP was a form of remote viewing. You traveled to locations as a disembodied spirit, a vaporous cloud of consciousness. But this was no ghost. Ghosts could not break through fences. Ghosts did not attack animals and devour their flesh!

And the most unnerving part of all was that . . . it felt good!

As frightened as he was, he felt strangely energized, fueled with anticipation and delight. He wanted to experience it again, if only to confirm it was real! One more time, for sanity's sake. Maybe there was some way to control it.

Tom located the occult book he'd checked out of the library and reviewed the chapter on the astral realm. It described the plane of consciousness immediately above the physical, the realm of the emotions where thought-forms lingered and souls departed to after death. It was here also that the astral body visited during sleep. As the living shell sank into slumber, the spirit wandered in an unconscious state to this other dimension, where the very landscape was transient and subject to the heart's desires.

Some people had the ability, natural or acquired, to enter the realm willfully. They were, thus, presented with a wealth of extraordinary possibilities. AP could be used to travel through time and space. One could explore the moons of Saturn, or visit the Serengeti during the Pleistocene. Many accounts of bilocation, accorded to saints and yogis, were in fact astral projections. They appeared literally in two places at once, at the blink of an eye! To perfect out-of-body travel was the goal of many a practiced magician, for it allowed transmigration to distant places, both in astral and (to the highly advanced) *physical* form.

Another phenomenon was the "doppelganger" or *tulpa*, as it was referred to in Eastern texts. This was the creation of a second entity, an astral double that shared the consciousness of the host. There were reports of holy men, especially in Tibet, who, through intense concentration and visualization, projected these tulpas to carry out a distant project, or serve as a stand-in for themselves. Once the project was completed, the astral double was reabsorbed into the host. An account of Alexandra David-Peel described a tulpa she created in the form of a short, fat monk. It accompanied her and her servants on a long journey, and took on a personality of its own. Soon, the party was asking about the "mysterious stranger" who had joined them. When she chose to reabsorb it, the entity offered great resistance, refusing to allow its destruction. The process went on for six months.

Tom reread the section, awestruck, and felt a tingle of excitement. Was this truly what he was experiencing? It seemed farfetched, yet it explained so much. His monstrous alter ego could manifest itself physically and was taking form as a living creature! It could reach into the most savage, primordial side of his fantasies, and act upon them.

Act upon them. He thought again about the attack on his father and the massacre at the farm. Could such a thing become dangerous? How could he learn to command such an ungodly force?

He thought about Julie. About the strange way *it* viewed her in the bedroom, with a yearning lust that bordered on carnivorous. It caused him to shutter. The possibility of sex had released something inside him. Those lustful impulses, normally corralled obediently in his subconscious, were loose and free to engage. He sensed that the "creature" savored that essence like sweet nectar. His withdrawal last night frustrated it. Sent it on a rampage.

If the pig slaughter was the result of his resisting sex, what if he indulged? Would that placate it somehow? Or make it worse.

He recalled how it savaged the hogs, remembered its hunger for Julie, and—

No! That would never happen!

Tom walked into the living room and grabbed the telephone. Crouched in a lotus position on the couch, he dialed her number. He needed to speak to Julie. Right now.

She answered in a sleepy morning voice, "Hi."

"How are you doing?"

"O-kay."

Hearing her voice soothed him with relief. The insanity of the past hour began to subside. "I guess we left things in a weird place, last night," he said to her.

"Kind of. I'm sorry," she said. "I shouldn't have come on so strong."

"Don't apologize, Julie. I was a little nervous. That's all. I was alone with you in your bedroom, and I got so excited I lost my focus. It was just so overwhelming."

"Really?"

"Julie . . ." He summoned all the charm he could muster. "You're the most gorgeous thing I've ever seen, and you were stripping naked right in front of me."

She snickered bashfully. "I guess it was quite a show."

"Knocked me for a loop."

"Next time I'll put on sitar music and do a feather dance."

"Good. I'll bring my camera."

"Tommy!" She laughed. "Thanks. I was a little worried. And just so you understand . . . I was nervous myself."

"You were?"

"Terrified."

Tom smiled, grateful for the disclosure. Thinking about Julie in her underwear, glowing in the moonlight, he felt a tingle of renewed desire. He needed to be with her again to undo last night's mistake. "Maybe we can get together, later."

"I don't know." She sounded doubtful. "My mom's on her way home. She'll probably be here in an hour or two."

He sighed, disappointed. Their wonderful chance for intimacy was lost.

They talked on for half an hour about trivial subjects. Neither addressed the awkward events any further. When he hung up, he felt greatly relieved, as though an enormous weight had been lifted. He returned to his bedroom and sat in his work chair.

Tom gazed at the creature model on the tabletop.

"What are you?" he asked aloud. "What the hell are you?"

The puppet stared back vacuously. It was only made of rubber and steel. The sheer insanity of it all caused Tom to laugh. He felt suddenly very foolish. "I'm going wacko," he chuckled. "This is all too much. No more animating. I need to stop it for a while." He looked again at the puppet, as though asking permission. "I need to stop."

And he *did* stop. For a while.

But he was animating it again before nightfall.

CHAPTER 50

MONDAY NIGHT FOOTBALL PLAYED ON THE OVERHEAD TV at Gary's Tavern. Long-legged farmers in jeans lined the bar like livestock at a trough, downing their beers and chatting. The tavern was a popular after-hours hangout. Its location just off Route 17B made it a favorite watering hole for both the local yokels, returning from the fields and factories, and the travelers staying next door at the Aspen Motel. Nina, the tavern's barkeep wiped a spill of Budweiser off the countertop as the Dallas Cowboys took on the Green Bay Packers on the small screen above. But tonight the game was largely ignored, and Nina was even asked to lower the volume on the set.

There was a heated discussion underway. Sam Whateley, the old hog farmer from Latham Road, sat at one of the side tables. Everybody had heard about the strange slaughter of Whateley's hogs, and the talk coming down sounded like a political debate.

"Pack of wild dogs, for sure."

"Naw, that don't explain the blood on the roof," said

Whateley.

"An eagle, maybe, or a hawk. I saw a red-tailed hawk take a raccoon once."

"No shit?"

"Just plucked 'im outta the tree like a piece of fruit."

"Well, this weren't no hawk, I'll tell you that."

"Grizzly bear."

"There ain't no grizzly bears in New York! Even a big Blackie couldn't have made this kind of mess. Besides which, there were no tracks." Whateley chugged at his third beer of the evening, and his gaze was intense. "I tell you, there's something abroad as shouldn't oughta be abroad, and I for one figger that witch out at Crohaven to be at the bottom of it."

"Stephen Parrish?" asked Carl the mailman. "Now, how do you figure that, Sam?"

"He was at my place just a while ago, him and that beanpole daughter of his. I was out slopping the hogs and caught him conjuring spells in my barn."

"He was in your barn?"

"Yee-up. There he was, a-rolling in the straw, singing and chanting, making noises as could rob a man's sleep for a week. Asked what business he had in my barn, he says he was a 'psychic 'vestigator' something or other. Fancy, newfangled word, I reckon. Don't need a college education to know a witch when I see one. No telling what kind of devilish powers he has. Had to take a pitchfork to him to get him out!"

"Aw, you're puttin' me on," another patron scoffed. "There ain't no such things as devils and witches."

Whateley looked at him sharply. "If'n you'd seen my hogs as they were, all torn up like they'd been chewed and spit out, you'd be wonderin'."

"But you're not saying Parrish had anything to do with *that*, are you, Sam?" asked Carl.

"Well, I figure it's kinda funny, him chantin' and raisin' a ruckus, and then my farm gets attacked by something such as never been around before. Caught a glimpse of it as I made my way back to the house. It took off from the roof of my barn like the biggest damn vulture you ever saw! It made a sound too. A scream as could not have come from anything born on Earth. Don't mind tellin' you, it had me trembling in my boots!"

There was an ominous silence as everyone sipped on his or her drinks.

"Always wondered if what they say is true," Pete Driscoll spoke up.

"About what?"

"About Parrish. I heard a story years ago that he died and came back to life."

"Yeah, I heard that too. Car accident, I think. Pronounced dead and everything."

"That's a load of hogwash!" contributed another man. "No one can come back from the dead, lest he's Lazarus who had the hand of Jesus to help him!"

"Or the devil."

"I think all y'all are a bunch of paranoid delusionists. Parrish ain't got no magical powers. Just a little twisted in the head is all. I heard he's a Buddhist."

"I heard he's a Hindu."

"Same thing."

"Meditates and believes in 'reincarnation.' Do you believe in reincarnation, Carl?"

"Sure, when I was in 'Nam. But that was the sixties."

"I believe I'll have another beer!" Laughter.

"Yeah, all those Hindus are witches, anyway. Ya ever see those statues with all the arms and elephant heads? Maybe those kind *do* reincarnate, figurin' they got nowhere else to go, 'cept to Hell."

"You think that's what Parrish was doing when he came back to life? Reincarnating?"

"The way I figure it, maybe he's Jacob Tornau, risen from the grave."

This caused a hush throughout the entire bar.

"Well, he lives in that big house, belonging to the 'black wizard,' and all. And there are all those rumors about him reading minds. What was that thing with the Wilkens kid? Wasn't he involved with that? Hypnotized the boy or something?"

"Sounds suspicious to me," said a familiar voice from behind. The men looked up, suddenly embarrassed. It was *Gerard Wilkens.*

Carl turned a whiter shade of pale. "Hey, Gee."

"How're you doing, Gerard?"

"Yeah, sorry about to hear about Connie."

Wilkens had the determined gaze of a man searching for meaning after a terrible misfortune. He had buried his wife only three days earlier. Poor Connie had ceased her long fight with the cancer at last.

Carl dipped his eyes uncomfortably. "We were just having a little discussion."

"So I heard." Gerard pulled up a seat beside them. "I figure if you're talking about Stephen Parrish, I ought to be in on it." He put his eyes squarely on Whateley as he said this.

Nina switched the TV channel to the news, hoping it would drown out the unpleasant discussion.

But no one was listening to it.

CHAPTER 51

THINGS LOOKED DIFFERENT AFTER YOU'VE SEEN THEM through the eyes of a monster.

Two more days of animating. Two more nights of eerie out-of-body travel. The framework of Tom's reality was beginning to blur. Yet he remained oblivious to any danger and continued on with his "project" like a compulsive nineteenth-century explorer searching for the North Pole.

It was Wednesday morning, three days after the hog massacre at the Whateley farm. The effects of astral travel and the long hours of stop-motion were taking its toll on him. He clicked off his last frame around 2:00 AM the night before and climbed into bed. His legs ached from the incessant journey back and forth from camera to tripod, and his eyes could barely focus.

But rather than sleep, he projected outward and found himself creeping through a deserted campsite deep in the woods. There were log bungalows filled with steel-framed bunk beds in a clearing of pine trees. The summer campers were long gone, but their astral patterns still lingered.

His diaphanous alter ego could sense the memory of children, sitting around a campfire, singing songs, roasting marshmallows. They delighted in ghost stories and cowered in dread at the night sounds. But they were gone now, and what remained was like a damp mist after a rainfall. Fau'Charoth took to the air and circled the shoreline, a famished predator in search of prey. Tom could feel its restlessness. It was hungry.

He awoke again at six-thirty feeling lightheaded and weak. As he rose from bed, the cool morning air caused another chill attack that left him shivering. He clutched himself and crawled back under the covers, the freezing tremors racking his body. Was he sick? Was there a flu bug going around? Or was this some new symptom of his bizarre condition? Tom lay in bed an additional hour, until his core temperature was restored. He wondered if he could make it to school. It didn't seem hopeful at that moment—with the ceiling spinning like a top above him.

How could I be such a dope? he scolded himself. Staying up so late to animate. Now he had to summon the strength to get to school. He clenched his teeth, pulled himself out of bed, and fiercely repelled any remaining chill.

I can't be sick! he thought to himself. *I need to see Julie today.* Their conversation Sunday morning had dispelled any immediate concerns about Saturday, but the last two days were awkward. He no longer reached for her hand. She had to take it. His arm didn't circle her waist the way it once did. And they kissed less frequently, like they were still finding their way back to one another. Was he afraid of her now? Had he lost that precious spark of desire?

Or was he fearful of that peculiar sensation he increasingly experienced whenever he looked at her. It was like Fau'Charoth lurked just beneath his skin, hungering for Julie. Ready to pounce like a lion on an antelope. It wanted a taste of her.

Tom dragged his shivering body into the bathroom and plunged himself into a scalding shower.

Two hours later, in school, he only felt worse.

He wandered the halls, disembodied and detached from everything. His mind was hazy, and he experienced moments of vertigo as though he were spiraling off his feet. During these spells, his vision shimmered slightly, veiled as if in a stupor. Walking through the building became an ordeal. His depth perception seemed reduced. Once he nearly bombarded into a door as though he had expected to walk through it. It was as if he couldn't distinguish illusion from reality.

He went into a bathroom and hid in a stall.

What's going on?

A wave of nausea struck him, but it didn't quite surface enough to vomit.

During his next class, Social Studies, he phased out and for a moment found himself floating above the classroom. He gazed down at his own body, slumped in his chair. Mr. Witkowski was lecturing at the front of the room about westward migration and the Turner Thesis. Hovering above, he saw that the tall man had a patch of baldness forming at the top of his head. As though sensing the boy's scrutiny, Witkowski called his name out. The voice jolted him back and caused him to gaze about disoriented.

"Are you getting enough sleep, Mr. DeFrank?" the teacher inquired.

"Yeah," he answered, wide-eyed.

Witkowski stood over him, studying the whites of his orbs. Tom knew what he was looking for—signs of drug use.

"Son, are you on something?" he asked in a low voice. The direct question startled Tom and caused him to flush red. There were gasps of hushed laughter throughout the classroom.

"No," he responded as sincerely as possible. "Well . . . I've been feeling sick all morning, and I took an antihistamine for my sinuses. I think it's the kind that makes you drowsy." The answer seemed to satisfy the man, and he kneeled down to look Tom evenly in the eye. "Why don't you go to the nurse, Tom? You don't look well at all."

Tom nodded gratefully to the teacher, trying to avoid thinking about his bald spot.

Back from the nurse's office, Tom shuffled past the crowd, making his way for the front of the library. He knew he had to get home. The nurse had granted him full exemption from his torment—a release slip for sickness. He could take the local bus from town and be home in forty minutes. And he would lie in bed until the world stopped spinning. No animating.

No more animating!

But he couldn't leave without at least seeing Julie and tell her he was leaving. This was their usual midday encounter spot, where they would meet for a brief chat and quick rejuvenating kiss. Tom saw her first, standing against the wall, going through her book bag. She had her hair tied back behind her ears. He was eager to see her, speak to her, touch her.

Something gripped him tightly in the stomach. That churning, like turbines in an engine.

His apprehension resurfaced like a deep-sea vessel. The world was spinning. He was suddenly very afraid.

Tom hesitated, and then turned and fled before she noticed him.

CHAPTER 52

"CYNTHIA, CENTER STAGE RIGHT," MISS DELMONTE directed, "and don't lose eye contact. David, speak up; I can't hear you." The actors complied, shifting their positions on the school stage. Behind them, a member of the tech crew was taking measurements off one of the new flats, which was undergoing a paint job.

The stage was expansive, somewhat larger than the small play required. The navy-blue curtains were drawn a third of the way in to reduce the excess space. Microphones were in place to enhance the sound, and the new lighting console was being installed backstage by technicians. Overhead, theatrical lamps shone down onto the proscenium. As the lights were adjusted, the gelled hotspots occasionally fell upon the performers in bright halos.

Miss Delmonte sat in the third row, taking notes on a legal pad as she watched the students on stage rehearse a scene from *Dark Victory*. She gripped the black rims of her glasses as though they were field binoculars.

"Project. You're not projecting," she called out. "David,

move closer to her."

Julie watched from stage left. She had just completed her walk-on, but enjoyed watching the others rehearse. David Jacobsen was performing the lead role of an English doctor. She admired David's performance. He was in just about every play Julie had seen in Chapinaw High, and was obviously very serious about acting. She regretted they hadn't found time to get better acquainted. Julie wished to pick his brain for advice about her own acting ambitions. David was a sweet guy.

She wandered backstage to where the techies were working. The lighting console was a five-foot rectangle of angled board covered with slide dials and knobs. Although her magazine sales weren't great, she knew her efforts had purchased a small part of the machine. Randy Moore, the lighting designer, stood on stage with a clipboard, cueing light positions just behind the actors. He called out to Alex Lugones at the console, who adjusted the settings. With each slide of a lever, a gelled light adjusted its radiance.

"Bring up number six about ten percent. That's good."

One of the overhead spots came on and shined onto the performers.

Janine Meadows came out of a dressing room with Suzanne. As female lead, she was on the set for most of the production. There was no avoiding her. Julie had managed so far to coexist with the girl, but Janine's presence had certainly put a damper on her theatrical experience. Try as she might, she didn't feel particularly welcome among the cast and was forced to keep company with the crew.

She felt a little lonely. According to Danny, Tom had gone home sick. He appeared more rundown than usual, claiming the flu. But she knew it was more than that. The boy had retreated emotionally since their heated petting session. Seducing him like a cheap hooker had not been her brightest idea.

What was she thinking?

Why don't I just doll up like a tramp and force the guy to have sex with me? Julie cringed, remembering herself in heels and nylons, barely able to walk, her face painted like a kabuki dancer. She deserved the "booby" prize of the year. No wonder Tom practically fled from her in terror. They say girls mature faster than boys do. Maybe he simply wasn't ready for it.

Julie sat alongside the flier cables, where she finished the remains of a Pepsi. Janine and Suzanne were talking in hushed tones, snickering. An occasional glance her way made Julie self-conscious. She hoped she was imagining it, but then she heard them hum a familiar theme song.

"Bah-dump. Bah-dump. Bah-dump-dump dump, da-dump!"

She recognized the theme from the TV show *Bewitched*, and frowned, knowing she had become the butt of their joke. Now, they were laughing outright. She turned her back, choosing to ignore them, but in an act of uncharacteristic camaraderie, Janine actually approached her.

"Hi, Julie."

"What's up, Janine?"

"Suzanne and I were wondering if you had spoken to your dad yet, and what he was planning to do about the 'situation' with Crohaven Manor."

"What situation?"

"You mean you haven't heard . . . oh, I'm sorry." A devious smile formed. "I thought you two could *communicate*. You know. '*Mind meld*'."

Suzanne turned red, giggling.

Julie tossed her soda can into an overflowing trash bin and began walking away. "Very funny. Hah hah."

"No, wait." Janine stopped her. "What we mean is has your father been aware of what's going on?"

She leered at her, impatiently. "Janine, what are you talking about?"

"My dad was at a bar the other night. *Gee* Wilkens was there, and he and some others were discussing how Crohaven Manor should be sold. They say it's a drain on the economy."

Julie felt her blood rush. "That's bullshit. It's a landmark."

"Nuh-uhh. Wilkens is petitioning the town council to reconsider. When they get enough signatures, the estate will go on the block. His company will buy it, and your dad will lose his job."

Julie was dumbfounded by the news.

"Yeah," Suzanne added. "Everyone's talking about it. I heard the churches are involved. They're concerned about your dad's anti-Christian practices and want him expelled."

"His *what*?" She was at the breaking point. "Suzanne, you're so full of it!"

"She is not," Janine defended her. "They're saying he's a deviant and a devil worshipper. They're gonna run him out of town."

"Don't say that about my father!" she shouted.

Her voice echoed through the rafters and distracted the performers on stage. David and Cynthia glanced back at them. Bill twisted in his chair from the lighting board. "Shhhh!"

But Julie felt her pulse rise. "That's a cruel and malicious thing to say, Janine!"

"I'm just telling you like it is." Janine shrugged and turned away, continuing with a whisper. "Hey, they got *my* vote, the perv."

Julie grabbed her by the shoulder, spun her around, and slapped her hard across the cheek. It happened so fast that Janine was stunned. For a moment, Julie could see the imprint of her own hand on the girl's face. "*There's* some hocus-pocus for you!" she shouted.

Janine let off a girlish growl and flung herself at Julie, grabbing thick handfuls of hair. Julie's head smacked against one of the flier posts, and it smarted terribly. She resisted the pain, tears forming in her eyes, and fought back. Unleashing her full fury, she pressed Janine to the wall and collapsed with her onto a pile of canvas flats.

"You bitch!" she screamed.

"Witch!" Janine countered.

Cast and crewmember gathered round. They were spellbound, watching the girls flail at one another. Some of the guys enjoyed the spectacle, cheering on their favorites.

"C'mon, Julie!"

"You can take her, Janine!"

"Somebody call someone!"

" 'Doctor Bombay! Doctor Bombay'!" There was laughter, now.

Julie managed to get the upper hand, tugging at the girl's sweater. Janine was on the defensive, not used to backing her taunts with action. Julie put a headlock on the girl, who struggled fiercely. Randy came in from the stage, joining Bill, who reached to get a grip on Julie. Together, they pulled her off the furious Miss Meadows. David and Cindy were watching now, as well.

Miss Delmonte stormed in. "What the hell is going on here?"

"Parrish picked a fight with me!" Janine shouted, held back by Randy.

Julie's eyes flared. "Bullshit!"

"Did too!" Suzanne rallied to Janine's support. "Out of nowhere, slap!"

"She's vicious! Just like her dad!" Janine accused.

Julie scowled and fought Bill's grasp on her arms. "You're the vicious one! You are! How dare you say that about my father!"

"Look, girls!" Delmonte argued. "I don't know what this is about, but I don't have time for it. I have a show to put on!"

"Not with *me* you don't!" Janine threatened. "I quit!"

Delmonte's eyes lit up with alarm. "Janine! What are you saying?"

"I'm not sharing the stage with *her*! Either she goes, or *I* do!"

Miss Delmonte looked like she was struck with a mortar round. "You can't do that. You're the lead!" she pleaded. Julie felt suddenly very sorry for her.

Janine pulled free of Randy. "Try me! I'm gone!" She made good on her threat and began walking for the exit. Everyone started looking about with doomed uncertainty.

Julie felt her heart plunge to her knees. The entire cast and crew had worked all month on this play. The first performance was almost a week away, and nobody could replace Janine in such a short time. She had the lead role. Like it or not, Julie was only a bit player, easily recast. She knew her neck was in a noose.

Miss Delmonte looked at her with a pained expression. "Julie, I . . ."

"Screw your play!" Julie shouted, making sure Janine heard her. "I'm out of here!" She rushed from the theater without looking back. Delmonte and the others were astonished. No one followed after her as Julie pushed her way out the side door. The bump on the back of her head was beginning to hurt, and she focused on the stinging, hoping it would distract from the real pain and rage she felt inside.

CHAPTER 53

TOM CRUSHED FOIL OVER A SMALL STRETCH OF WIRE armature. He was making another tree. There was so much he had to think about, and as his mind labored, his hands were kept busy building, creating, like an insect fashioning a hive. His fingers absently kneaded and bent the foil, giving it a sinuous curl. The new tree would be added to a grove that had sprung up from the artificial netherworld like alien fungi. It became almost a daily routine, as though the landscape was his private garden, and he tended its flora like a demented herbalist. Everyday, it grew more and more, expanding outward over the surface of the set, threatening to spread its tendrils into the room beyond like ivy vines over a mausoleum.

Though the chill attacks and vertigo had subsided, he was still too weak to animate. His head ached, and he sipped occasionally from a mug of Lipton's chicken soup. Grandma's "wonder drug" didn't seem to help with his particular ailment. Yet he couldn't keep himself in bed. The urge to work on his project was too strong.

The phone rang, and he went into his mother's room to answer it. It was Julie. She sounded upset.

"What's wrong?" he asked.

Her voice trembled. "I quit the play."

Tom slumped onto the bed. "You *what*?"

"I *quit*! They were giving me a hard time. I got into a fight with Janine Meadows."

"But why?"

"She called my father a devil-worshipper. She said people were trying to run him out of town, and I lost my temper. Then she threatened to leave if I didn't quit. So I quit!"

Tom slammed the phone against his chest, anger rattling his form. Damn them! "Julie—that's so unfair! You worked so hard."

"It doesn't matter," Julie dismissed it. "I was getting tired of it all, anyway."

"You *loved* being on stage."

"I'll find something better to do with my time. Who needs it?" She was trying to be authentic, but her voice didn't mask her disappointment. "I don't know what made me think I could act, anyway."

"But you *can* act. I watched you. You looked great up there."

"You mean it?"

"Better than that Janine Meadows any day. Miss Delmonte must be blind. Those thick glasses of hers need a cleaning."

He heard her sigh gratefully. "Thanks, Tommy. It

means a lot to me to hear you say that. I'll get over it." She paused and her voice shifted. "How are you feeling?"

"Me?"

"Danny said you went home sick. Are you okay, sweetie?"

"Yeah. Just a bug, I think. I'm fine."

But she didn't sound convinced. "Are you sure?"

Tom found the inquiring tone in her voice a little invasive. He'd forgotten how perceptive she could be. "Yeah. Why do you ask?"

"I don't know . . . It's just . . . I'm worried about you. You seem different."

Tingles of uncertainty raced up his spine. "Different? How?"

"You've been so tired and rundown."

"I haven't been sleeping too well."

"And . . . it's like you're afraid to touch me. I can feel it. We didn't hold hands once this week."

"Sure we did." He was hoping she hadn't noticed. "In the courtyard."

"It wasn't the same."

He shifted uncomfortably on the bed.

"Julie . . . I . . ." He owed her an explanation. She had always been honest with him, right from the start, and she deserved nothing less in return. He considered telling her about his recent "monster activity." He had already primed her with his flight dreams, so it wouldn't come completely out of the blue. Julie had a lot of experience with strange phenomena, and her knowledge of the occult would surely provide insight into his "condition." At the very least, it would shock her less than the average person.

Or so he hoped.

But what if it alienated her? Terrified her? What if she refused to be with him ever again? No. He couldn't tell her. "I don't know what to say. I guess I've been a little distracted."

Now she was exasperated. "Are you sure it's not about *us*? About the other night?"

A stabbing pain in his stomach. "No, Julie, it has nothing to do with that at all. It's something else, but I haven't figured it out yet." He hesitated again. "It's complicated."

"Fine. I'm a complicated person. So tell me."

"I can't. Give me time and I'll explain it to you."

She paused on the line, struggling to accept his words. He sensed she wasn't satisfied yet.

"Maybe you've been working too hard on your movie," she said. "You should take a break."

"Take a break from my animation?" His voice was suddenly stressed. "No. I can't."

"You can't?"

"I mean I don't want to. I'm coming down the home stretch, and I just have to finish this . . ." He wanted to say "story," but there *was* no story. The truth is he no longer knew *what* he was filming. His animation shots were just random movement exercises, devoid of plot or purpose, as though the creature's saga was not being recorded on film but on the fabric of his soul.

He wasn't making a film; he was keeping something alive.

Julie persisted, "Can't you put it down for a little while? I mean what's the deadline?"

"Julie, I . . ." He was growing defensive and had to contain himself. "It's what I do. I'm sorry if I've been distant, but I'm fine, really. It's *you* I'm concerned about." He was anxious to shift the subject, and he focused again on her situation. "This crap they pulled on you with the play. I'm just so angry that you had to go through all this. Is there anything I can do about it?"

She went silent, and it worried him. *Now* what?

"Julie?"

"No, thanks. I have to go."

"*What?* What do you mean?"

"I just need to think."

Silence. He struggled to break it. "Julie, please don't be angry with me."

"I'm not angry. I'll speak to you tomorrow. Try to get some rest, okay? I have to call my dad, now. Bye."

"Julie, wait—"

She hung up.

Tom was dazed for a moment as he put the phone down anxiously.

Did I just blow it with her? Damn it!

Why was he being so evasive with her? There was so much he needed to share, and instead he was putting her off, even *lying* to her. Now she was hurt, and there was nothing he could do to change it. Down deep he experienced a terrible notion of failure. He wanted to take her pain away and make everything better. As her "boyfriend," he felt it was his responsibility.

But he was *powerless.*

Nothing he could say or do could change things. The outrage buried deep inside, where it festered in his gut. There was a bitter taste in his mouth, and he paced angrily through the hall.

That damn play. It was all because of the damn play! Stupid actors!

How dare they treat her like that! She was a sweet, wonderful girl. Why couldn't they let her enjoy a simple part in a stupid high-school production? It wasn't fair!

Tom felt something well up inside as his anger reached a fever pitch. It occupied space in his solar plexus and threatened to burst forth from his ribcage. Suddenly, he hated that play. He hated the entire school. Before he knew what he was doing, he was heading to his bedroom, drawn to his netherworld, where he still had the power.

Maggie DeFrank nudged the door open to her son's room. From the bright lights inside, she could tell he was animating. Tom didn't like to be disturbed when he was doing his work. Lately, he had been so adamant about it, becoming grouchy at the slightest intrusion. You would think he was performing brain-surgery. But she had to tell him something important, and it would be brief.

"Tom?" she asked, entering the room.

His camera was set up, and he was busy moving that ugly model of his. All of his monsters were gross and scary, but that one was particularly frightening. It made her queasy looking at it. She rarely entered his room anymore, fearing she would upset some important object that had been carefully arranged. The room was such a mess, anyway. It wasn't even a room anymore. It looked more like a *jungle.*

Just look at him. He didn't even answer her. He was standing over the set, peering down at his creature as though it was all that mattered to him in the world. He wouldn't take a moment to acknowledge his own mother. Just stood there, with his back to her, like she didn't exist. *What's with this kid?* He was so much like his father, capable of deep pits of depression and obstinate self-withdrawal. Well, she wouldn't give him the benefit by getting upset over it.

She folded her arms resolutely. "I just wanted to say Paul and I have to drive to the city first thing in the morning, so—well—he's going to be staying over tonight. You can have the car tomorrow, if you need it. And the weekend after next is our big "trip" to St. Thomas. We'll be gone for five days, so let us know if you intend to stay home, or if you want to visit your Aunt Lucy. They're having a big Halloween party and would love to have you. Do you know what you want to do, yet? Tom?"

No reply. He didn't even look up. He just stood over

the model, still contemplating its next move, his fingers gripping its tiny ankle.

Now she was mad. He had no right to be so cruel. She did the best she could for him, all these years. It wasn't her fault his father turned out to be such a deadbeat. Every penny he ever sent she gave directly to Tom, which he squandered on this dreadful hobby.

All these monsters reminded her of terrible times. Even that puppet looked like the devil. How could he like such things? How could he embrace something so sinister, after what they'd been through?

If only he knew the pain she suffered for him.

She decided to leave the room in the same manner she came, with the boy intently focused on his animation. She refused to be insulted. Still, it wasn't asking a whole lot from him to give her a moment. He could've turned to face her. Answer her. Nod his head. Anything. He didn't have to pretend she wasn't there.

By the way he looked, his eye glued to that puppet, one would think he was in a "trance."

CHAPTER 54

A MOMENT BEFORE, TOM WAS ANIMATING. HE COULDN'T recall the instant he left the confines of his makeshift studio. His mind drifted from the process and focused on the emotions welling inside him. He thought about Julie again and the harassment she suffered backstage. The anger pitted in his stomach until it became a knot. There was a trembling in his solar plexus, a brief feeling of vertigo, and a bright flash of light against his pupils.

Snap!

Suddenly, he was there.

Cloaked in darkness, the deserted stage surrounded him. He—it—was standing before the newly constructed set. Flats of pinewood and fabric were built to resemble the interior of a stable. A papier-mâché horse's head hung outside a stall, and an authentic riding saddle was affixed to a nearby wall.

The creature opened its wings, feeling life stretch through its newly formed body like fingers through a gauntlet. It skulked about the stage in a crouched posture—head thrust forward, elbows held rigidly back. The claws on its hands curled like the teeth of a rake. It eyed the fake scenery with animal bewilderment. The flats were confining, and the creature snarled at them, snapping its jaws with a loud clap. It felt an inexplicable malice, the rage burning like coal in a furnace. Its tongue lolled within its mouth, slithering over long fangs that dripped wet onto the floor. A gurgling sound came from the back of its throat.

As Fau'Charoth walked beyond the set, the sharp taloned feet scratched the floorboards. It was surrounded with banks of rope and canvas flats that rested in piles against the far walls. The area was deserted, the crew having put down their work for the evening. Tools were ditched in open bins. Paint cans were laid out on pages of newspaper beside hastily cleaned brushes and rollers. The smell of fresh paint accosted its nostrils, and it bent to sniff, picking up the human aroma and astral memory left on the brush handles.

Lingering in the air was a familiar female scent. Its nose twitched, absorbing the fragrance with immediate identification.

Fau'Charoth recognized the location. Its primitive, wolflike mind sensed it was here for a purpose. A commanding force was driving it, and every fiber of its being responded. It filled with wrath and with that wrath came a terrible hunger.

A terrible need to destroy!

Zack McBride took the weed back from Jeff Plotnick and sucked in another long drag. It tickled his chest, and he fought the impulse to cough as his larynx tightened from the fumes. A cloud of well-being settled over him. His friend Jeff hadn't quite reached that state of euphoria yet. He continued to complain in a slow drawl, although his voice had raised an octave and sounded creaky like twisted straw.

"Lydia has to be the meanest girl I ever met."

Zack smiled. "She's a bitch, man. I told you."

"Ditching me like that in front of my friends. Thinks she's a queen, or something." Jeff scratched at his knee, which protruded from a hole in his jeans. "Why did she ever even agree to go out with me?"

"I don't know, man. She enjoys jerking your chain."

They sat on the steps to Senior Lane, their backs pressed to the cold brick of the High School auditorium. The school was locked secure for the night, but there was a large gray gate that closed off an entrance beneath an underpass. Zack had learned how to shimmy under it and gain access to the courtyard after dark. It was an ideal hangout. He enjoyed the quiet under the cool arc lighting of several lamps.

The evening air was brisk, and Zack's skinny arms were starting to feel the chill. He rubbed them through his jacket and glanced at Jeff, whose eyes were dulled over with a marijuana glaze. He took another hit on the weed, savoring the aroma. The reefer was giving him a solid high. Cliff Burke always provided the best pot. It was greener, more potent than the seedy crap from the city, like the difference between fresh produce and canned veggies. He took another drag, inhaled it deep, and began to offer sage advice to his stoned companion. The kid needed to relax.

A few Quaaludes might have helped, but he'd sold his entire stash once again to that senior, along with a bag of angel dust. He purchased an extra large amount, hoping Burke wouldn't get suspicious. Zack couldn't resist. The money was too good. He wondered what effect PCP would have on a kid like Jeff. Probably turn him inside out. Zack didn't care much for "dust." He tried it once and remembered it as a really bad trip.

"The problem with you is you're always a pussy for those types. You gotta learn to—" He was cut off by a loud crash.

For a moment he thought he imagined it. Sometimes pot caused him to hear noises.

But Jeff heard it too. "What was that?" he asked.

"I don't know. I thought it was the weed."

They listened. Again, they heard it. Crashes from within the building.

"What the hell?" Zack creased his brows. They were sitting against a wall that put the stage behind them. Maybe the techies were still around, installing heavy machinery, or something, for that new play.

But the crashes grew louder and more violent.

Zack's spine tingled. He crushed out the weed and put the rest of the joint in his pocket. Then he rose to his feet and began creeping around the corner to the front of the music building. Jeff followed, wincing from a head rush. He seemed about to keel over.

"Man, what *is* that?"

"Shhh! I don't know."

They neared the entrance, listening to still more loud bangs. Something was tearing up the stage. Vandals. It had to be. Zack hesitated. If it was some new rover pack, they needed to get out of there, or wind up piñatas in a gang fiesta.

They came toward the windows of the main entrance. Zack cringed as yet another thunderclap of tortured metal could be heard within. Whatever it was, it was totaling the stage!

And then they heard it. A loud guttural roar, like something from the zoo. It seemed to be coming closer. Zack and Jeff both stiffened, shrinking low in fear.

Cra-aash! The windows exploded outward, sending splinters of glass across the blacktop. The boys leaped aside as something huge and dark sprang out of the building. Great wings expanded, catching the air like a parachute. The humongous shape soared clear across the courtyard, landing in a crouched position atop the cafeteria. It stood there a moment, scanning the architecture. Then it twisted its upper body in their direction.

The boys were frozen as they gazed at the creature.

"What the fuck—"

Zack couldn't believe what he saw. His mind scrambled to identify it. His first reaction was that it was a bat. A giant black bat with a wingspan the size of a Buick. But as it rose to its hind legs, he could make out a long tail, and a human torso with arms and legs like—

No! It couldn't be!

Like-some-kind-of a-freakin'-monster-that's-what-it-was! They were looking at a monster!

"Oh shit, man, am I seeing this?" Jeff whined, doubting his eyes.

"It's there, man."

"I'm not seeing this!"

"Yes you are, man! It's for real!"

Standing upright, it was just over six feet tall, with an eleven-foot tail extending behind. The head was that of a lupine dragon with a pointed snout. Horns spiraled back from its brows. Its upper body leaned forward, elbows thrust back like a gunslinger about to draw. Four-fingered hands dangled from its wrists. The legs were triple-jointed like a bird's, each ending in sharp talons. Zack could not have known it, but he was looking at a giant, living incarnation of the little puppet that stood on the movie set of Tom DeFrank.

The creature gazed at the boys with predatory curiosity. It gave off a hideous snarl that sounded like a cross between a hound and a crocodile. Two pinpoints of yellow fire gleamed out from its wolflike face. Zack could see its head cock, the way his Labrador did when it was curious. But then its pointed ears fell back, the neck reached forward. It gave off another threatening growl, and Zack knew the monster was about to charge!

"Oh, shit!" His realization came with a start; they were trapped in the courtyard!

Zack grabbed his petrified friend. "Come on!"

He hauled Jeff backward and headed for the underpass.

Fau'Charoth dove down from the top of the dining hall and dropped to its feet near the edge of the courtyard. It leapt forward, landing on the palms of its clawed hands, and began loping like a wolf on all fours. The wings folded back at its shoulder blades.

They reached the underpass. Swiftly, he slammed his back to the pavement, and with one smooth move, slid his way crablike under the gate. But Jeff staggered and slammed headfirst into the bars. "Ow! Dammit!"

"Move your ass!" he shouted as Jeff flattened to the ground. Zack could see the dark shape closing in on them. The streetlamp glistened off its hideous features, a grotesque visage of scale and horn. Long fangs were revealed as its snout wrinkled, drawing the flesh off its teeth.

Jeff slid under the gate, but his midsection got caught halfway. Zack grabbed his shoulders and hauled him through, clearing the gate just as the creature crashed into it. Fau'Charoth's claw snatched the boy's sneaker. Jeff screamed. He was being pulled backward!

"Aaaaah! Zack!"

Zack gripped the boy by the shoulders, and heaved against the creature's savage strength. He feared it would succeed in dragging Jeff under, or tear the boy apart! In an act of desperation, he glared directly into the monster's yellow eyes and yelled at the top of his lungs.

"YAAAAAAUGGH!"

Startled, the creature dropped Jeff's ankle. Jeff jerked it free to safety. Fau'Charoth snapped its jaws at Zack, the snout reaching between the bars. It pounded at the metal in a frenzy of flailing claws and gnashing fangs. Then it stepped back and began ramming the gate. Zack and Jeff cowered in fright. The hinges of the gate began to creak like tortured metal, threatening to tear free. Zack felt his heart pound, praying it would hold.

Fau'Charoth withdrew from the gate, glaring at the teenagers. It continued to snarl, but its rage had been sated. It backed out of the underpass, shook its scaly wolf's head, and with an unearthly shriek, took to the air with great wings flapping.

Vanished.

Zack and Jeff stood petrified, listening.

The creature had swooped out of their view. It could *fly*.

He gazed up at the open sky above them.

Oh my God. *The thing could fly!*

Zack panicked. He grabbed Jeff and pulled him into the shadowy corner of the building. He looked in every direction. The sky was free and clear, and there was nothing to prevent it from swooping down onto them. But after a few excruciating moments, he dared to hope that the monster—whatever it was—had left for good.

He and Plotnick collapsed onto a patch of grass, still

trembling with fear.

"What the hell *was* that, Zack?" Jeff cried.

"I don't know!"

"Like the freaking devil, man!"

"Will you shut up?"

They could hear the building's antitheft alarm ringing. It had been set off the moment the creature burst through the glass. Zack knew the police would come to investigate shortly, but he dared not move. For once, he welcomed the sound of an approaching patrol car, with its siren and spinning red lights. He had a lot to tell them.

CHAPTER 55

TWO SQUAD CARS WERE PARKED ALONG THE CURB OF the school's front entrance. Zack's nerves were fried, and as he leaned against the car's hood, he could feel himself shaking like a jackhammer. His fear soon gave way to anger and exasperation as he tried to explain to the officer.

He took to shouting. "It was a *demon*, man! Like—with wings, and fangs, and it could fly!"

"All right! Calm down." Officer McFarlane had stopped writing in his pad as though he doubted their testimony. He had seen the shattered glass of the windows and damage to the gate, but appeared unconvinced the boys weren't involved.

"It was big," Zack continued in frustration. "Maybe eight or nine feet tall, and it looked something like one of those things on a cathedral. A gargoyle!"

Only ten minutes had passed, and he half-wished the creature would return, if only to convince Barney Fife, over here, that he was telling the truth. By the skeptical look in his eyes, the cop was far from accepting his monster-story.

"We told you everything we know. Can't we just go now?"

McFarlane shook his head. "You're not going anywhere. Not until the sheriff gets back." His nose twitched and he took a sniff. "Is that pot I smell? Hey, aren't you Frank McBride's kid brother?"

Zack frowned. He was afraid of this. Frank, his older brother, had been picked up once for marijuana possession. It did little for his *own* credibility.

Sheriff Kronin and his deputy were stepping over the rubble on stage. They wielded two large police flashlights and were shining the beams over the remains of the *Dark Victory* set. The auditorium lights were on, but due to the massive destruction of the lighting console, the power backstage had to be shut down. Too many lines had been cut, and they dangled dangerously on the floor. Cut was perhaps the wrong term. *Chewed* was more like it. Ozone from burnt cabling made the air thick.

Kronin couldn't believe the mess. The stage was totaled! The flats were collapsed and slashed as though by razors. Prop furniture had been overturned, and the curtain was torn down on one side.

"Careful over here," he addressed Chris Evans, his second in command. "There's broken glass." Several of the hanging lights had been trashed, the glass gels shattered about in colorful shards. *Expensive debris*, he thought. Each one of those bulbs cost a fortune. The lighting board was demolished too, as though someone had taken a sledgehammer to it. He could only imagine how much everything cost.

Chris shook his head. Whoever—or whatever—did this had done a thorough job. Beneath the debris, Kurt caught sight of a horse's head. His heart skipped a beat. For a moment he flashed back to the carnage at the Whateley farm, and it caused his stomach to flip over. Remembering the peculiar nature of that attack, he glanced furtively above to the rafters and fliers as though expecting something to be clinging to them, ready to pounce down on their heads. He wasn't sure what he was looking for, but he sensed he was dealing with a similar phenomenon. If so, they needn't limit their search to ground level.

What could do this, he wondered, *and why the stage of a high school? A disgruntled drama critic*, he mused. The plays were amateur, but they weren't *that* bad. He'd sat through several, over the years, and hadn't complained. *Poor kids*, he thought. *They had obviously worked very hard on this production.* Two of his three daughters still attended the school. Nancy, his youngest, had even expressed interest in auditioning for the musical come the spring. She had a beautiful singing voice. And Rosy was in the school band. She'd played in the orchestra twice already, once for *Brigadoon* and again for *South Pacific.* He still crooned "Some Enchanted Evening" now and then to get her to smile. They were going to be very disappointed that the musical, regrettably, would not be produced this year. The school budget could never replace the wrecked equipment in time.

"Hey, Kurt! Over here!" Chris waved for him, shining the light down on the wooden floor.

He followed the light beam and saw deep, long scratches in the shellacked panels, like the markings his cat made on one of his chair legs.

"What the hell is this?" Kurt asked aloud.

"Looks like somebody took a garden trowel to the floor."

"I doubt it. It doesn't look deliberate enough."

"You think those kids had anything to do with this?"

Kurt shook his head. "Naah. They could've run off when they heard the siren, but they stayed put. Besides, there's way too much damage for two kids."

They continued their investigation backstage and eventually searched the entire auditorium and surrounding buildings. Principal Harding had been notified, and he was going to contact the play's director and anyone else who was last to leave the premises. Kronin hoped they would shed some light on the matter, because so far he was coming up empty.

The rest of the school was devoid of tampering. There was no other damage anywhere. This disturbed Kronin for a particular reason. The boys reported the thing crashing *out* of the front entrance windows. The debris scattered on the courtyard was proof of that. But every door in the building was locked, and no other windows were broken. No signs of forced entry.

They could not determine how this thing had gotten *in*.

CHAPTER 56

TOM COULDN'T BELIEVE WHAT JUST HAPPENED. HE WAS standing beside the tabletop, in the middle of contemplating the puppet's next move, when suddenly *whoosh*! The scene shifted from his bedroom to the high school, like some lunatic film editor had misaligned his life's sequence. Could he have imagined it? Could it even possibly have been for real?

He saw it all, the back stage of the auditorium—demolished! Crashing through a window! And two kids were there. He knew one of those kids by name. They fled from him like he was a monster!

And he *was* a monster!

Tom began pacing. He held his head as though to take hold of his sanity. Almost immediately, he was shivering again. Another chill attack stole his body of warmth. He clenched his muscles and shoved his fists into his sides as the shocking cold stabbed at him. But even as he keeled over, clutching himself, he was delighted.

"This isn't happening!" he shouted. "This *can't be*

happening!" Part of him was frightened, but another part wanted to laugh. It welled up inside like a great joke. Then it burst out of him. "Hah!"

He laughed because it felt good. It felt *powerful*. He laughed because it had been deliberate, this time. He had, on some level, *willed* this thing to happen.

And it obeyed him!

CHAPTER 57

BY THE FOLLOWING AFTERNOON, THE NEWS HAD already spread like a brush fire throughout the school. As witnesses on the scene, McBride and Plotnick became local celebrities. Their descriptions of the "demon" made headlines in the *Times Herald-Record.* Though their testimony was compromised by the discovery of a marijuana joint, the bulk of the incident was described as "unexplained," leaving ample room for inventive speculation.

Zack McBride had been charged with a misdemeanor for drug possession, but given his assistance in the investigation, he was handed a slap on the wrist and a trip home with his parents. His father was angry with him, but accepted his story that it was "Frank's weed" he'd found in the closet. Older brothers could come in handy, sometimes.

McBride's monster was already a public legend. It grew in size, almost ten feet now, and acquired by some the ability to breathe fire. Kids were excited by the story, passing it around with relish. It was, after all, a welcome break from algebra.

Not all were amused by it, of course. Miss Delmonte was mortified by the destruction to the stage; her heart dashed to bits when Principal Harding told her the play was canceled. The cast and company were equally devastated. So much effort and nothing to show for it. It affected more than the dramatic and musical productions. All concerts, assemblies, and political rallies would have to be held elsewhere until further notice. Sadly, the school's budget could not restore the damaged equipment anytime soon.

Julie Parrish walked the halls in dismay. News of the vandalism shocked her. Why did *she* feel responsible? There were eyes on her at every turn. Every glance seemed laced with accusation. Obviously her dispute with Janine Meadows was being served up as grist for the rumor mill. Janine passed her briefly in the hall and gave her a startled look of suspicion. "How dare you show yourself, today" was the silent insinuation. Great! So much for noble sacrifice. She'd quit the play in order to save it. Now it was cancelled, and she was pegged the disgruntled actress with a vengeance. As though she were gloating over the news. She queried Randy Moore and Bill Lugones for details.

"The console looked like it had been stepped on by a giant," Alex said, shaking his head. "You should've seen the look in Mary's eyes. I thought she was going to cry."

"I had nothing to do with this, Alex," she implored.

"Of course not," he said, surprised by her guilty disclosure. Yet there was a hint of doubt in his voice, as though her very denial raised an issue of complicity. Julie decided there would be no comfort with any member of the play's company. Fear and paranoia were making mincemeat out of reason. She was becoming the only logical scapegoat. She had motive, and she had a reputation for being strange. Reality be damned.

She wished there were someone to whom she could talk. Someone who cared. *Where was Tom?* She couldn't find him anywhere. Was he still sick? Did he suspect her as well?

She ran into Danny and asked.

"I haven't seen him today," Danny answered. "I don't think he came to school. Too bad. He would have been thrilled."

"How do you mean?"

"Well, didn't you here about the stage?"

"Of course."

Dan raised his brows as though it were obvious. "Winged monster-demon?"

She blinked at him.

"It's just like the one he built! Like someone stole his idea!"

Julie's eyes glossed over as the craziest notion entered her mind. No. Can't be. It was totally insane. She felt her head go light, and her heart began to pound.

"I gotta go." She raced off. Dan shouted after her.

"Tell Tom he should sue for copyright infringement!"

She knew she had to call her dad. There was no time

to lose. She stopped as she neared her locker bank. Her shoulders dropped, dismayed. Taped to the locker door was a black pointed witch's hat. It was one of those cheap vinyl Halloween hats you bought from Woolworth's. Somebody decided it was appropriate attire for her.

Her vision blurred as tears began to form in her eyes. It was all happening again.

CHAPTER 58

THE PACKAGE ARRIVED AT THE ORPHEUS BOOKSTORE at 10:30 AM. The cost for overnight air freight from Saudi Arabia was outrageously high, but Humphrey Culhane had spared no expense in procuring the item as quickly as possible. Adding it to the cost of the volume itself (rigorously bartered for) his personal investment now exceeded ten thousand dollars.

Culhane removed the parcel from the box and found the book encased in burlap and wax-impregnated paper. Ghasem, his Saudi colleague, had taken special care in shipping it. Over the phone, the aged bibliophile seemed uneasy about the diabolical nature of the tome. Culhane caught a whiff of incense as he unraveled the burlap. Ghasem had apparently "smudged" it with smoldering herbs to dispel negative properties.

Culhane rubbed his fingers over the worn leather of its cover. The book itself was about the size of a photo album. The leather retained some rusty-brown pigment, but had been stained and glazed from finger oils. Its title was engraved with gold leaf.

The volume was an English annotated edition of the *Dæmonolatreia*, a *grimoire* compiled by Remigius in the late sixteenth century. Like the *Necronomicon*, it was a veritable cookbook of ancient spells, much sought after by sorcerers and demonologists. The pages contained blocks of Sumerian text, star charts, and incantations. Runes and sigils were carefully indexed, as well as diagrams of talismanic magic. The ten thousand dollars now seemed a steal to Culhane. The volume was obviously priceless, and he was glad to add it to his library. Only twelve additions were catalogued, and most were no longer accounted for. Many, he suspected, were destroyed. This one had been purchased from an Arabian scholar's private collection. If Jacob Tornau had owned a volume, it was assumed lost with his other possessions. Burned by the locals.

Impatient to begin work, Culhane left the store in the care of his assistant and retreated to his study. There he would remain for hours, combing the pages, deciphering phrases, and comparing them with the sketchy details of Parrish and Tom DeFrank. Nearly a month had elapsed since Stephen reported his bizarre findings in the tunnel. Culhane envied the man's discovery, and looked forward to examining the ritual site himself.

Crosschecking the mysterious symbol from Parrish's barn vision led to a generous selection of Voc Caru rituals. Culhane sharpened his gaze on one block of text, gratified that his hunch had been correct.

The phrase began with the word "Fau'Charoth."

CHAPTER 59

PARRISH ENTERED HIS CAR, AND TOSSED HIS SMALL bag of groceries onto the front seat. The bag spilled, and a can of chicken broth nearly rolled under the cushion, but he ignored it. He sat down and pulled open the newspaper he'd just purchased along with his other parcels. Mr. Van Owen, the proprietor of the small country store, had given him a pointed look when he selected a copy of the *Times Herald-Record.* Van Owen was always quiet with him. This morning, though, he was unusually vocal.

"Some news, today," he remarked, referring to the front page. Parrish glanced down at it, and his eyes widened with curiosity. Emblazoned in bold print along the top was the heading:

VANDALISM IN HIGH SCHOOL.
TEENS CLAIM TO SEE "DEMON."

His eyes darted back to Van Owen, but the man had already moved on to the far end of the counter, his back turned away. It made him feel dirty, somehow.

Seated in the old Chevy, he read the brief but pointed

article.

According to the story, the high-school stage had been vandalized, forcing the cancellation of the play. The only witnesses were two delinquent students who described seeing some kind of large creature. Parrish creased his brows, disturbed. Julie had called him the night before, heartbroken with bitter news. According to a rumor, Gerard Wilkens was once again launching his civil assault against Crohaven Manor. The news was delivered as a taunt from a cast member, and she had quit the play because of it. It bothered him that she was being harassed for his sake, and he regretted having to miss her performance. He had been looking forward to seeing her on stage.

Did I remember to tell her so? Damn his neglectfulness!

He pulled the Chevy into the street and made a quick retreat back to the estate. As he drove, he focused on each aspect of the story like a detective juggling clues.

Julie had quit the play. The stage was destroyed. By some kind of "monster," if the kid's testimony could be believed. Was there a connection? Sections of a puzzle were being placed before him, and he struggled to assemble them. A twinge of new comprehension entered his psyche. For weeks now, he had sensed a peculiar vibration in the air, a lingering sense of foreboding that was dark and pervasive. He attributed it to the phenomenon in the tunnel, an active current of negative psychic energy. But what he considered now was that this vibration was not simply a magical turbulence in the æther, but a *consciousness* unto itself.

An entity.

He decided to call Culhane immediately.

"The teens described the assailant as a winged demon-like creature, about eight feet tall." Parrish read from the article over the phone.

"Sounds like a drug-induced hallucination," Culhane insisted on the line.

"But it's not the first incident we've had. The Whateley farm was attacked last weekend. Some hogs were mutilated. Torn to shreds."

"Are you serious?"

"If it's a coincidence, it's a damn peculiar one. Whateley's already accusing *me*."

"Maybe he slaughtered the animals himself in order to put suspicions on you."

"Not likely. And there's something else. I'm sensing a strong negative presence in the æther. It feels to me more like an entity of some sort. Humphrey, I think I've been blind to the true situation here. Chapinaw may have an entirely new peril at hand. Something came through that portal. And it's still out there."

He heard Culhane shuffle and take in a deep breath of resignation.

"I didn't want to alarm you," Culhane began, "but I'm afraid you may be right. I can perhaps shed some light on it at last. I've located Tom's fragment and the name 'Fau'Charoth' in the *Dæmonolatreia*."

Parrish couldn't believe what he heard. "You have?"

"It's part of a ritual that dates back over eleven hundred years. Now, 'Fau'Charoth' is not a true name. It has been introverted from a longer title, which means the verse invokes that being, an atavistic spirit of some kind."

"You mean a *tulpa*?"

"Yes. A constructed entity, vivified by its creator, and enslaved into servitude. This Fau'Charoth was originally of pure elemental essence, perhaps with a fragment of animal consciousness. Whatever it was, it's a demon, now."

"A demon." The word gripped Parrish, and he glanced again at the headline of the newspaper. He knew now what they were dealing with.

"Yes. Cults like the Voc Caru often summoned demons as their strong-arms. Opening a portal to the dark world would be formidably dangerous without some kind of protection. Ages ago, they created this Fau'Charoth as a pure astral entity, then perverted it through ritual until it was totally dependent on the essence of the sorcerer. Using the passages in the *grimoire*, Tornau summoned it and infused it with his life force. He literally fed it parts of his soul like scraps of meat to a dog. At least until he was killed."

"And then what happened to it?" Parrish ventured. "This demon, after Tornau's death?"

"It should have suffered dissolution," Culhane surmised. "Cut off from the vivifying host, the demon normally disintegrates, reverting to its original essence."

"But suppose it didn't? Suppose some part of it managed to maintain its cohesiveness while trapped between planes of consciousness."

"It could have succored itself on other life forms—rats and cockroaches and such."

"Bats," Parrish said. "There are bats by the thousands in that tunnel."

"Bats. Well, that might have sustained it indefinitely, in a torpid state, but to evolve and manifest on this plane it would need to do more than just steal essence like a mosquito. It would need a greater host from whom to draw energy. And not just *any* host. For an astral demon to feed, the host has to project his life force intentionally. The relationship between entity and host has to be symbiotic. You might say the demon needs to be *revered*."

"It sounds like a religion."

"Well, think about it," Culhane offered. "A spiritual entity, inspiring devotion through fear or covenant, strengthening itself off the mental emissions of the worshippers. Sound familiar? That's how gods are created."

"So you're saying this demon has found someone *willing* to let it feed off his soul?"

"In a manner of speaking. A necromancer. A warlock. Someone with knowledge of the black arts. Perhaps someone with a score to settle. Did Tornau have any relatives?"

"None that we know of." He held the phone to his forehead, rubbing it across his brow, as he wrestled with his worst suspicions. He had put them aside these past weeks, comforted by Culhane's reassurances. They returned now with a vengeance.

The boy. It was the boy.

"What about an *unwitting* host," he asked. "Someone who provides the essential elements without full knowledge. Say for instance . . . a kid who draws monsters?"

"You're referring to Tom DeFrank again?"

"From what Julie describes, he's completely preoccupied with his hobby, to the point of autism. Lately he's become especially compulsive, working night and day."

"So he's dedicated to his craft. No harm there."

"But wouldn't an obsession with fantasy and horror movies provide an ideal environment for demon possession?"

Culhane laughed. "In and of itself, no. Most horror stories are in fact macabre morality plays. They don't engender evil in people. Rather they create fear and avoidance, and they're presented in too outrageous a fashion to attract the truly diabolical. I think if every kid who watches horror movies or draws monsters was able to conjure a demon, we'd all be in a lot of trouble."

"But Tom's an animator."

"Okay, so he draws *lots* of monsters. That in itself wouldn't conjure a demon, even if Tom were the 'anti-Disney'." He chortled at his own pun.

"No. He's not that kind of animator," Parrish corrected. "Not a cartoonist. Tom's a stop-motion photographer."

"Stop-motion? Oh-h, you mean like Harryhausen and that George Pal fellow."

"He builds little puppets and manipulates them for

each frame of film—"

"Wait a minute," Culhane interrupted. Parrish could hear the man shift excitedly over the phone. "Hold on. You mean to tell me . . . there's a *puppet* of this thing?"

CHAPTER 60

IT WAS NEAR SIX-THIRTY IN THE EVENING BY THE TIME Julie had the courage to ride her bike over to Tom's house. She wasn't sure what she expected to find. When he didn't show up for classes again, she grew worried. Nobody picked up when she called.

What her father revealed on the phone left her feeling untethered to reality. She had never allowed much reflection on the dark side of things. Life had certainly delivered its share of misfortune—her father's accident, the breakup of her family, the harassment of her peers—but she had refused to let it take root in her philosophies. If you searched for the evils of the world, you would find them—and worse, they would find *you.* She kept a vanguard against these dark thoughts, maintaining faith in a benevolent universe.

Evil could never prevail in an innocent heart, or so she wanted to believe.

But she was wrong. Innocence was not a panacea to wickedness, and even the noblest of souls could become a nest for the sinister. This was the claim her father was making.

And he was making it about Tom.

When she pulled into his driveway, she noticed the garage door was open and empty. His mother was probably out again, having gone on parental AWOL for another evening. Julie understood now how neglected Tom must feel by her, and how disastrous that neglect may prove to be. It made her indignant, knowing that much of the trouble might have been avoided if Tom had at least one attentive parent.

She rang his doorbell and waited. Tom appeared at the door, surprised to see her. "Julie. Hi." He was absolutely haggard. His hair was an oily mat with unruly, clumping strands, and his clothes were wrinkled. He looked like he'd just risen from bed, but by the circles under his eyes she suspected he hadn't really slept in days.

She stepped into the doorway and offered a kiss, which glanced off his cheek.

"Hi. I tried to call."

"I'm sorry," he said.

"Are you okay? You look—"

"I'm still not feeling too well. It must be the flu. Come in. It's kind of chilly outside."

"Chilly?" It was actually a warm evening. Julie noticed he was wearing a thick hooded sweat jacket over a flannel shirt, and there appeared to be another sweatshirt below that. She herself was sweating in a T-shirt and denim jacket.

They walked through the house. The living room was dimly lit. Tom offered her a drink, which she passed on. "But take something for yourself. You need plenty of fluids when you've got a fever."

"Fever?" He looked at her sidelong. "I don't have a fever. I'm freezing." He tucked his hands into his sweat pockets. Julie was seriously growing concerned. Was it simply the flu, or could it be something worse?

"Well, you should stay in bed. Take an aspirin. I'll cook some soup for you."

"Thanks. I'm not hungry, and I'll be fine. Just need some rest." He shifted the topic. "What's happening in school?"

"It's crazy. Did you hear about the stage?"

He glanced away, distracted. "Stage?"

"Someone trashed the auditorium!" Julie reported. "They had to cancel the play! Everything was destroyed, including the set and the new lighting console we worked so hard to purchase. Two kids said they saw a 'monster'."

His eyes lit up, but he struggled to appear nonchalant. "Really? A 'monster,' huh? I thought mine were the only monsters in this town."

Julie followed Tom into his bedroom. "It was in all the papers. Some of them are even calling it a—" Her eyes widened as though she had boarded an alien spacecraft.

"Oh my God!" she exclaimed.

The movie set, which stood above his two bureaus on a large plank of plywood, had grown like a fungus, extending now to much of the back wall. His twisted rows of aluminum foil trees had become a forest, with branches reaching beyond the painted backdrop. The magenta sky had spirals of pink and ominous clouds of charcoal gray looming over a Jovian horizon. A storm seemed to be forming in the distance. Jagged rocks with fingers like a gauntlet snatched up from the ground, amidst patches of moss and blue-green lichen. It was as if the lunatic dreams of madmen had gathered together to form a universe.

"You've been busy," she said with astonishment.

"Yeah," he shrugged. "I added a little bit every day, and it just kinda *grew.* I told you I was inspired."

"Inspired?"

Julie glanced around, a chill clutching her spine. And she noticed something else as well.

It *was* cold in this room. The temperature seemed to have dropped as much as ten degrees since they left the hallway. She reflexively tugged at the corners of her jacket to close it.

The camera stood in a corner on its tripod. The shelves above his desk were stocked with his animation models, mostly dragons, dinosaurs, and grotesque, misbegotten characters with scales and horns. Despite their ugliness, Julie had always thought of them as whimsical or cute, an extension of how she felt for Tom. But now she thought they were horrible, distorted creatures of the psyche, and her heart broke, thinking of the self-abhorrence that one must feel to identify with them. She was beginning to understand for the first time the world Tom lived in—a manufactured world that served as both a sanctuary and a prison. These creatures were his own mirror image, each one a reflection of some aspect of his soul. And none of them were kind.

The Fau'Charoth model stood on the set, wings folded at its back. It appeared to have just completed a step, and its gaze was lifted to Julie's face. It was looking right at her.

"Boy," she remarked tentatively, recalling Danny's description of the creature and how it paralleled the news reports. "He sure looks real, doesn't he?" Her hand reached out for it.

"DON'T TOUCH IT!" Tom shouted.

Julie snatched her hand back in alarm. "Sorry."

He apologized. "It's just that . . . I'm in the middle of a shot."

A projector was set up on a small table, directed onto the wall above his bed. A roll of film was already threaded. "I got more rushes back today," he said with artistic pride. "Would you like to see them?"

Julie nodded, still unnerved by his extreme reaction. He switched on the projector. The plastic Super-8 cartridge began to rotate on its spindle. "It's just a test, but I think I got some great moves in it."

He turned the lights off, and the room filled with darkness, except for the light of the projector. The bright flash on Tom's wall was replaced with glimpses of his eerie world. The miniature mountains and crushed foil trees became a phantasmagoric vista as the camera panned through the landscape.

Julie sat on the edge of his bed, inches away from the Fau'Charoth model. She could feel its gaze on her, and she glanced back at the rubber creature nervously. Yellow-gold eyes peered out from beneath its horned brows. The snout bore a frozen grimace of teeth. Julie felt a shiver, as though the model was peering into her soul. She had to remind herself that it was just a puppet, created step by step from clay to rubber and metal.

On screen, the puppet's animated image appeared in *life.* The demon fluttered down, the great bat-wings flailing. It dropped to all fours and then slowly erected itself. It was uncannily realistic, his best work thus far. The animation was smoother than his previous efforts, without the jarring stop-motion strobe of some of his earlier works. In a few short weeks, Tom had mastered the craft and could certainly rival any of the professionals currently at work in the field. Julie would have been delighted with him, if she wasn't so frightened.

Fau'Charoth took a few steps and made a quick turn to face the lens, its tail swooshing in a sinuous curve. Julie recognized its movements. They were similar to the Ymir, Harryhausen's space monster, but even more so they resembled Tom's *impersonation* of that creature. The way it twisted its torso and arched its back. The way the neck darted forward. Julie was looking at an animated doppelganger of Tom DeFrank!

She remembered the unrestrained enthusiasm he expressed when he described animating: how for that brief time Tom *became* his fantasy creatures, stepping into their bodies and moving about. He said he dreamed about it, as though his greatest wish was to shed his pitiful human form and lumber like a beast. She recalled the reports from school of the "monster with wings," rampaging through the auditorium, taking vengeance on the stage. Julie watched the image on the screen, and wondered: *Has he found a way?*

The animated Fau'Charoth continued to skulk through its nightmare world. On the tabletop, the puppet gazed at her. The combination of demon eyes made her tremble. Julie felt her cackles rise and a breathless feeling of panic. Her head lilted. She glanced about, unable to look at the screen anymore. When she could no longer take it, she stood up hastily and stepped away from the puppet.

"Turn it off," she gasped.

"Julie?"

"Please! Will you just turn it off?"

Crestfallen, Tom switched off the projector. The movie demon was banished, and she sat in the dark while he reached for the room lights.

"What's wrong?" Tom inquired.

Julie had to gather her thoughts, taking a deep breath. "What *was* that?"

Tom looked puzzled. "What's what?"

"That!" She pointed to the blank wall dumbly.

He shrugged. "It's just my animation."

She shook her head, dread consuming her. "No. There's something else. Something else going on, and you're not telling me."

They exchanged a penetrating stare, and Tom's denial

began to erode. He slowly paced about the room, as though struggling to conceive an explanation. "Okay. Okay . . . you're right. There *is*. I was planning to tell you, but I wasn't sure of it at first. I thought I was going crazy, and I didn't want to scare you away."

Julie sat down, trying to relax. Confronting him was not the way to go about this. She needed to gain his trust. Her eyes softened as she looked at the boy. "You won't scare me, I promise. Whatever it is, I want you to tell me about it."

He began to construct his thoughts, his reluctance replaced by a growing enthusiasm. "I didn't believe it at first, myself. It started when I began building this model. I thought they were just dreams. But they're *real*! It's . . . it's like it's *me*, but it isn't, somehow. At night, I go places, and I become this creature. It's just so amazing. Like having every one of your greatest wishes realized. Remember the dragon, Julie? I become a dragon!"

His eyes expressed a zeal that was vaguely familiar, and she realized it was the look in her father's eyes when he began his painting, the fervor of an explorer who had discovered a new continent.

"I wish you could be there with me! You get this incredible feeling of power! It's an emotional rush like nothing you can imagine! So invigorating. It's the most supremely satisfying thing I've ever felt in my life."

She listened uncomfortably. It confirmed her father's wildest and most absurd fears. But she refused to accept it.

It was utter lunacy! "Tom . . . are you saying you're some kind of *werewolf*?"

"A werewolf?" Tom gawked in astonishment as though the very term brought his ravings into check. "No! I don't transform into some hairy monster or anything. I dream about Fau'Charoth, and in my dreams, somehow, I become him. For real!"

Julie wore an incredulous smile as though questioning her own sanity. She rose to her feet, her face awash with trepidation. "Okay, you *are* scaring me now."

He opened his arms to reassure her, and reached out. She flinched fearfully, and Tom withdrew. A crushed look filled his eyes, and he pleaded softly to her. "Julie . . . you don't have to be afraid. It's still *me*. I'm still Tom. I just have this extraordinary new power, that's all. I don't know where it comes from, or why it came to me, but it's mine and I can control it."

"*Can* you?"

"Yes. I can."

"Tom. Listen to yourself. What about last night? The stage . . . those boys. Did you control *that*?"

Tom shrugged self-consciously. "I got a little carried away. It didn't hurt them. Just scared them a little. That's all. And that stupid play! I mean, they deserved it, right? For what they did to you."

She gazed at him in confusion, and then it occurred to her: "You did that for *me*?"

He looked to the floor, shielding guilt. "I got angry . . .

for your sake."

Julie softened her voice, conscious of her indignation. The last thing she wanted to do was stand in judgment of him. The boy needed help, and as her father pointed out, he needed to *ask for it.* She stepped up to him and gently took one of his hands "Tom. My dad thinks—"

His eyes sharpened, suddenly defensive. "Your *dad*? What does he have to do with this?"

"My dad thinks . . . you might be possessed by a demon."

The insinuation hit like an uppercut. "*What?*" She could see the betrayed look in his eyes. Tom gazed at her a moment, deeply smitten. He shook his head rigorously. "No . . . no. Not you too."

"Tom, sweetie, look at me," she pleaded, trying to recapture his eyes. "He's worried about you, and so am I."

"Your dad thinks *I'm* possessed? Your dad. The one they call a 'witch'."

The word stung her. "Don't call him that!"

"How dare he!"

"Tom—"

"Tell him to mind his own business. I can handle it."

"Tom . . . we've been to the tunnel."

Tom looked at her, stunned.

"We were there," she revealed. "We saw everything. Danny told me about the night you got lost in it. How you came out chanting spells."

"I wasn't chanting—Dan's got a big mouth!"

"Why didn't *you* tell me about it?"

"I don't know why. I wanted to . . . but I couldn't."

"You *couldn't*?" She gazed at him firmly. "Tom . . . Can't you see? Whatever this thing is, you're not in control of it."

"*No* . . . yes I am!"

"It's controlling you! You told me you never want anything to control your life. That's why you make puppets, remember? Well now *you're* the puppet!"

It was a clever twist of his philosophy, and she hoped it would penetrate.

But his behavior was that of a junkie defending his habit. "No! I created it! *I'm* the puppet master!"

"You have to stop animating. You don't know what you're doing. This demon was summoned through a blood ritual. And you were part of it."

His eyes were wells of confusion. "What are you talking about?"

She had to tell him. It was the only way. She fell frantically into an explanation. Tears formed in her eyes. "Your mom never told you. She wanted to protect you from the truth. When Tornau escaped, your parents were terrified that he might come back for you, so the police concealed your name from the records."

"Tornau—what? Julie! You're babbling."

"Remember the Tornau cult? The big raid at the farm when they almost killed the baby? Tom . . . that was *you*. You were the baby the cult tried to sacrifice."

Tom looked at her as though she had spoken in tongues.

He put a hand to the back of his head in a slow labored movement. "*Huh?* Wait. That's not possible."

"Think about it. The 'incident' your parents moved away from? It wasn't your grandparents. Jacob Tornau abducted you as a child. Six people were murdered as part of that ritual, and they were going to kill you too, but this one woman—her name was Sarah Halloway—she felt sorry for you because you were only a baby, and she didn't want you to die. So she informed the sheriff. But the cult escaped to the tunnel and performed the final blood rite, using *Sarah* instead of the baby. That painting on my father's wall, it's *her*! She died to save you, Tom. But this demon survived. And it attached itself to you."

He began to pace like an angry, overwhelmed tiger. "This is crazy!"

"Is it? Look at everything that's happening. This monster. That spell—"

"What about it?!" he shouted and then rubbed his forehead, trying to regain his composure. It was too much for him to absorb. "Look, Julie, I don't know what your father's been smoking in that haunted castle of his, but I don't know anything about demon cults or blood sacrifices, and I'm not a devil worshipper. This isn't witchcraft. It's not evil. It's *Hollywood*!" He hoped she could discern the difference between the two.

"I'm just an animator. *This* is what I do." He gestured about his room, including the set and the models in an all encompassing sweep. "It's who I *am*. I thought you understood that. I thought if *anyone* could understand, *you* could. Now you want me to give it all up because your dad has some wacko notions about possession?! How dare he judge me like that! This is all I got, Julie! It's all I got in the world, and if you don't like it, you can both *go to Hell*!"

Julie gasped as though she'd been slammed in the stomach. A shadow fell between them. He stood away, arms folded defensively, unable to look at her. He had hurt her in ways he could never comprehend, but he was at that moment devastated himself.

"Tom . . . you don't–"

"I think you should go now."

The words contained such finality that she felt her heart shatter. She gazed at him, struggling to find a way to close the chasm that had formed between them. He continued to stare into space, a million light years away. Julie watched him quietly, awaiting some retractile indication from him. But nothing came.

"Tom . . . please."

"Go! Go, before I *turn into a monster*!"

Julie fled from his room and ran down the steps from the living room to the main entrance.

She paused for a long while before the front door, staring blankly at the golden knob, knowing once she passed through the threshold she might never return. Her breath came in gasping sobs, tears streaking down her cheeks to her chin. She realized in despair the great irony: that both the men she loved dearest in life had been taken from her by mysterious forces from beyond.

Tom stood in silence, his head bowed heavily. He was in a stupor; barely comprehending that Julie was gone. One brief, angry exchange of words had obliterated their relationship, and a black hole of despair now formed in his chest. In a flash, he had plunged into a depth never before reached in his young life.

How could this happen?

He remembered her startling insinuation. It pummeled him completely out of his senses. And the way she cringed from his touch. The look of fear in her face that said "You are different. You are disturbed." All through his life, he saw that reaction in people's eyes. Friends keeping their distance. Relatives privately sharing "heartfelt" concerns with his mom. Counselors, psychologists, priests. A glance at his sketchbook was to them a glimpse into a troubled mind. He was a bad seed, tinged by the darkness. In need of salvation. He recalled the taunts and accusations from school. Monster-Boy. DeFrankenstein. Always it pushed him away, making him the misfit. The exile. Was there something wrong with him that people picked up on? A kernel of evil in his soul? He always wondered if any of it was true.

Now he knew for certain that—yes—there was something different and vile about him. He was tainted by the diabolical. Even as an infant, he had been selected by the dark forces, singled out from the scores of Crohaven children to succor the powers of Hell.

Tom sank to his knees, trembling. He raked fingers through his hair.

Was it true? Was he really that child, stolen and nearly killed in sacrifice? If so, did he have any recollection of it at all? Did a trace of cruel hands and dark robed figures lurk somewhere in his subconscious? And how did it affect him? Was there a blemish on him even now, a twin-pointed crease on his palm, a triple-six birthmark on his scalp? Maybe this was why his father left, and his mother withdrew emotionally. They sensed the change and no longer wanted any part of him!

Tears jumped to his eyes. He was a monster! An abomination!

And yet a woman died to save him.

This was the bitterest irony of all. Cut off from his parents' affections, he'd always felt undeserving of love. Yet this poor woman, this Sarah Halloway, deemed him worthy of rescue and was slain for it. He remembered the glowing portrait in Parrish's study, the mournful, familiar face that seemed to call to him from across time.

She died to save him!

Now he made allegiance with the very machinations from which she had spared him. He looked over to the model on his tabletop, and his vision blurred. No wonder it had bound to him. They were siblings of a sort. Demons summoned and rejected, alone in the feckless void of reality.

"Is that what we are?" he asked it aloud.

The puppet seemed small and innocuous, a construct of rubber and metal.

He heard the front door to the house open and shut.

Julie? Was she still here?

And then sanity returned.

"Julie!" He ran out of his room, hoping to catch her before she was gone, possibly forever. He needed her. He couldn't continue without her.

Far down the street, she was already peddling away on her bike. "Julie!" he called out to her, but she was long out of earshot.

"Julie, PLEASE!" He sprinted in a great effort to catch up to her. But it was too late. She had turned off the side road and was gone. He stood alone in the dark empty street. Far-off, he could scarcely make out the rotating beacon of the "eye of the dragon," traversing the night sky like a memorial candle for his dying love.

One last time, he shouted her name, but it was lost beneath all the barking.

Dogs were barking. Everywhere.

CHAPTER 61

JULIE LAY FACEDOWN IN HER BED, AND SHE COULD FEEL the dampness of her tears on the pillow. She drifted in and out of sleep, the heavy sadness like an anvil on her heart. The quiet splashes of the lake and the ticking of her nearby clock filled the silence. She felt the subtle rhythms of her body, the intake of air into her lungs, and the soft patter of her heart. Suddenly, as pinpricks of fear stabbed at her, she was alert. Her face and arms felt exposed above the bed sheet. The temperature in the room dropped to an unseasonable chill, and she imagined her breath as a white cloud of vapor. Her eyes cracked open, blinking through the darkness, because she fearfully realized *she was not alone*!

Fau'Charoth hovered above the girl as an ethereal specter. It could smell the sweet scent wafting up from her dormant form. The bed sheet, the clothing on her dresser, and much of the room caressed its nostrils with the same rich feminine odor. Though it could have manifested in an instant, snapping into material flesh, it chose to linger as little more than a conscious mist. It peered at the girl with perplexing fascination as it absorbed the energies of its host, miles away.

There she was, the mysterious presence that inspired so much anxiousness and desire. As it looked down at her, a terrible longing filled its being, a voracious hunger for emotional essence. Something was being withheld, and it caused the demon's host immense pain. Anguish filled it like a viral transmission. It felt empty, a vacuous hole, and the demon glared at the girl, confused in its primordial mind. For here was the source of the pain, and yet here the cure.

The girl stirred, and Fau'Charoth's ears pricked up like a dog. It listened to her breathing as its jaws lolled insatiably. She was food for the taking, completely vulnerable. The demon had eaten girl flesh before. Over the centuries, it had been conjured frequently with the ritual sacrifice of young women. Succored by their life forces, it then feasted on their meat like a true carnivore. Was it not the intention of its host that it do the same with this one? Was she not a morsel to sate its palate? It was tempted to take on its dense physical shape and spring upon her with tooth and claw, rending her to pieces. Its jaws would reduce her savory form to gristle, and the warm blood would flow down its gullet in delicious streams. She was an elixir waiting to be drunk, a banquet that would fill the coffers of its being and end the terrible emptiness that now plagued it.

But something prevented it. Somehow, it understood

that to do so would only engender greater pain. There was an awakening comprehension that what it needed was not present simply in her flesh. It longed for the sweet nourishment of her spirit, the soothing embrace of her affection. It hungered for her love.

A tingling occurred throughout its ætheric shroud. On an astral-molecular level, the demon's vibrations were raised, a feeling so strange and mystifying that the ghost creature wavered in uncertainty. Fearful of these new and beguiling sensations, it fled the room in a fury.

Julie sat up abruptly with a shout. She reached for her night lamp, and with a snap of the key, the room was flooded with light. Her eyes darted about, shaking with fear, as every shadowy corner revealed its contents to her. But she could find nothing of the intruding presence. The room was empty.

A few deep breaths brought her out of panic. Julie lay back in bed, drawing her knees up under the covers, where she clutched herself in a fetal position, and cried.

Fau'Charoth soared across the landscape, angry and driven. It made frantic and delirious spins through the air, as though to rid itself of a pestilence. The shift in its vibration caused it to experience things unknown ever to a demon of its kind. This new essence was like a cancer, attacking the very fabric of its composition, transforming it, molecule by molecule, into something new. Fau'Charoth was evolving. Its mind had been that of a wild beast, savage and untamed, without the capacity to distinguish complex emotions. But that was changing.

Rage! Lust! Hunger! These were sensations with which it was well acquainted. For centuries since its creation, wizards had evoked it, sustaining it on the darkest passions of the soul. Their twisted, demented minds had perverted its consciousness into a demon that thrived on such energies. But here was something different. Here was energy of purer substance, rich and more potent, more vital, capable of overwhelming ecstasies and devastating torment.

Here was love and anguish and despair.

Fau'Charoth lacked the intellect to define them. A poet might take them to task, but not an elemental creature, devoid of an advanced spirit. It was composed of emotional essence. Feeling and action were the same to it, and so it was compelled to obey the dictates of its heart, even as confined vapors, ignited, were compelled to explode.

The demon flapped its gigantic wings in frenzy, and flew off to the horizon, where a beam of light suddenly gave meaning to its rage.

A small airplane made its way to the landing field, guided to the runway by the rotating beacon. The pilot, Dick Livingston, was finishing his last flight for the day. Having shuttled three chatty passengers to Newark, he was returning now for the third and final time. The cabin was empty, and he savored the quiet. Three such trips in one day were an overload. In the distance, the main terminal of Sullivan

County Airport was a welcome sight. Livingston tapped his microphone once and transmitted to the tower.

"Hello Sullivan County, this is Fletcher Seagull ten-four bravo, making final approach. Over." He clicked a switch on the console, preparing for descent.

A woman's voice responded over the speaker. "Roger. Ten-four bravo is radar contact."

"That you, Lilah?" He smiled, recognizing the soft, sultry tones of the air-traffic controller's voice. The woman was a tall longhaired blonde, mid-thirties, who worked the night shift. Dick had met her twice, passing through the terminal, and it put a pretty face to the voice. Since then, she'd become his friend on the airwaves. The thought of her guiding him safely to the runway made his evening transports that much more endurable. He fancied one day asking her to dinner, but for now he'd settle for coffee and a doughnut. "Save me a cup of the good stuff. I'm coming in for the last time, tonight."

"Roger that, Dick. I break at midnight."

He sensed an invitation in her voice, feeling suddenly bold. "How's about meeting me in the commissary, and—"

Crash!

The airplane was violently struck on the wing, causing the entire craft to dip and jolt to the left. "HOLY—" Dick fought at the controls as something large and dark swooped past the cockpit window.

"Come again, Dick?"

"Something just winged me!"

"*What?*"

"Check your radar!"

"I'm checking. There's noth—wait, there *is* something. Too small for a craft."

"I see it dead ahead."

He craned his neck to follow the dark shape, which soared off toward the terminal. *What the hell is that?* Dick pressed his face against the window, brushing his fingers against the glass to rub away condensation. He caught sight of it again just before it vanished.

"Lilah?" His voice was excited.

Silence.

"Lilah, are you there?"

"We still have it on radar. Can you still see it, Dick?"

"No. It's gone."

Whatever it was, it was out of sight, and Dick furrowed his brows curiously. In all his years as a pilot, first for the navy and finally as a privateer, he had never once reported a UFO. Often he wished to, just to break the routine of air travel. Most reports described bright lights, saucer shapes, or luminous cylindrical objects and could usually be explained as weather balloons or the planet Venus. But what could he call this? A giant bat? Pterodactyl?

He puzzled, listening to expectant static on the cab speaker, until he noticed the gauges on his panel. The plane was quickly losing altitude.

"What the hell—"

Lilah's voice jolted him. "Dick, you're descending too

rapidly! Elevate to 1,601."

He grabbed for the controls as the runway appeared out of the clouds, racing toward him from below. The wing had apparently been severely crippled by this *thing*, and he was drifting uncontrollably in flight.

"Uhhh . . . Lilah? I'm having trouble here."

"Just maintain your present angle of descent. You're doing fine, Dick. Dick? Fletcher Seagull, do you copy?"

"Roger."

But he knew he was anything but *fine*. The air currents against his wings made an uncharacteristic wailing sound, like banshees heralding his death. This would be the landing of his life, if he survived. He gripped the controls fiercely.

"Clear the runway! I'm coming down!" Then he caught sight of the *thing* again. "There it is! It's heading for the hangar!"

It was way too big to be a bird. Not large enough to be another plane. It was black, and he caught a glimpse of leathery wings. Landing lights were blotted out by its passage as the great winged object glided to the Earth. As it cleared the runway, it veered off to the side of the building. Then it disappeared.

Down below, airport workers were rushing out of the terminal to the landing strip. They watched as the small craft descended rapidly toward the tarmac. One of its wings was torn, offsetting the wind drift. Dick had managed to direct the plane back to the runway and was struggling now to steer clear of the parked aircraft and utility buildings.

Bob O'Connell, the airfield supervisor, was shouting orders into a walkie-talkie, motioning people into position.

Workers held their breaths as the plane dove for the runway. Its wheels hit the tarmac, and it fell into a dangerous skid. Air pockets were formed within the crevasses of the damaged wing, causing it to veer to the left and right. Within the cockpit, Dick Livingston fought to steer the plane safely, but as he struggled to maintain control the craft sped off the airstrip and swerved toward the main hangar. Tires screeched, and Dick had time to glance over his shoulder as the wall of the building suddenly swiped him sidelong to a halt. He jolted violently, slamming his head against the window. And then everything came to a stop.

A siren was wailing. He heard shouts. The impact stunned him, and he lifted his head from the bloody window, feeling the sticky warmth on the side of his face. He reached for the buckle on his harness. A fire engine advanced to the crash site, red lights flashing, and he saw the familiar face of Bob O'Connell appear at his cockpit window carrying a large fire extinguisher. He gave the man a relieved thumbs-up—*any landing from which you can walk away*—and a cloud of white gas blotted everything out as O'Connell sprayed the entire engine.

From the outside, O'Connell could see the craft was totaled. It landed on its side, narrowly missing a head-on collision with the hangar's corner. The plane was squashed along the wall of the building like some huge fly mashed against a windshield. The left wing was crushed; and the right wing suffered a cruel gash that looked like three slashes of a machete. Curiously, it had made no contact in the collision. What could have caused it? Others joined O'Connell beside the craft.

"Let's get the man out of there," he commanded them to the cockpit. He knew it would take machinery to pry the doors open, but perhaps if they broke through the windshield, the pilot could crawl through. "Get me a hammer over here!"

The hammer broke through the safety glass. Dick coughed off the remaining extinguisher gas and looked out gratefully to O'Connell and the others.

Then he noticed how they'd all frozen in place.

Something growled.

In the alley, off to the side of the building where Dick's plane lay crumpled against the side, a hulking shape appeared. It leapt onto a large garbage canister now gazed at the workers.

"Holy Jesus," Bob O'Connell cursed.

It rose on its haunches, and two great wings unfolded. O'Connell's throat locked.

"Shit! What is it?!" shouted another worker.

Fau'Charoth had struck out at the rival night creature, which fell, defeated, from the sky. The demon snarled in challenge as it padded toward the winged object, a predator advancing on its prey. Startled humans were gathered about it, and as they looked up, the demon could sense their fear. Bright halos of energy radiated off their forms, shifting in color as their terror intensified. The demon's rage had reached a peak. Like a child in the fit of a tantrum, it needed to smash something.

Dick Livingston fumbled again with his harness. The damned catch was jammed! "Bob! What's going on?"

O'Connell and the others hesitated as the strange shape lumbered closer. It crept forward on its two legs, occasionally dropping to its forepaws, as though standing erect was strange to it. O'Connell stared at the creature and at Dick in the cockpit, uncertain.

"Jesus Christ," he repeated.

The demon roared and raced toward them in a four-legged gallop. The men scattered. O'Connell dropped the hammer and ran from the airplane.

Dick couldn't help noticing their hasty retreat. "Hey! Get me out of this thing!" He saw the hideous shape through the broken windshield. It was the same thing he had seen from the air, only now it was earthbound. An unidentified *stalking* object! His blood froze. The harness stubbornly fought his fingers, refusing to unbuckle.

With a leap, the demon closed the distance to the plane, pouncing on the nose. The impact crushed the aircraft down, and Dick found himself staring into the face of the yellow-eyed menace. It growled, and the pointed snout pressed forward through the empty frame of the window. It was inches away. The little nose twitched. Muscles tightened, lifting the lips from long pointed fangs. The demon gave off a wet gurgling snarl as it peered in at the pilot. The pointed triangle ears folded back in canine threat. Dick trembled, trapped in his pilot seat, gazing motionless. He could feel sweat spreading through his flight suit.

Fau'Charoth opened wide its jaws and snapped them forward. The fangs clashed together a finger-length short of Dick's face. He gasped aloud. "No, please, no, please, God, please . . . please."

A shot rang out. The yellow orbs glared in fury, but hesitated. Then it glanced away.

A distance away, as the workers cowered and watched, airport security officer Hank Gleason arrived, pistol drawn from his holster. He spied the strange creature on the nose of the plane, and without hesitation began firing rounds at it. The demon turned, startled, as the projectiles pierced its hide and chest. The bullets clearly penetrated, but seemed to have little effect.

The demon turned and gave off a shrill bark. Then it pounced free of the plane and was airborne, soaring toward the officer. Hank emptied his chambers into the flying monster until the gun clicked empty.

He ducked down and threw his hands protectively to his face as taloned feet fell onto him, crushing him to the ground. He struggled, feeling the immense weight of the creature.

It was standing on top of him!

It clutched at his side like a bird of prey. There was piercing pain as the claws penetrated his jacket. Hank felt himself hoisted as the great flapping wings launched the creature skyward.

His head fell back, cringing against the squeezing grip, and as he dangled upside down he saw the runway below flashing past him. His feet and arms flailed helplessly. He was being carried off like a rodent in an owl's claw! Instinctively, he reached up and grasped the creature's ankles, pulling his weight upward to relieve some of the pain in his side. Its skin was hot to the touch.

Higher and higher they flew, until the terminal grew small and the lamps of the airfield became bulbs of starlight.

And then there was a bright flash. Hank heard the creature let out a snort. It veered toward the light. Suddenly the man's eyes were blinded by the direct glare of the tower beacon.

Fau'Charoth gazed at the rotating shaft of light emanating from the tower. Its struggling prey weighed heavily in its claws. The demon intended to feast on its flesh, but the light distracted it. The glowing eye resonated with a familiar essence that filled it with longing. The demon soared toward the tower, carrying the hapless man aloft to the picnic clearing. The closer the beacon loomed, the more its celestial brilliance beckoned to it, until all other desires were forgotten.

As they descended, Gleason felt the talons release, and he was falling! Branches whipped him, and he grabbed out at them to break his plunge. A tree limb slammed him painfully in the side, and he tumbled to the ground, landing in a thick cushion of bushes. The man looked up from the brush, gazing into the clearing where the tall tower shined brilliantly with the rotating light. He had been abandoned by the creature, but sensed somehow that it was still nearby. Creeping out of the bush, he gazed up and caught sight of it. The winged beast was perched on the very peak of the tower like an aluminum eagle on a flag post.

Fau'Charoth clutched the metal of the tower, crouching low. It could hear the hum of vibrating motors as the great orb of light rotated. Its fingers passed over the hot glass, grasping the "eye of the dragon" in its claw, as though the cold metal of the scaffold held within it some meaning. The demon peered across the landscape, spying the picnic tables and the drive path through the forest. It knew this place and felt the trembling of familiar pleasures. They were but a memory, displaced by yearning and despair, yet they pierced the demon like a hot skewer. Again, its astral essence throbbed to the rhythms of human emotion.

It remembered the girl. She was gone now, her love withdrawn. Sorrow racked its soul, and it gave off a whimper. Then it threw back its head and let off a long mournful howl of animal torment. The wailing echoed across the clearing and traveled over the distant airfield, where Bob O'Connell, Dick Livingston, and the others heard it and cowered in awe and terror.

The creature lolled its head pitifully. Sorrow brought pain. And pain-rage!

With an angry swipe, Fau'Charoth pounded down on the beacon. There was an explosion of glass and electrical charge as the dragon's eye went dark.

Below, the security officer watched the creature attack the beacon. Sparks erupted from the scaffolding, and there was the shrill sound of tortured metal as the demon annihilated it. Then it launched itself back into the air and was gone.

CHAPTER 62

TOM AWOKE IN THE ARMCHAIR OF HIS LIVING ROOM.

Rather, it seemed he *faded back* into his human form, having never fully lost consciousness. He found himself flopped heavily in the sofa, chin to his chest. The image of the airport, the hapless face of the pilot, and the struggling of the officer he had nearly killed were just febrile memories, like images on the television.

He sprang up from his chair, looking about. His head reeled with vertigo. The churning sensation was dying down in his solar plexus. It felt strange and unsettling to be back in his body, as though it were suddenly too small and lightweight. The enormous creature shape was gone. The phantom memory of a tail and wings tingled like the "ghost limbs" of an amputee. As he walked through the house, he felt the instinctive need to draw his arms in to avoid crashing into the ceiling and furniture.

So much of himself at that moment was *not* Tom DeFrank.

Slowly he settled back into reality and experienced the

horrifying sensation that he was actually *stealing* himself back. Fau'Charoth was only reluctantly letting go. Something had changed in their connection. Where before he had been in command of his actions, albeit in an awakened dream state, he now perceived himself to be a mere passenger in another body. As though the creature had stolen his eyes and taken them for a joyride. It still thought like him. It still felt his feelings. But Fau'Charoth was no longer the emotional alter ego he'd considered it to be. The "demon" was a twin to his consciousness, but separate of body, soul, and *will.*

Julie was right. He *was* losing control.

Julie! He had been with her too! The creature paid a visit to her bedside, standing over her in an ætheric state. He remembered how small and sad she looked beneath her covers. He—it—wanted to touch her, hungering to be close. At first the desire was purely carnivorous.

But then some new and compelling emotions surfaced within it. These new feelings caused it anxiety. They were alien and incomprehensible. The demon reacted like a chimp puzzling over chords of music on a radio, until it destroys the set in frustration. He remembered its bewilderment and the terrible rampage that ensued.

It had nearly *killed* a man!

The creature was going to devour the cop like another hog in a pigpen! Had it not been for the distraction of the beacon tower, Tom would be a murderer!

And then Fau'Charoth destroyed the tower.

He raced out of the house and ran to the backyard, where, vaguely in the distance, he hoped to catch the light beam on the horizon. There was a slight drizzle. The sky was a dark canopy of mist and cloud, but the familiar beacon was nowhere to be seen.

"Damn you! What have you done?"

He would never willfully have destroyed the "eye of the dragon." He certainly never would have attempted to kill a human being. Tom was afraid now. Terrified of what he had unleashed. Yet part of him felt extremely angry and betrayed. He was tricked and misled by this *thing*—this thief of his soul.

If it was separate, then he wanted to confront it. *See* it with his own eyes! Tom made fists to temper his resolve. "Fau'Charoth," he spoke aloud, determined. "I know you're out there. Come forth!"

He listened and heard only the crickets and the light patter of soft rain. He tightened his fists. "Show yourself! I command you to show yourself!"

Something stirred in his solar plexus. The sensation churned and built into a spiral of energy. There was an explosion and a burst of light that Tom took for a thunderbolt. *Was he struck by lightning?* It was as if a large part of him broke off in a flash. The force drove him to his knees. His eyelids fell heavy and he thought he might faint, but he pried his eyes open and peered ahead.

There it was, standing before him beside the yard table and metal shed.

Fau'Charoth unfurled its wings and lifted to its full height, gazing down at its "creator." Tom's eyes widened at the sight of the beast, his limbs trembling, his mind racing with fright and fascination.

He often wondered what it would be like to see an actual dragon. In his youth, he had visited zoos, gazed at an elephant or rhinoceros and imagined he was looking at a triceratops. When he watched a monster movie, he tried to project himself into the hero or victim as they peered at the sci-fi creature. He often wondered what it would be like to stand in the presence of something so unique, so otherworldly. To see it moving, hear its *breathing*. Observe its flesh shifting over bone. Tom thought all these things in a millisecond, as though his brain was scrambling to process the incredible vision before him. There it stood! His same eyes, having witnessed the rhino and elephant, were now peering at the reptilian monster, this chimera from his imagination.

It looked the same as he had envisioned it on paper. The same lupine face he had etched in graphite now lolled at him. The same dragon tail now swished behind sinuously. Its posture was the one he had generated in his animation, moving with the stop-frame action of hundreds of work hours. Tom knew this creature intimately in his heart, and from his heart it had escaped!

It leaned forward, gazing at the boy with glowing yellow eyes, and as Tom gazed into its pupils, all energy drained from his form. He felt his consciousness drift—*snatched away*!

And suddenly he was gazing down at himself! It looked at the boy with beastly familiarity as the essence spread through the veins of its being. It felt strong again and issued a threatening gurgle from its throat. Tom knelt before it on the grass, a dormant shell, vaguely conscious. The pitiful human body seemed so frail and insignificant, a feeble vessel for its spirit. With one deadly swipe of its claw, the boy could be ravaged to a bloody corpse.

No!

Tom snapped back into his body with a gasp. His eyes darted about the yard, cowering from its threat. It was gone. The yard was empty once again. There was no indication that the creature had ever been there. For a moment he thought he'd passed out and imagined it. The droplets of rain had accumulated on his neck, and he was shivering. He couldn't recall how long he'd sat there on his haunches. The intimidating thoughts of the creature burned in his mind. Forcing life into his limbs, he raced back into the house, overwhelmed and desperate, and certain of what he had to do.

It was too much. Far too much for him to control.

Julie was right. He had to put a stop to it.

Tom stormed into his bedroom and gazed down at the creature model, which remained fastened to the set. He reached below, and with a quick twist, unscrewed the tie-downs that secured its feet to the base. Then he grabbed it up fiercely, preparing to tear the flesh off the jointed steel skeleton.

But as he held the puppet, his fingers sinking deep into the latex skin, something restrained him. It felt so perfect. The model was exquisite, the product of so much toil and creative labor. Tom felt angry tears form in his eyes. He didn't have the strength of will to destroy his own handiwork. It would be like shredding a piece of his soul.

Frustrated, he carried the puppet to a large wooden chest in the corner of the room, thrust the model into it, and slammed the lid down.

He collapsed on top of the chest, pressing his face to the wood, feeling relieved and exhausted.

And very, very alone.

Julie. He missed Julie.

"What have I done?" he cried aloud.

PART 3

CHAPTER 63

CHRIST ALMIGHTY.

Sheriff Kronin repeated it to himself again and again as he interviewed the airport eyewitnesses. It was half past nine on a Friday morning, and already there were news vans lining the roadway to the main terminal. He knew he should have ordered a press lockout. A cup of black coffee was gripped tightly in his hand, and he swallowed the scalding liquid as he toured the crash site of the airplane. Both the pilot and Hank Gleason, the wounded security officer, were undergoing treatment at the hospital. Kurt knew Gleason. He used to be an officer with the Chapinaw PD before accepting the comfy airport position. Hank was a good man, sober and reliable, and he wasn't prone to hallucinations. If he said he'd been plucked into the air by a flying monstrosity, well *hell*, you had to believe him.

Christ Almighty.

Another horror show. It was the third such incident in a week. This time, the thing, whatever it was, had attacked an airport in full view of at least a dozen people. And these weren't codgy old farmers or doped-up school kids. They were a seasoned shuttle pilot, a veteran police officer, and a score of skilled technicians—all of them credible witnesses. It would prove difficult to challenge their testimony, skepticism be damned. He passed a reporter from the *National Democrat*, but his scowl turned the man away.

The press was going to have a field day.

His office was already besieged with questions, and they were under serious pressure to quell a growing hysteria. He agreed to step up patrol and bring on additional constables, but these were indulgences at best.

"What do you want me to do, Bob?" Kurt argued when the hangar manager demanded an increase in security. "Do you want me to post every one of my men at the airfield every night? And what about the high school? They'd like the same thing. Then there's the bowling alley, and the shopping center. There's no telling where this thing will strike next. Maybe I should just cover the entire town with plastic and fill it with Malathion. Works on roaches, I hear."

He was frustrated. Three appearances by the thing and they still had no idea with what they were dealing. Tests on the hog corpses gathered from Whateley's farm were inconclusive. Dr. Adrienne McDowell at Cornell University had not been able to identify the saliva collected off the flesh. She claimed they lacked any of the known enzymes found in mammal saliva, yet the bite radius suggested a carnivore the size of a Kodiak bear, the largest predator on U.S. soil.

McDowell suspected an elaborate hoax of some kind.

All of Kronin's officers were engaged in the investigation. They followed standard procedure, dissecting every detail. But where did one begin? The targets seemed to have no association. A hog farm, a high school, and an airport. What was the connection? How does one track an aggressor with no physical restriction: a creature that could fly and seemingly appear and vanish at will? Where did it come from, and what attracted it? Did it act on its own, or was it under some commanding force? He knew it was beyond his scope of experience. Kurt's only method for dealing with the supernatural in the past had been to point and shoot. Only Stephen Parrish seemed to have any insight into the matter, but Parrish had his own problems. He was once again the subject of hysterical scrutiny, and to draw him into the investigation might prove disastrous.

CHAPTER 64

PARRISH SAT IN HIS KITCHEN WITH A GLASS OF JUICE and a half-eaten muffin on the table. The tinny voice of a portable radio was tuned in to WVOS, the local news station. He'd already heard the morning update twice and was well aware of the latest demon attack. In a call placed to the sheriff's office, he'd offered to examine the site himself, but Kronin strictly forbade him.

"You step one foot on that tarmac, Stephen," the sheriff warned, "and the press will be on you like piranha." Parrish reluctantly agreed. The airport was a media hotspot, and it was best to keep a low profile.

So in the midst of all the excitement, he was forced to "stay put." He listened intently to *Open Mike*, a call-in talk show. Today's topic: is there a monster loose in Sullivan County? Bud Thomsen was the show's arrogant host, and he handled the subject with his typical aplomb of singeing irony and hip skepticism. Parrish found his flamboyant irreverence annoying.

"Open Mike. You're on the air."

"Yes, Bud. Roy Schaeffer, here." The caller sounded young. Mid-twenties. "I was pulling out of the Sidewinder bar, driving north on 17B about midnight, when I *saw* it. *Big* mother—"

"Out kinda late, weren't you, Roy?"

"Well . . ."

"Boozing with your buddies?"

"Just a cocktail. I made a turn onto Starlight Road, and it came out of the sky. Landed for a moment on one of the electric towers."

"Really? What did it look like?"

"Like one of them whatchamacallits you see in the museum. A Wingasaurus."

"C'mon, Roy? A *dinosaur*?"

"Swear to God! It had a wingspan of about twenty feet."

"I think you had more than a cocktail."

"No, man. Honest to God."

"Get on the wagon, Roy, and get off my show." *Click!*

It was a typical report.

The show ran for two hours, and there were many similar calls from eyewitnesses, frightened school moms, and armchair demonologists, all voicing their best explanations and deepest fears. Speculation soared as to the nature of the beast. Theories ranged from extraterrestrial to magical, with the occasional "prehistoric throwback" tossed in. One caller said the "Chapinaw Demon" was a *Wendigo*, a forest spirit of the lost Indian tribes. A New Jersey resident insisted it was their own Jersey Devil, a mythical creature of the Pinelands, which had haunted the Garden State for the past 260 years. An ornithologist suggested that it might be an oversized condor, a *Quetzalcoatlus* that had wandered north from Argentina. The legendary "thunderbird" had a wingspan of over fifteen feet and was alleged to attack dogs and small children.

Whatever the theory, prehistoric or preternatural, people were readily accepting that there was a strange animal loose in the county, but for many it was a harbinger for greater evil. Halloween was approaching, and there was talk about putting a suspension on the festivities. Schools were canceling parties, and the big costume parade down Main Street would likely be axed as well. With all the fear of "demons," the atmosphere did not seem appropriate for fanciful spooks and specters.

As he listened, Parrish felt his intuitive hairs twinge. Dread could be a tangible thing. It was all about him, like a sticky pitch that clung to his skin. People were frightened, and it created a shift in the æther. All around him, rational thought was being controverted by fear and paranoia. If it continued to fester, there would be more demons. Not demons with fangs and wings, but monsters of a more imminent sort—demons of intolerance. An epidemic of hate and suspicion could surface that would tear the town apart. And he was ground zero for the assault.

But for now there was nothing he could do. Julie had already confronted Tom, attempting to dissuade him from his animation. The boy had refused, and worse. His emotional outburst had evidently triggered another rampage. It showed how dangerously things had progressed. Clearly the demon had taken significant possession of Tom's psyche, and enraging the boy in any manner could unleash it. The next course of action, he feared, would be far more severe—some form of controlled exorcism. But they were unprepared for such a direct assault, and to confront him forcibly could prove disastrous. You couldn't rip the demon out of Tom's soul without doing irreparable damage to the boy, and you risked another outburst from the creature. Even were they to succeed, the demon would likely flee to seek a new host, perhaps one less innocent than Tom DeFrank.

Parrish would need Culhane's assistance and was preparing another trip to the little bookshop in New York, where the occultist worked feverishly from the *grimoire*. Together they might find some answers. He only hoped it wouldn't be too late.

There was one small comfort. The creature had not taken a life. Not yet.

"Open Mike. You're on the air."

"Yes, Bud," the caller cleared his throat. "I've been listening in, and I have a thing or two to say." Parrish stiffened to the voice. It was *Wilkens.*

Thomsen paused on the line, adjusting his tone appropriately. "Nice to hear from you, Gerard. I'm sure all our listeners were sorry to learn about the recent loss of your wife."

"Thanks, Bud. She's in a better place."

So his wife passed away. It was the first Parrish had

heard of it. Poor Connie, he offered in silent condolence.

"Now, about this 'demon'," Wilkens continued. "It's evident that our community has come under diabolical assault, and I hate to say it, but I told you so. Or at least I told the folks down at City Hall a few years ago. I said plain and clear; you invite the devil into your midst, and demons will follow. I've been fighting this thing in my own quiet way, since the death of my son Joshua. You're all familiar with those sorrowful circumstances, I'm sure. Now, I don't mean to name a name, or point an accusing finger on your show, but I think we need to examine our consciences and do our civic duty for once and for all. Many of you may never have heard of Crohaven Manor or are aware of its history."

"You mean the Tornau murders?" Bud interceded. "I'm sure plenty of our listeners still remember those horrible days. I was in high school at the time, and two of the murdered girls were classmates of mine. Everyone remembers Jacob Tornau."

"Sometimes a devilish presence leaves a trail behind," Wilkens continued, "and it attracts evil like flies to the stench of rotted meat. I swear to you on the holy name of our Lord that the evils of Tornau have come home to roost. He has returned to his old house in human form and is conducting all manner of devilry on the *community payroll*."

"Huh," Thomsen commented. He was clearly out of his element.

"Now, I'm just a simple businessman. I run a string of appliance stores, Bud, and I would never hire an employee of questionable integrity. If I sensed they were corrupt, or possessed any degree of moral ambiguity, they're *fired*! Plain and simple. Now, here we have a building steeped in sinister activities, and what does our town do? It employs a *sorcerer* as its custodian! A man with ungodly powers of influence. I tried to have him fired, once. No, they said. Unconstitutional. So what can we do? We can attack the building itself! I'm lobbying to have the landmark status of Crohaven Manor revoked for good. Let's knock it down and sell off the property. Send the man packing, and offer him no succor in our town. Once the sorcerer is gone, the demon will follow. I promise you. We're holding a rally in front of City Hall next Friday afternoon. We need your support. In the name of my boy, Joshua, I'll be sounding the horns of Jericho. And the walls of Crohaven will come down!"

CHAPTER 65

CLIFF BURKE DROPPED HIS CIGARETTE BUTT INTO THE urinal and watched it swish around in the water as he flushed. He was in the high-school bathroom with Gunthur, keeping his usual store hours. Zack McBride pushed his way in, brushing past two underclassmen that were leaving.

"You again?" Burke grimaced, shaking his head laughing. "I don't believe this."

"C'mon, Burke," Zack pleaded. "I need some downers. I'm all on edge."

"Yeah, so I read. What did you do with all that stash I just sold you? Eat it? No wonder you're seeing monsters."

"It was real, man!" Zack protested. "Didn't you hear the news?" The "airport attack" had given credibility to his story, but the school rampage was old news now. His fifteen minutes of fame were up.

Gunthur snickered, "The guy's wasted."

Burke rinsed his fingers in the sink. "I don't like seeing my customers freaking out in the papers. It's bad for business. Before you know it, people start asking questions, and then I got problems. Did they do a test on you? 'Cause 'dust' stays in your system, man."

"They didn't test me for anything. They just found the weed in my pocket. That's all. I told 'em it was my brother's."

Burke smiled at Gunthur. "I bet he dropped the dust along with the weed. That'll totally screw with your head every time."

"He'll be seeing Tinkerbell next," Gunthur scoffed.

"I didn't have any dust!" Zack shouted. "I sold it!"

Burke's eyes went cold. "You *what*?" He gazed at the boy suspiciously. Sometimes he could smell trouble, and this kid was beginning to stink. Striking with the speed of a cobra, he grabbed Zack and shoved him against the wall. "Did I just hear right? You said you *sold* it? What am I, your fuckin' middleman? Did I say you could front my goods for profit?"

"Quit it!" Zack fought his grip nervously as Gunthur stepped over to assist Burke.

"What do you have, a little action over at the junior high school?"

"No! I don't!"

Gunthur grabbed the boy by the sides, and together they pulled Zack onto the windowsill. The window was open. Second-floor drop. Zack was hoisted nearly halfway out. More and more he struggled as his torso dangled over the edge. His head fell back and he got a startling upside-down view of the teacher's parking lot.

"Little pipsqueak!" Gunthur said. "We should let him drop."

"Who'd you sell the stuff to, McBride? Who'd ja sell it to?" Burke let his grip loosen. "Better tell me, boy, or it's a long way down!" Burke pulled him in and out of the window, each time a little farther.

"Okay—okay!" Zack shouted. "I sold my stash. A coupl'a times."

"To who, dammit?!"

"I don't know his name. Some kid. A senior. Tall guy, dark hair."

Burke exchanged a fiery glance with Gunthur at the boy's description. It was starting to make sense now. They pulled Zack back off the windowsill. His relief was short lived when Burke gave him a swift punch in the stomach. Gunthur followed up with some pounding of his own while Zack McBride received his first dose of anger vicariously aimed at Kevin.

Kevin was napping on a bench in Senior Lane. He had a magazine over his face to shade him from the light, so he didn't see the angry figure vault into the alcove. The magazine was snatched off his eyes, jolting him awake, and there was Cliff Burke's mug in his face.

"You hear about Zack McBride?" he asked. "Somebody beat him up real bad."

Kevin feigned ignorance. "Who?"

"McBride. You know, the kid in the papers."

"Oh, yeah. Saw a 'demon'." He sat up, ignoring Burke as he rose to his feet to stretch nonchalantly. "Must've been high on *dope*."

"Seen any 'demons' of your *own*, lately?"

"Just you."

"Lately, I've had this uncomfortable feeling that I've got a tail on me, like I need eyes on the back of my head."

"Would be an improvement. Why don't you check with your doctor?"

"Shut up!" Burke snapped. "I know what you're up to. You've been hitting . . ." He lowered his voice to an intense whisper, aware of eyes around them, "you've been hitting up my 'clients' for stash. Stop screwing around! If you want to see 'demons,' you come to the source."

"Suck moose."

Burke shoved him in the chest. "Man, I gotta teach you some respect. You got no fear of us whatsoever, do you?"

Kevin met his leer and matched it.

"So what are you gonna do, huh? You gonna nark me out? Is that your plan? A little you-or-me, 'this town ain't big enough' bullshit? What the hell is your problem, Kevin? We used to be friends."

"Used to be. I cry every night over it."

"You know, I'm getting sick of this petty vendetta of yours. I didn't do nothing to you. I just screwed around with some pussy, and she wasn't even yours! You gotta let it go, man. Kathy's gone! This won't bring her back."

It was like pulling the pin from a grenade.

Kevin grabbed Burke and slammed his back against the wall. "Don't say her name!" he shouted. "Don't you EVER say her name. I don't even want you THAT CLOSE TO HER! Now you listen, man, 'cause I'm the 'exorcist'! I'm gonna rid this town of 'demons' of all kinds, starting with you!"

With an angry toss, he threw Cliff Burke against the benches. Burke lost his balance and fell hard. When he got back to his feet, Kevin had already left the lane. He glared with enmity, knowing Kevin's wasn't an idle threat. Burke knew the final round had begun.

CHAPTER 66

THE NETHERWORLD SET WAS COMING DOWN. TOM TUGGED at the aluminum foil trees until they were torn free from the baseboard. He wasn't gentle. The trees were wrenched and mangled, revealing the sparkling foil beneath their painted bark. There was a sense of urgency as he dismantled the landscape. Bit by bit, it came down. The fragments of forest and Styrofoam mountain were hastily stuffed into black garbage bags. Within minutes, the room was thoroughly deforested, scoured, and cleansed of the alien vista. He felt a pang of regret, staring at the barren wall behind his dresser. The Jovian skyline was gone, retreating now into the recesses of his mind. He cringed as he destroyed his handiwork, but he drew strength knowing that with every savage wrench he was reclaiming some control.

The dreams had abruptly ceased, as though stashing the model away was enough to banish the demon from his psyche. Or perhaps, Tom considered, Fau'Charoth had abandoned him for a worthier vessel. Whatever the case, his dreamscapes were as barren as his waking life, devoid of color and joy. Nevertheless, its influence was still pervasive. Temptation pulled strong. He could feel its tow on him, like a lasso, whenever he neared the chest. The old wooden cabinet had become his own personal Pandora's Box. Inside, the model still waited for him. The sight of the netherworld set invaded his fortitude, whittling at his willpower, and he knew he had to destroy it or be lost. It had taken him all week to gather the strength to tear the set down. He was in the constant throes of withdrawal, like an addict strung out, desperate for a fix, but it got easier every day, and he was convinced he was on the road to recovery.

The real agony was at school. His heartache over Julie was unbearable. He had not managed to catch even the most distant glimpse of her. Whether by accident or design, she was nowhere to be found. It seemed she stayed clear of the lunch area and detoured every possible way from her usual route. Passing their meeting spots was like being impaled on a lance, yet he wandered by as often as he could, peeking from corners, hoping beyond hope to find her waiting for him. But he knew encountering her by accident in the hall would be devastating. What if she ignored him or scowled at him? What if he saw her *with somebody else*? He had known her for less than two months, and already it was agonizing to be without her. Tears stung his eyes as he thought of their time together.

Danny and Kevin were both stunned to learn of his breakup. He fiercely refused to discuss the details, until he had to steer away from them entirely. He walked alone for long hours after school, wandering aimlessly through town, dumping quarters in video games at the convenience store. Coming home offered him no relief. He felt bitterly isolated, lashing out at his mom for no reason. There was nowhere to go, no one to whom he could turn.

Tom sighed and began carrying the refuse out of the room.

As he stashed the bags alongside the curb of his driveway, the Monstermobile pulled up unexpectedly. Tom saw his friend behind the wheel. "Kev?" he asked.

Kevin stared out at him with troubled eyes. "Taking out the trash?"

"Yeah."

"Me too. You got a minute? We need to talk." He left the car and headed toward the house. Tom assumed he wanted to discuss his situation with Julie, and felt at last willing, even grateful, to talk about it. But then he noticed Kevin was carrying a duffle bag. *The* duffle bag.

Walking deliberately into his house and room, Kevin looked around at the debris of the set. "What happened here? A tornado? Your mom let you keep your room a mess like this?"

"She doesn't come in here anymore."

"Why not?"

"She's afraid to," Tom said. "Last night she plopped a basket of laundry at my door. She wouldn't even bring it in."

Kevin raised a question with his eyes, but quickly dismissed it. He plopped the duffle bag onto the unmade bed and pried it open just enough to expose its contents. Inside was the large Ziploc bag of marijuana. Joining it now was a series of smaller bags filled with pills and a white powdery substance.

Tom looked at them uncomfortably. "More drugs?"

"I've been buying it off Burke's little 'clients.' Mostly Quaaludes and some angel dust. Cost me a fortune."

"Jesus, Kev." Tom looked away, nervously rubbing his temple. "What are you gonna do with it?"

"Relax. It's evidence. The sheriff needs evidence for a search warrant. Now he's got it."

Tom dropped his shoulders in relief. "So you're going to the police?"

"Eventually. Not yet, though. I need something more to tie it all together, but I'm gonna nail the bastard. Maybe bring down the entire operation."

"What, you're gonna take on the mob, now?" He didn't like where this was going.

"No, but if I hang on a little longer, I might be able to tag his source. I know he has a contact somewhere in Yonkers. I figure he'll go for a run there soon. Maybe I can follow him."

"Why can't you just drop it off at the sheriff's and be finished with it?"

"'Cause if I just wanted to blow the whistle on the guy, I would've done so already. But this is my game, Tom, and I gotta do it my way."

"You're crazy, Kev, and you're in way over your head."

"Chill out. I know what I'm doing."

"So what did you bring it here for?"

"I need you to hold the stuff for me."

Tom's eyes widened. "*What?*"

"I had a run-in with Burke, today. He's definitely on to me. If anything happens, I want you to turn the stuff in. Whatever you do, don't touch it. I wrote a long letter in there too. Explains everything."

"Awww, man! Kevin, why are you doing this? This is crazy! It's not your problem."

"He's selling dope to *kids*, Tom! I'm *making* it my problem."

Tom was angry now and took to shouting. "Yeah, the trouble is it's *my* problem too. Mine and Danny's! They beat the crap out of us to get back at *you*! You think you're this caped crusader, taking on the bad guys—"

"I know, I know—"

"—but you keep forgetting there are consequences for your actions."

"I didn't forget. I know what I'm doing, Tom. This has been building for a long time. After Kathy, I had to do something. Me and Burke have this coming. You're right; we are like Batman and the Joker. Tied together by destiny. Eventually someone's gotta go down."

"I think that's a load of crap!"

"True." He smiled. As he spoke, he reached into his jacket pocket and pulled out what looked like a voodoo blow dart rolled out of paper. Tom paled as Kevin pulled out a lighter.

"What the—what are you doing?"

Kevin lit the joint. The little point glowed like the evil eye of an imp. Then he brought it to his lips and drew a breath. "I thought we might celebrate Burke's imminent downfall with a ceremonial toke. Some of his own stash. What do you think about that?"

The wisp of herbal fume made Tom choke. "What do *I* think? I think you've flipped your gourd. Put that away! My mom'll be home soon."

"I thought you mom doesn't come in here. C'mon, one puff. You can drop your 'anti-drug' convictions this one time."

"The whole point of having convictions, Kevin, is that you *don't* drop them."

"Oh, bullshit. Just take a lousy puff!"

"No! I'm not doing it. You shouldn't either. It brings you down to Burke's level. I thought you wanted to be better than him."

He inhaled again at the weed, and his voice started to crack. Already his eyes were taking on a dull glaze. "I *am* better than him. Smoking this pot demonstrates my superiority over my adversary. It's like eating his heart. C'mon, man, share this with me. One puff won't kill you."

Tom hesitated as the marijuana was offered to him. He didn't want to let Kevin down. He hated drugs and everything they represented, but that wasn't the reason. At that moment, looking at the burning tip of that joint, all he could think about was how it might affect his condition. *How it might arouse the demon.*

"Kevin, I can't."

"Try it."

"I don't want it!"

Kevin practically stabbed it into his lips. Tom swiped it out of his face. The joint went flying to the ground. Kevin stared down at it, and then at Tom, angrily.

"What the hell's wrong with you?" he said, retrieving the joint from the floor.

"I don't do that crap, and neither should you."

Kevin glared at him, suddenly incensed. "Well, what the hell do you know, anyway? You live in a goddamned fantasy world! At least I'm willing to try things. I'll tell you the difference between you and me, kiddo. You're wrong; I'm *not* some superhero fighting for truth and justice. I stole this dope because I could *get off* on doing it. It thrills me 'cause it's *real*! It's not some monster world I dream about for excitement. There is *real danger* here, and I'm willing to take my chances, because it's better than doing nothing and dreaming about stuff all the time. You're like a nagging kid brother to me sometimes. Tagging along and always criticizing. What do you know about the real world? It's like you're in a giant egg and you only know what you read on the inside of your shell."

The words pierced Tom deeply. Moisture soaked his eyes, and he fought off the tears. If only it was true, he thought to himself. If only I could be that innocent again.

Silence weighed heavily between them. Remorseful, Kevin shook his head. "Damn. I'm sorry, Tom. I didn't mean it. I don't know what I'm sayin' half the time."

"S'all right." He struggled to conceal the gloss in his eyes.

"I'm really sorry about you and Julie. You two really had something. I know what it's like to have your heart smashed."

"Yeah. I guess you do."

"I wish I could say 'it'll pass.' But it doesn't. It fucks with your head, until you want to kill yourself. That's why you gotta find something bigger to think about. You gotta *do* something. It's the only way, man."

A tear escaped Tom's eye, and he turned away to wipe it.

Kevin looked distant, scanning Tom's display shelves, where the monster models were gathered like a Greek chorus. A faint grin appeared on his face as he reflected on Tom's handiwork. "You're really talented, Tom. The way you can make these things and bring them to life? Man, that is *epic*! You're like a crazy genius or something. You're gonna go far with this stuff. I wish I could do something like this."

"Kev . . ."

He turned to Tom. "So are we clear? Can I leave the stash with you?"

Tom sighed. "Yeah . . . I guess. But only for a while."

"Your mom won't go snooping through your stuff?"

"No."

Kevin looked around the room and saw the big wooden chest in the back. Before Tom could react, he had lifted the lid up.

"How about in here?" he asked. Tom's blood turned to ice as Kevin tossed the duffle bag into the chest, ignoring its contents entirely. "That'll do. Maybe if you have a padlock for it."

Tom exhaled. *Fine*, he thought. *Keep all of the evil in one place.* He gave Kevin a studied glance, trying to penetrate the older boy's aloofness. "Are you sure you're all right?"

"Sure." He smiled and ambled for the door. "Like a bat outta hell."

He left Tom alone in his room.

Tom sat quietly for a moment, pondering everything Kevin had said. There was a lingering dread, and a foreboding that clutched tightly to his heart. He could hear the Monstermobile pull out of the driveway and peel off with a thunderous engine roar.

CHAPTER 67

KEVIN PULLED THE MONSTERMOBILE INTO THE LOT OF the Mini Mart convenience store and parked it off to the side, where he sat listening to Led Zeppelin. Two kids were making out in the car next to him. The girl couldn't have been older than thirteen. She had long dirty-blond hair and wore a sleeveless turtleneck that the boy was struggling to remove. As it passed over her arms, it got all bunched up, binding above her chin like a straitjacket. The boy continued to kiss her torso as she fought off the shirt. She barely filled that training bra.

As Kevin watched them, the kids peered over, noticing his gaze. He expected a dirty look, but instead the boy came out of the car, followed by the girl. She didn't bother to put her shirt back on, but crossed her arms teasingly over her chest.

The boy knocked on his window.

"Hey? Do you think you could buy us some brew?"

"What?" Kevin asked.

"C'mon. We'll share it with you." He held out a ten-dollar bill. Kevin had him pegged with a glance. Barely sixteen. Mother's car. Learner's permit. He frowned and shook his head.

"Please?" the girl asked, shivering against the chill in the air.

The boy leaned closer, whispering. "We can take a ride somewhere. Carla's real hot tonight. You can have her when I'm done."

Kevin cringed, but hid his reaction. He glanced at the girl and saw the bloodshot look in her eyes. Something triggered a protective response. He looked past the boy, directly at her. "Aren't you Jeff Bryant's kid sister?" Bryant was a former classmate, doing time as a juvenile.

"Yeah," she answered, surprised. "So what's it to you?"

"Do your parents know you're out this late?"

Her eyes froze on him. Before he knew it, he had stepped out of the car and was approaching her, ignoring her skinny date. "You live in Langley, don't you? C'mon, I'll give you a ride home."

The boy stepped in front. "Whoa! Hey! Like hell you will!"

Carla scowled. "I ain't going nowhere with you, perv!"

Kevin frowned. "You don't learn from your brother's mistakes, do you?"

"Oh, fuck off! Eddie, let's get outta here. Creep!"

Eddie and Carla returned to their borrowed cruise machine and sped off. Kevin felt stung for a moment and remembered when he was that young and stupid.

He went into the store and bought a bag of Doritos and a package of Slim Jims with cheddar cheese. Talk of brews made him thirsty, so he picked up a six-pack of Bud. The man at the counter knew him well enough not to proof him. Ironic, since he'd just recently turned eighteen and could've used a legal ID for the first time, rather than his fake one. He heard they were talking about raising the drinking age to twenty-one and wondered how they were going to pry beer cans away from nineteen-year-old college kids. Dampers. Nothing but dampers ahead.

He returned to the car, and that's when he saw three figures approaching him. They carried clubs and a bicycle chain.

Shit.

It was the Three Stooges.

Burke and Finch shuffled deliberately behind Gunthur's lumbering physique. They stood between him and the Monstermobile, probably waiting in ambush, and Kevin knew they meant business.

"Where ya going, Marshall?" Burke spoke out. "We gotta talk."

"Yeah, man. It ain't cool what you're doin'."

"Gotta take your medicine."

Kevin feigned motion to the left and then lunged for his car. They were on him in a second, dragging him around to the back of the store. His bag fell to the ground, one of the beer cans popping open, spewing a fountain.

The area was empty, save for a large garbage canister

and some empty crates. A loud humming emanated from the refrigerator systems, and there was a foul smell of spoiled meat. An alley cat meowed in warning and scurried off in the path of the assailants. It all happened so fast. Kevin hardly had time to react.

He took the first club in his chest. It knocked the wind out of him and filled him with fire. The second came down on his head, but he twisted in time for it to land on his shoulder.

"Fuck!" The pain made him furious.

The third club hesitated. He pounced on Burke, forcing him to the wall of the building. Another club tore his scalp, but he ignored it, banishing the pain from his mind.

"You couldn't face me alone, bastard? You gotta hide behind your goons?" His voice gurgled through coughed-up blood.

Burke pushed him away fiercely. "Damn you!" he hissed.

Gunthur's chain swiped Kevin hard above the ear. It knocked him senseless to the ground, and he almost blacked out. He felt a boot in his stomach. Lenny's boot, he was sure of it.

Then another from Gunthur. For a split second, Kevin saw Burke's club coming at him. No hesitation this time.

Thwack! The impact to his skull was tremendous. Kevin's head exploded in pain.

"Had to be a smartass," Burke snarled. "Couldn't mind your own like I told you to."

Kevin was on the ground now, looking up. Blood burned

his eyes, streaming from his temple. He felt nauseous, swimming out of consciousness.

If you're gonna do something, he thought.

Thwack!

Do it right.

Thwack!

Then he was gone, his mind snuffed out like a candle.

"That's enough, Burke!" Lenny yelled. "You're killing him!"

They looked down at Kevin, who lay still on the pavement. His eyes were gazing blankly through slits. "Oh mother . . . !" Gunthur said.

"I think he's dead," Lenny yelped. "You *killed* him, man!"

"Shut up!" Burke stared down at the body and poked his toe into Kevin's side, searching for movement. The boy was as still as concrete. "Shit," Burke said.

"Awww, man. This sucks man!" Lenny was already losing it, raking curled fingers through his hair. "Alcatraz. This shit is *Alcatraz*."

"See what you made me do, you stupid son-of-a-bitch?" Burke resisted an impulse to kick the body.

Lenny was about to bolt. Burke grabbed his shirt. "Where do you think you're going?"

"We gotta get outta here!"

"We can't just leave him, man. Too many people are gonna ask questions."

"What are we gonna do?"

"Shut the hell up, dammit! I'm thinking!"

They watched him anxiously as he clutched his club tightly, watching droplets of blood drip from its end. Then he set his mind on a solution.

Burke went to the silver Trans Am and checked the ignition for the keys. They were there. He glanced around nervously for passersby then climbed into the cab. The engine started, and the Monstermobile came silently around the building toward the others.

"C'mon," he called out, motioning them to drag Kevin's body over.

They were especially skittish as they carried Kevin to his automobile. He was limp and heavy in their arms. Gunthur and Lenny seemed squeamish, trying to avoid the blood.

"Put him in the front seat. I got an idea," Burke ordered as he went to retrieve the beer cans that had fallen to the ground.

Burke drove the Monstermobile, the car of his nemesis, to the outskirts of the county on Route 52. Kevin lay still against the side window of the passenger seat. The blood was crimson and clotted on his skull, but it was hidden well in the darkness of his hair.

Gripping the steering wheel tightly, Burke cursed aloud repeatedly. Damn it!

He didn't need this. It wasn't his intention to take things so far, but he didn't have a choice. With his insider knowledge, Kevin's threat was significant. He had to be taken out or else it would lead to an avalanche of dire consequence. Pushing drugs in a high school was a federal offense, and he was no longer a minor. That meant no juvie hall. This was serious prison time he faced.

He had to shut the kid up. Solve the problem.

Well, this was one problem that was solved for good.

Trouble was it created many others. Now he was looking at a murder rap.

Shit, shit, shit!

He glanced at the rearview mirror. His Jaguar followed close behind like a jungle cat. Gunthur was driving. He wouldn't let Lenny behind the wheel under these circumstances.

No more fuck-ups.

Every car they passed was a threat to them.

There was a spot Burke knew of where the road climbed to a crest. Just beyond it were a steep incline and a hard right turn. "Kenny's Corner" it was named, after a driver who had once hydroplaned over the railing to his death. It was a notoriously dangerous spot, especially hazardous in the winter months. At least two accidents had occurred here of which he knew. This would be the third.

Burke pulled the car to the edge of the road, a short distance above the infamous curve. He rubbed his shirtsleeve over the wheel to remove fingerprints and did a thorough job wiping things clean. He'd have to burn his clothes. Burn everything. He'd burn Gunthur and Finch too, if he could. Reaching over, he pulled Kevin's limp form toward the driver's seat and placed his hands on the wheel. Burke had generously drenched him in beer, so he smelled strong of alcohol.

Burke scanned the roadways. It was clear of any approaching traffic. Then he stepped out, reached in to put the transmission into "drive," and let the car lunge forward on its own. The Monstermobile barreled down the incline toward the railing and crashed through.

In the driver's seat, Kevin's mind swam momentarily into consciousness. His eyes focused briefly as the Trans Am plummeted down the hill. He didn't have strength to scream. The numbness had already robbed his body of pain. Any additional sensation was snuffed by the first impact of the car against an outcrop of rock, which snapped his neck.

It toppled eight times before crashing.

CHAPTER 68

THE SKY WAS OVERCAST WITH A SHROUD OF WHITE sheet that threatened to burst into a downpour. Perhaps it was the damp, chilly air that made this morning especially grim. Or perhaps it was the way students were gathered in little groups throughout the halls, the way students always gathered when there was *news.*

Tom sensed the disturbance from the moment he entered the school. His stomach tightened with dread. Danny stood alone beside his locker, and he appeared stunned.

"What's going on?" Tom asked.

"Tom . . ." Danny began. "Oh my God."

"Where's Kevin?"

The boy looked at him with such a dazed and fragile expression that Tom knew the answer before it was spoken.

He just *knew.*

Dan paused, and his look spoke a thousand words. "There was an accident."

Tom stiffened. He walked off with long deliberate strides, too angry to speak. Dan followed him. His hands were clenched into mallets. He used one against a locker cabinet. "Damn it!" Again and again he pounded it, until the pain made him stop.

"I knew it! I *knew* this would happen! That son-of-a-bitch!"

"Who?"

"You *know* who!"

"Tom . . ."

"*What?*"

"It wasn't Burke. It was a car wreck. He crashed off that curve on Route 52."

Tom looked at him, flabbergasted. "*Kenny's Corner?*"

"They found liquor. They said he was drinking."

"No," he countered furiously. "That's not what happened."

"Tom, he was speeding all the time. We both know it."

"Bullshit!"

He wanted to argue, but couldn't find the words, so he stormed off by himself, lost and inconsolable.

It wasn't *right*! It *couldn't* be!

Tom refused to believe what he heard. He skipped his first class and wandered the halls, unable to contain his emotion. It would cost him detention, but he didn't care. Kevin was dead. He considered going home. But instead, he sneaked into the basement and found a quiet spot in the boiler room, where he sat, dodging the maintenance men until he got his head straight.

The basement was dim and musty. Once before, he had

stolen back here to "get away from it all." He always knew where the dim quiet places were. They offered sanctuary. The roaring of ventilation motors could be heard, drowning out the voices above. There was a pile of old *Penthouse* magazines in a corner, and maintenance uniforms hanging on the pipes. Tom retreated to the darkest recess he could find. He pressed his back against the brick wall and sank to the ground. There, he reflected on his friendship with Kevin, cut down, like the boy himself, way too soon.

It began with a Cyclops model he'd brought to art class. He was proud of his handiwork, and needed to show it off. When kids in the class seemed duly impressed, it groomed his ego enough to keep the figure with him at lunch, eager for attention. He got more than he expected. Kevin Marshall, the cool rogue, was eyeing his goat-legged monster with interest.

As the older kid came over, Tom assumed the worst, but then—

"Whoa! *The Seventh Voyage of Sinbad*, right?"

Surprised, Tom answered with a grin. "That's right."

"I love that film. I love all those Sinbad movies." It turned out Kevin Marshall was a fantasy and SF film buff.

"No shit, you *made* this? I can't believe it." He held the model like it was a priceless relic, studying every detail.

They talked all afternoon about seven-headed hydras and sword-fighting skeletons. About the virtues of stop-motion over *Godzilla* suits, and why Dino De Laurentiis should never have remade *King Kong*. Tom had won a new friend.

Over the year, Kevin would change his life. He introduced him to the blue-collar ballads of Bruce Springsteen, the devilish twangs of Black Sabbath, and a new paradigm of life that shattered the confines of Tom's eggshell existence. The word "adventure" took on new meaning. It wasn't something you read or watched on a screen. It was something you survived and talked about. Adventures could be created from the simplest act of rebellion, the token theft from a dime store, or driving with the headlights off. "Counting coup"—that's what he called it. Testing fate with a smile. Kevin taught him how to be "cool," how to live on the edge, and how to have fun. All it took was a fool's confidence and a world without boundaries. And now he was gone. Tom always wondered what it would've been like to have a brother. Now he knew what it was like to *lose* one.

Tears came at last, and they blurred his eyes. But they didn't banish the anger. He felt robbed. Why would Kevin be so careless? It didn't make sense. He was a fighter pilot behind the wheel, keen and alert. He never drank before driving. And if he wanted to kill himself, he would have chosen a more original crash site.

Kenny's Corner?

It lacked imagination. It was almost a cliché. Too easy. Too convenient.

From the moment he learned the news, the only thing he could think of was Burke. He wanted to believe it was Burke. He needed to place blame.

Burke was the only thing right now that made sense.

Tom confronted Burke in the lunchroom as he wandered alone with a vacant stare. There was no sign of Gunthur or Finch. That was suspicious in itself.

"Got a guilty conscience?" Tom inquired as he stood in Burke's path.

It jolted the senior. "Only from what I'll do to *you*, if you don't move," Burke threatened.

But Tom stood his ground, challenging him. He felt powerful, as though grief had tempered his mettle into cold steel.

"You bastard," he said. "I know it was you."

Burke became unusually sensitive. "Watch your mouth, DeFrank." He tried to shove Tom aside. Tom stood rigid, pushing back.

"What the hell's your problem?" Burke glared.

"I *know* you did it!"

"Like hell. I had nothing—"

"Bullshit!"

"Listen DeFrank, Kevin was reckless. He got what was coming to him."

"Yeah? Convenient for you," Tom baited, "No nark reports from the grave, right, Burke?"

If it was meant to catch his attention, it worked. Burke's eyes went frigid with a silent "what-did-you-mean-by-that?"

"You know what I'm talking about," Tom added. "Had to shut the guy up, didn't you? Well, maybe his *secrets* didn't die with him!"

It pressed a trigger. Burke detonated, tossing a wild blow to Tom's face. Tom dodged it, the knuckles grazing his scalp, and then he slammed Burke with an uppercut.

Danny Kaufman was sitting down to eat when he saw a startling sight. Tom DeFrank had just *walloped* Clifford Burke full in the jaw! The older boy lost his balance with the impact, crashing onto a tabletop. The table collapsed, spilling milk cartons and sending a group of girls scurrying to safety. But he recovered quickly, jumping at Tom with a vengeance.

A crowd flocked to the skirmish. Burke sent a powerful swipe to Tom's cheek that caused him to stagger back. Arms were flailing wildly, and Danny could not see clearly. He pushed his way through the bewildered throng, hoping to determine who was "winning."

But nobody ever "wins" a high-school brawl. Chaos ensued as bodies jumped into the fray; some to separate the combatants, others to egg them on. The entire incident lasted all of ten seconds.

"I'm gonna kill you, man!" Burke hissed at Tom, blood dripping from his mouth.

Tom fought off the gripping hands. "I guess you got a taste for it now."

And then the lunch police arrived. Teachers put an end to the violence.

Danny watched as the two foes were dragged apart and hauled off to the front office. He tried to make eye contact with Tom as they left, but Tom was oblivious.

From a distance away, Julie Parrish also watched, ducking behind her schoolmates, and a tear welled up in her eyes for Tom's sake. When everything had calmed down she sought Danny out for the details.

CHAPTER 69

"DAD," JULIE SAID INTO THE PHONE WHEN HER FATHER picked up. "There's trouble!"

"What is it, Sprite?" Parrish answered from his end. "I can barely hear you."

She glanced around to see who might be listening. The school payphones were a bank of unsheltered boxes on a wall right in the center of the hall. There was very little privacy when using them. As it was, the bustling of between-class students made it difficult to speak, let alone hear her father's voice. She was forced to shout, and was afraid her own voice would carry. She cupped her hand over the receiver and spoke in a harsh whisper. "Tom's been in a fight. His best friend Kevin Marshall was killed last night."

"*What?* That's terrible."

"I've never seen him so angry."

"Where is he now?"

"The principal's office. They'll probably send him home. Danny says he blames this bully, Cliff Burke. They got into a big brawl during lunch. Dad, what do you think might happen? I mean—with Tom's condition?"

He paused on the line. Julie felt herself trembling. She thought of the school and the airport. They were trivial matters compared to this.

"I don't know, sweetheart," he said. "This can only make things worse. I'm going to New York later this afternoon to discuss the matter with Humphrey. I think you should—"

"Let me come too," she interrupted.

Silence, as he considered. "Julie, I don't think your mother would allow—"

"I'll give Mom a call and smooth things over. Dad, I have to come. I know things about Tom that neither of you can possibly know. I can help!"

He paused again. "You may be right. I need to drop by the Municipal Center, first, to talk some sense into the town council. Did you bring your bike?

"No, but I can walk it."

"Four o'clock in the City Hall parking lot. Be careful, Julie. Stay off the street."

"Why?"

"Today's the rally."

"Oh." She forgot it was Friday. The Wilkenses' anti-Crohaven rally. She took her father's warning to heart, but this was something she had to see.

CHAPTER 70

AT THE END OF CLASSES, DANNY CAUGHT UP WITH TOM in the nurse's office. He sat alone on a cushioned bench with an ice pack to stem the swelling of his right cheek. It was gonna be one hell of a shiner.

"Hi," Dan said. "Does it hurt real bad?"

"No," Tom replied glibly. "You should see the other guy."

"I did. It looks like you mopped the floor with his ego." Dan smiled. "Everybody's talking about it. That was one incredible right hook you gave Burke. He's gonna be feeling it for a while. So what did Harding give you?"

"Suspended." He rose up from the bench. "And, starting Monday, two nights detention. They were 'lenient' with me 'cause they figured I'm upset about Kevin. Meanwhile, the murderer gets off scot-free."

"Tom . . ."

"He did it, Dan. He killed Kevin. I've got the evidence."

"What evidence?"

He told Dan about the drugs Kevin had stashed with him. Dan went pale.

"So Burke knew about it and wanted to shut him Shit. This is bad."

"Tell me about it."

"What are you gonna do?"

"I'm gonna do what Kevin wanted me to do. Turn it First, I gotta go home." He looked at Danny earnestly. " you think you can come over later? I don't want to be alon

Danny sighed. "Sorry, I can't. Annette's shopp with my mom, and I gotta watch my little brother. W about your mom?"

"She's leaving with Paul to St. Thomas. She'll be g till Tuesday."

Danny stifled his rolling eye. "You get the car at leas

"Yeah."

"Well, you can drop by if you want. We should ch on memorial services for Kevin." Danny walked him to door, then brushed him with a thoughtful look. "Oh . . . I saw Julie before. She's really worried about you."

Tom looked at him surprised. "She is?" His he trembled.

"You should give her a call."

"Yeah. Maybe," Tom said, reflecting. There was a g tening in his eye, but then he set his jaw rigidly. "I can't th about that now. I gotta grab a bus. Speak to you later."

"Hey . . . Tom . . ." Danny warned. "Don't do anyth stupid."

He sighed. "I'm just going home, Dan."

"I know," he added with concern. "Don't get lost."

CHAPTER 71

WHEN TOM GOT HOME, HE FOUND HIS MOM PACKED and ready to leave. Franklyn's BMW was parked out front. Maggie had bags gathered by the stairwell. They were rushing to catch an evening flight from JFK Airport, when Tom gave her the unsettling news about Kevin's death. Rattled, she made a pathetic attempt to offer sympathy. He couldn't tell if she was genuinely saddened or just inconvenienced by the need to offer comfort. She kept looking at the big clock in the living room and to Paul, waiting in the kitchen, before she finally took to scolding him for fighting.

"I can't believe you got *suspended*! Tom! What were you thinking?"

Tom was surprised by her reaction. "The kid deserved it."

"That's no excuse! You don't solve anything with violence. I didn't raise you like that."

"Sorry."

Again, she glanced at the clock. "What am I supposed to do with you?"

"Nothing! As usual."

"I can't leave you here alone if you're going to be like this."

"*Sure* you can!" he yelled, suddenly incensed. "What difference does it make? You never give a damn, anyway!"

"That's not true!"

"It *is* true! Dammit it, Mom, when's the last time you—"

"Don't shout at me!"

"You never even—"

"Well what am I supposed to do?" she challenged. "You keep locking yourself in your room with those damn MONSTERS! Think about *me* once in a while!"

Tom stared at her, dumbfounded. This was *madness*! He threw his arms up, "Go to Hell!" and stormed into his bedroom, slamming the door. Then he sank slowly to the floor.

His face was red, and his eyes ached for tears. How callous could she be? He had just lost his best friend, his *best friend*, and she was lecturing him about violence! The anger caused his heart to pound. It tightened his gut into a knot. His hands trembled, and curses gushed from his mouth in a harsh whisper.

I never want to see her again! I'm sick of her and I never want to see her again EVER!

His head went light. His churning emotions concentrated into a ball, and he began to feel that peculiar sensation in his solar plexus. Blood rushed from his face in realization.

Oh my God.

Alert to the danger, Tom leapt to his feet. *No.* This

can't happen. He hadn't animated in a week, and he was nowhere near the puppet. This could not be happening! He clutched his abdomen tightly, fighting the drift in his consciousness. He could feel the chill entering his body. Calm down. Get a grip. He took a series of deep breaths, sweeping the aggression out of his system.

Let it go. Let it go, man. Get a grip.

He made himself a blank slate. He purged himself of the intense rage.

At last the surging in his midsection died down. His hands ceased to shake, and his breathing took on a normal rhythm.

The danger had passed.

Tom sighed with relief and pondered how closely he had come to disaster. If he had lost control, if he had let his emotions erupt any further, the demon might have—

No!

Not to his *mom*!

He sat on his bed, exhausted.

His vision blurred as he thought of Maggie. All his grievances against her suddenly vanished. The emotional fortress built over the years had been breached. His eyes released a flood of tears, and he felt only a deep longing to be close to her again. To bridge the rift in their relationship and repair the damage. He realized that, despite all his efforts to shut her out, he needed her after all.

There was a soft knock at his door, and Maggie appeared. She wore a sullen expression, like one about to confess to a crime. He turned away, as though his tear-streaked face would offend her, but she came quietly to his side and put a hand on his shoulder.

"I've been to Hell, Tom," she said. "A long time ago."

"I know."

"So . . ." She paused and sat on the bed beside him. "You did find out. I thought you might have. How did you learn about it?"

"I just figured it out. It's not important."

"I almost lost you," she said. "You were stolen from us. I would have told you, but . . . it was so many years ago, and I didn't see the point. That was the most terrible day of our lives."

Tom sighed, accepting the reality at last. His mind was filled with questions. "How did it happen?"

Maggie sighed as the memory darkened her features. "We were in a parking lot, loading bags into the car. We turned our backs for a minute, just a *minute*, Tom, and you were gone. Someone came out of nowhere and just swept you away. It was horrible. Your father went completely berserk, out of his mind. We called the police immediately, but I was afraid we'd never find you again."

His voice was jagged with sobs. "Sorry you had to go through all that."

She took his head and pressed it softly into her bosom. Then she kissed it, passing her fingers through his hair. "You were such a beautiful baby. You were almost bald for a long time, and you had this silly crooked smile. To think

I almost lost you to those monsters . . ." She inhaled in an involuntary gasp. "I should have told you, but I wanted to put it out of my mind and never think about it again. I wanted to forget it ever happened."

"But some things don't simply go away because you want to forget them, do they, Mom?" He looked up at her.

"No. I guess I was fooling myself. I thought we were safe from him. I thought we had gotten far enough away from it all. But when I see all *this*," she gestured to the creatures on the shelf, "I wonder if he didn't touch you in some way."

Tom felt stabbed by this. "Mom. It wasn't Jacob Tornau that touched me. It was you and Dad, always fighting and shouting at one another. Making me feel like . . . a monster." His throat locked. "Like it was my fault you hated each other."

Maggie blanched. "Of course it wasn't your fault, Tom. I never hated your father, and I never blamed him for what happened, either. I was there too, that day. It was my responsibility as much as it was his. But he never forgave *himself*. He wanted to be Superdad, and your abduction crushed the life out of him. I don't think he ever trusted himself after that. He didn't feel he could take care of you anymore. He just gave up on life—on the three of us as a family. I put up with it as long as I could. I put up with it for *eight years*, but then I had to move on."

Tom looked at her blankly, overloaded with emotion.

"I'm sorry about Kevin, Tom," she continued. "I really

am. You lost your friend. I know how much it must hurt, honey. I'm truly sorry."

There was another knock at the door. This time it was Paul standing there. "I don't mean to interrupt, Maggie, but I need to know if we're still going. It's getting late. The rush-hour traffic . . ."

She looked into Tom's eyes. "Do you want me to stay here with you? Should I cancel the trip? Tell me what I should do?"

He stared into space, succumbing to a rush of feelings, and had to hold back more tears. *I don't want you to* stay, he thought. *I want you to* care.

Paul's eyes went to his digital clock impatiently.

"Honey?" she repeated. "Should I stay with you?"

Tom raised his shoulders with a relinquishing shrug "No. It's okay. Go."

There was a long pause as Maggie fenced with guilt and desire. Her expression was forlorn and tortured. She glanced toward Paul, who stood by the threshold with his arms crossed. Then she turned back to Tom with a decisive look.

"It's just for four days," she explained wistfully. "The tickets are nonrefundable."

Tom stifled a sigh, trying to mask his disappointment. "Okay."

"You can have the house and the car all to yourself. It has a full tank of gas. Invite your friends over if you get lonely. We'll be back on Tuesday night."

"I'll be fine, Mom," he assured them, big trooper and

all. His eyes were beginning to glaze again and he blinked off the moisture. “Nonrefundable” repeated through his head.

“Thanks, guy.” Paul smiled. “The next time, you’re coming with us. We’ll do the city and take in one of those science-fiction conventions.”

“Yeah. That’ll be fun,” Tom said. And he meant it, as much as he could mean anything at that moment.

CHAPTER 72

CROHAVEN MANOR WAS UNDER SIEGE. THE VILLAGERS were storming the castle, wielding not torches and battering rams, but picket signs, pencils, and clipboards.

"Sign the petition!" Dorothy Bottoms, a lector from St. John's Presbyterian, shouted in front of City Hall, where a table was erected for their rally. The table had poster-sized prints of the infamous estate and copies of old newspaper articles detailing the atrocities of Tornau. With the weather cleared, a late-afternoon crowd of students, shoppers, and happy-hour drinkers gathered. Stacks of fliers were quickly dispersed among them.

Dangling from the branches of a big tree was a large winged demon. Some imaginative artist had built a scarecrow Fau'Charoth, drawing from the sketchy descriptions in the papers. It was composed of black trash bags and painted Styrofoam, with a papier-mâché head. It had lemons for eyes. The presence of the gangly, wind-animated monster rammed home the group's agenda.

Emily Driscoll and her husband handed out petitions.

Others were clutching signs that proclaimed "SELL CROHAVEN MANOR!" and "NO WITCH HOUSES IN CHAPINAW," while a third read "TORNAU II," a direct reference to Parrish. There were copies of the newspaper articles announcing the "demon" attacks and transcripts of the radio reports.

Gerard Wilkens dispersed them like campaign fliers.

"Let me tell you about Josh!" he shouted. "Let me tell you about my boy."

His voice boomed above Dorothy's, relating the unfortunate account of his son's suicide. It was his *cause célèbre*, and he spared no expense in bringing as much attention to the rally as possible. Eight of the protestors were in his employ. The G. Wilkens Appliance outlets were shorthanded that day, with all his key personnel recruited to attend the rally. The rest were wary citizens from the local churches with a bone to pick about witchcraft. Their intention was clear: remove the warlock from Chapinaw, and the demon would follow.

"It says in the Bible," Wilkens quoted, "Forswear ye of wizards, mediums, or spiritists, nor seek out soothsayers, lest ye be defiled by them! Those who do these things are an abomination unto the Lord!" He was reading chapter and verse off a card. Despite his recent loss, Wilkens seemed like a man reborn, filled with energy and fierce with purpose. He still wore his black mourning suit, but retained his famous tan fedora as a symbol of his relentless spirit. He had set aside his grief and blazed onward like a soldier in battle. It was a holy war he was fighting. Josh had been its first casualty. Connie the second. *He* would not fail them. This simple, civil action had become his crusade, and every signature he drew from the crowd was a victory.

" 'I will be swift to bear witness against sorcerers'!"

People gave them startled glances. Many of the newcomers had never heard of Crohaven Manor and were surprised to learn of its history. To the older residents, however, the sale of the "devil estate" was long overdue. The building was already perceived as a nucleus for sinister activity, and its caretaker was an easy target. The strange new phenomenon simply added to their suspicions. There was an evil abroad. Folks were frightened, and fear abhorred a vacuum. It needed a point of origin. Someone to blame. It was their way of taking control of the intangible, quell the hysteria, fight demons with angels.

"God only knows what he does in that building all day long," Emily stressed. "They say he communes with the dead. What's he doing with their *souls*?"

"He *died*, once. I read about it in the papers," Pete Driscoll added. "He *died*, and came back to *life*. Doesn't that tell you anything? I mean, if Heaven won't keep him around, *I* sure as hell don't want him."

"I believe in religious freedom as much as anyone," Dorothy said to another. "I have friends who are *Jewish*. But this man goes too far. I hear he can read minds. I can't sleep at nights thinking about it. It's like he's crawling around inside my head. Do you want your children living in a town with a—with a *vampire*?"

"*Cool!*" some of the kids shouted playfully. "Let's put a stake through his heart!"

"Yeah, throw him in the lake and see if he floats!"

CHAPTER 73

WAS IT PRIDE THAT CAUSED STEPHEN TO COME HERE today? He reflected upon it as he sat in the office of George Neuhaus, head of the town board. He'd been warned not to venture anywhere near Main Street. Avoid the rally at all cost. Keep a low profile. He was an exile in his own community, forced to elude the crowd by stealing into a back entrance like an infamous outlaw. It made him take stock of his life, wondering if any part of him deserved such incalculable persecution.

All this evasiveness left him feeling impotent. Part of him wanted to face his aggressors and confront their accusations directly. Most of all, he wanted to exonerate himself and quash the fear that was careening through the æther like sulfurous fumes. It was suffocating.

"They're having a vote tonight." George scratched the white hair on his head. "We'll contact you with the results. I'm not sure what more I can do for you, Stephen. You've been a good employee. You were the only one who would take that job at the time. I never could figure your fascination with the place. Most people steer clear of it, saying it's haunted. I'll be sorry to see you go, but I have my hands tied on this one."

"What if I talk to them?" Parrish offered. "Assure them that this 'demon' has nothing to do with me."

"You'd be talking to a wall. The folks out there have their minds set. They're looking to blame somebody for this thing, and you're a perfect scapegoat, what with your special *talents*, and all. Besides, Gerard Wilkens has been lobbying to shut the place down for years now, and he's finally got the public's ear. You have to realize Wilkens thinks you're the devil *incarnate*. He blames you for his son's death, and now his wife's as well."

"That's rubbish!" Parrish said. "When are you going to realize you're dealing with a lunatic?"

"He's a madman. No doubt about it. But there's a method to his madness. He happens to be an astute businessman, and will likely profit handsomely from his personal vengeance. It's not the first time he's had his sights on that property. He filed an offer back in '77 to buy it, and just submitted a comprehensive proposal from his partnership of investors to purchase the estate and some surrounding farmland. There's talk of a new access road from Route 17 that would make the territory ripe for development. The only thing that's stood in his way before is the New York Historical Society. They insist the mansion's some kind of architectural treasure. But with the right amount of signatures, he could force us to overturn its landmark status and sell the property to him. God knows, the town could use the revenue. It's a done deal, Stephen. Word to the wise, me to you? You should seek new employment."

CHAPTER 74

JULIE WALKED INTREPIDLY TOWARD THE MUNICIPAL Center. She knew of the rally, of course, and had been warned to avoid it, but unlike her father, she couldn't resist seeing for herself. In front of City Hall, she saw the angry throng, heard the shouts, and read the protest signs. The makeshift Fau'Charoth billowed from the tree, and as she drew closer a clipboard was shoved in her face.

"Sign the petition!" Dorothy Bottoms shouted at her, waving the petition. Julie glanced over its content, feeling her blood boil. The crowd surrounded her, Parrish haters, all of them, making their insinuations, lost in ignorance and medieval accusation. Well, she was a Parrish too! Suddenly she despised the woman with her smug, self-righteous grin. And then she heard the belligerent venom-filled voice of Gerard Wilkens.

"Sign the paper! Help rid the town of the evildoer!"

Something snapped.

Julie snatched the clipboard from Dorothy, hurling it to the pavement. She shoved the startled woman aside and grabbed at the first protest sign she saw. "Sell Crohaven Manor" was wrenched from a man's grip.

"Hey!" Mr. Driscoll shouted.

She tossed it to the street where a passing auto swerved to avoid it. Then she grabbed another sign—this one a curse on her dad—and ripped it free. Julie waved the sign, parting the spectators before her, and swiped it across the tabletop. Papers flew everywhere. Two men attempted to restrain her. Bodies surrounded her small form until she was trapped on all sides. She struggled as they closed in. The table overturned as hands gripped her wrists, and an arm encircled her waist from behind.

She fought them off fiercely, kicking and swearing. "What's wrong with you people?! He didn't do anything to hurt you! Not one of you!"

Confused faces. Some filled with doubt, others with guilt.

But Wilkens pointed an accusing finger at her. "You stay away from here, little girl! You're not wanted here! Everyone, this is the witch's daughter! She looks sweet and innocent, but she played as much a part in my son's death as the man himself!"

"Liar!" she struggled. "He was my friend! You treated him like a *dog*!"

"The fruit doesn't drop far from the tree."

She met the poison in his eyes. "We didn't kill your son, Mr. Wilkens! *You* did!"

Wilkens glared with outrage. He seemed like a wild

boar about to charge.

The man holding Julie released his grip with a gasp.

He fell away, clutching his shoulder where it was crunched. Julie turned to see her father fending off another man. The crowd recognized him instantly, and there were gasps of alarm.

"That's *him*!"

"*The witch-guy!*"

Tall and intimidating, Stephen Parrish stood among them like a vengeful archangel.

Hungry for blood, some closed in on him but were astonishingly brushed aside. A backhand sweep sent one man careening to the ground. Another keeled over, clutching his stomach. Julie watched as Parrish floated past them, deflecting their blows, twisting their arms backward in painful holds. He seemed to move in slow motion, taking deliberate strides, the swift actions of his hands a blur. She recognized some of the stances from his exercise.

Tai Chi. A form of Eastern meditation. It was also a highly advanced *martial art.*

He continued until he stood directly in front of Gerard Wilkens and met his squinty-eyed gaze. "Leave my daughter alone," he said in breathy challenge. Enraged, Wilkens took a swipe at him, but it was deflected. Parrish curled his arm past the man's fist and twisted his elbow in a defensive hold. The man was wrenched to the ground, moaning. He hissed with malice, but the pain was debilitating. Parrish glared down at him.

"You fear me, don't you, Gerard? For the past three years with your hateful campaign, you've never once confronted me yourself. You're afraid to look at me. You see something you don't want to face. You call me evil. You want to believe I'm the devil. But all you see in me is a reflection of Josh. You see your boy staring back at you through *my eyes.* Have you ever looked through the eyes of another person? Have you ever seen yourself through those eyes? Because I have, and I'll show you what it's like."

He gripped the man's wrists firmly, staring into his pupils. Wilkens resisted, but was mesmerized. The man's grip on his flesh seemed to burn, and there was an electric tingling up his arms, into his spine and neck, until it reached his skull. Images synapsed in a cognitive stream. He saw his own face, bitter and punitive, heard his own ugly words of threat. He felt constricted. Entombed in total blackness.

"Do you feel it, Gerard?" Parrish hissed. "Do you feel your son's terror? Can you see the darkness?"

Wilkens spasmed. "Let go of me, damn you!"

He remembered the confessional. The planks of black wood, crushing in on him. "No!"

His son's voice. *Let me out, Dad! Let me out! Let me out!*

Struggling against confinement. Pounding the wood in terror! *Let me out! Let me out!*

"*No-o! Damn you! Damn you!*" Wilkens pulled free of the psychic's grasp, lost in a maelstrom of guilt, and fell crying to his knees. The crowd watched as Parrish stepped away from the man, leaving him broken and defeated.

Parrish stared down at Wilkens, and half-whispered an axiom.

" 'Beware the fury of a patient man'."

He then went to Julie, who gazed at him in wonder. The crowd parted like the Red Sea around them, but he no longer noticed. His eyes registered enormous pain for her as he took her aside.

With a single whir of its siren, a police car pulled to the curb. The sheriff and Deputy Evans stepped out, with Kurt Kronin speaking in a megaphone to the remaining spectators. "ALL RIGHT, CLEAR OUT," the mechanical voice boomed. "ALL OF YOU. MOVE ON." Kronin read the scene in an instant—bewildered bystanders looking like they'd witnessed an accident, Gerard Wilkens on his knees bawling, and there was Stephen Parrish, standing off with Julie like a cornered tiger with its cub.

The crowd dispersed quickly after that. Evans helped Driscoll and her husband restore the table and retrieve the scattered papers. Dorothy looked to Wilkens and tried to help him up, but he shook her off, still traumatized by his vision. Kronin deliberately addressed him with the megaphone. "YOU TOO, GERARD. LET'S GO."

Wilkens rose to his feet, jolted by the shrill voice, and caught sight of the witch man and his girl as the sheriff escorted them off. Whatever remorseful epiphany he might have experienced was already lost in a new wave of hatred.

He gleamed after the father and daughter with fell intent.

Kronin shook his head as he walked the Parrishes to the old station wagon in the community parking lot. "God damn it, I warned you. I told you this would happen. Someday, Stephen, you're going to use that extra-special talent of yours to steer *clear* of trouble. These folks are frightened, and you're not helping much."

"I have a right to protect my daughter."

"I know," he conceded. Parrish sensed it had been a long couple of weeks for the man.

The sheriff was at his wit's end. He surveyed the buildings around him as though looking for an element of normalcy. "I don't know what gets into people. This whole town's chasing shadows. With what's been happening, who can blame them? Now maybe they're just looking for a 'monster' to pin it all on, but dammit, Stephen, I'm no *psychic*, but I've a hunch you've got more to tell me. That you're the man with the answers."

Parrish exhaled resolutely. "You don't want 'answers,' Kurt. What you want is some reasonable explanation so that you and your town can go back to sleep. I can't give you that. But I can tell you this. There *is* a monster loose in Chapinaw, and it's not *me*. Rather I'm doing everything I can to stop it. So I'd appreciate it if you could keep the torches away from the castle long enough for me to finish. After which, they can burn the place to the ground if they like."

Kurt studied the psychic, hoping for details, but assumed

none were forthcoming. He knew they were matters best left unspoken, beyond his comprehension, likely beyond the scope of reason. He rubbed the phantom pain in his shoulder and walked off with his shuffling stride. As he glanced back at Parrish one last time, he couldn't help thinking the man had his finger in a dike that was about to break.

Julie stepped to the passenger side of the car, expecting her dad to follow. But Parrish stood alone for a moment, lost in reflection. She returned to his side.

"What is it?"

He looked at her with a painfully troubled expression. "I'm sorry, Julie . . . I'm sorry. I never intended for you to get involved in all this."

Her throat locked.

"I wanted to see you in that play. I really did. It would've made me proud. It *makes* me proud just to think of it. I'm so proud of you."

Tears welled in her eyes. "Daddy."

"I want so much to be a better father to you. Your mother's right. I should try—"

But then she was hugging him, crying softly into his shirt. He felt her warmth and, like an icicle melting in the sun, slowly returned the embrace.

CHAPTER 75

TOM DIALED JULIE'S NUMBER ON HIS TELEPHONE, listened to the first ring on the line before hanging up in a panic.

What could he say to her?

He wanted desperately to speak to her, but the little courage he had was slipping away. The memory of his last cruel words shredded his conscience into confetti. He had practically thrown her out of the house! What could he possibly say to make up for that?

With a sigh of defeat, he hung up the phone and sat at the kitchen table. His stomach groaned with hunger. His mom left him several frozen entrees in the freezer, but he was too distracted to think about eating. Instead, he retreated to the living room. The evening found him abandoned in his own house, and for the first time he could recall he was actually afraid of being alone. Solitude brought contemplation, and his mind was filled with preposterous ideas. He was sinking into a pit of despair. There was no escape.

"Don't get lost," Danny had said. Already he couldn't

find his way back.

The rooms were oppressively quiet, and he paced from one to another like a caged animal, desperate for distraction. He sat in front of the television, surfing through syndicated repeats and news programs, anything to escape from his thoughts. But his mind kept returning to the tragedy.

Kevin was dead. The thought of it caused his eyes to glaze. Danny mentioned memorial services. He wondered whom he should call. Having met Kevin's adoptive parents only once, it would be awkward to speak with them. He hadn't accepted the death yet, and the thought of going to a funeral seemed premature. It was too much for him. He needed to rest. He needed time to think it all out. He needed to speak to Julie.

Tom wondered if Julie had heard the news. There was an official announcement over the school PA system. Surely she would want to speak to him about it, offer condolences, if nothing else. It gave him a reason to call, and that would allow him an opportunity to apologize. With all his nerves engaged, he returned to the telephone, rang her number again, and this time was rewarded by a voice. Her mom's. She seemed a little surprised by his call, but friendly and concerned.

"Hi, Tom," said Ellen over the line. "No, Julie went to the city with her father."

"The city?"

His heart sank. If Julie was with Parrish there was no telling what they were discussing. Her dad might at that very moment be convincing her to stay away from him. He felt his chances of reconciliation melting away.

"Well, can you tell her to call me as soon as she gets back? I don't care how late. It's really important."

"How are you doing, Tom," Ellen asked, concerned. "Is everything all right?"

"Yes. I just need to speak with her."

"She's been so quiet lately. I know you two had a quarrel."

"Kind of."

"I'm sorry. It's made her very sad, and I know she still cares deeply for you."

It brought tears to his eyes, and his throat locked. "I hope so," he said, his voice trembling with emotion. Julie's mom always liked him. Her comforting words made him feel forgiven. If at least one of her parents could be in his corner, he had a chance. But then Parrish wasn't against him, he reminded himself. Quite the contrary. Parrish was concerned for his welfare. He regretted now that he hadn't accepted the man's help.

"I'll have her call you as soon as I hear from her," Ellen continued. "I do hope you two can work things out. You were so good for one another."

"Thanks, Mrs. Parrish," he said, "That means a lot to me."

"Have a good night, dear. Don't hesitate to call if you need anything else."

She hung up. Now he would sit and wait. Every minute seemed like an eternity.

CHAPTER 76

AS THE LIGHTS WITHIN THE ORPHEUS BOOKSTORE WERE shut off, shadows seemed to ooze out of the mysterious volumes on the shelves. It was an eerie, haunted place after dark. Humphrey Culhane bolted the front door and reset the "Closed" sign over the window. Then he motioned to Parrish and Julie to follow him into his study as the Chinese door chimes jingled behind them.

Julie was distracted by the many curios in his display boxes, and she wished she had time to explore. The store smelled of pipe tobacco and exotic incense. Culhane's burly presence was a comfort to her. She hadn't seen the man since she was a small child, and she remembered his furry chops with fondness.

"I'm worried about Tom," she said with concern. "When I heard about Kevin . . ."

Parrish sighed. "I'm afraid it's put him in a volatile state."

"As though things weren't dangerous enough," Culhane agreed. "Now the kid's mourning the death of his best friend. It's a powder keg waiting to explode. I apologize now for not taking you more seriously in the beginning, Stephen. We might have averted it all had I simply heeded your initial suspicions."

"This is all *my* fault," Julie said suddenly. "I watched it unfold for two months, but I never suspected anything."

"No one could've anticipated any of this, sweetheart. Even I had my doubts until I mentioned the puppet to Humphrey."

Culhane looked to Julie. "The puppet was the key to the entire mystery. You see, to invoke a demon, you have to condense its attributes into a visualized form. It's usually a figurine, something that determines its shape, and it becomes a terminal for the psychic emanations of the host. When Tornau first summoned Fau'Charoth, he must have had an idol of some sort."

"The small wooden carving I found by the firepit," Parrish recalled. "It had the features of a wolf. A wolf with wings."

Culhane nodded, intrigued. "A wolf. Yes. The wolf image is often used in this sort of demon forging, but sorcerers fail to realize that in doing so they incorporate elements of the animal's true nature. Wolves have a strong will and an indomitable spirit essence. That's why they are so revered in Indian cultures. Wolf demons are not easily mastered, and they often turn on their creators."

"The face in the drawing kind of resembles a wolf," Julie observed, studying Tom's sketch, which was laid out on the desk. "Except for the scaly parts."

"Yes. It seems Tom embellished it with his Hollywood imagination. What he's done in effect is design a demon more lethal than even Tornau could conjure."

"Wonderful."

"Welcome to sorcery in the modern age, my dear," Culhane guffawed. "Before we had witches and warlocks. Now we have *animators*!"

Parrish reviewed the mystery step by step. "So the puppet anchors it to this plane of consciousness. And every time Tom animates—"

"He invigorates it into being," Culhane concluded for him. "In effect, he completes a process already engaged. I had dismissed the possibility that a sixteen-year-old boy with no applicable skill in the black arts could successfully conjure a demon. To do so requires intense visualization. Even for the adept, it's a daunting task, requiring years of practice. But the ceremony was already at an advanced stage of completion. The demon was half-formed and trapped in an ætheric state. And then Tom comes along with his hobby. Stop-motion generates a field of concentration very akin to an invocation rite. The mind stays focused on the puppet, visualizing its every move. A very strong mental impression is maintained. In Tom's imagination, it comes *alive*. Combine that with the spell, coursing through his subconscious, and the demon is conjured." A gleam came to the man's eye. "It's really quite remarkable, Stephen. This boy would provide the most excellent opportunity for study."

"This boy is a dear friend of my daughter," Parrish reminded. Julie glanced at him appreciatively.

"Yes, of course," the scholar conceded. "But forgive me my scientific enthusiasm."

"I'm trying to determine its pattern of behavior," Parrish said. "It might have followed an ætheric trace to the Whateley farm, but why attack the high school, and the airport? What's the common link?"

"*Me*," said Julie. "I am. I've been to all those places, recently. It attacked the airport the night I confronted Tom. The beacon was . . . special to us." She exchanged a daughterly glance with her father. "Nothing 'happened'." Parrish dropped his eyes, bemused.

"Tom mentioned he was having flight dreams?" Culhane asked her.

"A few times," Julie answered.

"Clearly, the demon is using his astral body as a vehicle. You see, the astral body is composed of *emotional essence*. Everything Tom feels becomes enmeshed in its vaporous orb. The demon clings to it and feeds off it like a parasite. As it does so, it sublimates Tom's feelings and acts upon them as though they were its own. It becomes a sort of doppelganger, an extension of his subliminal will. Since the astral body remains connected to the boy in life, he *vicariously witnesses* it all through a trance state."

"He called it 'invigorating'," Julie quoted. " 'Like having every one of your greatest wishes realized'."

"I'm sure it must be," Culhane gleamed. "Flying about

on the wings of a demon that seemingly obeys your deepest desires. But eventually the tables turn. It develops a will, a *personality* of its own, and you lose control."

"How intelligent is it?" Parrish asked.

"It's smart. Not to a man's degree, but it has the instincts of an animal, and an intuitive connection to Tom's psyche. It knows what Tom knows."

"Can it hurt him?" Julie asked, worried.

"Not deliberately. That would be like hurting *itself.* But with each turn it'll dominate him more and more, steal his essence until it can manifest independently at will. In time, the boy will diminish and be reduced to a mere shell, a vessel from which to draw energy."

She glanced anxiously. "But we're going to stop it, right?"

Culhane offered a reassuring smile. "Yes . . . yes. Your father and I are well into it, my dear. We are fortunate enough to have the very source material for Tornau's spells right here," he tapped the *grimoire* proudly on his desk, "and we'll send this thing back to the abyss it came from. Banish it, before . . ."

"Before what?" Julie asked.

"Well, let's just say the demon was summoned for a *reason.* We know that Tornau was attempting to create a dimensional rift, a portal to the darkest regions of the astral world. He summoned Fau'Charoth to keep watch over the threshold. But something went terribly wrong. Perhaps they performed the ceremony too late. Or some important step was overlooked. Or perhaps . . . it rejected the soul of

Sarah Halloway, a grown woman, instead of an infant."

"It rejected Sarah," Parrish considered. "So she got her revenge on Tornau, even as she was sacrificed. An ironic form of justice. Almost poetic."

"Whatever the cause," Culhane continued, "the powers overwhelmed them, and they were destroyed. The demon was stranded in a limbo state until a suitable host appeared."

"Tom," Julie said.

"He awakened the demon from its torpor. A fissure between worlds has been forced ajar. It's leaking a trail of negative energy that's tethered to the demon. As it wanders, it tugs at the fissure like a loose thread on a sweater, tearing it gradually wider. In time, any number of ungodly things could come through."

"*That's* a cheerful thought," Julie mused.

"We'd better get back," Parrish said, checking the clock above Culhane's desk.

"Good. I'm long overdue for a trip to the country, and damned if I'm going to let *you* have all the fun! Meanwhile, sweetheart, you should call the boy and convince him to see us. And we'll need to speak to his parents."

"His dad's AWOL. Somewhere in Florida. And his mom's useless. Probably away."

Culhane shook his head. "Then the intervention will be our responsibility. Parents these days—they don't have the slightest reckoning of what their children are doing. Drugs. Gang violence. Black magic. It's a pity."

Julie felt a tingle of excitement as she went to the phone.

CHAPTER 77

THE PHONE RANG ONLY ONCE. TOM SNATCHED UP THE receiver and nearly dropped it putting it to his ear. "Julie?" he asked expectantly.

There was a moment of silence, and then he heard a familiar chuckle. "Monster maker! No, it's not your spooky girlfriend. But don't worry. We'll take care of her after we're done with *you*."

Tom's blood went cold. He crushed the receiver in his fist. "Burke!"

"Sneaky little creep. I should bust you up for that stunt you pulled today."

"You killed him," Tom hissed. "You cowardly bastard. You killed Kevin!"

"Aw, you think you're so smart. I don't know what he told you, but you better keep your mouth shut. You hear me? Fair warning."

"Murderer."

"Yeah? Well, say one word about it and you're next. Then we'll have some fun with Little Miss Magic! You know, they used to burn witches around here. Maybe we'll have ourselves a little Salem barbecue."

The words were like venom in Tom's ears. "Stay away from her! You go near her, and I'll take everything to the cops."

"I thought you'd say that. Thanks for confirming it, though. It makes life easier, figuring what I gotta do. Later for you!" He hung up.

Tom remained on the line, breathing heavily. He listened to the silence for almost a minute before he placed the receiver down, hands trembling.

"It's *busy*," Julie announced to Culhane and her father as she heard the annoying signal on the line. Tom didn't have many friends. Who could he be talking to? "Maybe his mom *is* home."

"Good," Parrish said. "At least he'll be looked after. That should buy us some time. We'll try again before we leave."

"Stupid! What was I thinking? I blew it!"

Tom was frantic. His rage had given way to fear as he considered Burke's threat. Why did he announce his intentions so defiantly? Threatening to go to the cops? What an idiot! Now, Burke knew *everything*. If Burke had killed Kevin, his old buddy, without a second thought, how much less would he think about killing *him*?

Suddenly Tom felt vulnerable. Kevin had entrusted

him with a mission, and now there was the risk he wouldn't live to complete it. They were coming for him for certain.

He went to the front door and bolted it secure. He double-checked the garage door as well. Windows were closed and latched. He shut off all the lights so the house would appear empty. It was almost nine o'clock, and the streets were quiet. On a Friday night before Halloween, people were not likely to respond to shouts for help. Just the neighborhood kids having a blast, they would assume. All in good fun. Boys will be boys.

Damn! What a time to be alone.

"I need to get out of here," he said aloud, grabbing a jacket from off the sofa arm. He thought a moment about Julie's phone call and regretted having to miss it.

Julie! Burke threatened to attack Julie too! What if they went after her first?

He was on the verge of panic, feeling helpless.

"Okay, Julie's in the city with her dad. She's safe for now. It's me they're after." But where to go? The police! His mom left him the car. He could drive to the police station and bring the "evidence" stashed in his room! That was the plan all along, right? Blow the whistle on the guy. Put him away for life, not only as a drug dealer, but as a *murderer*, too. At least he would be safe. *Julie* would be safe. And then Kevin would get his revenge. Tom felt excitement. Here was one last adventure from his friend. It was as if Kevin was guiding him from beyond the grave.

He raced to his bedroom. Where was it? The blue

duffle bag with the drugs. Then he remembered Kevin had tossed it into his chest. He went to the wooden box, opened the lid—

—and saw the puppet of Fau'Charoth gazing back at him! It lay toppled on its side just below the duffle bag. The glass eyes peered out at him.

Tom stared transfixed, his entire mind pulled into its unwavering gaze. In that moment, all fear left him. His shoulders dropped, and he felt like he was being enveloped in a diaphanous veil of tranquility. *All would be well now*, he thought. Nothing could harm him. He was safe and secure, and knew clearly what he had to do.

He lifted the puppet and felt the familiar texture of its rubber skin. Then he carried it to the tabletop above his dresser. The alien landscape had been torn down and discarded, but it didn't matter. There wasn't even film in his camera, but it didn't matter. He need simply take hold of his creation, and everything would be fine.

Somewhere in the world, winds were blowing.

Click!

and the Earth was turning.

Click!

Seasons were changing, winter–spring–fall, but not in this room.

Not so long as dragons needed life.

In the kitchen, the telephone rang again. Tom didn't hear it. The model was being animated on his desktop, and in that "netherworld" of his mind, his creature rose from its slumber and took wing.

"Now there's no one home!" Julie shouted, exasperated, as she let the phone ring for the tenth time. "Where did he go?"

"Memorial services, perhaps?" Culhane offered. "Or to a friend's?"

"He might be with his friend Danny. I just hope he's not alone." She felt a twinge of regret. Maybe it *hadn't* been such a good idea for her to come to the city. She might've been with Tom right now.

"I'm sure he's fine," Parrish comforted her. "But we'd better get home."

"I'm about ready," Culhane said as he packed the remaining books he needed, including the *Dæmonolatreia*, into his portfolio. He also took a roll of parchment, an assortment of ink pens and brushes, some jugs and bottles, and a strange cloak that looked like a ceremonial robe. "I hope you have a warm spare room in that mansion of yours, with hot running water. This is so exciting! I've been to every corner of the globe. Bangkok, Haiti, Ethiopia, and from right in your backyard, Stephen, you bring me a demon!"

CHAPTER 78

"LATER FOR YOU!" BURKE SLAMMED THE PHONE down and fell back into his chair. He knew it was risky threatening DeFrank, but maybe it would keep the little creep quiet long enough for him to figure things out. The whiny bastard. That remark in the lunchroom about "nark reports" had caught him completely off-guard. Kevin had evidently brought a conspirator into his little scheme, and now the shithead could make his life a living hell. Burke needed to put the fear of God in him but *good*. He hoped DeFrank was squirming.

Maybe threatening him wasn't enough. There was only one way to solve this. The kid had to be taken out. The girlfriend too, probably. No telling what she knew. He would enjoy nailing her scrawny ass.

He dialed the phone and called Gunthur.

"Yo," Gunthur's guttural voice answered.

"It's me. Where's Lenny tonight? We got business to take care of."

The road to the Chalet was lined up with cars. The parking lot was full to capacity. It was a busy night for the club. The building was a two-level ski lodge owned and operated by the nearby Revele hotel. Off-season, it was converted into a disco nightspot. The red scaffold of a ski lift stood off to the side, overlooking a steep incline of forested hillside. In the coming months, snow would transform the area into a white paradise.

Loud music could be heard from within. It was the big Halloween weekend, and the Revele was sponsoring a gala party for its guests. Outsiders could enter for a fee, and costumes could be obtained through the concierge. People were sauntering to and from the building, wearing gaudy masks and elaborate outfits. Two women strutted along the road as the Jaguar drove by. They were dressed like Vegas showgirls, in sequins, feather bolas, and *little else.*

"Whoa!" said Gunthur, gawking at the long-legged beauties. "Gotta get me a piece a' that."

"Don't embarrass me in there," Burke warned. "We're just gonna go in and find Lenny."

Lenny Finch hadn't made it to school. The chickenshit wouldn't answer his phone and was probably ducking low. Burke figured murder wasn't on his top-forty list. Too bad. He was there when it all came down and was up to his neck in it. Hiding wouldn't help him for long, and Burke didn't trust him not to squeal out loud during one of his personal soliloquies. It was better if they all stuck together. There was more work to do. Another bug to squash.

He pulled the Jaguar into an available space along the road, behind a black Mercedes. As he emerged, he felt a cold shiver gazing at the baroque display gathered in front of the lodge. Something about it reminded him of a sinister carnival. The Jaguar keys jiggled in his hands as he dropped them into his pocket. He wasn't feeling particularly festive.

The interior was noisy with disco tunes and chatter. The decorators had done a fancy job with candlelit jack-o'-lanterns and paper skeletons. The room was dim, with lightning strobes flashing to the beat. Disco Mardi Gras from hell. Partygoers pranced about behind masks. There were zombies, Jedi Knights, and caped vampires. Don Quixote tilted toward an imaginary windmill; Sherlock Holmes sucked on a plastic pipe. And then there were the girls. Sorority chicks and high-school cuties decked out in black spandex catsuits and rented fairy gowns. Their sexy bodies shimmied to the dance music.

Burke took in the spectacle with a sweeping gaze. He hadn't expected such a bacchanalia. Under better conditions, he might have enjoyed himself. As it was, the nocturnal fiesta only added to his anxiety.

A Lugosi-tuxedoed bartender was filling complimentary glasses of champagne at the liquor station, with several waitresses distributing them on trays. Gunthur grabbed two glasses from a barmaid witch, handing one to Burke. The waitress gave the boys a studied glance, assessing their age.

Burke felt uncomfortably conspicuous without a costume. He downed the bubbly in a quick gulp to soothe his nerves.

"Where's Lenny?" asked Gunthur. "I don't see him anywhere."

"He's up in the box." Burke pointed to the sound booth.

They made their way through the crowd. Burke could see Lenny sorting the LPs. The kid looked very preoccupied as they approached him on the platform. He wore a black satin shirt and polyester slacks that made his legs look like saplings. It didn't count as a costume, unless he was impersonating someone innocent.

"Lenny!" Burke put a hand on his shoulder, and the DJ nearly dropped his *Tavares: Greatest Hits* album.

Burke read Lenny's startled gaze with amusement. He had to shout above the music. "What's with you? You act like I'm a ghost."

Lenny fumbled to regain his cool. "Hey, guys. Come to do some dancing?"

"Cut the crap! I didn't see you in school today."

Lenny's eyes wandered to the dance floor. "Yeah. I wasn't feelin' too great. Upset stomach. But my boss couldn't find a replacement, so here I am. I feel like I'm gonna puke."

"Well, suck it in. We gotta talk!"

"Cliff, I'm in the middle of my shift!"

"Put on something long. Then come down to the basement."

Lenny frowned and put a Blondie mix on the turntable.

It gave them exactly fifteen minutes to chat.

The basement below the lodge was cavernous and had a number of side chambers like catacombs. Incandescent bulbs glowed from dangling sockets. The light was dim and failed to illuminate the darker corners. Flanked by Gunthur and Finch, Burke wandered to the farthest end of the cellar. The air was musty; crates of incoming goods were stored against the walls. Vintage wine bottles were shelved horizontally on wooden racks.

"Make it quick!" Lenny demanded. "If Perry finds out I left my post, he'll fire me!"

Burke hesitated. "We've got more work to do."

His eyes squinted with dread. "What do you mean?"

Burke described his phone call with Tom DeFrank.

"Awww shit!" The tendons in Lenny's neck went taut. "DeFrank? That little pipsqueak? You gotta be kidding me."

"He's little, but he's got a big mouth. He could do a whole lotta damage."

"Fu-uck!" Lenny grabbed his hair and turned around like he was going to retch. "This is the pits, man. This is the goddamn pits. We're doomed."

"Will you relax?"

"Relax? We fuckin' killed a kid, dammit!"

"Shut up, Lenny!" Burke snapped at him. "We *had* to. Kevin knew too much. He was a snoop. He was gonna finger both of us. We had to eliminate him."

"Yeah, but now we have another snoop."

"That's why we gotta take care of it."

"We?" Lenny took a few steps into the shadow behind a crate. "No way, man. I've had enough. This is all your fault, Cliff. I don't want anything more to do with it."

The temperature dropped to a death freeze.

"Lenneee," Gunthur chimed in.

"I don't like your tone," Burke warned.

"Well, *screw you!* Kevin was right about you, man. You're a fuckin' maniac!"

"Don't push it, Lenny. That kinda talk can get a guy hurt."

Lenny bolted for the stairs.

Burke and Gunthur jumped for him, but Lenny was quicker than both. He shoved Burke aside, slammed Gunthur hard in the stomach, and ducked underneath his reach. Then he grabbed a wine bottle and shattered it against the wall, brandishing the jagged bottleneck at them.

Burke raised his palms. "Calm down, man."

"You stay away from me, or I'll cut off your faces. I swear to God. I want out of this. This is your fault, you bastard. You killed the kid. I was just there for the ride."

Burke and Gunthur found themselves cornered in an alcove, the frantic teen in front of them. Wine dripped from the broken neck of the bottle, splashing crimson to the floor. The last chords of Blondie could be heard upstairs. Lenny stood defiantly. He continued whimpering incoherently to himself. All Burke could make out was "gotta cut to the chase."

"Lenny. Put the bottle down. We're gonna figure this

out. I promise. We can handle it."

Then something dark *materialized* in the shadows behind Lenny. It stood on a large stack of crates, rising up from its haunches.

Burke and Gunthur stiffened, but Finch went on with his tirade. Hysterical gibberish poured from his lips, oblivious to the menacing shape that loomed behind him.

"Sure, you can handle it. Like you've been 'handling' me from the very start. I'm tired of getting jerked around!"

It crouched in silence directly above the kid. The dim light of a bulb cast an eerie gleam over its features. Something was familiar about it. In a millisecond, a crazy image flashed through Burke's brain—that of a sketchbook and a scribble drawing of "Gunthur's old man." It let off a growl like the rumble of a death engine.

The expression shifted in Lenny's eyes as he became aware of the giant presence behind him. He turned just as a claw gripped the boy by the shoulders and hoisted him up. His jaw dropped in terror.

"Holy shii—"

But he didn't have time to scream.

A snout with gaping fangs clamped onto his face. His muffled whimpers were mixed with the demon's guttural snarl as it wrenched him about like a rag doll. Its fangs minced the flesh of his cheeks. Blood and saliva streamed about wildly. Lenny's fingers raked at the creature's muzzle.

Burke and Gunthur froze in terror.

The creature blocked their escape. They struggled to

get past the flailing limbs of boy and demon. Nearly half of Lenny's head was now engulfed in the creature's maw. The tremendous strength of its jaws was like a hydraulic press.

And then there was a sickening *crunch* as the front of Lenny's skull crushed in like a melon. A spurt of gooey brain matter and part of his cranium shot across the distance, hitting Burke on the neck as he ran by. With a final yank, the upper half of Lenny's head was torn free and tossed across the room. It splattered on the floor and skid like a raw pizza.

Fau'Charoth tossed the decapitated corpse aside and shook its head like a dog. Messy droplets of blood sprayed the room. It focused on Burke and Gunthur. Keen yellow eyes blazed at them, and it snarled with recognition as they raced for the stairwell.

The demon leapt off the crates and charged.

Burke clawed at the doorknob at the top of the stairs.

The door mercifully opened, flooding the stairwell with light and the sounds of partying. Burke and Gunthur scrambled through and collided with a Kiss wannabe swigging a coke. The man went flying off his platform shoes and into one of the barmaids. Glowering in anger, the Paul Stanley look-alike cursed aloud.

"Motherfuck—"

Then he caught sight of Burke's bloody neck.

Immediately all eyes were on the boys. There was laughter from some, suspecting a gag.

"Ugh! That's just gross, man!"

Burke and Gunthur staggered and fought their way to the front door.

The basement entrance exploded as a very large *thing* came through.

It stood upright, momentarily disoriented by the loud noise and flashing lights. Then its chest bulged with a great intake of air, and it bellowed ferociously.

The roar snapped people alert. This was no Halloween trickery. No sci-fi movie prop the Revele had rented for the festivities. They were looking at a living, breathing monster. Something unnatural. Ungodly. It was alive, and deadly in its intent.

Chaos ensued. People collided with one another, yelling and screaming in a frenzy to get away. One man dressed like a pirate crashed into the snack bar, trapping a Charlie Chaplin against the wall. Bags of chips and cookies tumbled in a sloppy mess.

A paunchy matador fell to the ground, trampled by the onrush. Two zombies went toppling directly through a large side window.

Jack-o'-lantern candles squashed over, and soon there were drapes and paper decorations on fire. A spilled bottle of whiskey from the bar carried the flames across the dance floor.

In the mass confusion, people crushed themselves into the exits, all the while gazing back at the creature in terror. It snapped at them from the distance. Gunthur and Burke were nearly at the door when they were overtaken by the stampede. Suddenly the squeezing bodies fighting to get out compressed them.

The disco lights continued to strobe, creating white hot flashes of terror.

The head of the demon twisted to and fro, snapping at the heels of terrified humans. The great bat wings flapped in agitation. Through fire and smoke, it searched for its prey. The wolf nostrils scanned for their trail, twitching against a multitude of human scents.

Then it located them.

With a great leap, it launched onto a wall, scaling quickly up the side and crept upside down along the ceiling rafters like a great bat. High above the flaming dance floor it crawled, until it reached a skylight.

CHAPTER 79

BURKE AND GUNTHUR FOUGHT THEIR WAY CLEAR FROM the lodge. All around them, people frantically raced out of the building, stampeding the scene like antelopes escaping a predator. Some of them tumbled into the pool and splashed about struggling to stay afloat. Others left through a back terrace exit and actually toppled into heaps down the steep ski slope. Those who made it safely to the parking lot piled into cars and took off in a mad rush, jamming the drive in a gridlock until no one could move.

"Where did that thing come from?" Gunthur cried out as they maneuvered past the congestion to the roadside.

"How the hell should I know?" Burke shouted back.

The distance to his car seemed endless. As the Jaguar came into view, he fumbled with the keys, hands shaking wildly, when he heard another crash of glass behind them. He turned to the lodge and saw the skylight shatter.

Fau'Charoth broke through the skylight and loomed over the rooftop, a cathedral gargoyle come to life. Flames rose up from the room below, the lodge ablaze with tongues of fire that ripped through the windows. The creature roared above the din.

Horrified, some of the onlookers gazed up in awe at its terrible splendor. The demon spied its prey from the distance. It took a tremendous leap and sliced the air toward them.

Burke struggled to get his keys into the car door. "Fucking hurry up!" Gunthur screamed as he finally slipped the key into the groove.

With a flip of the latch, the car door opened. Burke turned to Gunthur and his eyes froze, seeing the demon glide like a hellish kite into the space above them. It rammed Gunthur from behind, sending him crashing to the pavement.

The hulking boy fell into a death match with the demon. Gunthur fought it off, wrestling with his burly arms. He screamed to Burke. "Cliff! Help me!" Burke cringed at the sound, but he continued to methodically climb into his car. In that moment, he discovered something about himself. Kevin was right. He didn't care. Confronted with the brutal slaying of his friend, his sole concern was for his own survival. He plunged the keys into the ignition with an eerie, trancelike detachment and was rewarded with the loud roar of the engine.

Burke looked back only once and saw Gunthur flattened to the ground, the demon clinging to him like a bird of prey. Its tail whipped about in excited arcs as its fangs ripped out the boy's throat. Then the jaws crunched onto his chest, tearing through ribs like they were toothpicks. He saw the demon rip up a mouthful of Gunthur-gore and swallow it with a gulp. He steered the car free of the space, ramming the Mercedes in front, and sped off with a loud screech.

The Jaguar raced down the winding back road. It careened around a curve and nearly upset itself. Burke's eyes darted nervously into the rearview mirror. He felt lucky to be alive. The overcast sky was black, except where the clouds had parted, allowing some moonlight to bathe the landscape in blue.

Burke looked again in the mirror, wary of pursuit, and saw a dark wet splatter on his neck. Something pink was glued to his nape. He pulled it free and saw that it was some of Lenny's brain matter, which had splat on him when the kid's head burst. He flicked it away in disgust. A tremor of guilt made him wince, but he shoved it off vehemently. Lenny was dead. So was Gunthur. *I'm alive. I survived. Deal with it!*

His hands trembled, clutching the steering wheel, as his mind spun with a kaleidoscope of horror-show images. *What the hell was that thing?* A freaking movie monster from some old horror flick! Yet he recognized it. The ugly wolf face, those bat wings. It looked like the sketch! That insane scribble drawing by Tom DeFrank, the one he had joked about, saying it looked like Gunthur's dad.

He began laughing hysterically. "Gung-ho! Gung-ho, you finally got your ass chewed out by your 'old man'!"

Suddenly it made preposterous sense. DeFrankenstein had actually built a monster!

Shifting his gaze to the rearview mirror, he frantically scanned for the creature. And then something swooped through the reflection.

Burke caught his breath. *It's after me!*

It flew out of range, but he sensed it was near, dangling at the fringe of his awareness. Burke felt suddenly very vulnerable, like a blind man in a room with a killer. He slammed his foot down on the accelerator, and the Jaguar lurched forward. A green road sign flashed. The highway entrance ramp loomed in the distance. *Gotta get off this road. I'll be safer on the highway.* More lights. More cars to get lost in. He had to ditch this thing fast.

Whump! It crashed down on the car roof!

"God damn it!" he shouted, steering hard to the left.

He missed the exit. The car roared past the narrow offshoot. Hope drained from him as he saw the desolate blackness ahead. No streetlamps to guide him. He was driving through Hades on the river Styx, fleeing the maw of its sentry.

"Shit!"

Whump! It slammed again onto the roof, causing the sports car to skid.

"Leave me alone!"

Burke couldn't believe it. He was under siege by a demon. This harpy—

Whump!

—from DeFrank's monster factory.

"Fuckin' motherfuckin' DeFrankenstein!" he shouted,

outraged.

Whump! The screeching of metal followed the crash this time as the entity's sharp claws raked across the roof surface. The car crushed under its weight, and Burke knew the thing was clinging to the top. He swerved sharply, trying to dislodge it. Above him, the ceiling was beginning to cave under its pounding fury. He could hear its guttural growl. Then a claw smashed through the side window, grasping blindly for the driver.

"Yah! Get away from me!"

He slammed the breaks. The car halted violently, and he was thrust into the steering wheel. There was searing pain as his nose hit the rim. But the demon was tossed forward, plummeting to the road ahead. Vision shaky, he saw the demon crouched in front of the headlight, momentarily subdued by the impact. He floored the accelerator, scorching tire rubber as the car jolted forward, ramming the creature full in the chest. It smashed into the windshield, shattering the glass instantly, and rolled back over the roof out of sight. Burke sped onward, his eyes dashing wildly in search of it.

Was it gone? Did he kill it?

Some moments of blessed silence. He cried aloud in relief.

But several breaths later came another *Whump*! The creature had returned with renewed frenzy. He heard more tortured metal, accompanied with snarling gurgles, and realized with terror that the thing was only *angry* before.

Now it was *pissed*! Claws ripped through the roof as it growled fiercely. Burke cried out in a childish whine.

Fau'Charoth clutched to the speeding auto with a vengeance. It opened its wings, catching the sweeping air like a parachute, and lifted with a tremendous heave. The Jaguar left the ground, its engine racing loudly as the tires spun in empty air.

Hoisted on demon wings, the airborne car glided a full hundred feet like a launching plane, before it plunged back to the road surface. The impact jarred the demon's hold, and it swooped off, leaving the car to careen wildly. Burke fought with the wheel, struggling to regain control. He screamed aloud as the road suddenly vanished, revealing sky and wilderness.

Forced by its own momentum, the Jaguar skidded over the edge of the pavement. It tumbled down a grassy hill, toppling over three times before resting at the base of the incline.

Burke awakened. He had been stunned unconscious. His entire body ached, and his head suffered a painful wound. He found himself upside down in the overturned car. How long? A minute? An hour?

The smell of gasoline violated his nostrils, and he panicked, struggling to extricate himself. The roof had crushed against him under the weight of the car. He was trapped. Was that smoke he smelled?

"Oh God! He-ellp!"

Crash! God answered with a demon. It slammed now

onto the exposed underside of the wrecked auto. Burke screamed as the creature raked ferociously at the floorboards, trying to reach him. Part of the metal gave way, and he could feel the sharp talons on his calf.

It raked at his flesh, and withdrew. Then it pounded again, ripping past the floor. Burke gazed wildly about in the darkness as he struggled. Upside down, in the passenger seat beside him, he thought he saw the blood-smeared corpse of Kevin looking at him.

The car exploded into flames, turning the Jaguar into a pyre for Clifford Burke.

Engulfed in flames, Fau'Charoth rose into the air like a fiery phoenix, before disintegrating with a flash.

CHAPTER 80

TOM SCREAMED. IT SHATTERED THE TRANCE LIKE A gunshot.

The bloodthirsty images fled, replaced by the dark surroundings of his bedroom. He found himself kneeling rigidly beside his tabletop. The churning in his solar plexus settled down and extinguished. Tom clutched at it with his free hand, pressing away the lingering sensation. Then he saw the motionless Fau'Charoth figure still in his grasp!

He released the model in alarm. A miniature human puppet was held in its jaws, crushed between its epoxy teeth. At what point in his trance he had pulled the little figure off his shelves and fed it to the creature, Tom wasn't sure. It already seemed like many hours ago, but the images from the Chalet were razor crisp in his mind. He remembered everything, the fire, the onslaught—the awful sound of Lenny Finch's head crushing. He remembered the final screams of his nemesis Clifford Burke and the blaze that consumed him. In disgust, he plucked the tiny mannequin out of the demon's mouth and tossed it. The shivers were already starting. His whole body was shaking.

Reeling with nausea, he wiped his mouth with the back of his hands, expecting to see them covered in red. They were clean. The metallic taste in his mouth was not blood, but the *memory* of blood from his walking dream. Yet it was vivid and frightfully real. The flavor made bile rise in his throat, and in a panic he ran into the bathroom and emptied his contents into the bowl. He then went to the sink and pushed his face into the running faucet stream. Gulping and spitting, he struggled to cleanse the taste away and finally gazed at his face in the mirror. The reflection showed only a frightened boy and not the monster he envisioned. There was no smear of gore across his face, no sign of dripping fangs, and yet the flavor was still there. He trembled with the thought that it would *always* be there, haunting him like the "damned spot" on Macbeth's hand. He had shared the creature's bloodlust, experienced it to fruition. Now the cost would be charged to his soul.

He was a murderer.

"God!" he screamed, wringing his head with his hands. "What have I done?"

Three people, possibly more, were killed from the creature's rampage. Burke, Finch, and Gunthur were all dead. He felt no satisfaction at their loss, only sudden and unbearable guilt. Vengeance he decided was a bitter fruit, devoid of sweetness.

He wandered through the house, glancing back tremulously at his bedroom door as though its gravity could snare him and pull him back in. He checked his watch. It was later than he thought, nearly two-thirty in the morning.

Another shiver attack. His blood felt like ice in his veins.

Tom sat on the living room couch, trembling violently, and pulled his legs up to his chest. His breathing was labored, close to hyperventilation, and he wondered if he was going into shock. Traumatic experiences could propel a body into catatonia. The entire system shuts down. People died from it.

"No!" He shot to his feet again, succumbing to a shudder. He fought it off, resisting the pain and paralysis, and knew he had to get out of the house. Away from *it*.

"What do I do?" he said desperately aloud, knowing the answer to the question even as he spoke it. There was only one place he could go to for help, only one person to whom he could turn. He went to the kitchen and wrestled his set of car keys from the cupboard where they hung. Then he pulled his hooded sweatshirt from off the sofa arm and put it on as he left the house.

Outside it felt like winter.

The street was silent and deserted as he parked his mom's Chrysler along the houses bordering White Lake. He extinguished the ignition and stepped quietly out, feeling the breeze off the water that stabbed at him like needles. He clutched himself as his teeth chattered. Julie's house was dark. No one would be up at this hour. But she had to be home by now. Tom crept up the drive and walked around the building until he reached her bedroom window.

Apprehension gripped him. He felt like a thief, but he pressed on until he was clutching her windowsill. Her room was located conveniently on the first floor, but the ground receded slightly. Balancing himself precariously, he peered through the glass.

In the darkness of her room, he could see Julie sleeping soundly in her bed.

She looked very peaceful, a pink blanket tucked just under her face and arms. Desperate, Tom tapped his fingertips against the glass. After a moment, Julie stirred and awakened. Her eyes opened and gazed at the window.

She saw Tom and gasped.

As her eyes registered, she immediately sprang from the covers, reached over to her lamp and filled the room with light. Then she was beside the windowsill, unclasping and lifting the pane. "Tom! Oh my God!" she yelled, gazing wide-eyed at the boy.

"J-J-Julie . . ." His voice was a whimper of sadness.

"Come inside." She forced the window open as far as it could go. Tom struggled over the pane. She gripped his arm and helped pull him through. "I've been trying to call you all night. We even went by your house, but there were no lights on, and all the doors were locked. Where were you?"

He looked at her, imploringly. She could see the terror in his eyes, and her heart froze.

"Tommy? Are you all right?"

"Don't know. I'm c-c-cold."

Julie immediately grabbed the covers off her bed and wrapped them around him. He crumpled into a ball on the floor, grateful for the blankets, and Julie's body warmth within them. She sensed his confusion and realized something terrible had happened.

"What is it? What happened, sweetie?"

"Julie . . . I . . ." He sounded exhausted, his voice heavy with despair and regret. "I did a horrible thing. I'm sorry . . . I'm . . . so . . . so sorry."

She put her arms on him, but he cringed back in fright, a doleful look in his eyes. "You sh-shouldn't . . . you shouldn't touch me . . . you c-can't."

But she embraced him nonetheless, fearlessly clinging to him, offering safety and salvation. He melted into her arms, crying softly. Her presence was a salve to his tortured conscience. Tears filled her own eyes as she felt his anguish.

"I d-didn't mean it to happen. Didn't mean it." He shuddered violently. "S-so c-c-cold."

Julie stood up decisively. "You're going to the hospital. I'm gonna wake my mom."

Suddenly he grabbed her arm and looked at her with resolve.

"No! J-Julie . . . I n-need to see your father."

His request both surprised and delighted her. She flung her arms around him again. "Yes. You must. But sleep now." She helped him onto her bed, where he collapsed beside her and fell immediately into a troubled sleep. She curled up beside him, listening to his deep breathing, and decided to let things rest until sunup. She would explain everything to her mom in the morning—after she had spoken to her dad.

It could wait until then.

At daybreak, she immediately called her father.

"There's a very strange report on the news," Parrish said grimly over the phone.

"Oh?" Her blood went cold.

"Sprite, you need to bring him here as soon as possible."

CHAPTER 81

PARRISH'S STUDY AT CROHAVEN WAS FILLED WITH A warm glow as the late afternoon sun came through the large windows. Tom sat heavily in the man's armchair. All about him were the paintings he had so admired nearly two months ago. He now looked upon them with despondency, as though their purity assailed him.

For hours, Parrish and Culhane discussed with him every aspect of the demon. He thoroughly recounted everything he had experienced from his discovery in the tunnel onward. He described the flight dreams, the confrontation with his father, the awakening of lust that led to the pig massacre. Finally, he chronicled the demon's terrible onslaught at the disco. Many of the events seemed hazy, as though his mind was resisting the memories; and his head was bowed through most of it, lost in his own self-reproach.

Julie paled, listening to the horrible accounts, but she put a supportive hand on his shoulder to reassure him that he was no longer alone.

Culhane stood by the easel, where Parrish's work-in-progress was replaced by a large parchment. Carefully inked on it were foreign verses similar to the "spell." The nearby desk held a formidable volume, the *Dæmonolatreia*, which was bookmarked with slips of paper. Tom listened to the man's theories and felt a growing anxiousness, as though Culhane was deliberately trying to diminish his responsibility in the affair.

"But it's *me*," Tom insisted. "It feels what I feel, and it does what I want."

"On an *empathetic* level," Culhane explained. "What we are talking about is an 'embodiment of dark passions.' The demon feeds off your emotions and, in a way, shares them. What actions it takes after that, well, you have no control—"

"Tom," Parrish interrupted, "you mustn't blame yourself for what happened last night. The monster exploited your darkest, most elemental aggressions. We all have those feelings buried inside us, the remnants of our primal beginnings. It's the reality of being human. But it's the nature of our character, our ethics, and our values that determine what feelings we *act* upon. They serve as barriers to those dark impulses. The demon circumvented all of that."

"But I *created* it," Tom argued.

Culhane shook his head vigorously. "No. You're a clever lad, but don't over-credit yourself. What you created was its 'icon.' The puppet anchors it to this world, much the way an idol did in ancient religions. By animating it, you were in a sense *worshipping* it, focusing your mental and emotional energies: anger, fear—

"Love?" Tom inquired.

Culhane raised his brows. "No, 'love' exists on a higher plane. A demon knows nothing of love."

Tom met Julie's eyes briefly, repeating to himself. "A demon knows nothing of love?" The words didn't ring true to him. Even as it knew his own heart, he knew the demon's *soul.* It had grown into far more complicated a being than Culhane surmised, possessed of complex emotions.

"I'm not so sure," he said. "When it attacked Burke, it was *protecting* me. And the airport . . . it wasn't just a rampage. It was experiencing my pain. I think . . . it was *heartbroken*."

Julie's eyes widened, abashed.

Culhane scoffed with laughter. "My dear boy, I'm sure what you sensed might have *felt* like love. Someone your age is barely equipped to even comprehend what love is. The emotion has so many baser facsimiles. Lust, jealousy, cathection to name a few. Even the definition of love can be elusive. Lord knows *I* never had a clue."

Tom listened, conflicted. He wasn't sure what he was feeling. The demon had committed horrible crimes. It killed people. Tom knew he had to put a stop to it. But he knew also that the creature was an ally of sorts, bound to his emotions. It had obeyed the whims of his heart, however unfortunate, the way a loyal dog obeys its master.

"I know it sounds strange," Tom said, "but I can't help having sympathy for it. You don't know it the way I do.

It's lost and confused. I sense . . . a terrible loneliness and despair."

"Tom," Parrish said. "You're projecting. These are your own feelings, echoing back."

"No. Mr. Parrish" Tom countered. "It's been a slave for *ages*. It never knew any other life, but it's changed, now, and in constant agony. I feel responsible for its pain. For its even *being* here. You told me it was created pure, and then perverted into a demon. Is there any way to reverse the process?"

"Reverse?" A spark of intrigue entered Culhane's eyes, but he quickly dismissed it. "No. For that you would need the spirit's full name, and there's no record of it. 'Fau'Charoth' is a conjunction of its true title, which is now lost to the ages. I'm afraid there's no way to recover the missing parts."

"Well, it's not fair," Tom protested. "Even for a demon. It's not its fault."

"Mr. DeFrank," Culhane addressed him firmly. "Let's be clear about things. This isn't some beloved *pet* that's gone rabid. We're talking about a diabolical entity, conceived in evil, and by its very nature evil to the core."

"No! It's not. It's an *animal*. You said so yourself. Animals can't be evil. They don't have that choice. Evil's . . . a *human* privilege. If there's any evil in it, it comes from me."

Culhane went silent, impressed with the boy's acumen.

"All right, then," Parrish interceded. "The issue now

isn't one of blame, Tom, but *accountability.* Will you be accountable for this entity you've unleashed? Because only with your complete focus of mind and will can this thing be stopped. Can we count on that?"

Tom walked heavily about, torn by the decision. He stopped before the portrait of Sarah Halloway. She seemed so lost and sad to him now, and he felt shame under her gaze. *What happened to her?* Was she lost now, for all eternity? Was that the reward for her redemption?

For saving him?

He thought about the bond he shared with the demon and the joyful flights he'd taken with it before it all went bad. The memory of the night's bloodshed came back to him. He sighed with resolution. "I have to destroy it. There's no other way. I have to destroy the puppet. I tried once before. But maybe now . . ."

"You'll need to burn it," Culhane said. "At the ritual site."

"Like a cremation," Julie suggested. "It would offer some closure."

"Yes," Parrish said bleakly. "But I'm afraid it won't be quite that simple." Even as he said this, he scanned the boy with his eyes. Tom felt again the eerie sensation that he was being probed.

Engaging his spectral vision, Parrish re-examined Tom's aura. Where before the demon was a mere parasite, clinging spider-like to his halo, it now pervaded every inch of his astral body. Parrish frowned with dismay.

"What did you see?" Tom asked.

"It's your aura. Your astral field is severely contaminated. What was once merely an attachment has now enveloped your entire orb of energy. You and the demon have totally merged in spirit. Every time you touched the model, Tom, the demon took a piece of your soul. Now, it wants the rest of it."

Tom nodded, letting the fateful words penetrate. "Then what can be done?"

"I am calculating a spell to separate your auras," Culhane explained, gesturing to the parchment behind him. "We'll need to return with you and the puppet to the demon's port of entry. The threshold has been held ajar all these years. So long as the demon has an anchor here, the door will remain open. Once we've severed your bond, burning the puppet in the fire will hopefully untether the demon to this world. This will send it back to the abyss and close the portal."

Tom gave a relinquishing sigh. "Sounds like a plan."

"Go home and retrieve the puppet," said Parrish. "Together we'll head to the tunnel."

"I'll leave now," Tom said. "I think I can drive." He reached into his jeans for the car keys.

"I'm going with you," Julie volunteered.

"No, Julie," Tom objected. "I have to go alone. This is something I need to do by myself. If I arrive with anyone else, it might sense a disturbance of some kind. I'll be okay."

"Are you sure?" she asked.

"Tom's right," Parrish agreed. "He needs to face it alone. Any one of us could alert it to our intentions."

Tom went to the door. Parrish met him there, speaking softly. "Tom. Be careful. If it should emerge, it will defy you now to protect itself. Don't underestimate it. The demon is very powerful, and it has many means of deception. It will attempt to trick you and steal your energy. Remember that it comes from the realm of the *astral*, where all things are commanded by passion."

"I'll remember."

"But remember also, you are the wellspring of its power, the source of its very existence. Its strength is *your* strength. Whatever it can do, *you* can master as well. You must fight it; however, it might oppose you and reclaim dominance over your life force. Only then will you defeat the demon."

"Tom . . ." Julie approached him once more, throwing her arms around him. "Please be careful."

He nodded, allowing a smile to break through his grim countenance. "I'll see you in a bit." And then he left them.

In his departure, the three remained lost in thought. At last, Culhane rubbed his hands together. "Well, aren't *we* a cheerful bunch? Look alive, folks. We've got work to do." They scrambled to their assorted tasks.

CHAPTER 82

"EVIL IS A HUMAN PRIVILEGE," CULHANE REPEATED Tom's words, a smile pursing his lips as he worked. It was a remarkable statement from a boy so young. Tom had a reckoning far beyond his years. He understood that all "evil" originated not in some elusive Hell dimension, but in the human heart. Where it went from there was another issue entirely.

Culhane didn't believe in Hell, or at least in a Biblical one. But he understood the principles of thought-form creation. As a repository for emotional consciousness, the astral world was the canvas of the imagination, governed by desire. Its molecular structure was manipulated by consciousness, the landscape literally *transformed* by our thoughts. What we believe in, so we *create* with our minds. Over the millenniums, mankind had fashioned an afterlife of its own design, replete with a topography, inhabitants, and tangible phenomena. Its many levels encompassed the vast distinctions of paradise and purgatory; the splendid light of Elysium, the plutonian darkness of Hades. When asked if Hell exists, Culhane's glib response was often "It does now."

Thousands of years of depravity had constructed on those lowest planes an abyss of hopelessness, where lost souls found a home for their basest fears. Were they scorched by undying flames and devoured by demons? Only if they believed so.

Culhane didn't envision a devil, either. There was no supreme hierarchy of evil. Satan was simply a mythological icon, cultivated by Judeo-Christian doctrines, romanticized by Milton. But there were legions of malevolent souls who would choose to impersonate such an entity, feeding off the fears and hatred of mankind for their own aggrandizement.

Tornau was such a spirit, and he had labored long to become a demigod over his followers. He sought to enter his own twisted realm of fire and brimstone, using the blackest forms of magic available. But something went wrong. Something caused him to fail.

Or *did* he fail?

What destroyed the magician on that fateful night? Had the final sacrifice been truly rejected, the flame should have dissipated. There would have been no signature of the event for Parrish to perceive. Tornau and the others would simply have left in failure, unscathed. Yet something else occurred. Some colossal power was unleashed, consuming them. It seemed the cycle *was* completed, the barrier to the dark realm pushed asunder. But how?

Culhane crinkled his brows, speaking aloud. "The

baby was not consumed. The vital seventh sacrifice was not completed. That portal should never have been opened. Yet it was." He pondered the riddle, exasperated. What was he overlooking?

From what Parrish described in his barn vision, the fire in the pit *reacted* to the boy's presence. It reached out with fiery tendrils to caress the toddler's living flesh. Like Abraham to God, Tornau had willfully offered the child as sacrifice, but fate had intervened, and like Isaac, the boy was spared.

God was content with the offering and bestowed a blessing upon man and child.

What if Tornau's *intention* to sacrifice the baby was likewise sufficient?

Culhane reviewed the most fundamental rule of magical practice: all of magic was a process of mental focus—psychic emanations of the mind. It wasn't through the rending of flesh that human sacrifice gained its potency but through the malice and hatred of the perpetrator. Flesh was redundant.

If so, then Tom *was* the seventh sacrifice. The cycle *had* been fulfilled!

If this were true, then Tornau must have been unaware of his success. Escaping the police, he attempted desperately to repeat the final ritual. Killing Sarah was as much a vengeful act as a ritualistic one, but in the end it was pointless. Gratuitous. When he thrust the poor woman into the flames, he must have expected her body to catch fire in an agonizing spectacle. Instead, she passed through the threshold. The demon realm had been accessed. The door was already open!

"Dear Lord," Culhane muttered. This would mean that the signature pattern of Tom's aura was imprinted on the vortex. It was like a key that would reactivate the portal.

It wasn't the demon that kept the gateway ajar. It was Tom!

"My God," he spoke with dread, "if the boy rekindles that fire . . ."

CHAPTER 83

Tom pulled the car into his driveway and sat for a moment peering up through the windshield to his bedroom window. Apprehension filled him. He brushed it away. His mind needed to be clear of his intentions, or else the creature might be aroused. The sun hovered close to the horizon, but it was still daylight. He couldn't recall any occasion of the demon surfacing during daytime. Perhaps it was nocturnal and couldn't materialize under sunlight.

Tom entered the garage and located an old canvas knapsack. Into it he stuffed the largest flashlight he could find, a can of lighter fluid, and a box of sturdy wooded matches. Then he proceeded through the inner entrance to the kitchen.

Everything was as he had left it. He went into the fridge and poured himself a glass of juice, less because of thirst and more because of a need for routine. The world was as it had always been, before this demon took wing. It functioned under the same habitual laws. Gravity still chained him to the earth. There were unwashed pots in the sink and orange juice in his glass. Life was open for business as usual.

With that same nonchalance, Tom took a deep breath and carried the knapsack toward his bedroom. A Billy Joel song lingered in his head. He didn't particularly like the song, but it had a bouncy rhythm and served as a distraction.

His heart pounded as he approached the room.

His door was still ajar from the previous night. He poked it aside and entered his "studio," peering into the room like a burglar. It seemed larger, somehow, yet familiar and comforting. Cluttered in the usual disarray, it offered no threats except to the squeamish. Dragons and dinosaurs stood on the shelves. Cavegirl Raquel Welch still greeted him alluringly from the wall poster. His bed beckoned to him with the promise of badly needed sleep, and standing on the empty tabletop above his clothes dresser was his demon-creature stop-motion model.

Tom reached for the puppet—

Snap!

—and was immediately pulled into another world.

CHAPTER 84

PARRISH LOADED TOOLS FROM THE TOOL SHED INTO THE back of the station wagon. He tried to anticipate everything they might need, including hand shovels, axe, and flashlights. He gathered some dry branches from a nearby hedge and as much kindling and firewood as he could find. These he placed in a drawstring bag. Julie was in the basement, fashioning garden fence posts into torches. Light was a necessity, as much as they could manage. When Tom returned, they would drive together to the tunnel and enter as soon as the sun had set. He regretted they couldn't begin sooner, but sundown was swiftly approaching, and the bats had to vacate first. He didn't want them trapped in another onslaught of wings. The risk of getting bitten was too great. Bats could be rabid.

In spite of their dire circumstance, Parrish felt in better spirits than he had for some time. Tom was being cooperative. He sincerely wanted to set things right, and with Culhane's help they had a good chance of success. Much would change after that. The Tornau mystery was solved, and with the banishing of the demon, Parrish believed his purpose in the small town would be completed. He decided to leave Crohaven Manor and start a new life. Neuhaus offered him a generous severance package if he resigned voluntarily. Perhaps he would move back to the city and take up on Humphrey's offer to show his paintings. He promised most of all to be a more attentive father to Julie.

With an enthusiastic lift, he shut the tailgate of the station wagon and turned just as someone he presumed to be Julie entered his peripheral vision. "Julie, I—" he began, then froze.

Gerard Wilkens stood there, aiming a shotgun at his chest.

What is this place?

Tom gazed at the vista in utter disbelief. He was standing before an alien landscape. Far in the distance were stark, grotesquely chiseled mountains that rose up like jagged fingers. The stone pinnacles scratched at a sky splashed with violet and magenta clouds. There were eerie, twisted trees, devoid of foliage, with limbs that tapered and branched like antlers. He knew this landscape. He had labored many hours to construct it. It was the "netherworld" of his movie set!

"This is crazy," he said aloud. "I must be dreaming. This has to be another dream!" But his senses were filled with it. It was undeniably real. His feet were pressing deep into spongy reddish earth. His nostrils twitched to

the smell of plant growth.

Tom recalled reaching for the demon puppet in his bedroom, and at the instant of contact, he was pulled bodily into this imaginary realm. Everything was as he'd built it, and yet there was so much more. The landscape went on for miles, well beyond what he conceived. As he gazed about, he imagined he could walk on into infinity. The air was cool, and there was a breeze rippling through his shirt. At a loss for what else to do, he began walking across the plain, feeling the squash of moist earth beneath his feet.

The netherworld was barren and lifeless, devoid of any movement, unlike in his films, which he populated with denizens of rubber and steel. He wondered if any of his creatures were here. Was Gothmaug the dragon here? He remembered how Gothmaug had been killed by Fau'Charoth in a stop-motion battle. This was its domain. It dwelled here alone, unchallenged. But where was it then? Where was the great monarch of this demonic empire?

"Wait a minute!" His blood chilled. "If I'm here, then Fau'Charoth must be back home!"

Frantic, Tom began running wildly, making a mad dash for the horizon, but the mountains loomed ever farther ahead. It was as though he was treading air. As he ran, his head grew light, energy draining from him with each step. His limbs felt weak, until he could barely sustain himself to stand. Finally he collapsed, and the mossy netherworld ground struck him in the face.

Julie sat on the front porch, staring at the cemetery across the road. She watched the last specks of sunshine disappear below the horizon. The sky was now awash in orange and purple as the clouds darkened. Hundreds of tombstones reflected the dimming light. She had gathered the last of the fence-post torches, four in all, which she wrapped with a tight strip of cotton cloth. Each was soaked in alcohol, from a bottle she found in the basement, hoping that it would burn effectively. The thought of returning to the tunnel, especially in the dark of nightfall, was frightening, but she knew she would be going with Tom and the others. It was an urgent task, yet soon it would be over.

Where was Tom? She checked her watch. It was already late. He was taking longer than expected. Julie hoped everything was okay.

Something caught her eye across the road. The big mausoleum was there, just beyond the cemetery fence. Its imposing structure was now a silhouette in the twilight sky, but the familiar square shape had changed. Something stood atop the structure.

Julie gazed at it, setting the torch at her feet. The shape, whatever it was, stood perfectly still, and for a moment she thought it might be another structure, an angel statue, which aligned visually with the mausoleum. It was tall, with a curled triangular outline. She squinted at it.

And then the shape *moved.*

Ever so slightly it twitched with the wind and began bending upright. The curled outline unfolded, revealing wings that fluttered once in the breeze. The head lifted, revealing horns that swept backward.

It was the demon! She recognized its shape from Tom's model. It stood atop the mausoleum, slowly reviving as from a deep sleep!

Julie remained perfectly still, catching her breath. She rose to her feet in slow, subtle moves. It appeared to be looking right at her! She didn't want to jar its attention. Slowly, she backed toward the door.

It was there, *watching her.* She was sure of it.

Her heart jumped as it rose on its haunches and took an abrupt leap to the ground. Vanished out of view beyond the fence and stones, she could barely make out its form as it passed between the headstones. She made for the front door and quickly forced herself inside.

"Dad! Mr. Culhane! It's com—" Julie gasped in horror.

Parrish knelt in the center of the foyer. His eyes darted into hers to calm her. "Julie . . . shhhh." Standing above him, shotgun in hand, was Gerard Wilkens.

Her hands came up to her face.

"Be quiet, girl!" Wilkens warned.

Bitter with hatred, he seemed to have aged overnight. His gray hair had bleached to a bright white, and his face was a mask of tragedy. What remained of his sanity could not be told.

Julie's heart hammered madly. The man held the barrel of the shotgun only inches from her dad's face. His finger rested on the trigger as though he might send an impulse to it at any second. The charge would travel the neural pathways from his disheveled brain until they reached the tendons and muscles of his finger, which would contract ever so slightly to constrict the mechanism and send an ignition through the gun's chamber—exploding a cartridge—*killing* her father.

"Daddy."

"It'll be all right, honey. Just stay calm." The psychic's pupils rolled to the side until they focused on Wilkens. "Gerard . . . please . . . you don't want to do this."

" 'I know even where Satan dwells'." The man quoted from scripture as though it was the only language he had left. " 'I will scour the serpents from the land of Canaan'!" And then there was a pause as a new light of recognition entered his eyes. They shifted to Julie. "You said I killed my boy."

"No," she pleaded. "Mr. Wilkens, I didn't mean—" She caught movement through the window, felt the door at her back, and shrank slowly away from it. Her eyes darted nervously. She knew it had cleared the gate and was heading over the front lawn. *The demon was coming!*

"We don't have time! You gotta—"

"You said I killed him!" Wilkens repeated, delirious, tears streaming from his eyes. "Why would you say such a thing? I would never hurt my son. I loved him so much, and now he's gone." His eyes sharpened cruelly on Parrish. "You mesmerized him. You put the devil in his head."

"No, Gerard, I was only trying to help him."

"You tempted him with evil thoughts, and he went into

the abyss where there is no salvation!" His voice was a jagged muttering of sobs, but his grip was firm as steel on the shotgun, which remained poised at the "witch-man."

"That's not true, Gerard. Your boy isn't suffering," Parrish assured him softly. "No loving God would make a boy suffer."

Just then, Culhane came obliviously down the steps. "Stephen, I have to speak with you. It's very important."

Startled, Wilkens turned to the stairwell and fired a warning blast from the gun. It missed Culhane by inches, punching a huge hole in the wall beside him.

"Oh shit!" Culhane cowered from the blast. He peered up in utter bewilderment.

"Humphrey! Get down!" Parrish shouted. Wilkens re-aimed the shotgun on him.

Frantically, Julie's eyes shifted from the crazy armed man to the window's view just outside, where she knew the creature must now be mere yards away.

"Mr. Wilkens, please!" she implored. "Josh was my friend. He wouldn't want this! You've got to listen! We don't have time. It's *coming*, Mr. Wilkens. Dad, it's *coming*!"

Parrish met her eyes, alarmed.

"Shut up!" Wilkens shouted.

He gripped the gun shaft until his knuckles grew white, and his fingers trembled. He began whimpering again, barely audibly at first, as though he was reciting a prayer of some sort. Parrish could discern the verse of the rosary. The man stiffened and sharpened his gaze anew. He stepped around until his back was to the door, eyes fixed on Parrish with Julie beside him, and Culhane still crouched low in the stairwell.

"You see this gun? Josh killed himself with it. I saw my boy *splatter* his brains out with this gun. You know what that's like? Your child's brains splattered on the carpet right before your eyes? You'll see now, 'cause I'm gonna show you." His head turned to Julie, and Parrish's jaw dropped with dread.

With a sudden jerk, he shifted the barrel of the gun to Julie's face. "Now I'll send *her* soul to the devil, in exchange for my boy's!"

"No-o!" Parrish screamed. He leapt to his feet.

With an earsplitting crash, the front door exploded inward as the demon Fau'Charoth pounced into the chamber. The impact jarred Wilkens aside just as his shotgun discharged. Julie fell to the floor, feeling the shellfire ring past her ear. It shattered a pottery vase and part of a tapestry on the back wall.

Forced by its own momentum, the creature swept passed them, colliding into the mantle. It swiftly regained balance and crouched menacingly, snarling at the humans. Pinpoints of yellow fire blazed from its sockets.

Everyone stood shocked, staring at the creature.

Astonished, Culhane responded first. "My God, Stephen! Look at it! A complete physical manifestation!"

With Wilkens distracted, Parrish pulled Julie toward him. The demon stood upright, hissing at Wilkens, its eyes filled with deranged fire as he faced the Satan of his nightmares. It circled the man on nimble legs and reached out for him with a snatching claw, its tail swishing back and forth in serpentine sweeps. Julie watched its movements with startled recognition, having seen them first in Tom's film and now here *in the flesh*. It was his vision of monsterdom brought to life.

Wilkens swung his smoking gun around and fired a blast into the demon. The shot took the creature square in the chest, forming a wet black hole. Fau'Charoth jolted back on impact, snapping its jaws.

Julie threw her hands over her ears, cringing from the blast.

"I know you, dragon!" Wilkens cried in triumph. "Old serpent which is the devil!" He pumped the chamber of his gun and fired again at the creature. The shot went wild, taking a section off its wing.

"Get thee behind me, Satan!" Wilkens fired the remaining shells, shattering part of the creature's skull! Then the gun clicked empty.

The demon stood wounded before the man. Several sections of its body were gored from the blasts. Its head was missing a horn as well as an entire side of its face.

Tendrils of flesh stretched over the glistening wounds, shimmering like black worms into place, until the creature was whole again! Its yellow-flame eyes restored, it glared defiantly at the bitter human, jaws snapping in fury.

Sensing a bloodbath, Parrish pressed against Julie and

Culhane. “Quick! Upstairs!”

As they raced up the steps, the demon launched itself with full force at the shotgun-wielding man. Wilkens disappeared into the kitchen and collapsed backward, the full weight of the creature on him. He fell beneath its fangs, which delivered the retribution his soul cried out for. Parrish and Julie winced at his screams of agony, not daring to look back. It was all over within moments.

CHAPTER 85

PARRISH AND THE OTHERS REACHED THE THIRD FLOOR and entered the study. They slammed the heavy oak doors and barricaded them with furniture. Even fortified, the doors looked like a feeble barrier.

"It won't hold up for long," Parrish said.

Julie looked wildly to her father. "What's happened to Tom?"

"I don't know, sweetheart. We need to protect ourselves right now."

"Perhaps I can hold it at bay," said Culhane. He frantically pulled objects out of his supply bag. The first was a large bottle of sparkling white powder. He uncorked it and began to shake the contents liberally about the edges of the room.

"Dusting for roaches?" Julie asked.

"It's sea salt," he explained. "It creates an aura of pure essence that repels dark presences." He then took up the *Dæmonolatreia* and began leafing through the volume where it was bookmarked, muttering verses aloud.

"There is a warding spell I discovered that might work. Here!" he shouted, pointing to a talisman. "A circle of protection. Clear the center of the room!"

Fau'Charoth skulked about the lower floor, sniffing the wood of the steps as it reached the stairwell. It was reluctant to climb them. The building was filled with strange, abrasive energies that assaulted its composition. Long cleansed of disharmonious vibrations, the mansion was filled now with a serene, positive essence, repugnant to the demon's nature. It sensed a greater concentration of this essence at the higher levels and so hesitated, pacing about like an animal leery of the poacher's net. Yet the men presented too great a threat to ignore, a threat even its brutal mind could comprehend. The demon stepped cautiously up the first set of stairs, using its fore claws to test the surface. Its wings were folded tight at its back, and its tail dangled in midair behind it. Building resistance to the polar charge of the æther, it then leapt the remaining steps before reaching the third and final level of the mansion.

"Chalk! I need chalk!" Culhane shouted. Parrish handed him chunks of white oil pastel from his art kit and bent to assist him in scribbling a large circle on the wooden floor. Julie's eyes darted to the barricaded door, even as the two men labored like sidewalk artists on the warding sign. The talisman took shape, a series of overlapping lines within a six-foot circle that spanned the center of the floor. There was barely enough pastel to complete it, and the stumps of white crayon were reduced to waxy smears as they closed the final axis.

"I hear it!" she whispered. They froze, listening to the scratch of claws outside. Loud snorts and heavy breathing could be heard just beyond the door. It was sniffing them out like a hound. Julie moved behind her father.

"Stand within the circle," Culhane commanded, clutching the *grimoire* to himself. He held it open, peering down at its pages, and licked his lips in preparation. The strange pictoglyphs and words were beyond the scope of the average man, but Culhane enlisted his advanced knowledge of the ancient arts to decipher them. The three stood tightly within the circle and faced the coming onslaught.

The demon roared, and the door crushed inward, forcing aside the barricade. As the doors splintered into shards, Fau'Charoth poked its scaly, horned head into the study. It immediately cringed back from a wave of forbidding energy. Julie was amazed that a substance as pure and simple as salt could repel it. But it persisted with a growl and stepped fully into the threshold. It bared its fangs at the humans.

The three remained poised in the warding ring, exposed and defenseless, but trusting to the scholar's spell. As the demon ventured forward, Culhane began reciting aloud.

"Aga mass ssaratu! Ia mass ssaratu!
Nanna Zia Kanpa! Nebos Athanatos Kanpa!"

It hesitated and shook its head like a dog. The demon eyed the burly man curiously, ears pricked up, as it took another cautious step. Culhane bellowed with a powerful voice.

"By Shamash the Mighty, I command thee!

"By Enki, Lord of All, I command thee!

"By Marduk, the Great Magician of the Gods, I command thee!

"Turn around. Arise and go far away!"

The ancient verses rumbled through the chamber. The demon roared in defiance and frustration. It pushed against the space between them, but was restricted by an oppressive barrier it could not penetrate. Little sparks burned across its flesh, followed by streamlets of smoke and the smell of ozone. Fau'Charoth snorted, its lupine face registering pain and outrage. It paced back and forth about the perimeter, blinking and flinching as if stung by a hornet. Julie held on to her father, watching with amazement.

But with every painful step, the creature grew more resistant to the energy field, adjusting its vibrations until it withstood the pain. It lurched back into a crouching position, and with a bold swipe struck at the man holding the book. Its claw broke into the barrier, striking Culhane in the chest and sending the three colliding out of the circle. Parrish wrapped his arms around Julie as they plummeted and slid to the far corner of the room. Culhane collapsed to the side, and the old volume went flying from his grasp. Terrified, he braced himself against the wall, expecting his death within an instant.

But the demon struck first at the *grimoire*, perhaps threatened most severely by its contents. The creature hauled up the book and rended it savagely with tooth and claw. Paper and leather flew about in fragments. Culhane watched dismayed as the creature sated its frenzy against the book, finally tossing it with a crash through the large picture window. It then turned angry eyes toward him!

The burly man pulled himself deep into a corner as the demon lunged. Throwing his arms up, he yelled and fought off the powerful jaws as they snapped down at him. It gripped him painfully with its claw, and then its powerful fangs reached down and bit deep into his corpulent belly. The man seethed in pain, pressing against the creature's face, trying desperately to fend off the savage teeth.

"To-om!" Julie screamed in horror.

The name had an electrifying effect on the demon. It immediately halted and withdrew its attack, leaving the man withering in pain. Its eyes focused on the girl and her father, blazing with fury. It raised up to its full height, faltered a moment and then . . . *collapsed weakly to the floor*!

"To-om!" the voice called to him. It was Julie's voice, reaching beyond time and space. Tom responded instantly, jolting himself alert. "Julie," he said aloud. Somewhere she was in trouble, and she needed him. His head reeled, but he pulled himself upright from the ground where he had fallen in a faint. All about him, the netherworld landscape was still present, but it seemed to flicker like a mirage. He could catch glimpses of his bed and desk as they eased in and out of his consciousness.

He was still in his room!

The demon had tricked him! This was an illusion!

Tom focused his thoughts, grimacing tightly, and made fists at his sides. With sheer effort, he willed himself back to reality.

In that instant, the alien tableau faded, replaced by the mundane view of his bedroom. He hadn't collapsed at all, but remained upright, his body rigid, even as his consciousness had been stolen and catapulted to that *other* realm. It was deception, as Parrish had warned. The demon was diverting his attention, trying to steal his life force. Still clutching the puppet in his hand, he was unaware that at that very moment, at Crohaven, its demonic double was keeling over in weakness, its energy siphoned off by his will.

With one swift action, Tom lifted the model from the tabletop and stuffed it deep into his knapsack. Then he took a step, felt his body reel with vertigo, and quickly left the room.

CHAPTER 86

PARRISH AND JULIE WATCHED IN BEWILDERMENT.

The demon had collapsed, and for a brief instant, actually seemed to *fade*. Its physical body shimmered as though close to dissolution. But its stubborn flesh clung together.

Cringing in a corner, Culhane curled his mangled form into a fetal position. He clutched at the torn flesh of his belly and watched as Fau'Charoth struggled to rise to its feet. The room's distance away, Parrish looked anxiously to his friend. Culhane was moaning in pain, but not seriously harmed. Not yet. The creature stood between them, eyeing the man with ferocious purpose. It collapsed again and lolled its jaws like a tiger succumbing to tranquilization.

"Is it dying?" Julie asked.

"No," Parrish whispered. "Just weak. It's Tom. He's resisting it." Julie's heart leapt with hope. But how long before it regained its strength?

Seizing an opportunity, Culhane crawled back toward the warding circle and balled himself up at its center. Alerted by his movement, Fau'Charoth suddenly leapt to its feet and snapped its jaws at the man, but the warding energies were again in effect. It yelped like a dog as the sparks of energy jolted it, forcing it back. Parrish exchanged a glance with Culhane, pleased that the wounded man was momentarily safe within the circle. In its weakened state, the demon dared not challenge the barrier.

It seemed distracted, and focused on maintaining its composition. Could they make their way past it? Parrish took a tentative step toward the door. Just then the creature snarled angrily and looked at them. No. They were trapped. Julie glanced up and saw the attic panel just above their heads.

"Dad! The attic!"

Parrish reached up, snatched the pull cord and tugged. "Come on!" With the groan of spring hinges, the panel swung down, and a jointed ladder dropped heavily to the floor. Up the small gantry of steps they climbed, passing through the narrow opening to the dark attic. Parrish reached behind for the ladder and heaved it up, allowing the panel to rise again with a jerk.

Seeing them vanish into the ceiling, the creature made a feeble lunge for them just as the door slammed shut. It shook its head, warding off dizziness, and then roared with the full charge of its lungs.

Making his way out the front door, Tom suddenly toppled and fell to the grass. He felt his strength draining again, and it was only through sheer effort that he avoided passing out. The world spun around him, and the light of the nearby streetlamp seemed to brighten and fade in a pulsating rhythm. Tom gritted his teeth and rose up to his knees. He pounded his fist to his side.

"No!" he shouted, fighting off the vertigo.

Again, the demon faltered, staggering this time against the opposite wall. A bookshelf crashed loudly to the floor, causing an avalanche of volumes on the creature's back. It shook them off violently. Then it paced about the room, snarling with frustration, shunned by the paintings and mystical curios on display throughout the study. A febrile presence pervaded the images, and the demon shrank back from them like a vampire from a cross.

It saw the art board with its ink-lettered parchment and determined its purpose. With a savage swipe of its claw, the yellowish paper was slashed to an illegible mess. Culhane winced in pain, his labors destroyed.

The demon peered at the man, its snout just inches beyond the spell's wall. It sank to its haunches, its growl rumbling like an ancient motor, as the sustaining life force was drained off from miles away by its host. In its fiery yellow eyes, the man could see the soul of a monster twisted and malformed from ages of hellish servitude. Tom was right. It was a sorrowful, pathetic creature, writhing through an existence of unending torment. He could almost pity it.

Tom made it into the car and tossed the knapsack on the front seat. Somehow he resisted the flow of energy and mustered all his strength to fire the engine and pull out of his driveway.

The roads were dim as the final sliver of twilight sun dropped below the horizon, but the autumn moon was at its fullest. Some jack-o'-lanterns were burning on front porches. A skeleton was tied to a neighbor's streetlamp, smiling with a cartoonish death grin. But the street was strangely quiet for Halloween, the result of the near moratorium of the holiday traditions. There were not the usual trick-or-treaters going door to door in little ghost and goblin suits. The Chalet attack had filled all the papers and news channels. A perverse terror had descended on the town. Only the most intrepid would venture out tonight.

Tom drove with determination down the empty suburban streets. His eyesight was hazy, and at times he saw flashes of that *other* world. He feared that at any moment he might be sucked back into its eerie landscape. The Chrysler spun its wheels and sped away. When at last he was free of the residential streets, he zoomed onto the main road, headlights blazing, and was off for Crohaven.

"Listen," Julie said to her father. It was deathly quiet in the study below. She and Parrish huddled together in the dark, cramped quarters of the attic. The sloping walls of the ceiling squeezed them into the narrow triangular space. The scant floor was cluttered with boxes and rustic furniture.

Julie's nostrils twitched to the stale air, which smelled of cobwebs and old secrets. A single window loomed at the far end, overlooking the gable of the second story.

They listened to the silence. "What's happening?" she asked.

"I don't know," he answered.

Tom steered onto the dark forested road, its heavy canopy blocking out any light from the moon. The little car bounced off some steep hills. Only two miles left. He raced the accelerator, picking up as much speed as he could.

His eyes began to dim again, and he struggled to stay alert. The trees twisted into strange configurations, and the landscape suddenly shifted to a mountainous terrain. Spindly cliffs of stone, like cathedral spires against magenta clouds.

"Get away! I don't see this!" he shouted, banishing the alien mirage from his eyes.

The car barreled around a curve. Crohaven Road loomed ahead, and he barely adjusted his speed enough to make the turn. The tires skidded and screeched as he careened wildly onto the narrow road. *Damn!*

Almost there. He glanced at the knapsack as though expecting the creature model to spring out and attack him.

"I am the puppet master! I am the puppet master!" he repeated to himself.

Empty fields were about him. Just around that bend, the cemetery would appear. He pressed the gas pedal to the floorboard, feeling exhilarated.

Suddenly a shape appeared in the road, reflecting the headlights.

"I don't see this!" he shouted again.

But the shape didn't vanish. It was a *deer.* A deer was standing in the road!

"Shi-it!" he yelled, steering wildly to the side to avoid impact. The doe leapt terrified into the brush, white tail flagging in distress, but by then the car was out of control. It careened over the roadside, crashing through an abandoned stretch of wood fencing and settled into a ditch.

Breathing loudly, Tom gunned the engine, but the back wheels were hopelessly entrenched. Soil was tossed up in a spray. He was grounded, less than a mile from the Crohaven Estate.

"Damn it!" he shouted as he grabbed the knapsack, extinguished the engine, and crawled out the car seat.

Moisture immediately penetrated his sneakers as he stepped out of the car. He had landed in a small creek. The walk up the incline to the road seemed endless, but he trudged along, carrying the bag with its precious contents. When he reached the crest, he bent over, exhausted. His energy was waning again. Staring off, he could barely see in the distance the looming structure of Crohaven Manor.

It was the last thing he saw of the *real* world before losing consciousness.

Rejuvenated by the new flow of energy, the demon skulked below the panel where the father and girl had vanished. It ignored the man in the circle, who was no longer a threat, and peered at the cord dangling from the ceiling. Though it was cunning enough to comprehend the device, the panel entrance was pathetically small for its hulking form. Instead, the demon stepped back to the center of the space, sniffing the air. It crouched tightly and leaped toward the ceiling with the full thrust of its legs. Culhane watched in alarm as it crashed into the ceiling, creating a hole above.

Julie crept aside just as the attic floor below her buckled. The creature's head and claw cleared the jagged wood before disappearing again. "It's back!" she yelled as Parrish hauled her away. He studied their surroundings, desperate for an escape plan. It was only a matter of time. The creature would reach them if they stayed here. There was only one route left to them. The rooftop!

He grabbed a chair from the clutter of furniture and rammed it against the small window. It shattered, taking the wooden frame with it. "Julie, we have to get to the roof!"

"*What?*"

"Trust me." He put his back to the window opening and began reaching out to the roof frame. "Pull on my shirt until I can climb free."

She hesitated, but another leap from the demon caused the floor to shake. It was coming through! She grabbed the front of her father's shirt and tugged, preventing him from toppling back, even as he climbed precariously out the window.

Gripping the slanting sides of the roof, Parrish managed to clear the window. Julie released her hold as his torso disappeared outside. His upper body now dangled from the building, clinging precariously to the roof peak. Carefully, he swung his abdomen from side to side up until his legs cleared the attic window and swung around the arched edges. Then he hauled himself up. A few breathtaking moments later, he was safely on the rooftop.

Crash! The creature leapt up, this time clinging to the crevice created in the attic floor. The hole was large enough for it to protrude. Julie glanced back in terror as its head appeared through the attic floor. She was *alone* with it!

"Julie!" called her father from outside. "Give me your hand!"

She recoiled. This was crazy! But the demon was climbing through just a few feet away. Parrish's hand showed outside the window, and she grasped it firmly, her back to the window as her father had demonstrated. He pulled tightly, hauling her bodily out the window. She suddenly found herself dangling from his one hand in midair!

She looked down and let out a gasp of fear. A three-story drop below her.

"Julie! Look at me! LOOK AT ME!"

She gazed up at her father, whose eyes burned with strength, and then struggled with her free hand to reach his other hand. With his strong grip heaving at her, she was swung over to the slanting roof and pulled up free and clear—

—just as the creature's claw snatched out for her.

The claw missed her sneaker by inches. The two of them crawled away from the corner, balancing perilously on the roof peak.

When he came to, Tom was lying face down in mud. He couldn't be sure if it was real mud, or more illusion, but it was wet on his cheek, and there was the very frightening sensation that he was sinking into it. In a panic, he lifted his head and opened his eyes to a thick mist.

All around him was a bog, like some primordial swamp. Tall reeds and cattails surrounded the pool he was immersed in, and the sound of crickets and katydids chorused from all sides. There was a stench of crude oil that sickened him to his stomach. As he pressed his hand down, he could feel the black sticky substance give way beneath him. His lower body was restrained, and he realized it had already sunk below the surface of the pasty muck. He was still clutching the knapsack, but it seemed immobile and hopelessly stuck.

Asphalt! The black substance was asphalt! He was in a tar pit!

Visions of mammoths and saber-tooths struggling to death filled his head. He squirmed desperately to free himself, but his legs sank deeper with each stroke. The suction was pulling him under. In a claustrophobic frenzy, he tugged and fought against the tar. His lungs filled with air, gulping it down in quick gasps.

"This isn't real! This isn't real!" he shouted. "There

are no tar pits in New York!"

He swung his free hand out, and felt a dry patch of grass to his right. Stretching with all his might, he reached what seemed like a strong root. It resisted to his pull, and he gripped it tightly, hoping to extract himself. But the sticky tar gave way even more, and though he clung to the root frantically, his body sank deeper into the prehistoric swamp.

"Fight it!" he commanded himself. You can't give up!

But the tar, illusion though it might be, sucked him into its maw, until just his face and arm remained above the surface. He continued to grip the root, his only hold on life, with the last vestige of strength in his body.

He was drained to total exhaustion. The fumes from the asphalt were making his head light, and soon his lids were heavy, unable to stay open. He knew the black mud was simply a metaphor, ripped by the demon from his subconscious, but it was deadly effective. His limbs were frozen, except for the free hand clinging to hope in the form of a twisted growth of plant, and he knew then that he would die in this dream hell.

"Julie . . ." he cried out, defeated. "Julie . . . I'm sorry."

Scarcely a mile away from where Tom's car lay off the roadside, his spirit lost in an ethereal bog, Julie and Parrish stepped cautiously across the pinnacle of the roof. It slanted at a steep angle on either side of them, and they straddled the peak, making way for the chimney at the far end. Its craggy surface of brick offered some possibility that they might climb down.

Julie led the way. They were closing the distance to the chimney, when there was a loud crash. Less than ten feet behind them, the demon had pounded its fist through the angled surface of the roof.

Startled by the sound, Julie took a misstep.

"Careful!" Parrish shouted.

Her ankle twisted, and she fell to her chest on the roof. With a scream, she gripped at the peak, but missed when her sneakers slipped on the surface.

"Julie!" Parrish reached for her too late, and she began to slide down the slanted roof! Instinctively, she pressed her palms against the tiled surface, and the coarse texture miraculously brought her sliding to a halt. There she lay, seven feet below the roof peak, with a scant distance to go before a three-story plunge.

She didn't dare to breathe.

"Julie! Julie! Reach for me!" her father called from above.

To her right, the creature pounded through the structure from within the attic. The concussions threatened to send her sliding again.

Oblivious to the demon's rampage, Parrish flattened himself to the surface of the roof, gripping the sharp edge of the peak with one hand, stretching the other toward Julie. "Julie . . . You've got to reach me!"

"Daddy," she cried, too frightened to move.

His arm stretched until his joints and tendons ached.

His fingers burned with the strain, but they were still a good foot out of her arm's reach. Thinking fast, Parrish grabbed for his belt and unbuckled it. With a swift pull, he removed the belt from his jeans and whipped it down to her, clutching the leather strap tightly. It extended to just above her head.

"Julie, *now*!"

She swallowed hard and flung her hand up to grab the belt. She clutched the buckle just as her feet slipped farther toward the edge. The leather pulled taut, but she was held secure. She gripped at it with her other hand, holding on for life. With a tremendous effort, Parrish pulled, trying to haul her back up the roof surface. She kicked and dug desperately with her toes.

Just then, the creature broke completely through. It splintered the remaining planks of wood and brushed them aside. Then it crawled out to the surface of the roof.

Neither Julie nor her father dared to look. They could feel its motions and hear its breath as it gripped the tile surface with sharp claws and pulled itself up to the pinnacle of the rooftop.

Parrish lay prostrate on the peak, his right arm outstretched, holding the leather strap as he struggled to pull his only daughter to safety. The demon stood perched a mere ten feet away from him, its wings riding the air currents like an eagle. He refused to acknowledge it.

CHAPTER 87

WITH EACH NOISY SLOSH, TOM FELT HIMSELF SINKING ever deeper into the tar. His right hand still clung tightly to the root for salvation, his left to the knapsack, which was now lost beneath the surface. But his thoughts had drifted into a hazy surrender, no longer fighting his inevitable doom. The oppressive black muck constricted his chest, making it nearly impossible to breathe. His gasps for air were labored, and his strength dwindled.

In some dim place of his mind, he saw the plight of Julie and her father. The demon's eyes captured for him their hopeless stand on the rooftop. Though nearly engulfed by the asphalt, Tom stirred to the vision. Some small spark of hope remained inside him. The desire to rescue his girlfriend kindled a new fire.

He remembered the words of Parrish: You are the wellspring of its power, the source of its very existence.

The voice seemed to speak to him from afar. Its strength is your strength. Whatever it can do, you can master as well.

Tom closed his eyes, attempting once again to fight the

demon's grasp on his mind. "It's an illusion. An illusion. I'm not here. It's not real." But the tar resisted. The thick fluid crushed against his chest, the fumes suffocating him. Try as he might, he could not break free.

Then a queer logic pervaded his thinking.

"You fool! It's not an illusion. It IS real," said a voice, his own mind answering back.

He trembled in uncertainty. "It's an illusion. It has to be."

"No!" the voice countered, "You are not in your world. You are in the realm of the astral. Illusions and reality are the same."

He felt his grasp on the root loosen slightly as he dropped farther into the abyss.

The astral world . . . where all things are commanded by passion.

It tingled at his cerebrum, a peculiar notion just beyond his comprehension.

Illusion. Reality. The same!

Astral world . . . where all things are possible . . .

There was a spark of understanding, an epiphany that deconstructed his very concept of reality. He realized he was straddling the gap of consciousness, caught at the crossroad of two dimensions. Somehow, he was simultaneously in his world and another and could choose between them. If he chose his own reality, then he was lying facedown by the roadside, unconscious and paralyzed, and all of this was a fatal illusion. But if he chose the other reality, then he was in an alternate realm, sinking in a pool of tar. If that were true, then he had traveled to this place physically. The world about him was not a mirage but real molecular matter, constructed by the demon to entrap him.

The tar was real. The fumes that assaulted his nostrils. Real! Every particle of his body, his clothes, his backpack, even its contents were duplicated in an astral matter, malleable to human thought. His mind was the architect of all he perceived. He could change it. He could leave this place!

Outrageous! Too incredible to believe, but in that hopeless moment, his mind opened to the impossible. He recalled reading about it. Saints and yogis bilocating. Instantly appearing in two places at once.

Glitch! His paradigm shifted, breaking the continuity. Tom pondered. He struggled. He sought the answer.

The demon could transmigrate from one place to another using his astral body—his soul*—as a vehicle. It could physically manifest itself, flesh and blood, in whatever place it desired. If the demon could do it, then* so could he*!*

Tom clenched his eyes shut. He envisioned Crohaven Manor and saw again the dangerous plight of Julie and Parrish. Adrenaline pumped through his veins, and his strength was suddenly restored. Pistons of willpower sent energy churning through his system, until he felt his body aglow with a fire. The molecules of his flesh began to vibrate wildly like an engine roaring to life. With a keen inner sight, heightened by his animator's imagination, he imagined the front yard of Crohaven. He saw the building's face and the weeping willow. He focused on the gazebo, with its circular tiled roof, until the image was crystal sharp in his mind.

His body was blazing now. An aura of bright radiation surrounded him. His left hand clutched the canvas strap of the knapsack, buried beneath the asphalt, while his right continued to grip the root.

Taking a deep breath, he braced himself—

I . . . am . . . THERE!

—and released his hold on the root!

Snap!

With a flash of light, the tar pit vanished around him. He felt himself floating for a brief instant in a void of bitter cold. Bright colors swirled around him. His astral shape followed the path set by the demon in a stream of consciousness. Even as it sucked and pulled at his essence, it formed a channel on which to travel, drawing him like a magnet through ætheric space, until his own mind charted the course to his selected destination.

Snap!

Then he rematerialized onto a small sloping circle of tiled rooftop!

The clean air of the night caressed him, and he gasped heavily at it, filling his lungs. It took him a moment to register what had happened. As the landscape filled his peripheral vision, he knew where he was.

He was lying facedown atop the gazebo of Crohaven

Manor! His body was clean of the tar, and it gave off a faint shimmer. Glancing over, he saw that the knapsack and its contents were still in his grasp!

"Jesus!" Tom said, astonished. He had managed to teleport himself.

He lifted his head, gazing to the top of the mansion.

Above, Julie and Parrish were prostrated on the roof surface, the man struggling to pull his daughter to safety. Fau'Charoth stood a scant few feet away, poised to attack them.

Tom stood up on the gazebo, clutching the knapsack. He unzipped it and pulled out the demon puppet, holding it aloft.

"Fau'Charoth!" he shouted at the top of his lungs.

The demon startled and turned to its "creator." It saw the rubber icon in his hand and growled menacingly.

At that moment, Parrish was able to hoist Julie up the final inch and haul her over the surface of the roof, until he held her safely in his arms. She embraced him, feeling the warmth of his love. "Thank you. Thank you," he whispered to the heavens.

Looking past his shoulder, Julie saw a startling sight. There was the boy standing atop the gazebo, puppet in hand. "Tom? Oh my God! Tom!" From below, Tom looked up at her and gave a wave of acknowledgement.

Parrish turned to see him and was amazed. Tom sparkled with a halo of energy so bright that he seemed like an angel.

The snarling demon snapped its jaws at the boy, flailing

its wings. Then it stood upright in defiance and roared.

Tom faltered, nearly dropping the puppet, as a stream of essence drained from him. "No!" he shouted, forcing life back into his limbs. "I won't let you. *I'm* the puppet master!"

Now it was the creature's turn to stumble as it relinquished a fragment of its stolen energy. It fell into a crouch, shaking its head dizzily.

"*I'm* the puppet master!" Tom repeated, lifting the model again. "I control you!"

Enraged, the creature flapped its wings and launched into the air. In a swooping arc, it flew high into the night sky, soaring above the mansion. It circled in flight and began diving toward the boy.

"Tom!" Parrish shouted. "Get out of there!" Julie clutched at his arm in fear.

Tom watched as the airborne demon dove at full speed for him. It let out a high-pitched shriek of challenge as it fell in swift descent. The boy crouched to the roof, threw his arms up, bracing for the attack.

"I defy you. I defy you. I'm the master!"

Whoosh! The demon sped past him overhead, claws slashing at him. Parrish saw a flash of light as the two beings, twins of the same soul, collided in space. But a cushion of astral energy shielded Tom from its blow. The claws were turned harmlessly away.

Unscathed, Tom looked up in surprise. Miraculously, he had summoned the power to resist it. It was as if he reversed the pole of his energy like a magnet, repelling the creature with a psychic blast.

"That's right!" Parrish shouted encouragingly. "Fight it, Tom!"

He could hear the voice of the angry demon as it swooped above him. It rose into the air, wings flapping furiously, and dove at him a second time. Tom prepared himself for another assault.

Whoosh!

Another flash of light as the demon bombarded him. This time a claw broke through his wall of resistance and slashed his shoulder. He winced in pain, but it was not severe. It flapped its wings into yet another aerial ascent, climbing higher into the sky until it was merely a speck in the clouds. Parrish and Julie followed it, seeing it circle and begin a final assault. It passed over them, casting a shadow in the moonbeams.

"This isn't good," Julie cringed tightly to her father. "Tom!"

"Here it comes again!"

From below, Tom felt the hairs on his neck bristle and braced himself for another juggernaut. He could feel its rage as it dove for him with lethal intent. Bracing himself on the gazebo, he gripped the small point of its pinnacle and focused his mind.

"I defy you. I defy you. You cannot harm me."

The wind roared with its onrush as the demon hurled itself straight for the boy. Tom clenched his teeth, awaiting its impact.

"I DEFY YOU!"

The creature rammed him with full force, and there was an exploding flash. Boy and demon were catapulted into space as their opposing energies collided. The top of the gazebo shattered.

Parrish watched astounded as their bodies repelled one another with a violent pulse. The demon was tossed heavily into the nearby willow tree's leaf canopy as Tom fell onto the soft grassy cushion of the lawn.

His spectral vision engaged, Parrish could see the blazing auras of both. They were aglow with the same spectrum of ætheric light. As Tom strained and rose to his knees, a bright line of luminescent energy extended from just below his chest. It traveled like an ethereal leash to the willow tree. There, it joined to the creature at its solar plexus. Parrish watched as Fau'Charoth fell out of the branches and fought it off savagely, a wild beast ensnared.

"Look!" Parrish directed to his daughter.

"What is it? What do you see?" She squinted, failing to discern it without astral sight.

"Tom's captured it with his cord! He's reclaiming its substance!"

He observed with astonishment the legendary "silver cord," so prevalent in occult literature that tethered the astral and physical bodies together. Boy and demon were connected by this ghostly filament, and as the demon took to the air, it stretched and pulled taut, glistening with astral light.

With eyes closed, Tom concentrated fully on the cord.

Even as the demon attempted to escape, the silver thread thickened and grew brighter. The aura around the demon brightened as well, resembling metal being heated to a molten stage. It twisted and tossed in the air as Tom wrangled it from the ground like a cowboy tugging at a roped steer.

Around and around, the demon swooped, a kite on a string. The cord glowed to a brilliant white. The demon struggled fiercely, but it weakened and lost its composition, until with a sudden burst it dematerialized into a cloud of luminous energy. Like thick vapor into a vacuum, the energy was sucked into the "straw" of Tom's silver cord, entering back into his body. As the last puff of demon mist passed into the thread, the glowing tendril began to fade, withdrawing into the boy's ribcage.

Tom collapsed to the grass, lying still. Silence engulfed the estate.

From the roof, Julie could hear him moan slightly. He turned to his side and rose on his palms and knees, clutching at his midsection in pain. Even as it entered him, the demon fought containment and pounded with a vengeance against his restraint. It churned at his guts now, burning with vehemence. He knew it would not remain shackled for long.

"Julie!" he cried, rising limply to his feet.

She called back, "Tom! Are you all right?"

"Mr. Parrish. Get to the tunnel! I can't hold it for long! Get to the tunnel, now!"

He searched the grass until he found the puppet,

crumpled in a fetal heap on the ground, and then he gathered up the knapsack. Forcing the puppet into the bag, he turned again to Julie and her father, who were making their way across the rooftop.

"I'll meet you there. *Hurry!*"

Parrish watched as he clutched convulsively at his stomach, fearing to see the creature emerge once again. But Tom held it tight, resisting the pain.

Then he made fists at his sides and dropped his head down in concentration.

"*Tunnel!*" he shouted.

For an instant, his halo began to sparkle with feathers of light, until his entire body filled with a bright, ethereal glow.

Before the eyes of man and girl, Tom vanished in a flash.

Julie gasped, "What happened?"

Parrish was stunned beyond words. "My God, he can *transmigrate*."

He didn't know how, but he knew they were in the presence of miraculous events.

"But where did he go?" Julie asked, frantically.

"Did you hear him? He said 'tunnel.' He's already there!"

"We need to follow him! This way!" Julie shouted, pointing ahead. The crevice created by the demon offered a safe entry back into the attic. They carefully straddled the roof peak and dropped through the jagged hole.

Parrish found Culhane still curled up in a ball within the

warding circle. He was limp and barely conscious, bleeding profusely from his stomach, which he held firmly with one broad hand. Julie winced at the sight and turned away.

"Julie," Parrish commanded. "Call the sheriff and request an ambulance." He addressed his friend, gently turning him over, "Humphrey."

The man stirred with a groan, and his eyes opened, grateful to see the man and girl beside him. The faintest hint of a smile appeared on his burly face.

"Stephen. You still live? Blessed be."

Parrish nodded. "Are you in serious pain?"

Culhane blinked. "Got . . . *divorced* once. That was *worse*, I think."

He pulled his hand away, allowing Parrish to examine his wound. His skin was torn and severely ravaged about his stomach and chest, but protected as it was by a formidable layer of fat, there were no vital organs punctured.

Julie grabbed the phone from where it had toppled and made the call to the sheriff's office. She wrestled with questions and cut it short with the simple phrase "demon attack." Then she hung up the phone and joined her father. "They're coming," she announced and then asked with concern. "What about Tom?"

Parrish grabbed a clean piece of muslin from his art table and held it to Culhane's wound. He looked into the man's eyes. "Hump, Tom's reclaimed the demon inside him, but not for long. He's at the tunnel already, waiting for us. We need the spell. Where's the spell?"

He moaned in delirium. “Destroyed. You must . . . *stop him!*”

Parrish’s heart sank. He exchanged a worried glance with Julie.

“Hump. What happens if Tom burns the puppet without the spell?”

An agonizing pause, and then—“. . . can’t separate their auras. The demon . . . will take Tom’s soul with it . . . into the demon void.”

Julie blanched. “*What?* We have to get to him!”

“Julie, wait!” Parrish shouted, but she was already out the door. He called out to her as her footsteps receded down the stair below. “Whatever you do, DON’T LET HIM BURN THAT PUPPET! I’ll be right behind you!”

He turned again to Culhane, who was on the verge of passing out, and began fashioning a makeshift bandage for his wound. Culhane gripped his arm tightly.

“Stephen . . . very important.”

He struggled to raise his head. “So foolish . . . I never considered . . . Tornau didn’t fail . . . just never realized . . . the child offering was sufficient. Cycle completed.”

Parrish met his eyes. “Humphrey, what are you saying?”

“You mustn’t let Tom get too close to the fire. The boy . . . his aura signature . . . will fully activate the vortex. He’ll open the gate to Hell!”

CHAPTER 88

DARKNESS.

Tom caught his breath, fending off the stabbing chill. Blackness enveloped him. Was he blind? Had his corneas been damaged by the searing cold of inter-world travel? Seized with panic, he grappled frantically at his bag, searching until he located with relief the large flashlight in the pouch. He switched it on and was rewarded with its bright light. Incredibly, he found himself in the black recesses of the tunnel. Its darkness was as oppressive as he remembered. For the second time in an hour, he had focused his mind and was transported in a flash to another location.

But there was no time to dwell on miracles.

His body shivered violently, not only from the icy chill, but from the physical exhaustion of restraining the demon within him. Another shudder attack gripped him, jolting him fiercely. He clutched his sides, gritting his teeth, as his innards quaked. The demon wanted out. He imagined it ramming against his insides, clawing at his intestinal walls, but he held it fast with a tempered restraint.

Tom peered down the tunnel, where the moonlit sky was a barely discernible circle of steel gray. Still no sign of the others.

Where were they?

He stood beside the ritual site, unable to proceed. He would have to wait for them to arrive, and every second was a torment. In a feeble attempt to distract from the pain, he set the large flashlight upright so that its harsh beams could illuminate the walls. He then gathered fragments of unused firewood from around the circle and piled it into the circle of stones. It would speed things up at least if the fire was already built. It would also add much needed warmth and light. Feverishly searching for additional fuel, he grabbed the empty leather satchel, which was brittle and dry, and stuffed it into the pile.

Guano covered everything. He recalled reading that it made a good fuel source. Most of the bat droppings were dry and powdery, but some were fresh, and he wiped his smeared fingers with disgust onto his pant legs. Bat carcasses littered the corners of the floor, creating a stench of fetid rot. He twitched his nose.

Pulling the can of lighter fluid out of his bag, he pulled up the spout and let the clear liquid drench the contents in the fire circle. Thank God for the matches he brought! The box felt like salvation in his shivering fingers. He flicked a single wooden match, and set it ablaze. Immediately the scent of burning petrol filled the chamber, and the shadows receded like black spiders into dark crevices. The fire warmed his heart and body. It burned less than a foot in height, but to Tom they were the flames of Pentecost.

As the tongues of fire danced, the chalk on the walls shined in reflection, revealing the arcane symbols. They were like hideous road signs guiding him now, on his hellish journey.

He glanced at the decrepit robes decaying in piles on the floor and felt a tingle of morbid curiosity. Picking up the flashlight and aiming it close, he reached for one of the crumpled vestments. He pulled at the hood. There was the rasping sound of stiffened wool as the cloth gave way. He then gasped in horror as the flash beam revealed the nightmare below.

Beneath the robe was a desiccated skeleton, crushed and malformed. It was literally flattened and merged with the stone like a paraffin figure that had melted under tremendous heat. The empty sockets wailed silently at him from beyond the grave. He stepped away in revulsion, feeling his body tremble, and clutched again at his midsection.

Just then the fire roared as though a tremendous draft had soared through the tunnel. The flames grew bright and stretched upward. There was a burst of new light within the firepit. A pillar of revolving phosphorescence began to form, churning at the core as if it were a tornado. It glowed an odd violet. And it was *cold*, a scorching cold like the space between stars. A howling wind filled the tunnel. Tom gazed at the fiery maelstrom of pure energy as it rose to the very top of the chamber. All darkness was now obliterated, replaced by its otherworldly glow. Tom blinked against the brightness, protecting his retinas against the piercing light.

He reached into the knapsack and withdrew the creature puppet, gripping it firmly in his hand.

Julie ran until she thought her legs would fall off. Her thighs were burning as she sped beyond the cemetery and onto the service road. Gravel crushed under her feet as she followed the ancient rails that led to the tunnel.

She came to a stop.

The black entrance stretched ahead. Her knees quivered, and she bent over to catch her breath. Clutched in her hands were a flashlight she managed to take from their stash and one of her makeshift torches. With a quick flick from a butane lighter, she set the torch ablaze. The flame on the cloth billowed from the top. In the distance, she heard sirens approaching the mansion. Help was on the way. She needed only to find Tom and keep him comforted until her father arrived. Then all would be well.

All would be well, she told herself, even as she took her first tentative step toward the blackness, armed with her light sources.

"Tom?" she called, hearing her voice bounce across the stone surface. No answer. She held herself against the chill and called again. "Tom! Are you in there?" In the distance, she thought she saw a campfire glow. It encouraged her, and she thrust the flashlight and torch ahead.

Just then, a sudden burst of light caused her to leap

back. She threw her forearm before her eyes, squinting against the brightness. A draft of wind roared past her into the cave. The torch flame fluttered. When her pupils readjusted, she gazed with alarm at the core of the tunnel, where a pulsating star now burned.

"Oh my God! Tom!" She ran toward the glow, fearing what she would find.

The patrol car pulled into the black gate of Crohaven, lights and siren blazing. Others would follow. The troopers were also on their way. In the distance, Kurt Kronin heard the wailing of the ambulance he'd radioed. He and Deputy Evans left the vehicle, weapons drawn. The building was ominously quiet, but in the glare of the headlights, Kurt could make out the damage. The front entrance was a shambles of splintered wood, as though a pickup had crashed through it. The rooftop (he'd grown accustomed to looking *up*!) was similarly smashed, a gaping hole in the surface. Something huge had broken in and out again. He glanced at Evans, fearing what might lurk within the looming structure. His shoulder tingled with ancient pain.

A figure appeared in the ravaged entrance. They thrust their weapons out in unison.

"Hold it right there!"

Parrish froze in the glare of the headlights, his palms face up. Kurt focused on him with relief. "Stephen! You almost gave me a heart attack."

The psychic walked toward them. Evans noticed his

hands were bloody.

"What happened in there?" the sheriff asked.

"The demon attacked us," Parrish spoke hurriedly.

"Where is it?"

"It's gone for now. You'll find what's left of Gerard Wilkens in the kitchen."

"Wilkens?" Kronin was stunned. "It killed him?"

"I'm afraid so. And my friend on the third floor needs medical attention immediately. No time to explain. I have to catch up to my daughter. She's with Tom DeFrank, and they're in danger!"

The name triggered a flare in the sheriff's eyes. "Tom De—*what the hell?*"

"Kurt, I have to leave *now*!" Parrish forced his way past the officers.

Kronin pressed a palm to his chest. "You aren't going anywhere . . . *alone*."

As Julie neared the fire, she saw a fantastic sight. In the firepit was a pillar of rotating lavender flame. Standing before it like a petrified statue was Tom. He stood transfixed with puppet in hand, a black silhouette against the shimmering conflagration. There was a roaring wind that moaned like souls in purgatory.

"Tom!" she called above the torrent.

He turned to her, and his eyes brightened with relief. His face looked callow, and he was clearly on his last legs. She stepped quickly to embrace him, but he put out a forbidding hand.

"Stay away! I can't hold it much longer." He pressed a hand against his stomach in a spasm of pain. It made Julie wince.

"Where are the others?" he asked.

Julie filled with dismay, unable to answer.

"*Julie*," he pleaded. "We need to begin the ritual! *Where are they?*"

"Tom . . ." she tried to tell him. The look in his eyes shattered her. "Tom . . . we can't."

Tom gazed at her bewildered. "What are you saying?"

Tears streaked her face. "The spell. It *destroyed the spell*! We can't perform the ritual without it."

What? His eyes glazed over in understanding, and he wavered in sudden panic and uncertainty. She felt helpless.

Tom convulsed again. Confusion tore at his fortress of will, and in that moment the demon broke through his restraint. He spasmed, dropping the puppet, as a pulse of energy ripped out of his midsection.

Snap!

A dart of glowing ectoplasm shot from his solar plexus. It streaked past Julie, and the demon materialized in a flash *behind her*!

Julie froze and turned with a scream just as the creature's claws wrapped around her and snatched her into the air. Tom watched in horror as Fau'Charoth held the girl aloft above its head. She dangled horizontally, struggling in its grasp.

"Julie!" he cried, as the demon bellowed ferociously in triumph.

Horrified, Julie fell into a swoon, whimpering in fear. Tom immediately snatched up the puppet from the floor and held it outstretched toward the creature. With the girl tight in its clutches, the demon locked eyes with him in a challenge of wills.

"Don't you hurt her!" Tom shouted. "Don't you dare hurt her, you *bastard*!"

It snarled, showing the length of its canines to its "creator."

"Let her go! Damn you! I command you to let her go!" Tom focused his inner strength, hoping to reclaim the demon once again inside him, but the creature was powerfully resistant. He could feel its will braced against him like steel. He gripped the puppet, crushing the rubber flesh to the "bone," and held it up to the fire as a threat.

Fau'Charoth snarled in lethal warning.

Another light appeared, approaching from the entrance. Bright flash beams bounced with the arrival of two men. It was Parrish, flanked by Sheriff Kronin. Both were shielding their eyes against the spectacle of the purple fire. Drawing nearer, their gazes filled with shock and terror as they beheld the display.

"Holy Jesus!" the sheriff yelled in alarm. He could barely comprehend what he was seeing. There before him was a blazing pillar of flame that stabbed back to his memory in the barn. Beside it was a terrible *thing* that fit every description of a demon he had ever heard. And Tom DeFrank, the boy he had saved as an infant so many years ago, clutching a puppet before the flame.

"Julie!" Parrish cried out to his daughter. The girl was held supine in the grips of the monster. Aghast, Kronin reached for his weapon.

Hearing her father's voice, Julie swam back into consciousness and felt the hot grasp of the demon on her legs and back. Its grip was so strong she feared it would wrench her apart.

She turned to Parrish. "Daddy . . ."

Kronin pointed his firearm at the demon—

"Get down, Stephen!"

"No! Don't!" shouted Tom.

—and fired two rounds into its side. It responded instantly. With a swift action, it swung Julie under the crook of its arm, holding her firmly as it lashed out with its free claw.

The sheriff couldn't get another shot off before the claw gripped him and pulled him in. Kronin threw his left arm up. The demon grabbed it in its jaws, the fangs slicing deeply into his forearm. He felt a crunch as the demon pulverized the bones below his wrist.

While the sheriff screamed, Parrish rammed the large flashlight like a club on the creature's face, causing it to drop the police officer. With a backward shove of its claw, it swiped him aside. Parrish collided painfully with the stone wall.

"Daddy!" Julie cried as the man fell to his knees,

clutching the back of his head. Returning its attention to Kronin, the demon slammed its foot down on the sheriff's chest, forcing him to the ground. He hollered in pain.

"Fau'Charoth!" Tom shouted to distract it. It shifted its gaze to the boy, with Julie still held tightly under one arm.

Kronin squirmed beneath it, drawing his gun from below the creature's bulk. He fired it point blank into the creature's belly, emptying the chamber. Black ooze issued from the demon's wounds.

Momentarily stunned, the demon stepped back as the gun clicked on empty. The wounds glistened in the purple glow. As the man tried to rise, it flapped its wing wildly, swatting him like a fly. The sheriff was sent careening backward. Tom heard his body plummet onto the gravelly surface, followed by loud groaning.

Both men were subdued, and still the demon clutched the girl like a rag doll.

Once again, Tom held the puppet to the flame, with no alternative except to plunge it into the blaze. He felt the seething not-of-this-Earth cold as his knuckles drew near.

Fau'Charoth growled threateningly and lifted Julie to its snout. Glaring into Tom's eyes, it brought her into its open jaws—

—and closed them onto her delicate midsection. The snout buried beneath her shirt. Julie felt the wet fangs as they pressed down against her bare skin, threatening to mince her into pulp. She gasped aloud and began breathing tremulously. Hot saliva soaked through her clothing.

Tom froze, perceiving its intent. One more gesture toward the fire and Fau'Charoth would tear out Julie's belly. Painfully, he withdrew the puppet from the flame, but held it firmly before the firepit.

Stalemate.

From the ground, Parrish watched helplessly as his daughter quivered in its jaws. He coiled like a cat about to pounce.

The creature bit down slightly, and Julie cried out in pain.

Tom shouted to him. "Don't move! Nobody move!"

His face was pale and anguished. He gazed at Julie, and despair swept over him. There was nothing he could do to save her. The demon would crush the life out of her and destroy the only love he ever knew.

The only love he ever knew.

There was the slightest tingle in his ætheric pathway to the creature.

He paused, alerted to a new idea.

A demon knows nothing of love, Mr. Culhane had told him. Yet Tom sensed there was more to this demon than the man guessed. Though conceived in evil and succored on the blackest milk of human wickedness, it had grown beyond its original design. Its soul, now free of the magician's influence, was coupled to his own and had tasted the sweetest of human passions. As he stood helplessly before the fire, desperate to save the girl he loved, Tom felt the faintest shimmer of that love echoing back to him.

With renewed hope, Tom seized onto the emotion and

let it wash over him. It filled him with yearning and tender affection. Tears filled his eyes, and he gazed pleadingly at the creature. "Please . . . please," he implored. "You know you can't do this. I feel it in you."

Empathic energies coursed through him and channeled through their ephemeral link. Tom felt a quiver in the creature's will and gathered new resolve. His eyes pierced into its soul, and he sensed its pain and confusion. The many centuries of cruel isolation, and unbearable loneliness.

Then he spoke knowingly in a broken voice, addressing the girl.

"Julie . . . It won't hurt you."

She twisted her head to him, hanging like prey from its terrible jaws.

"It won't hurt you because . . . *I* would never hurt you. I love you, Julie. I love you."

He let his mind flash to their meeting and to their first intimate exchange. Their warm embraces and passionate kisses and the simple pleasure he felt at her touch. He deliberately relived every moment as a precious memory cradled in his heart. Then he looked at her, caressing her longingly with his eyes. As she dangled perilously near death, he imagined the tremendous pain of losing her.

Passion filled him. His eyes welled up with moisture. He sensed the feelings transmit to the demon. They were like an elixir that poured into its soul. The yellow demon eyes gazed into his own. The tight muscles of its snarl relaxed, until the wrinkles of its wolf snout softened. Julie could feel the jaws open as the fangs withdrew from her midsection.

The demon wavered slightly. It lowered to its haunches, still clutching the girl, but removed its mouth from her body.

Parrish watched with hope, sensing a change in the demon's composition. With his astral vision, he could see Tom's aura take on a resonance of pure love. It radiated like a blue-white halo, brighter even than the conflagration in the pit. In a stream of consciousness, it extended threadlike to the demon's chest. The tenuous filament was aglow with Tom's passion for his daughter, and it filled the demon like a vessel. Soon it burned with the same brilliant illumination, its vibrations elevated by this unique new energy. The indomitable wolf spirit rebelled against the demon nature, and it was transformed.

"I love her," Tom pleaded as tears dripped from his eyes. "Please . . . let her go."

The demon brought the girl tenderly to the ground, releasing her from its grasp. Julie recoiled and drew back. She saw the demon crouch to its forepaws, its features *docile* and forlorn. There was something almost mournful in the beast's demeanor. It looked at her with doleful eyes. She felt a sudden rush of sympathy as she crawled away.

Parrish immediately reached for her, clutching her dearly to his breast.

Tom and the demon stood apart from one another, hearts beating in unison. He watched, grateful and relieved as Julie and Parrish withdrew to safety. He gazed at the "monster," this creature of his design, connected in spirit before him. He saw it, as though for the first time, in all its magnificence. The sheer majesty of it overwhelmed him.

His entire life, he had imagined the *dragon.* The *behemoth* from time's abyss. Horned and fanged, with armored skin, aflight upon wings of triumph. He had cherished its colossal strength and ferocity when it had been indomitable and unconquered. And here it stood before him, humbled and subdued, smitten by love. His heart broke for it, overwhelmed by its loneliness, and he felt a dire need to touch it.

But in that moment, an explosion of light filled the chamber. The purple fire that had raged undisturbed now churned with activity. An orb of white pulsating energy materialized within the pillar of flame. The vortex shone brilliantly, and then a tongue of white plasma shot out of its core.

It blasted into the tunnel wall, searing a hole in the stone!

Parrish gaped at it wildly, and Julie clutched him in fear.

Another lance of plasma shot like a laser bolt from the vortex.

Tom fell back and looked at the creature with apprehension. It shrank back, fearful of the vortex.

A loud humming emanated from within the fire as the white light flashed. Currents of electricity gesticulated from the blaze.

"What's happening?" Julie cried out to her father.

He threw her to the ground as a shaft of fire struck above him. "The vortex is opening."

Tom ducked in alarmed, dodging the energy blasts.

Parrish called out to him, "Tom! We need to get out of here!" He looked at the tear in the fabric of time and space. The orb seemed about to explode. They were witnessing an inter-dimensional rift that would destroy all of them if they stayed.

But Tom held his ground, standing before the cosmic fury.

"It wants me," he spoke aloud with sudden realization. "I'm the seventh sacrifice."

Parrish pulled Julie to her feet. Together they were braced to make a headlong dash to safety. "Tom! Come with us!" he shouted.

"I can't!" Tom shouted back. "I have to close the portal!"

"You have to come, now!"

"No! Get out of here before it's too late!" Tom exchanged one final look with Julie. His eyes glazed, but he forced them clear with steely resolve. "Take her and get out!"

"No-o! Tom!" Julie nearly pulled free of her father, but Parrish held her tight.

Tom looked again at his demon.

The creature remained poised before him, ears arched forward like a dog's. Its eyes were locked with his own, and he searched its thoughts, wishing it could speak to him, hoping desperately for an answer. Fau'Charoth stared back, its primitive mind racing through centuries of memory. Then an answer came. It channeled from demon to boy and reverberated through Tom's mind. In the creature's consciousness, he found a memory—an *ætheric fragment* from a spell made long ago—and he brought it forth to his tongue.

He gazed at the demon and spoke it aloud, "Your name is *Fauglorum Anacharoth*."

He held the puppet to the fire.

"Fauglorum Anacharoth! I RELEASE YOU!"

He tossed the puppet into the pulsating flame!

"No-o!" Parrish shouted in alarm. Julie screamed.

The puppet vanished with a flash into the white void, and immediately the room filled with a gale force. It was as if the very atmosphere were being sucked into the vortex. Parrish and Julie clung together, pressing themselves to the wall.

Fau'Charoth howled and was immediately enveloped in white fire. It reeled up, tossing about as its flesh was incinerated, the glowing fragments pulled into the cyclone of energy. Tom watched in horror as his demon was torn asunder. Chunks of it gyrated through the air as they were sucked into the closing threshold. He felt his own consciousness fragment as well, his very thoughts soaring with the wind into the vortex, and he clutched at his midsection as though his entrails were being ripped out.

The maelstrom churned as a bright circle of fire, feeding its essence into the core.

The brightness was blinding. Parrish and Julie were forced to shield their eyes.

The last of the demon matter shot into the void, and the vortex closed with a deafening cataclysmic peal. The purple flame dissipated, and the room filled with clinging shadows, cast by the light of the dying fire in the pit.

All was deathly still once again.

Parrish's body shook uncontrollably, but he forced life into his limbs and pulled himself upright. Julie still clung to him, trembling. They heard a moan to their left and were rewarded by the sight of Sheriff Kronin, clutching his bloody forearm, but alive and mobile.

Julie looked about. "Where's Tom?"

Parrish scanned the darkness with dread. The area surrounding the firepit, where the boy had been standing just moments before, was empty. He immediately leapt to the circle of stones, darting about it. "Tom?"

"What happened to him?" Julie cried out in fear. "TO-OM! Where are you?!"

There was no sign of Tom DeFrank anywhere. He had vanished with the flames.

CHAPTER 89

ANOTHER POLICE CRUISER HAD JOINED THE SHERIFF'S car outside the tunnel. Officer Evans saw Parrish, Julie, and the sheriff straggling out of the entrance. Kronin had his forearm wrapped tightly in shirt cloth and was obviously in deep pain. Evans immediately reached for his car radio and called for another ambulance. "Officer needs assistance at—"

"Belay that!" Kronin called out to his deputy, wincing as he walked. "I can make it. Just get me to County General."

"Is my friend okay?" Parrish asked.

"He's on his way to the hospital. What happened in there?"

Nobody answered immediately. The girl was obviously distressed, crying profusely beside her father. It caused the officer to question. "Was anybody else hurt?"

Kronin hobbled into the backseat of the cruiser. "A boy, Tom DeFrank is—"

"Missing," Parrish finished.

"DeFrank?" Evans seemed puzzled. "A report just

came through. They found a boy unconscious beside his car about a mile back. No ID, but the vehicle was registered to a Margaret DeFrank."

Three faces simultaneously registered their surprise.

"*Tom?*" Julie's heart filled with hope. "I don't understand."

"I do," Parrish said, but fell silent as they entered the car.

Tom lay in a coma at County General Hospital. His skin was clammy and pale, and his body temperature had dropped to hypothermic levels. With treatment, he was restored to a healthy 98.6 degrees, but there was no reviving him. The doctors were baffled by his condition. EKG scans revealed only faint brain activity. No major injuries were found, except for some minor bruises and abrasions. They tested him for drugs and other contaminants, but his system was clean. The boy hovered near death, and no one could make a prognosis. There was no physiological cause for his condition, and so the physicians concluded it must be psychological. With his mother out of town and his father unreachable, they put him under surveillance and left the matter to the police.

In the rooms nearby, Sheriff Kronin was recovering from a crushed forearm and upper chest lacerations. Humphrey Culhane was likewise treated for wounds from a mauling. His belly required extensive suturing to close the wounds. The bite marks corresponded with those suffered by the late Gerard Wilkens, who was undergoing an autopsy in the morgue. The animal responsible was not identified, but its saliva was strangely clean and free of bacteria. Also peculiar, the wounds suffered by Culhane and the sheriff showed signs of rapid healing.

Kronin lay in bed, tossing restlessly. He opened his eyes and saw Parrish standing over him. The chief physician was nearby, glancing over a chart. Kronin groaned. Lifting his arm revealed a new white cast. "How's the boy?" he asked.

"He's in a coma, Kurt," Parrish answered. "It's been hours."

"Tom DeFrank has suffered a severe psychological trauma," the doctor informed him, "and is in a deep state of catatonic shock. We're monitoring his condition, but in cases like this the best we can do is wait."

Parrish leaned closer to the sheriff, whispering, "Kurt. There's little time left. If I'm to save him, I'll need complete access and privacy."

Kronin looked to the physician. "Doc, by order of the Chapinaw Police Department, I'm granting this man complete authority over Tom DeFrank. Give him whatever he needs, and see that he's undisturbed."

The doctor turned to Parrish. "Are you a physician?"

"No," Parrish replied. "I'm a psychic."

Stunned, the doctor raised his shoulders to Kronin in a shrug. "You're the sheriff."

Parrish was left alone with the boy as the staff continued to monitor his life signs.

It was clear to him now what remarkable event had taken place and how his body had miraculously turned up nearly a mile from the tunnel. The demon's engulfment of his aura had generated an ætheric field around Tom's entire flesh. It was this cloud of luminous energy that was so prevalent in his last spectral examination. The boy's body was no longer grounded to the physical plane. He had been encapsulated in a bubble of highly active astral matter. A mere thought was sufficient to send a projection of himself to another location.

His body was found lying by the roadside unconscious, his car entrenched in the mud. Desperate to get to the estate, Tom must have *bilocated* to Crohaven Manor. With much of his astral body already tugged to that region in the form of the demon, he simply relinquished the remains of his orb and allowed it to transmogrify into a second dense shape, a manifestation separate from the demon and himself.

The boy Parrish and Julie had witnessed from the rooftop was a completely solidified astral projection of Tom DeFrank. It was this astral double, possessed of Tom's consciousness, which confronted the demon and was pulled into the vortex, leaving behind his comatose body. The endeavor came at a costly price. The human shell in the hospital bed was nearly devoid of spirit-essence. Parrish knew that if any hope existed, it lay in his ability to project to the other side and locate Tom's wandering soul somewhere in that terrible void. It was a task he could only pray he was equipped for.

A deputy was posted outside the room to prevent intrusion by curious reporters. During those hours, the psychic simply sat in an armchair, engaged in meditation. Occasionally, he took the boy's hand in his own and whispered gently to him. Other times he was heard to mutter strange phrases under his breath and to seemingly dance in his ethereal Tai Chi exercise. The nurses and practitioners were put off by their limited access, fearing some arcane form of voodoo was being practiced on the patient, but since the man's actions were endorsed by the Chapinaw PD, they didn't intrude. Only his daughter Julie entered during his seclusion.

Despite the press lockout, the story leaked to the reporters, who hovered like vultures for tidbits of information. The town was furious for details and anxious for closure. The attack on the Crohaven Mansion was the climax to an astonishing series of events, starting with the bloody massacre at the Chalet. A raging fire had consumed the ski lodge, and with it most of the evidence. The word "demon," introduced in the early reports was later dropped and replaced by "unknown assailant," as the more bizarre details were duly kept from the public. Rumor and speculation persisted, however, and the little town became tabloid fodder for years. Roswell and Amityville could now claim a mate in Chapinaw, a place of devilish intrigue and unexplained phenomena.

Stephen Parrish wrote an account of the story himself. The Tornau affair was now just a precursor to the complete saga, which had a suitable ending at last. With Culhane's influence, an occult publishing house released *The Crohaven Demon* in 1982. The book crossed over into the mainstream and became a nonfiction bestseller. With all the mysteries put to rest, and his need for an ascetic lifestyle abandoned, Parrish voluntarily left his post at Crohaven Manor and moved back to New York City, where his daughter later attended Hunter College. The Crohaven property was eventually purchased by Wilkens's consortium of investors, the mansion leveled, the gardens and cemetery dismantled and relocated. An access road from the Route 17 highway plowed through the dense forest, scouring much of the countryside with new development. Fast food restaurants filled the area, along with a strip mall and car dealership. Many locals grumbled that, despite the cleansing, evil had retained its hold on the region. Today, on the legendary site of the Crohaven Estate, once the stomping ground for psychics, wizards, and demons, there now stands a Home Depot and Kmart shopping center.

Parrish returned to painting his beloved astral visions. His art pieces were eventually displayed in a gallery in SoHo's art district. Although they sold moderately well, his pseudo-metaphysical style did not achieve status until the "New Age" movement of the late 1980s. Collections of his work were later published in a popular form. An accomplished artist and author, Parrish attained local celebrity status in the town of Chapinaw. He was invited back to speak at seminars and graduations.

Kevin Marshall's funeral was a solemn event held on the quiet Sunday afternoon known as All Saint's Day. Julie Parrish stole away from the hospital long enough to attend the service with Danny Kaufman. The presence of Tom DeFrank was sorely missed.

EPILOGUE

Tom was falling. His body was weightless and without form, but he could feel the terrible velocity with which he plunged. Upon entering the vortex, he experienced the shock of ungodly cold. The brightness of the portal vanished, and his spirit dropped through a dark vacuous space. It was the blackest void imaginable. Sightless, soundless, it stretched on to infinity.

I am lost, *he thought*. This is Hell.

And as he thought the words, so did it appear.

Thunder boomed, and bright flashes revealed a sky of rolling black clouds over a turbulent sea. The black waves thrashed; above a canopy of billowing clouds that glowed red like embers stretched beneath a cauldron. Mountains rose out of the sea, and soon the waters receded into a stark, barren desert with ashen sand. Smoke and fire spewed from the conical peak of a towering volcano. The landscape was drawn from his mind. It was his vision of Hell. Of Mordor with its Mount Doom. All around him he felt, clinging to his mind like a malodorous pitch, the raw emotions of hatred, anger, and fear. His every moment of rage and despair was captured and concentrated, returned to him now, magnified a hundredfold.

He was alone in the abyss, and yet he was not alone. He felt the presence of the demon all about him. It was still merged with his essence, conjoined to the pulse of his spirit. His ætheric body was tossed and buffeted through the nightmare dimension, and he feared he would remain here forever.

Yet even as he feared the loss of his very consciousness, there suddenly appeared a glowing star amidst the black. It broke through the thick canopy of clouds and beckoned to him. With the speed of a bullet, he hurtled toward it and was catapulted into a bright realm.

His spirit eyes adjusted to the light, and he discovered he was standing in a meadow. All about him was a vista of incredible beauty. There were mountains as glorious as the Rockies, snowcapped and steeply peaked. The hills about him were heavily forested with verdant green trees and bushes. Giant sequoias reached to the blue sky, ferns and orchids growing thick at their bases. It was the primordial world as it stood long before the encroachment of man; and like Adam, Tom found himself a stranger in Eden.

He walked in the crisp air and felt a wind about him. There was a sudden and queer absence at the center of his being, as though a part of him had fragmented and broken free. He then realized the demon presence was no longer there.

He heard gentle footfalls of an animal behind.

Turning, he saw a wolf had come to him. It stood off about twenty feet, gazing with alert familiarity. Its fur was gray, its eyes yellow-gold, lined with black, and it had a glorious set of feathered wings folded at its back. Short pointed ears stood high on its head as it approached the boy cautiously.

Tom kneeled without fear, looking at the animal with instant recognition. The wolf stopped an arm's length away, timidly reaching forward with its snout. The muscles in its limbs were taut, prepared to bolt with the slightest indication of threat. Yet its yellow eyes stared boldly into his own with the proud majesty of a wild creature. Its lips stretched back into a canine grin, tongue lolling out with an animal's delight. Tom reached out and placed his hand tenderly on the wolf's head, burying his fingers in the tawny fur. He caressed it gently, scratching the ears until it panted affectionately.

Then he spoke the name again: Fauglorum Anacharoth.

He spoke its true name, long hidden in the demon's psyche, and knew that the chains that bound it were forever broken.

The wolf's eyes blazed with gratitude. The spirit that was once the demon Fau'Charoth raised its snout to the sky and let out a howl that was a long sustained note of farewell. The great condor wings opened proudly, the pinion feathers spreading wide into a serrated fan. Then it faded from view.

With the winged wolf gone, Tom felt very alone. He

wandered through the forested hillside, staring at the blue sky, wondering to what heaven it belonged. Was he dead? Was this to be his place of eternal rest? He dwelled on it, but only for a moment as his soul fell into complete exhaustion. He closed his eyes and took in a deep breath, absorbing the tranquility that surrounded him.

Then a soothing, familiar voice called his name. He felt himself drawn to it, and surrendered to the momentum of his spirit.

Tom awoke with a start and found himself in a hospital bed with Julie and Parrish peering down at him. Murmurs had alerted them to his revival, and they stood now above his bedside, relieved and concerned.

"Hey-y!" Julie greeted him with a delighted smile. "How's it going, buddy?" She took his hand and held it soothingly.

He blinked several times. His eyes were saucers of bafflement as he dwelled deeply in silence, and then bolted upright in bed.

"What happened?" he shouted. "I . . . I was . . ."

"Shhhh. Tom, take it easy," Parrish said as he put a gentle hand on the boy's chest and eased him down. "You've had quite a trip."

Tom lay with eyes wide, glancing at his surroundings. "Where am I?"

"In the hospital. You've been in a coma for almost thirty hours. We nearly lost you."

"Thirty hours? It feels longer."

"Can you recall anything at all?" Julie questioned.

"It's all very blurry to me now," he explained, attempting to retrace his fragmented memory. Tom described in vague detail his terrifying journey through Hell. How he was suddenly catapulted free, enveloped in a white radiance that transported him to a higher plane.

He described the glorious place he found himself and his encounter with the winged wolf.

"It wasn't a demon anymore," Tom recounted. "It was changed. Something transformed it."

"Love," Parrish surmised. "You taught it to love, and the experience elevated its being. It was no longer ensnared by the demon world. You set it free, and in turn it pulled you from the abyss."

Tom once again fell distant in contemplation.

"It was beautiful, that place I was in." He smiled at the two of them. "One day, I'll have to paint a picture of it." He turned to Parrish in wonderment. "I thought I was gone for good. But then I heard voices calling my name, and I followed them. It was *you*. You and one other."

"You heard a woman's voice."

Tom peered at him earnestly. "Yes."

"It was Sarah."

Parrish's eyes shined, contentedly reflecting on his own experience.

In a deep trance, he had traveled to the "other side," searching for Tom's wandering spirit. For a time he was cast completely adrift, with no sign of Tom at all; then he was met by an ethereal female presence. Her features were deliberately obscured, as though she feared judgment from him, but he was able to intuitively breach her veil. Parrish recognized her as the spirit of Sarah Halloway, not lost to annihilation as he had feared, but free and exalted by the act of her own sacrifice. She returned again to save the boy she knew only once as an infant.

It was Sarah who guided Parrish to the whereabouts of Tom's soul, providing a beacon for his consciousness. When at last they had located the boy, they called out to him and led Tom to the physical plane.

"You brought me back," Tom said gratefully.

"Yes."

Parrish held the boy's hand. Tom felt again that peculiar electrical current coursing through him, but this time it was welcome and familiar. Something friendly and intimate was passed between them. Then the psychic withdrew, allowing his daughter to steal the boy's attention. Soon the two were conversing lightly, even laughing, as he left the room.

Julie crawled onto the bed and nestled on him lovingly. She gave him the warmest hug she could muster. Tom smiled.

Totally rejuvenated to face the world. Or something to that effect.

Also available from Medallion Press:

FOREVER will you SUFFER

g.a.r.y f.r.a.n.k

ISBN#1932815694
ISBN#9781932815696
Gold Imprint
US $6.99 / CDN $9.99
Horror
Available Now

c.h.a.p.t.e.r 1

This is Hell on Earth: Mount Moriah Cemetery, treeless and broiling hot from the ferocious July sun searing everything, including me. It's like being sautéed in a frying pan. The two headstones are the only things that distract me from the heat. I'm deeply sad; tears well in my eyes, blurring the world like a Monet painting.

Mari Anne Summers Beloved Mother, Wife 1940 – 1996	Allison Beth Summers Beloved Daughter, Sister 1976 – 1996

I've come out here for eight years on the anniversary of the car accident and it still hurts so damned much. The therapists all said it would take time. Fuck time.

My father doesn't come any more. Five years ago, he met Marilyn, a woman in her thirties, and remarried. For the first time since Mom and Allison died, he was getting on with his life. I thought I'd be happy for him, but after Marilyn convinced him to put us behind him, I'm pissed that he doesn't come around.

A blank space for my father waits next to my mother's name on the tombstone and another, with Allison's name and dates, is just to the right. And yeah, there's another space on the tombstone next to Allison's name, but I don't look at it. They should all be empty.

I kneel before the headstones and look from one to the other as if my mother and Allison sit there, hanging out.

"Another year," I say. "I'm still in New York." I glance at my mother's headstone. "And still single." There's some comfort in this monologue; it's a connection between here and hereafter. Maybe God opens up a radio frequency down to the living so that my mother and Allison can hear me and know that I still care about them.

My mother would tell me to get on with my life. "I'm living. I have my gigs and my job at the bookstore. I just can't keep a girlfriend for very long, that's all." Looking around the cemetery, I wish things were different. "I miss you guys so much."

The man who slammed head on into them at sixty miles an hour didn't die. Mr. Walker couldn't explain what happened, though he said he didn't do anything wrong. Bullshit. Was the car possessed? He said that he was driving along and then the car took off on him. Serene Southern Drive turned into a collision scene so brutal that they had to pick pieces of bark from Allison's skull and—it was just real fucking bad.

My mother and Allison were driving to the supermarket

for groceries. The seatbelts had been released seconds before the accident. The police said the two belts hadn't even fully retracted. What the hell happened? The only answer my father and I got was that it was a malfunction. They hadn't gotten them completely on yet. Who expects a sixty-seven-year old man to suddenly play hot rod chicken?

"Sometimes I think about getting the old band together. It's kind of in honor of you guys and doing tributes and making you proud of me. I think it's just so I can see Katarina again. But after all that happened, it's a bad idea." I sigh. "I'm not as together as I want to be. None of my relationships last more than six months." I shake my head. "You don't need to hear this . . . shit. Yeah, I've been cursing a lot lately. Better than punching people." I stand up. "I just wanted to say hi and ask you to give Grandma and Grandpa my love." I glance up at the sky as if my grandparents are looking down on me.

Is there an afterlife? Do we reincarnate for another go round? I'd like to think there's something more than worm food waiting for me at the end of my life, but I can't say what. Maybe I'll see my grandparents, my mother and Allison; maybe I'll see New York City one more time.

"See you guys soon." I don't actually mean it. I just say it like I do to practically everyone I know. I'm about to walk away from the graves, when something like someone's tentative touch brushes my arm. I turn back, half expecting to see Allison standing there with her teenage girl smile that melted all the boys' hearts.

A hot breeze abruptly kicks up.

"*Take care, Rick,*" a woman whispers like a breeze.

But no one's here, just my anger, loneliness, and me. Fifty yards away, a man in shorts and a T-shirt digs at a fresh grave. He shimmers like a mirage in this retched heat. He stops and stares at me. Goosebumps break out on my skin and I shudder with fear that I can't place. Why be scared of a gravedigger?

"Take care."

The heat must be messing with me; I usually don't hear people's voices trickle through my brain. I place a stone on the top of each headstone and offer a prayer of safekeeping; I'm not a religious man, but for family, it feels right.

I head back to the old, dirty taxi waiting on the narrow road that runs through the cemetery. A growing pile of dark earth obscures the gravedigger, but it's strange that he's digging someone up. I shudder again. It's just my imagination running away with me.

I'm mildly annoyed that my nerves are getting the better of me when I should be somber and peaceful. The memories of my life before the accident are good and that's what I always hold on to when I go home.

The breeze swirls up from the ground, sighing with desperate loneliness that sends a chill through me. I imagine that a sigh so terribly alone should be reserved for very old widows, widowers or . . .

Knock it off, Summers, it's bright daylight in the middle of July. The dead don't come out this time of day, only at night when it's not this blisteringly hot. Maybe they're smarter than we are.

The driver's door closes as I get back in the cab, lost in sadness and memories. I stare back up the hill at the two headstones. I don't want to leave, but how long am I going to sit here, especially with the cab's meter running? The trip back to the city shouldn't take too long, though I'm in no rush to get back to my apartment that's going to be Hellish with useless fans barely pushing suffocating air around.

"I'm ready," I say and the cab pulls forward. "Back to the city."

I start sweating almost immediately and then I get a strong whiff of rotten meat.

"Wanna turn the A/C on?" I stare at my mother's and sister's headstones, then others that dot the green grass as the cab slowly pulls away from the curb. Something thumps against the driver's side of the car and the back tire rolls over it.

"What the hell was that?" I cautiously move to the window and look out. Nothing. I glance out the back of the car.

The cab driver lies on the road behind us, his head attached to his body by bloody strands of muscle, his eyes staring blankly after his car. I'm suddenly nauseous, made worse by the stench, and light-headed from the abrupt unrealness of the taxi cab driver lying on the road, practically decapitated. My sweaty hands stick to the vinyl seats and I wipe them on my pants.

"Hey!" Stricken with a sense of dread, I turn to see who's driving. A woman's face reflects in the rearview mirror and I think: *she's dead.* The thought zips through my mind, exploding like a Fourth of July firework. The driver is a dead woman in her mid twenties. *Maybe she's not dead.* But her skin is that odd shade of dead blue that you see in zombie movies.

I look over where I saw the gravedigger. He's face down on the ground and it looks like the coffin lid is open. *Ah, crap.*

I glance back at the driver. It's definitely a young woman. My curiosity is stronger than my good sense to flee and I lean forward. My big mistake. The driver's head turns slowly on a stiff neck.

Your neck would be stiff too if you were dead in a box in the ground for—

I gasp and throw myself back. The dead doll eyes tremble and stare through me. The lips, devoid of color, form a wordless sigh. The make-up covering the bullet hole in her forehead is gone, leaving a blackish-red circle filled with thick ooze. A fly crawls around the circle looking for something to eat. But it's not until I hear a sound, a word, that I realize I'm in a shitload of trouble.

"*Rick.*"

My heart races in my chest. My breath is so unsteady that if I try talking I'll stutter. But my mind's not working to speak. What would I say anyway? Please stop, I'd like to get out now? Yeah, like that happens in all the horror movies.

I don't know how the dead girl got out of the grave, but I'm not staying in here. I grab for the passenger side back door handle, but the lock descends into the door and all I can do is jiggle the handle.

Okay, Rick, stay calm. Stay calm? I can't catch a good breath between the terror that's crushing me and the unbearable heat that's tortured by the smell of this thing. I roll the window down, but no one's around to help me. I glance back at the hideous driver, then stick my head out the window to breathe the hot air. The heat slams against my face, but at least it's better than the stench of the driver. I draw in a deep breath, grateful for the cleaner air.

The front passenger window rolls down. Reflected in the side mirror, the dead girl, pretty but for the damned bullet hole in her head, leans over. "Rick," she says, "Pull your head in before it gets ripped off."

Her eyes stare, but I doubt they see. They seem to quake in their sockets, the iris trembling very quickly from side to side.

"I'll take my chances out here, thank you." I look at anything but her because when I do, chills run through my body and I want to scream.

"I can't afford you getting hurt," she says, her words coming slowly from a thick tongue that hasn't spoken since before the bullet sank into her brain.

"You may not be aware of this, but you're dead and you're stinking up the car!"

"Deal with it, Rick." The woman pulls the taxi over. The driver's door opens, then the driver's side back door opens and she pulls me into the car. Her hand tightens around my ankle and the cold of her dead hand freezes my skin through my sock.

"Let me go!" Panic sets in and I kick at her, but she avoids me.

"We have plans." Her other hand grabs my bare leg. I gasp in pain from her icy touch. She yanks me back in with strength belied by her thin body. "Now sit still." She slams the back door, gets in the front seat and we're off.

I sit up and rub my leg, trying to get some warmth and feeling again. "What do you want from me? Where are we going?" The stench twists my stomach and even breathing through my mouth is bad, because the stink of decay sticks to my tongue and forces its way down my throat. If I pass out, it'll be a saving grace. Maybe then my heart will stop jackhammering in my chest. "What are you?"

She just laughs.

The smell intensifies and I sit as far from her and as close to the window as I can, trying to breathe in any air that isn't tainted with death. It's no use. Then the nausea wins. Holding my breath only lasts a few seconds and the next breath I take is like swallowing thick bile. I'm gonna vomit.

I squeeze my eyes shut and the little food in my stomach forces its way out between my teeth.

"That is really gross," the woman says.

"And you're a ravishing beauty." I wipe my mouth with

the back of my hand and try to breathe through clenched teeth without losing the rest of my stomach.

"Why, thank you."

I keep my eyes closed and focus on Kerri and the breath exercises we've done together. Yeah, that's it, breathe slow and deep, ignore the smell of—forget it, this isn't working at all. I might as well just—

"Oh, Rick, did you make a mess back there?" The woman sighs angrily. "Now the car's gonna stink."

"Right. As if it didn't reek before." I keep my feet away from the mess on the car floor. "What do you want from me?" No matter how hard I try to keep my voice steady, it trembles and I feel like a little boy who's scared shitless. Okay, I may not be a little boy, but I'll own the scared shitless part. My hands and jaw tremble and I wonder if it's from my heart doing a staccato in my chest.

"You'll see. We're going to a familiar haunt." The woman turns her head and her mouth stretches in a rictus grin.

Suddenly, the radio snaps on. "Truckin" by the Grateful Dead rolls out of the front speakers.

I jump and gasp.

"How *apropos*. It has indeed been a long strange trip." She chuckles dryly. "I could really use a drink. Judith hasn't talked much in the last few days."

"Who's Judith?"

"I was Judith Baxter until my husband put a bullet through my brain because his dinner wasn't hot enough. Men are such bastards. For you though, I am death, come to claim you and your beloved."

"My . . . ? I don't have a beloved."

"Yes, Rick, you do."

I try the door handle more aggressively, this time to no avail. I'm shaking and I can't stop. I'm seconds away from wetting myself, or soiling myself, or both, and neither sounds appealing. "Let me out of here!" The door jiggles, but nothing more. I roll both back windows down, hoping the hot breeze will pull some of the stench out. Either it's lessened or I'm getting used to it.

"Where are we going?" I demand of the dead woman, but she says nothing and all that answers me is the Dead's Bob Weir singing how cities across the country are really all on the same street. *Okay, Rick, it's time for a plan.* I stare out as we come to the cemetery gates. I can fit through the window. Better than staying in the cab ride to Hell.

As soon as the taxi comes to a stop, I try throwing myself out, but I'm not as fluid as I'd like to be and instead of floating out the window, I get my upper torso out first, then push off the seat with my feet. Suddenly the window rolls up, pressing into my stomach. I gasp and try pulling myself back in.

"All I ask is that you sit still," Ex-Judith Baxter says. "We have somewhere special to go to. But you can't do that, can you?"

The window rolls up, cutting into my stomach. I wince and groan in pain.

"What is it?" Judith asks. "A little pain? How high

do you think the window can go before you suffer bodily harm? Another two inches? Three?"

The edge of the window presses painfully into my stomach. "Let me go." Tears spring from my eyes.

"What do you think'll happen? The window's not sharp enough to pierce flesh, so that leaves internal injuries. If the window closes too much, something inside you will rupture. You may not die, but you will be damned uncomfortable. By that point, of course, you'll be useless to me so I might as well let the window keep rolling up until the dull glass ruptures the rest of your organs and your body breaks in two."

"Open the fucking window!" The pressure worsens as the window tries closing. My back is pressed against the window frame, wrenching my spine. "Okay! I'll come in!" Sweat drips in my eyes, blinding me. Tiny little white dots blossom in my vision. My heart thuds like war drums in my brain. The pain rolls in waves to my feet and my head. If she doesn't let me go soon, I'm gonna pass out.

"Hm. Do you think your spine would crack in two, paralyzing you before the window cuts through you?"

I imagine what she said, is going to happen any minute. How much longer until my spine snaps? The pain takes my breath away until I'm suffocating and drowning in the thick heat and the pain explodes in my back. "All right! Let me go!"

"What?"

I feel close to being crushed as the glass inches higher.

Another inch and something will explode, crack, or break and I'll be dead. "I'll do what you want."

"That's real good of you." Her sarcasm drips like the sweat down my back.

Suddenly the pressure of the window draws back and I take a deep breath, afraid at any moment residual pain will cause something to pop, like my spleen, and it'll be all over. I fall back in the car and stay on my side, praying the pain in my back subsides quickly. "God damn it!" I shout, pissed, more than anything else. My spine is sore and no matter how I move, it hurts. At least lying down I can't see the dead woman. That makes me feel somewhat like the universe isn't totally fucking me.

Maybe this is a joke. Maybe someone's doing this as a practical joke. The woman's really alive but made up to look that way. Right, and for a practical joke I'd love to smell like death, too.

My friend, Dallas Richards, once said that in the face of the incredible or unbelievable, it's easier to go by the theory that such things can't be, than to accept the evidence and facts that are in front of you. He's right.

I don't have any more escape plans. The door's locked and the window's set to kill. The stench seems to have lessened and that's about all I'm thankful for. My heart rate's slowed to its usual rhythm and all symptoms of passing out have receded. Whoever this woman is, she's got my attention. All I can do is stay calm and enjoy the ride and the music. Mitch Ryder sings about the Devil in a blue dress and I think, no, today, she's in a green summer dress.

* * *

After ten minutes or so, the pain in my back's subsided, though it still hurts when I move. I sit up and look out at the passing scenery. The taxi speeds along Route 3 heading away from New York and jumps on Route 17 North. The stench is all but gone and since I agreed to behave, Ex-Judith hasn't tried killing me.

I've attempted conversation, to find out more information, but she's silent and I get this sinking sensation because I know where we're going. Ex-Judith hasn't said anything, but I know this area.

We take the new Route 4 fly-over too fast, heading west in the direction of Fair Lawn, a town I know too well; it's where I grew up and fell in love with Katarina Petrovska. I wonder how she's doing: did she ever kick the drugs, or did they kick her to death?

Katarina was part of the old band, TwistaLime, a bunch of addicts. Drugs, sex, porn, alcohol. You name it, we could addict ourselves to it. Yet, even wasted we were a good band, playing gigs at local bars, dreaming of bigger things. It wasn't until friends started dying that the whole thing fell apart. What a damned shame.

Ex-Judith speeds the car onto the Broadway exit off Route 4, then slows and stops at the red light by McDonald's. Flies race into the cab, swarming around Ex-Judith but she doesn't wave them away and when they land on her face, she lets them crawl. She suddenly catches one and slowly pushes her fingers into her mouth, chewing on the fat fly.

I shudder and turn away, about to retch again.

She accelerates and takes the turn I hoped she wouldn't take, the one that leads to Kat's house.

Maybe this is just a short cut to somewhere else. But the dead woman stops the cab in front of Kat's house, behind a teal Corolla.

"We're here. Get out." She slides the shifter into "Park" and stares at the house. She suddenly spasms, choking on something—her tongue? The fly? Her body flails around, arms swinging like a marionette's, jerked back and forth, up and down. "Not here, not here, not here, not here!"

I grab the handle and the door miraculously opens. Wonderful. Of all places for the damned thing to finally work. I get out quickly and slam the door.

"I have to find her!" Her head jerks toward the open passenger window and her dead eyes narrow and her gaze is pure hatred. "I will bring her. Don't leave or I will find you again!"

The car accelerates away with "Crawling" by Linkin Park blaring over the tinny cab speakers.

THE DREAM THIEF

HELEN A. ROSBURG

Someone is murdering young, beautiful women in mid-sixteenth century Venice. Even the most formidable walls of the grandest villas cannot keep him out, for he steals into his victims' dreams. Holding his chosen prey captive in the night, he seduces them . . . to death.

Now Pina's cousin, Valeria, is found dead, her lovely body ravished. It is the final straw for Pina's overbearing fiance', Antonio, and he orders her confined within the walls of her mother's opulent villa on Venice's Grand Canal. It is a blow not only to Pina, but to the poor and downtrodden in the city's ghettos, to whom Pina has been an angel of charity and mercy. But Pina does not chafe long in her lavish prison, for soon she too begins to show symptoms of the midnight visitations; a waxen pallor and overwhelming lethargy.

Fearing for her daughter's life, Pina's mother removes her from the city to their estate in the country. Still, Pina is not safe. For Antonio's wealth and his family's power enable him to hide a deadly secret. And the murderer manages to find his intended victim. Not to steal into her dreams and steal away her life, however, but to save her. And to find his own salvation in the arms of the only woman who has ever shown him love.

ISBN#1932815201
Gold Imprint
US $6.99 / CDN $9.99
Available Now
www.helenrosburg.com

erin samiloglu

DISCONNECTION

There is a serial killer on the loose in New Orleans. Someone is branding, stabbing and strangling young girls. Their mutilated bodies are being found in the depths of the Mississippi River.

Beleaguered Detective Lewis Kline and his colleagues believe the occult may be involved, but they have no leads. And the killer shows no sign of slowing down.

Then Sela, a troubled young woman, finds a stranger's cell phone in a dark Bourbon Street bar. When it rings, she answers it. On the other end is Chloe Applegate. The serial killer's most recent victim.

So begins Sela's journey into a nightmare from which she cannot awaken, a descent into madness out of which she cannot climb . . . as she finds herself the target of an almost incomprehensible evil.

ISBN#1932815244

Gold Imprint

US $6.99 / CDN $9.99

Available Now

www.erinsamiloglu.com

L.G. Burbank

Presents

Lords of Darkness

Vol I:

The Soulless

An unlikely hero . . .

Mordred Soulis is the chosen one, the man ancient legends claim will save the world from great evil. There's only one problem. Before Mordred can become the hero of mankind, he must first learn to embrace the vampyre within.

A forgotten race . . .

With the help of a mysterious order, a king of immortals and a shape-shifting companion, Mordred is set on a dangerous course that will either save the human race or destroy it.

A timeless struggle . . .

Journeying across the sands of the Byzantine Empire; in the time of the Second Crusade, to the great Pyramids of Egypt and then on to the Highlands of Scotland, Mordred will face the Dark One. This evil entity is both Mordred's creator and the Soul Stealer he has become. As champion of mortals, Mordred must accept his vampyre-self . . . something he has vowed never to do.

DANIEL'S VEIL

R.H. STAVIS

Daniel O'Brady is a burned out cop. When he sees a child blown away by her own father, he's seen one murder too many. Grief stricken and questioning the validity and purpose of his life, he takes off for a drive in the countryside. Daniel's bad day is only beginning.

Regaining consciousness after the single car accident, an injured Daniel sets out to find help. What he finds is a quaint little village full of people who are more than happy to help him. He's given medical aid, food, clothing and shelter . . . and no one will take a dime from him. If that's not strange enough, after a few days in the tranquil town he discovers an odd house surrounded by streaks of an odd blue light. He decides to investigate.

Dr. Michael Hudson is a scientist bent on proving the existence of supernatural phenomena. His life is consumed with passion to prove his theory, to the exclusion of all else. When his research leads him to a house outside a small village in Northern California, he packs up his team and his equipment and sets out to document and prove his long-held belief in another dimension.

What both men discover will change their lives, and alter their souls, forever.

shinigami

django wexler

Shinigami: In Japanese folklore, a spirit
that collects the souls of the dead.

At age fourteen, Sylph Walker died in a car accident. That turned out to be only the beginning of her problems . . .

She and her sister Lina awake to an afterlife, of sorts — the world of Omega, ruled by cruel, squabbling, and nearly all-powerful Archmagi. When Lina finds a magical sword of immense power, she becomes the unwilling epicenter of the conflict. The sisters are forced to join the Circle Breakers, rebels sworn to prevent the tyrants from expanding their rule.

Lina, bearing the ancient artifact, is hailed as the Liberator — the latest in a long line of heroes expected to destroy the Archmagi. Sylph finds herself at the head of the rebel armies fighting to take back the land and the lives of its people. But what kind of a land is it? Is Omega really the world that lies beyond death? And who is the legendary Lightbringer, a being greater even than the Archmagi?

ISBN#1932815716
Silver Imprint
US $14.99 / CDN $19.95
Epic Fantasy
October 2006
www.bloodgod.com